Indulgence

<u>Other Books</u> by
Cap Parlier:

<u>Anod series</u>

The Phoenix Seduction (1995)
Anod's Seduction (2004) [reprint of The Phoenix Seduction]
Anod's Redemption (2004)

—

Sacrifice (2000)
The Clarity of Hindsight (2016)
Apocalypse Endeavor (2019)
Indulgence (2021)

—

<u>To So Few series</u>

To So Few – In the Beginning (2014)
To So Few – The Prelude (2014)
To So Few – Explosion (2015)
To So Few – The Trial (2016)
To So Few – The Verdict (2017)
To So Few – Frustration (2018)
To So Few – Deflection (2019)
To So Few – Hunter (2020)
To So Few – Struggle (2021)

—

<u>and with Kevin E. Ready:</u>

TWA 800 - Accident or Incident? (1998)

—

These and other great books are available from Saint Gaudens Press at http://www.SaintGaudensPress.com
Visit Cap Parlier's Web Site at: http://www.parlier.com

Indulgence

by
Cap Parlier

SAINT GAUDENS PRESS
Phoenix, Arizona & Santa Barbara, California

Saint Gaudens Press
Post Office Box 405
Solvang, CA 93464-0405

Http://www.SaintGaudensPress.com

Saint Gaudens, Saint Gaudens Press
and the Winged Liberty colophon
are trademarks of Saint Gaudens Press

Print edition ISBN: 978-0-943039-61-9
Ebook edition ISBN: 978-0-943039-62-6
Library of Congress Catalog Number - 2021941913

Printed in the United States of America

DEDICATION

To all of the families and friends of addicts who have suffered and endured the trauma of proximate drug addiction. While your suffering may be passed or ongoing, there is always hope for a better tomorrow.

To all citizens who are attracted to psychotropic substances and found themselves on the wrong side of the law, especially those who injured no one and damaged no property. Freedom of choice in the privacy of your home should have never been a crime. There must be a better way.

To every individual who reads this book and thinks about what might be in a better tomorrow.

—

ACKNOWLEDGMENTS

First and foremost, I must recognize the extraordinary contributions of John Richard and my wife Jeanne for their critical review. They challenged more than a few elements of this story. Their constructive criticism made the story better. The mistakes, typographical errors, and the content are the author's responsibility, not theirs.

The premise for this story rest solely and completely with the author, no one else.

I also offer a big shout out to the editorial and administrative staff at Saint Gaudens Press, Inc., for their expertise, compassion, and professionalism. I am a most fortunate author to have found the connection. Thank you ever so much.

—

1

"**I** love these parties," proclaimed Sandra 'Sandi' Morrison, the oldest of the professional women. Sandi was also the tallest and most buxom of the three women. Her light brown, slightly wavy tresses extended to just below her shoulder.

"These fellas are always very generous, in addition to respectful and gentle," added Juliette 'Juli' Mason, the most petite of the three women. Her short auburn hair was her most distinctive feature, or her prominent bosom, depending upon one's perspective.

For Laura Simmons, the evening's entertainment had been gratifying, above average on the scale of pleasure. "Yeah, the guys stepped up their game." Laura was the third and youngest of the trio who had worked together, when a group was sought for such occasions. She was slender, the middle height of the three women, and kept her curly, light brown hair to upper neck length. Laura had used some of her extraordinary income to permanently remove all of her body hair below her neck. Yet, it was her perky breasts that seem to garner the most attention from men and women. "We'd better get back, or the boys might start thinking we're in here playing by ourselves."

They all laughed. Juli was the last to finish relieving her bladder. The three naked women freshened up, hugged collectively, then returned to the expansive and airy living room.

"We decided to zone out without you," announced Theodore 'Ted' Graves, the youngest of the three men. He was a 45-year-old, Fordham educated lawyer for John Baxter's bank.

John Baxter was the successful, 53-year-old, chairman, president and founder of Golden Nugget Bank, who organized and sponsored these evening playtime sessions. John had been one of Laura's regular customers since she had turned professional six years ago. He was already passed out, completely naked on the carpeted floor.

"The ecstasy and poppers were perfect for the sex, tonight," Sandi declared, "but a little mellow yellow after the excitement would be an excellent ending." Ecstasy, among other names and more properly known as MDMA, enhances pleasure, increases energy, empathy, and amplifies sensations. Amyl Nitrite, also known as poppers, Rush and many other names, is a muscle relaxant that makes penetrative sex easier, less painful, and arguably more enjoyable.

The third man, Michael 'Mike' Ignatius, the 47-year-old, vice president in Baxter's bank, was already in oblivion like his boss, only in a recliner rather than on the floor.

"I'm going to take my hit. Do any of you ladies want a dose?" Ted said, looking at the women.

"What have you got?" asked Sandi.

"Heroin aerosol," Ted answered.

Sandi looked at Juli and Laura, who both nodded their heads in agreement. "Looks like it's unanimous," Sandi responded. "Do you have enough for all of us?"

"Sure. John picked up a new inhaler at the store yesterday afternoon, and Mike and John have only taken one hit each, so that leaves eight remaining for the rest of us."

Juli did not wait and gestured for the inhaler. The 'psst' of the inhaler signaled Juli dosing. "Oh, yes," she said, handed the small inhaler back to Ted, and settled in a large, overstuffed, single chair. Oddly, as she laid her head back into the cushions, she draped her legs over the arms of the chair, as she descended into her own oblivion.

"There goes Juli," observed Sandi, as she looked to Laura.

"See ya later, ladies," Ted said, as he inhaled the spray and handed the small container to Sandi. Ted found his own place on the floor and laid down spread-eagled.

"Are you going to do it, Laura. I've never done this stuff," Sandi admitted.

"I've done it a few times." Laura reached for the inhaler. She inspected it. The small metallic bottle with a yellow nasal nozzle had the official markings, labeling, and government tax stamp with a clear, prominent title—**HEROIN AEROSOL**. The small integral counter displayed the number '6.' "Looks like the real stuff." Laura handed the inhaler back to Sandi. "Your choice, my friend. I don't think anyone will mind if you choose to leave." Laura looked at John and the object of her attention. Laura decided to enjoy one of Baxter's attributes a little longer, before she dosed up on the drug. "Want to join me?" asked Laura.

"No thanks. I had plenty a few hours ago." Sandi was holding the inhaler as Laura stood.

Laura reached out and embraced Sandi in a friendly hug, then kissed her on the lips. "What are you going to do?" she asked, as she reached for the inhaler.

"I don't know, Laura. I've never had the nerve to try heroin. I'm scared."

"Well, Sandi, a couple of thoughts for your consideration before I check out. First, the inhaler," she said and held of the dispenser, "is a proper, government certified device with the regulated quality, established dosage, and safety. Second, spray is harmless . . . as long as you don't overdo things."

"How do you know how to avoid overdoing it?"

"Stay to the dosage. It is controlled. As long as you don't take too many doses at one time, you will be fine. The high lasts a couple of hours, and then you come out the other side."

"What about addiction?"

"The key is not using this stuff regularly. I think I recall that the warning that comes with the inhaler is something like using one dose a day for two weeks can cause dependency, so just don't do that. I've only done heroin maybe a half dozen times in the six years I've been a professional. I have never felt an urge for more."

Sandi considered Laura's words, then announced, "OK. I'm going to try it."

"Sounds good. Before you take a hit, find a place to crash. It works fairly fast."

Sandi did as Laura suggested and chose one of the two open couches. She sat down at the end, looked at Laura and smiled, and then squeezed off a dose into her right nostril. Sandi shook her head rapidly as she felt the initial sting of consumption, placed the inhaler on the coffee table, and lay back on the couch rather than laying down entirely. She mumbled something that was unintelligible to Laura, and then even the mumbles vanished to silence.

Laura was the last of the partyers to seek oblivion. There was plenty of room on the couch with Sandi, so Laura took the inhaler with her as she laid down on the remainder of the couch. She took one last look, inserted the inhaler nozzle in her right nostril, and squeezed the side tabs of the nozzle down, injecting a mist of dissolved heroin into her nasal passages. The sting of the initial exposure passed swiftly as the waves of the familiar warm embrace rolled through her body, and a sense of buoyancy and flotation overwhelmed her. A blurry yellow glow filled what remained of her consciousness that added to the warmth of the cocoon that enveloped her, then the glow faded. *This feels so good and heavenly.*

What is that banging? It is so distant, but I hear it. Where am I? Laura remained motionless with her eyes closed. Her eye lids were so heavy. She felt like she was still floating, and yet she was also aware of her slow descent back to normalcy and consciousness.

Some unseen person squirted something into my nose. In a flash, Laura sat bolt upright with her eyes wide open and gasping for air. She quickly glanced around the room. John Baxter and Mike Ignatius were dressed in bathrobes with their hands handcuffed behind their backs and being led away by two uniformed police officers.

"What the hell?" Laura exclaimed, as she continued to take in the scene. She noticed that it was daylight outside. The shadows suggested it was early morning or late afternoon. Laura could not remember which way the back windows faced.

Laura tried to stand, but a hand held her down. She looked to the person restraining her. He appeared to be a Hispanic man in a nice light grey suit with a blue tie on his white shirt. The gold police badge hung by a simple ball chain around his neck.

"Just sit still, young lady," the man said. "Do you want a robe, or are your clothes handy?"

"In one of the back bedrooms. I am not particularly modest, but I am quite hot."

"OK. Out of professional propriety, I will grab a robe. Just stay here for the moment."

Ted Graves had a shirt, trousers and shoes without socks on, and he was seated in the dining room beyond the living room with another suited officer questioning him. Both Juli and Sandi had robes on with uniformed officers questioning them in opposite corners of the living room.

The suited police officer returned with a terrycloth, white robe. Laura donned the robe and tied it up. She did not want the robe since she was already hot without it, but she also did not want to offend any of the police officers in the house.

"What is going on?" she asked calmly.

"We had a failure to appear warrant for Mister Baxter."

"What for?"

"Securities fraud on a rather large scale."

"What about Mister Ignatius?"

"He was arrested for obstruction of justice. He decided to resist arrest. Now," the man said, "who are you?"

"Who the hell are you?" Laura asked a little more strongly than she intended.

The man smiled in a patient, tolerant manner. "I am Detective-Sergeant Rod Ramirez, Badge 1-8-9-6-3. Now, I will ask the questions, and you will answer." Laura nodded her consent. Rod shrugged his shoulders, lifted an eyebrow, and gestured—well?

"My name is Laura Simmons."

"Are those your given and family names, or your professional name?"

"My name since birth. Am I under arrest?"

"No, you're not. You aren't even under detention or restraint. You can walk out of here right now. Well . . . after you put on your clothes. We're simply gathering facts for what we encountered in serving these warrants and making these arrests." Ramirez lifted what appeared to be a nuclear-hardened iPad and inserted his left hand in the strap on the back. He touched the screen several times. "Do you have a middle name or names?"

"Yes . . . Lynn."

"Thank you. What is your contact information?" asked Ramirez.

Laura gave the detective-sergeant her residence address, telephone numbers both professional and private, and her eMail address. That seemed to satisfy the detective.

"Thank you." He touched the screen several more times, then scrolled through several more screens. "You will be happy to know you have no wants or warrants, and not even a parking ticket." Laura nodded her head, although he was not looking at her. "I see you are a professional, properly licensed, and your medical certificate is current. Everything appears to be legal and proper. Thank you for that, Miz Simmons."

"Thank you for acknowledging it, sir." Both of them chuckled. "May I ask a question here?"

"Sure. Shoot. I'm in no rush."

"Did you give me something when you arrived?"

"Yes. We gave you a snort of Narcan to bring you around. We figured all of you had taken at least one blast from the heroin inhaler," Ramirez said, glancing at the dispenser on the table. "We couldn't wait for each of you to come around, and we didn't want to transport you to detention to sober up."

Naloxone hydrochloride, commonly known as Narcan or Evzio, blocks the cerebral effects of opioids and their synthetic alternatives. It is intended for use in over-dose situations, but it can be and has been used for rapid recovery from opioid consumption.

"Wow! That was my first time. It's like a slap in the face."

"It does work. We try not to overuse it. Now, back to my questions. Whose inhaler?"

"I think it belongs to Mister Baxter, but I don't know for sure. I checked it. The inhaler has the government tax and anti-counterfeit stamp."

"Yes, it does. It is entirely legal. We'll trace it if we need to do so. What other drugs, if any, did you consume this evening?"

"Ecstasy. Would you like to see the wrapper? I also have a poppers inhaler. Would you like to inspect that?"

"No and no . . . not necessary."

"The ecstasy came from Mister Baxter as well, I do believe, but the poppers were mine," Laura volunteered.

"Were you here in a professional capacity?" asked Ramirez.

"Yes."

"Were the other ladies as well?"

"You'll need to ask them. I didn't ask them. I know they're both professionals as I am, but I don't know what arrangements might've been made with either of them."

"How much were you paid?' Rod asked.

Laura stared at Ramirez as she considered her answer. "Is that relevant? I would rather not have that information in the public record."

Rod Ramirez smiled as he took a moment to consider his response. "Very well. No, I do not suppose it is relevant. I was just curious. So, what do you know about John Baxter?"

"I have known him for roughly three years. He has been a regular customer of mine. He has always been a gentleman, and a gentle and respectful lover. I know he is a bank president."

"Do you use his bank for any banking services?"

"No. And, he never pressured me to do so. I try to keep my professional and private lives separate."

"So, you are saying that if you had been using his bank and then he became a customer, you would have terminated your use of the bank?"

"Yes, that is exactly what I am saying?"

Ramirez nodded his head and tapped his notebook several more times. "Do you know why he was arrested?"

Laura's brow furrowed, and she shook her head. "You said securities fraud. I'm not sure what that even means in practical terms. So, I guess the answer is no, I don't."

"He never mentioned securities trading or his bank's securities trading activities?"

Laura chuckled softly. "No. We never discussed his business. I have no idea what any of that is, and I doubt I really care."

Ramirez nodded his head and tapped more into his notebook. He took the iPad off his left hand and laid it beside him on the coffee table. "OK. That's all I need, for now. Just for clarity, the information you provided to me is subject to perjury laws. Do you wish to amend any of your answers?"

"No."

"Very well, then. You'll remain a person of interest by your association with Mister Baxter, professional or otherwise. To avoid any problems down the road, I'll strongly urge you to keep my office informed of any travel you may conduct beyond the state borders. Do you understand these instructions or guidance?"

"Yes."

"Thank you for your candor, assistance and patience. Now, if you please, I would ask you to get dressed and depart the premises since this is not your property." Ramirez extended his right hand to Laura. They shook hands, then Laura went to the back bedroom where her clothes and purse were located. By the time she dressed, checked to make sure she had everything she arrived with, and then she returned to the living room, Ted, Sandi and Juli were also dressed and standing in the atrium by the front door. The police officer stood on the periphery of the atrium, not talking and only watching.

The senior police officer, also in a suit, said, "You are free to go. Please do not go far without informing us of your whereabouts. Thank you for your assistance."

No one responded. Laura, like the other women, had arrived by Uber.

Ted apparently had his personal vehicle, a silver, Mercedes-Benz, S 560 4MATIC sedan with tan leather interior. He stopped to face the women before he reached his car. "It has been a troubling morning. May I treat you ladies to breakfast and give you a ride home?"

Sandi looked at Laura and Juli, received an affirmative head nod, and then answered, "Sure, we're game." She took the front passenger seat. Juli and Laura took the comfortable rear passenger seats. Everyone buckled up.

Ted drove several miles across town to a high-end specialty restaurant known as "Awaken." They all remained silent during the transit. Ted had been to Awaken before. The acting *maître d'hôtel*, or perhaps just a receptionist, welcomed him by name, and led him and his three guests to a back-corner booth that, given the morning's patronage, offered some privacy.

Juli and Laura scooted across the cushioned seats on each side. Sandi sat next to Laura, and Ted was the last to sit, taking a place next to Juli. Each of them examined a menu.

"Nice place," Juli observed.

"Yes, it is," Ted responded. "It has an elegant ambiance and great food. I often come here for business breakfasts or for occasions such as this."

"Wow!" Laura exclaimed. "I just saw the clock on the wall. It's 10:20 in the morning."

Graves glanced at his wristwatch. "My gosh, it is."

They sat in silence. The waiter brought their drinks and took their orders.

When the waiter completed his task, Sandi looked directly at Ted Graves. "What the hell was that all about?" she asked, presumably referring to the arrest of Baxter and Ignatius.

"I presume the police informed you that John was arrested under multiple warrants related to an allegation of securities fraud. Mike was arrested for obstruction of justice and resisting arrest. I've got a lot of work to do to get up to speed with these charges and the bank's normal business. Give me a fews days to sort thing out. I should be able to tell more after I've figured out things."

"Yeah, that is what they told me," Sandi added. "But, what does that mean to me, to us," she said, gesturing to the women at the table.

"Unless you gave the police officers false information, I suspect it is over and done for each of you. To my knowledge, none of you were involved in Baxter's or the bank's activities."

"I have my checking and savings accounts at the Golden Nugget Bank," Juli offered.

"That is not a problem, unless you were involved in Baxter's securities activities. I am under retainer as the bank's legal counsel, so I cannot go farther than that. I can each of you, the bank is quite solvent. Did the police ask you or did you tell the police about your bank accounts?"

"Yes. They asked if I had dealings with the bank. I told them of my accounts. The officer asked me a number of other questions about my business with the bank. Should I move my banking business from the Golden Nugget?"

"You need to seek legal counsel for that decision," Graves answered.

"You're a lawyer. Advise me," demanded Juli.

The waiter returned with their meals, placed each dish before the correct person, and asked if there was anything else the group needed. No one spoke. Ted shook his head. The waiter left them.

"I can't, Juli. I'm serving as legal counsel for the bank. I'm controlled by attorney-client privilege. Your question is marginally at the face of that obligation. I must respectfully decline."

"What about the drugs?" Juli asked, much more nervous now.

"The drugs have nothing to do with the bank," Ted answered.

"Are we in trouble for the drugs?" asked Sandi.

"The police saw them and know we used them," Laura responded.

Graves smiled. "No. There is no problem with the drugs. They were all government certified substances . . . unless one of you ladies had any illegal drugs in your possession."

"How do we know?" Juli pressed.

"I should have asked before the party. I assume each of you is current with respect to your license and medical certificate," Ted said and looked at each woman."

"I am," answered Laura.

"As am I," Sandi added.

"Me too," Juli finished.

"Then, you are in compliance with the law." Ted looked again at each woman. "Prostitution was legalized and regulated eight years ago. Drug use was legalized and regulated by the government six years ago, quite like alcohol was after Prohibition nearly a hundred years ago. Once again, unless any of you were in possession of illegal substances, what we did last night, and this morning was perfectly legal and above board."

"What do you know about John Baxter's arrest?" Sandi asked.

"Basically, what you know. He was arrested this morning."

"Yeah, but what did he do?"

"I have not seen the legal documents, yet. I don't know. I'm not his personal attorney. Whatever it was, it was apparently outside the sphere of the bank's board of directors and the official business of the bank. I've got a lot to learn in the next few days, especially since I know the board is going to ask me about their liability. Beyond that, I can say no more."

The four of them ate in silence for several minutes. They all seemed to be enjoying the food.

As they neared completion of their meals, Laura was the first to speak. "Thank you for last night, Ted. You guys were great."

"Hear, hear," added Sandi. "We should be paying you guys for performances like that."

"You're most welcome, ladies. Money very well spent, I must say. I hope whatever it was that happened this morning passes quickly. I look forward to the next session."

"We're always ready," Laura said.

Ted paid the bill. The ladies thanked him for breakfast as they walked out. Graves drove each of them to their apartments. Sandi and Juli lived in the same complex. Laura was the last to be dropped off.

Graves stopped in front of Laura's apartment building, put the car in park, but left the engine running, presumably for the air conditioner. He turned down the radio to a low but still audible volume. "I'm going to be pretty busy for the next few days, I suspect. When things begin to stabilize, I'd like to see you, perhaps take you to dinner or something."

"I'm always available, Ted."

"Thanks. I admire your skills, but I'm impressed by your intellect. I 'd like to get to know you better."

"As you wish, Ted. As I said, I'm always available." Laura smiled, sensing where Ted was headed. "The evening hours are my business hours."

"Understood. I'll gladly pay the going rate for a few hours of your time, perhaps even a night."

"Your choice. The more notice you give me, the better I'm able to accommodate my other customers."

"Also understood, and I shall respect your constraints." Ted looked intently into Laura's eyes. "May I kiss you?"

"Yes."

Ted leaned across the console, reached to gently touch the far side of Laura's head, and kissed her passionately. Laura responded in kind, kissing him with comparable enthusiasm. They stopped and restarted several times.

"Thank you for everything this morning, Ted. I truly appreciate you taking care of us."

"You're most welcome. I'm just sorry it happened the way it did. It was a beautiful night."

"Thank you. We try."

"I'll call you when I get a handle on things. Thank you, Laura." Ted leaned across and kissed her one more time quickly.

"Take care. Have a great day." Laura unbuckled, got out of the car, and walked several steps toward the entrance to her building. She twisted to look back at Ted, waved, and then blew him a kiss. She heard the car drive away. Laura was tired. She was ready for some restful sleep.

—

2

The last few days since the party had been a bit out of the norm. None of the unusualness affected Laura's business, but still, she wanted a break from all the craziness. Kelly's invitation to lunch at her house seemed like just the ticket for her distraction from the bumps and grinds of life.

Kelly Joubert, née Henry, had been married to Assistant District Attorney Raoul Joubert for five years. She had been friends with Laura Simmons since elementary school, through high school and college. Their two families had lived just a block apart through all of their school years. Kelly was eight months older than Laura, but they had actually been in the same classes more often than not. She remained a stunningly attractive, brunette, who prided herself in her appearance. She was always well kept, as they say. Kelly's engagement to Raoul had been a bit of a shock to Laura for the swiftness of their engagement but mostly for their 13-year age difference. Kelly had confessed to Laura alone, other than Raoul, that she had missed her period and self-tested positive for pregnancy, which in turn convinced Raoul to do the right thing. She miscarried two months later, but that reality did not alter their plans. Laura served as Kelly's maid of honor. They all had enjoyed the wedding, but the new relationship euphoria dissipated swiftly. As Kelly's best friend, Laura witnessed the deterioration of her friend.

The Jouberts lived in a magnificent home in an upscale neighborhood, thanks to Raoul's inherited wealth. The couple enjoyed the full-time service of a housekeeper and a chef. She enjoyed a bountiful life but remained profoundly unhappy.

Laura rang the doorbell and waited.

The Joubert housekeeper, Angela Sanderson, answered the door. "Good day, Miss Laura. Great to see you again." She opened the large, heavy, polished oak door wider, stood aside, and continued, "Miss Kelly is on the patio. She has been eagerly awaiting your arrival."

"Thank you, Angela." Laura walked through the atrium, as Angela closed the door behind her. She knew the way through the living room, the sunroom, which only saw indirect sunlight, and out onto the partially covered patio. "Hey, sweetie," Laura announced as she approached.

Kelly stood to greet her friend. She was wearing a lightweight, very airy, ankle length, brilliantly colorful floral print dress that would normally be referred to a muumuu, but she hated the descriptive term. Kelly opened her arms to embrace her friend and held her tightly.

Laura readily noted that Kelly was not wearing anything underneath the dress.

Kelly whispered in Laura's right ear. "I'm so glad you could come. I really needed to talk with you, eye-to-eye." They unclutched.

"I'm underdressed," Laura said, glancing at Kelly's coiffed hair, painted face, and brilliant dress, then gesturing with her hand to her usual off-duty attire of jeans, plain T-shirt—this one light pink in color—and sandals.

Kelly gestured to the chair next to her around the large, round, covered, picnic table.

Before Laura could sit, Angela placed a fresh mojito—the sweet rum Cuban cocktail—in front of her, and she noticed that Kelly was halfway through hers. "Starting a bit early, hon."

"Oh, don't give me any crap. I enjoy a good mojito, and I know you do too."

"True." Laura wanted to change the topic. "How have you been?"

"Before we get into any of that, I want to hear more about your excitement. I saw the arrest on the news night before last and read the newspaper story."

"Like I told you on the phone, yesterday, I was working an all-night party with some bankers and a lawyer, when we were interrupted by a small squad of police officers. They broke open the door, although I was still under the influence. I saw the door—very expensive door."

"Wow! That must have been scary."

"Not so much. All of us were crashed out in a heroin fog . . . very mellow . . . until the rude interruption."

"I saw on the news that the perp the police arrested was the banker John Baxter along with his deputy Mike Ignatius."

"Yep, that's it. I had a date with the lawyer and third man at the party, last night . . . ."

"Who was that?" Kelly asked.

"I cannot say, Kell. It was still business."

"OK, OK, sorry. I didn't mean to pry. I know you are very respectful of your customers."

"Thanks, Kell. Yes, I am. They respect me, and I respect them."

"So, what happened after your interruption?"

"They questioned us, then let us go. I found out later that each of us were interviewed a second time. Mine was yesterday morning. Nothing fancy. Just clarifying details."

"What did Baxter and Ignatius do to warrant that kind of an arrest?"

"That answer is a little more complicated. The newspaper account was fairly accurate to my knowledge. From what I understand, so far, Baxter apparently carried out some bizarre securities trading scheme, certainly not on the Bernie Madoff scale, but still, it must have been very serious, because Baxter is still in jail. Ignatius was bailed out day before yesterday. I have no reason to doubt the newspaper account that Baxter ignored a subpoena or a warrant, or something like that, which pushed the police to take more aggressive action."

Kelly took a sip of her drink and smiled. "How was the party?"

"Much better than average actually. We have done that group several times. They have always been quite imaginative, generous with their pleasure and money, and very respectful. All three of them are valued customers."

"All sex?"

"No, actually. They took breaks. We had some munchies and drinks, and we talked about politics, economics and such. These guys, all three of them, are experienced and know what they are doing. We also had some F2F for their viewing pleasure."

"You've always been into that," Kelly observed.

"Yes, I have. I take great pride and pleasure in being an equal opportunity lover. Now, enough of my salaciousness. What is going on with you?"

Laura saw emotion drain from Kelly's face. Her expression turned dark.

Just then, Angela reappeared and announced, "Lunch is ready, Miss Kelly."

Color returned to Kelly's face. She looked at Angela and acknowledged, "Thanks, Angela." Kelly looked back at Laura. "Shall we?"

The two women stood and took their drinks with them. The large, polished oak dining table had two, place settings, with a larger than modest green salad with shrimp, flakes of mahi-mahi, fresh tomato wedges and bacon crumbles. Large glasses of iced tea and water were at each place. Angela refreshed the mojitos. They took several bites in silence. The house chef, Michel Herriot, appeared at the passageway.

"Excellent job, Michel," Laura said.

Kelly looked to her left and added, "Yes. Perfect, Michel. Thank you. This will be more than enough for us."

"Merci, Madame Kelly," he answered in a distinctly sophisticated French accent. Michel bowed his head slightly and returned to the kitchen.

When Laura was sure Angela and Michel were gone, she lowered her fork, leaned toward Kelly, and said very softly, "Do you want to talk?"

Kelly shook her head. "Not now. After lunch."

Laura nodded her agreement, sat up straight, and took another bite.

After several minutes, Kelly opened a rather innocuous set of conversation topics about sports, pending concerts and the latest movies. Laura played along, keeping the tone light and upbeat, as she followed Kelly's lead. The avoidance was obvious, and Laura did not want to interfere with Kelly's mindset.

Neither one of the ladies finished their salad. They stood, thanked Michel and Angela, who were both eating their lunches at the kitchen table. Kelly led Laura back outside and placed her mojito glass on the table, but she did not sit.

"Do you want to get in the pool? It is nice and warm."

Laura had work appointments beginning in the early evening, so she was not particularly enthusiastic about negating her hair and light make-up, but Kelly's mood was far more important. "I didn't bring my bikini."

"No need," Kelly said and lifted the dress off, over her head, in a single graceful move. She was a little fleshier than Laura but just as well groomed.

"What about Angela and Michel?"

"They've seen me naked many times. Oh hell, Laura, they join me sometimes. I've never known you to be modest or bashful."

"I'm not," Laura responded and began undressing. "I never want to offend anyone. I was just checking."

Kelly stepped down into the water and sighed with pleasure. Laura was only a score of seconds behind her. Kelly walked toward Laura, wrapped her arms and then her legs around Laura. "You have always been very special to me, Laura Simmons."

"And you to me," Laura replied. "Something is really bothering you, Kell. What is it?"

Kelly did not loosen her embrace. "I am not happy."

"That's not good. What is making you unhappy? What do you want to do?"

"In one word . . . Raoul."

"I thought you loved him."

"I did. I do in a form. He is a good man for the most part." Kelly looked all around them. "He provides well and has been very generous, but he is cold, distant and unemotional. Hell, sex is just slam-bam-thank-you-ma'am, and I don't even get a thank you." They both laughed. "He never tended to my orgasms. I actually considered hiring you to service him, to keep him happy, so I didn't have to do that. You're so much better at that than me." She paused and held Laura's eyes. "Have you ever done him?"

"I try to avoid talking about clients, but in this case, I'll make an exception. No, I have not, and I don't know any of my friends who have."

Kelly released Laura, swam away a few strokes, returned, then stopped at arm's length. Raoul, my family and his family continue to harp on me about my dependence on Xanax. It's the only thing keeping me going."

"It can be addictive, can't it?"

"Yes . . . as I have been told a million times. I've been to multiple counselors, therapists, specialists and whatever to find a better way. I've tried to wean myself, with a doctor's assistance, multiple times. I even tried a rehad center a couple of years ago."

"Damn, Kell. We've been friends for 20 years, and I knew none of this. I didn't know you were struggling. I thought you had the perfect life."

"I was too ashamed, too embarrassed. I hid my addiction from everyone. Even Raoul doesn't know the whole story, but he knows most of it. He constantly rags on me. I'm an embarrassment to his profession."

"Oh, Kell, I'm so sorry. You said you've done a treatment facility. How was that? I've never talked to anyone that has done one."

Kelly smiled. "It was freedom, Laura. It was no walk in the park, but it was freedom. I did not have to listen to or deal with Raoul or my family. I'm really tired of being condemned as some human addict."

"Can't blame you there. Why don't you divorce him and move on, if you're that unhappy? Go to a happier spot."

"Even the answer to that question is embarrassing," Kelly said and leaned back to float without words for a few seconds. Laura waited patiently. Kelly stood and stepped toward Laura less than an arm's length, this time. "I will confess to you, but I want this strictly just between us. I could not even admit this to my therapists. Also, I know this is going to sound very shallow, but I've become too accustomed to the money and what it can buy." Kelly smirked and nodded her head rapidly several times. Laura did not react. "I know, I know, that is so shallow, but it's the truth. You don't need to tell me how foolish that is. I know it is, but it's how I feel. I haven't worked in my life, and I don't really want to start now. Yes, I have a college degree that my parents paid for, but there is nothing I want to do for my own income." Kelly paused, smiled and winked at Laura. "Well, I have seriously thought about your profession, to be candid and forthright."

"Kell . . . ," Laura stopped when Kelly raised her left hand palm forward.

"This is a topic for later discussion. I don't want to get into it now. Let me only say here, I have always enjoyed sex. I still do . . . just not with Raoul . . . well and others before him."

"Have you asked him?"

Kelly laughed hard for a handful of seconds. "He would go ballistic . . . for a host of reasons, not least of which is he would see my feelings as an insult to his manhood. He is a traditionalist, so much so, I am fairly confident he has never stepped out and had an extramarital affair."

"He is rather rare, then, from my perspective. Kelly, a majority of my customers are married, and every one of them claims their wives aren't interested in sex. Heck, Kell, I have a couple of female customers who are quite like you. I only say this to encourage you not to discount the potential."

"Oh, I don't. I am only telling you how I feel at the moment. Like I said earlier, I have seriously thought about engaging your services . . . openly . . . as a gift to him."

"I will not urge you to do anything like that."

"Why?"

"Wrong reasons," Laura responded. "But, I'll do whatever you want me to do and whatever will be helpful to you. I've always been your friend, and I'll do whatever will best help you."

Kelly stared at her girlfriend for several seconds, then shook her head and waved her hand. "We can talk about all of that later. Sex was not the topic on my mind at the moment." Kelly paused again to search Laura's eyes.

Laura showed no emotion or reaction. She wanted Kelly to have all the room she needed to go in whatever direction she wanted to go. One of Laura's many skills was listening. Some of her customers just wanted and needed her to listen. She knew how to listen without judgment.

Kelly shook her head, broke eye contact, and said, "I'm thinking about going to go into an indulgence camp."

"Oh, Kell, why? You can afford the drugs. You aren't a threat to society. Why would you do that . . . give up your freedom?"

Kelly chuckled softly. "Refuge . . . to put it plainly. I'm tired of Raoul's condemnations and harping on me. I'm not giving up my freedom. I'm reclaiming my freedom. If he decides to divorce me, then so be it. I'll not resist. Plus, if he divorces me, I think he'll be more generous . . . to buy me off. I just can't take that step on my own volition. I suppose this is a way of forcing his hand."

"Odd way to do it," Laura murmured.

"Yes, perhaps so, but I see it as reclaiming my freedom. I've done my research. I know what I'm getting into, and I'm comfortable with those constraints," Kelly said and waved her hand again. "Plus, I intend to try some of the other drugs."

"You don't need to go to the camp for that. You can get whatever you want. Hell, Kell, I can do it with you, if you want. I haven't done benzos like you are doing, but I've done most of the others at one time or another."

"A generous offer, my friend, but I'd still have to come home. I can safely hide out at the camp, and I think it's the most attractive option. I don't have to listen to him, hear from him, or see him if I don't want to do so." Kelly looked at Laura, as if she wanted or was expecting a response. Laura remained quiet and neutral. "I didn't tell you all this because I wanted you to talk me out of it. I have only one purpose. You're the one person, including my husband, his family, my family, neighbors, or anyone else, who I know will not judge me and I can trust . . . and more importantly, I have one request. Please come and see me, Laura."

"Sure, Kell. I've never been to one of those camps. But, I think one condition is relevant and germane." Laura stopped, raised her eyebrows, gesturing for a response. Kelly nodded her head. "I don't think I can just show up. So, once you get settled and check things out, call me, or send me a text or eMail. I'll come to you right away."

"That's agreeable." Kelly extended her arms for hug. Laura took the gesture and stepped into Kelly's embrace. "Thank you, Laura," she whispered into Laura's ear.

"You're most welcome."

"Now, I'm beginning to chill."

"Me too."

Kelly chuckled and nodded to the patio. As they stepped out of the pool, Angela appeared with a towel spread in her arms. She wrapped the towel around Kelly, then did the same for Laura. The two stood still and quiet for several seconds.

"Do you need anything else, Miss Kelly?" asked Angela.

Kelly looked at Laura. "Do you have time? I don't want to interfere with your work . . . er . . . pleasure."

The two women giggled together.

"What time is it, anyway?"

"It's not quite two, ma'am," Angela responded.

"Sure, I've got time."

"Then, if you would, Angela, fresh mojitos are called for . . . us."

"Yes, ma'am. Right away." Angela retrieved the two barely touched drinks on the table and returned to the house.

Laura followed Kelly's lead and used the towel to finish drying off. Kelly draped the towel over the patio chair and sat down. "You can dress if you wish, Laura, but unless you object, I'm going to enjoy the warm air."

Nakedness did not bother Laura whatsoever, especially since she knew neither Angela nor Michel would be offended.

Angela placed the fresh drinks in front of each of the women. "Anything else, Miss Kelly?" she asked.

Kelly gestured to Laura, who shook her head in the negative. "Thank you, Angela. I think we'll be fine for now." Kelly waited for Angela to close the door. "Now that we've dispensed with business. I've got some more curiosity questions."

"Fire away."

"Going back to the party, were the police interested in you or any of the other ladies?"

"Not really . . . only in so much as we might be aware of John Baxter's activities?"

"Did they ask about the sex?"

"Not that I'm aware of, but I didn't really ask Juli and Sandi. The detective who questioned me asked how much I was paid. When I pushed back, he backed off on that aspect. So, no, they weren't interested. They did check to make sure our licenses and medical certificates were current, but that was it."

"Was your date personal or professional?"

"It was business, but who knows. He was showing more than typical customer interest, but for now, it's all business. He wanted dinner, conversation, and eventually, sex, so it was an expensive evening for him."

"What is the difference between business and pleasure, or customer and friend?"

Laura smiled and chuckled. "In one word, money. In my profession, it's a fine line beyond the money."

"Would you have sex with me?"

"As a friend or a customer?"

"Well, to tell the truth, I hadn't thought of that question until you asked. I suppose the correct answer, given my feelings at the moment . . . a customer initially . . . perhaps eventually as a friend. Are you going to have to testify?"

"Wow! That was quite the abrupt transition."

"Sorry."

"No, no need. You've a lot of things on your mind," Laura said. "No, I don't think I will. I know nothing relevant to Baxter's activities at issue. To your previous point, the medium answer is it depends upon what you want or what you wish to achieve. I'll only remind you, sex is my business and I've yet to offer free samples. I'm not Costco."

Kelly laughed heartily—the best Laura had heard her laugh all day. "No that you're not. The fact is, I don't know what I want. The thought just popped into my head. I remember those days when we were young."

"Yeah, me too . . . with warm memories. I'll only say, we were children then. We're adults now. Have you been with a woman?"

"No, but I've thought about it."

"Well, that's a start. When you're ready, I'm always available. As I said earlier, I'm an equal opportunity lover, and I've learned well how to love a woman. When are you planning to enter the camp?"

"Day after tomorrow."

"Keep me informed as you go through this, Kell, and you tell me when you want me to visit, or you want to talk, or you're ready to come home."

"I won't forget. I've another curiosity question."

"Sure. Shoot."

"I haven't seen your parents in . . . what . . . 10 years. How do they feel about your profession?"

"My mother is more accepting, but my father less so."

"How does your mother accept it?"

"She has talked to me numerous times since I started and proclaimed my chosen profession. She knows I'm enjoying myself and making good money. She says as long as I'm happy and legal, she can support my choices."

"And . . . your dad?"

"He's still very much old school. He believes prostitution is a sin and must be condemned, even though it has been legal and regulated in this state for six years or so, and in practice since recorded human history began."

"That must be very hard on you," Kelly observed.

"I wish it was not so, but I don't control my father's feelings or opinions, and I'm not willing to comply with the ancient morality of the Victorian era that grips my father."

"You must be disturbed by your father's rejection," Kelly said.

"Oh, I don't think he has rejected me. He's just reflecting his struggle with the changing times. He disapproved of the state reforming the laws regarding prostitution. And then, Congress displayed the audacity to repeal the federal drug laws in part and reformed the remainder to regulate street drugs like alcohol and tobacco. He's still civil when we have family gatherings and such, and I do my best to avoid the topics that upset him. Mom does her best to dampen his anger, but there are flair ups now and then. What about your parents?"

"I don't have the same problem you do. My parents are pleasantly oblivious to my struggle."

Laura considered Kelly's words. "It sounds like you're on better terms with your parents. Don't you think you should talk to them?"

"I wish I could, but to be honest, I think there is a very thin line between their acceptance and the kind of condemnation you face from your father. No, I can't talk to anyone other than you. I know you accept me as I am."

"I do."

"Thank you for that, Laura." Kelly paused and held Laura's eyes. "Now, I'm mindful that you're a working woman, and after our dip in the pool, you have some prep time before your first appointment."

"Thanks, Kell, but I'm here if you need me. I can cancel my engagements."

Kelly smiled. "You're so generous and warmhearted. You always have been, but no, I think I've accomplished what I wanted with our lunch meeting. I'll probably not see you again until we meet at the camp, but I'm most grateful that you're willing to visit." Kelly stood and held her arms out. Laura followed, and the two women embraced. Kelly whispered in Laura's ear, "You are my best friend, Laura Lynn Simmons. I love you."

"I love you," Laura whispered back.

They disengaged. Laura nodded, stepped to her clothes, and dressed. Kelly chose not to do so, and she chose to just watch Laura. The two women walked together to the front door. Neither Angela nor Michel appeared. Laura noted with pleasant surprise that Kelly showed no sign of modesty as she opened the front door. Laura took a quick scan out the door. The trees, hedges and other vegetation shielded any would-be critical observers. They embraced each other again, said their goodbyes, and Laura wished Kelly good luck.

Laura settled and buckled into her small, pink, MINI Cooper car. She started the tinny engine, then turned to wave goodbye to Kelly who was still standing in all her glory at the front door. As Laura approached the front gate, the large, pseudo-iron gate opened automatically. She also noticed in her rearview mirror that the gate also closed automatically.

The 15-minute drive back to her apartment went smoothly with very little traffic, leaving Laura alone with her thoughts. Before she reached home, Laura shook her head like shaking off water or some enveloping fog to get her mind focused on what lay ahead for the late afternoon and evening. She had a full dance card, so it was going to take concentration and focus to manage her time properly. There was so much of this afternoon that she needed to think about, but business was business, and the customer always came first.

—

3

The detectives' bullpen had remained comparatively quiet through the morning and lunch. Rod Ramirez had a rare few hours at his desk and prided himself in catching up on his paperwork.

"Ramirez," called his boss, Captain Johnny Johnston, chief of detectives.

Rod stood and walked to Johnston. "You rang, *el jefe?*"

Johnston gestured for Rod to enter and close the door. "Where are you on the Baxter case?"

"I reviewed all the reports from the team and added my summary earlier this morning. The package was sent to and receipt acknowledged by the district attorney's office just before lunch. The lead prosecutor said she was happy with the reports. Baxter's bail was denied by the court as a flight risk, and he was transferred to county jail, yesterday. So, the case belongs to the district attorney now."

"Excellent. Does she think you'll need to testify?" asked Johnston.

"We didn't discuss that at all, but my guess is no . . . unless they want to present the conditions of his arrest."

"OK. Then, I can take this one off my list."

"Yes, Captain. I think you can."

"Well done, Rod. It could've gone south. You managed it well. Now, you've got the governor's commission on drug policy."

"Yes . . . not high on my list of things to do."

"Understood . . . but this is important, and I know you know that."

"Yes, I do. We start in less than an hour at the Regent Hotel. The president of the commission indicated we needed a welcome session this afternoon with the real work starting tomorrow morning. The first two sessions—today and tomorrow—will be closed door, then the third session will be a public event in the hotel's auditorium. I'll be out of pocket for the rest of the day and the next two days. I expect to be back in the office on Friday. I'm not quite sure what to expect in either the closed or public sessions, but hey, I've certainly seen the before and after of these changes."

"Yes, you have, which is also why you were chosen by the mayor and the chief to represent law enforcement."

"Thank you for your confidence and the chief's."

"Sure. Completely justified. Keep me posted as best you can. I expect headquarters is going to want a 'how's it going' report. Don't be surprised if the chief calls you directly, but just in case they call me, I'd appreciate any progress report you can offer."

"Sure thing, boss. No problem."

Captain Johnston nodded his head and then gestured like he was shooing a fly.

Rod returned to his desk. He had just logged into his office network account when Bob Lewis scooted his chair over to Rod's desk.

"Is our star pupil in trouble with the principal?" Lewis asked.

"Naw. He was just checking on the Baxter case and offering encouragement for this damn commission meeting I've got coming up."

"Are you going to tell 'em the facts of life?"

"I don't know about that, but everyone certainly knows how I feel about the drug policy change."

"Yeah, but will they understand?"

"That's the $64,000-question, isn't it?"

"Give 'em hell, bud."

"Thanks, Bob.

Lewis pushed himself back to his desk. Rod turned back to his computer screen and logged in again, since his access had timed out. He checked his Inbox—nothing new. Rod completed his reading of the crime statistics summary in advance of the commission meeting. He was comfortable with his position and the basis in fact of his report to the commission. Rod figured he would go over to the hotel a little early.

Rod arrived 20 minutes ahead of the scheduled start time, found the small conference room in which they would hold their initial meetings, found a peripheral chair, even though the place tags had already been set out. He waited patiently for the others to arrive. Several members walked in just before their scheduled start time. Rod greeted each member of the commission as they arrived. The whole group had met a couple of times at the state capital campus. They knew each other and their backgrounds.

Detective-Sergeant Rod Ramirez was one of seven members of the governor's commission on drug policy and the only current frontline law enforcement officer. The commission carried out their general initial session to open their review conference. Rod has his material organized and was ready to go.

The opening less-than-half session covered the latest administrative details including their planned social encounters during the conference. Rod continued to learn more every day he worked on commission matters. He always sought to contain his sense of frustration, disappointment, and even an element of betrayal by the government with the demonization of psychotropic substances. Learning was good, but so many years had been lost.

The drive home proved uneventful with moderate traffic. The police communications over the dedicated, installed radio remained routine and unexciting. Fortunately, there were no distractions. Since he did not check onto the network, he did not have to checkoff. Rod marveled every day at the sense of sanctuary and warmth he felt when he turned the corner on their street. He smiled on sight of their modest suburban home with its mature trees, constantly green faux-lawn in deference to the persistent water crisis, and the drought-resistant hedges, bushes and plants that kept their property appearing so plush, despite the persistent water crisis. He remotely opened the garage door, pulled his car in, parked, shutdown and closed the door behind him.

As he entered the house and kitchen, he heard Marci before he could see her. "You're home early. Is everything OK?"

Rod grinned broadly when he saw her in her shorts and T-shirt, yet covered partially with her full apron. "The judge adjourned us after he opened the meeting." They kissed more meaningfully than just a peck. "Since it's going to be a busy couple of days, I thought I would come home early for a nice family dinner. We've a working dinner tomorrow night."

"So, I'm not invited."

They chuckled together. "No."

Rodrigo 'Rod' Ramirez and Marcella 'Marci' Ramirez were both 35-years-old, still in good shape, and had been married for 17 years. Rod had served four years in the U.S. Marine Corps right after they were married, rising to the rank of sergeant before his enlistment was up, and then he joined the police force. They had one daughter—Bella Joy Ramirez—who was all of 15 years old, going on 30, not a perfect student but better than average, an accomplished striker on her school soccer team, and more headstrong than either of her parents wished.

"Go get changed, then set the table," Marci commanded.

Rod did just that, changing into loose shorts and a T-shirt. He turned on the TV, changed the channel to the local news, and set the table in short order. The broadcast covered the latest traffic accidents, actions before city hall, and the weather. If they had acknowledged the opening of the commission's work, they may have covered it earlier in the broadcast. "Do you need any help?" Rod asked.

"You just did it. Thanks, hon. I'm just finishing up Todd's Hot Dish. It'll go in the oven shortly."

"Love that stuff." The rice, crumbled and browned hamburger, and mushroom soup casserole had always been a family favorite.

"I know you do. We all do. Bella should be home any minute." Marci closed the oven door.

Rod jumped in and washed the pots, pans and utensils Marci had used to prepare the ingredients. She took off her apron, hung it up, and hugged her husband from behind. She kissed a bare spot on his lower neck.

Just then, Bella entered and shouted, "Get a room." Her thick shoulder length dark brown hair had been pulled back in a braided ponytail she preferred from soccer practice. Bella's post-pubescent body was maturing nicely on her slim 5'10" frame. She had exquisite full lips, near perfect complexion, and light brown, almost golden eyes. Bella was Marci and Rod's only child.

They all laughed. "You've seen worse," Marci responded but did not release her embrace. Rod finished up his task.

"Yes, I have," added Bella.

"Do you want to freshen up" Marci asked their daughter.

"How long do I have?"

Marci glanced at the oven timer. "About 15 minutes."

"I took a shower after *práctica de fútbol*, but a quick sponge bath would cool me off a little from the walk home." Bella was not a fluent Spanish speaker, but she liked to use what she could. Both her parents spoke good, passable Spanish as their second language.

"You've got time."

Bella departed to her room and bathroom.

Rod finished and turned around in Marci's arms, still holding each other. "How was your day?"

"Pretty ordinary" she answered. "More importantly, how was *your* day?" she asked with emphasis on the pronoun.

"Low key by my standards. The commission opened, but Judge Kendall just set the stage and adjourned."

"Tomorrow's going to be a full day."

"It appears so. I give my report first thing in the morning—top of the agenda."

"Good luck. Would you like a glass of wine?"

"No, thanks. I'll pass tonight."

Bella returned and added with a light-hearted tone. "Give it a rest, you guys."

They all laughed. Marci and Rod disengaged. The oven buzzer sounded. Marci turned off the oven, while Rod grabbed two hot pads, retrieved the rectangular casserole dish, and placed it on the table with two other large hot pads placed by Marci, who then grabbed the salad from the refrigerator. Bella poured three large glasses of iced tea for each of them.

They sat in their usual places at the small, round, kitchen table with the two women on either side of Rod. Bella offered grace to bless the meal.

Each of them served themselves. They discussed Bella's schoolwork and soccer practice. Everything seemed right with the world around them.

"I want to hear about your commission meeting," Bella declared.

"Not much to tell at this point," answered Rod. "Associate Justice Kendall opened the meeting with a summary. We discussed the background, and the charge from the governor and legislature, then we approved the agenda."

"Can I see it?" Bella asked.

"Well, I guess so, after dinner. It's not marked, and the judge didn't indicate it was sensitive or confidential, so yes, I think you can see it."

"Cool. It's a big topic at school. We're all interested."

"I'm sure," Rod said.

"Papa, didn't you tell me there was a public session after your closed-door meeting?"

"Yes. It's only closed-door for efficiency. We've a lot of ground to cover in a day. The results will be presented to open the public session, day after tomorrow."

"Can I go?"

"It's a school day," Marci interjected.

"Mom, this is really important," protested Bella. "It may be a once-in-a-lifetime event. It's the talk of the school. Even the teachers are talking about what the commission means and what its potential impact will be on our community."

"How do you think everyone feels?" asked Marci.

"Well, there is resistance . . . people who think we should go back to the way it was . . . and crack down harder on drug users and pushers."

"Are they the majority?" Rod asked.

"Oh hell no."

"Bella, please," Marci protested her daughter's language.

"Sorry, Mom. We just all want to know the results."

"Bella," inserted Rod, "we're only an advisory panel to the governor and legislature. We'll decide nothing. We're only going to review our status and progress so far, as well as any changes to the system."

"I've no idea how all this is going to turn out."

"Yeah, Dad, but you do have an opinion. I was old enough to remember the news reports from the time of the change when they talked about the way things used to be."

"Well, I've been in law enforcement since just after you were born. From my perspective, it is a world of difference."

"Yeah, but do you support the change?"

"Yes, Bella, I do. Tomorrow morning, I'll report the crime statistics, and the data we have is undeniable. From my perspective, we have less overdose deaths or danger, less crime virtually across the board, and less trauma on the community. However, there are costs associated with those improvements."

"Like what?" Bella asked.

"For one thing, the suicide rate is up. over the last six years of the SCIP Act. Some of our people, including our priests, will not be tolerant of that cost."

"That is sad, but can you tell the difference between intentional versus accidental?" asked Bella.

"Not from my perspective. The medical professionals on the panel will have to pass judgment on that question. Yet, my opinion is, there appears to be far fewer accidental overdoses . . . certainly not like we used to see years ago. But we shall have to see what the others say."

"Then do you support the SCIP Act changes?" Marci asked.

"In short, yes. From a law enforcement perspective, we appear to be more balanced and focused on the root causes of crime. There are tweaks we can and should make, but in my humble opinion, we, and here I mean all of us, are far better off with the SCIP Act than we were with that damnable war on drugs nastiness."

"Back to my earlier question . . . ?" Bella said.

Marci looked at Rod, who subtly nodded his consent.

"Very well," Marci answered. "I'll send a note to the school tomorrow, and we'll go together to hear the summary results and public testimony."

Bella smiled broadly. "Thanks, Momma . . . and Papa."

All three of them had finished their meal. Rod asked, "Is everyone done?"

Bella did not wait for the answer. She started clearing the table, stored and refrigerated the leftovers, and jumped on the dishes. Marci and Rod marveled at their daughter, and repeatedly glanced at each other for reassurance that it was real. Neither of them moved as they enjoyed their daughter's performance.

"OK. Dishes are done," Bella announced. "Thanks for a delicious dinner, Momma."

"You're welcome."

Bella looked directly at her father. "You said I could see the agenda after dinner."

"Yes, I did." Rod stood, went to his collapsible case, retrieved the agenda, and handed it to Bella.

After their daughter read it several times and studied the contents, she said, "Wow! That's pretty broad."

"Yes, it is."

"What's this Black Hole prison thing?" asked Bella.

"We haven't really talked about that aspect of the reforms, but it's the end of the road for habitual or dangerous criminals, who've not responded to lesser punishment and attempts at rehabilitation. We don't have capital punishment anymore. When a criminal gets to that end stage, they go in and only come out when they pass. It's only about containment. At the Black Hole stage, there's no parole, release or commutation. There is only survival until eventual death."

"That sounds very harsh," Bella commented.

"It is," answered Rod. "It's intended to be. At the Black Hole stage, the state is no longer concerned with the criminal's welfare—only public safety."

"Are you going to talk about these Black Hole prisons at the public session?" Bella asked.

"It's on the agenda, so yes, that is the plan."

"OK, Papa. Thanks for sharing it with me. Now, if you will excuse me, I've got homework to get done before bedtime." Bella did not wait for a response and departed for her room.

Marci and Rod stared at each other for several more seconds.

"What have they done with our daughter?" Rod asked.

Marci smiled broadly. "She is really engaged with this question, and it sounds like her friends are too."

"I suppose that's a good thing, but I hope she isn't too enamored with the drug policy stuff."

"I don't think so. We've been pretty open with her, and I think she understands. Are you curious?"

Rod stared sternly at Marci. "To be honest, yes, I suppose a little. But I entered the Marine Corps and then the police force when we had random piss checks. Things have changed, but for the police, not so much. We haven't had a piss test in several years now, but the force is still a socially very conservative organization. They know we dabbled with pot after I left the Marine Corps, but I'm not willing to challenge their position today. Are you curious?" he asked emphasizing the pronoun.

"Yes, I am, and I freely admit it. But my curiosity is not sufficient to experiment without you."

"Well, it's not going to happen anytime soon."

"So be it. I'm still with you." Marci stood, checked the kitchen to make sure everything was in order, and went to the family room.

They watched some sitcom episodes, although Rod's thoughts were clearly on other matters. Marci recognized the state and knew better than to interrupt his thoughts. After a couple of hours of ordinary entertainment, the

Ramirez couple headed off to bed, said goodnight to Bella, tended to their nightly hygiene, and retired to their bed. They both read their books. Rod lasted less than Marci and was soon fast asleep.

—

4

Molly Pritchard, a junior at Bella's high school, had organized the pool party the week before. Bella and Gretchen had walked over to Molly's house since their homes were only separated by a couple of blocks. The perfect day and sunny weather made the afternoon distraction a welcome change in the mid-spring season. The warmer than usual air made the coolness of the pool water quite attractive.

Gretchen Gisela 'GG' Hessian was Bella's oldest friend. She was a strikingly gorgeous young woman with shoulder-length, curly, blond hair, sky blue eyes. Gretchen was a couple of inches shorter than Bella.

The third of the *tres amigas*, Christie Theriot, was the shortest and youngest of the three of them. Her bobbed, dark red hair always made her stand out in a crowd. She had already told them she would be late since her mother insisted she go shopping with her. Christie laughed when she told them she would carry her bikini in her purse and change once she arrived at Molly's house. She always wore the skimpiest version of a bikini. Bella and Gretchen were both just as comfortable as Christie to get naked in the sunshine, but they were less willing to be on display with barely covering bikinis that were in style.

Molly answered the door and welcomed her two friends to her home. She was one year ahead of Gretchen and Bella in school. The girls had known each since middle school. Molly told them where the snacks and drinks were, and she informed them that her parents were out shopping for the afternoon.

"There are a lot of folks I don't recognize," Gretchen observed.

"Yeah," responded Molly, "some seniors I know and mostly kids in my class. You guys always fit right in with any group."

"Thanks," Bella added, "we try."

"Where Christie?"

"She should be here in an hour or so," answered Gretchen.

"Changing room is down the hall." Molly pointed down the hallway to the right. "Girls on the right. Boys on the left." The doorbell rang. "Excuse me," Molly said and turned to the door. "Mingle," she added over her shoulder.

Both Gretchen and Bella wore light airy wraps over their bikinis. They chose to retain their wraps for the time being.

"Hey, girls," said a young man Bella did not recognize. "Welcome." He held two red plastic cups. "Would you like some punch?" Gretchen took a proffered cup.

Bella held up her hand. "No thanks."

"OK. Suit yourself. Please allow me to be the first. If either or both you would like a stiff dick to play with, just let me know. I'm your man," he said with a broad smile.

"You're very generous, but no thank you," Bella responded.

"Me too," added Gretchen.

"If you change your mind, I'll be here for you, either of you."

Bella only nodded her head and moved past the young man. They made their way through the throng of scantily clad males and females to the kitchen. Bella noticed the large punch bowl with several stacks of upside-down red cups. She looked for and found the cooler she was certain to be around. Bella searched quickly for her favorite, Fanta Grape, but she found nothing even remotely close. The silver can she sought finally caught her attention. She reached through the ice chunks and cold water to extract a Diet Coke can.

"The punch wasn't good enough?" Gretchen asked.

"We've talked about these situations before, GG. How do you know what was in that cup, or in the punch bowl for that matter?"

"You've gotta trust someone, Bell."

"I know hardly anyone." She popped the top of her can with the corresponding 'cush.' "The risk is simply too great." They worked their way outside and to the far side of the pool where the only two unoccupied lounges sat in the shade. "My parents taught me long ago to be very careful taking any food or drink from a person I didn't know and explicitly trust with my life."

"That sounds really severe."

"Perhaps so, but I believe their teachings are accurate and appropriate." The two girls settled onto the lounges. "Both my father and my mother have told me stories of how girls got into trouble drinking spiked punch. I don't need to learn that lesson. I trust my parents. I'll stick with that."

They watched the busy scene of girls and boys in the pool, milling around on the patio engaged in unheard conversations, and moving in and out of the house. Bella had always enjoyed people watching, and today was a good opportunity.

"My parents never taught me about not trusting the punch," Gretchen mumbled, verging upon inaudible with the cacophony of teenagers at play.

"You must judge for yourself. I just believe my parents, and I believe they're trying to keep me safe while I fly farther from the nest."

"They've also let you try stuff."

"Yes, they have, and I'm grateful. I've learned early that tobacco makes me sick—no interest in that crap, in any form. I don't even like being around people who use the stuff. Just smelling smoke makes me ill. And, kissing someone who has been smoking is like sticking your tongue in a full ashtray. Yuck!"

"My parents just pretend smoking doesn't exist," Gretchen observed. "They do almost the same thing with alcohol, although I know they drink when my siblings and I aren't around. My brother got drunk one time, and they didn't react so well. I've tried to talk to them about it, but they GAF me off every time, so much so that I've stopped asking."

"I'd offer my parents," Bella said, "but I know they'd never agree, because they would see it as interfering in your family affairs."

"So, I guess we'll just do girl talk."

"Works for me. Hey, do you want something more to drink?"

Gretchen laughed heartily. "Yeah, I learned my lesson from my bestie. I'll take a Diet Coke as well."

Bella laughed. "Good girl. I'll be right back. Save our chairs."

"Will do."

Bella rose from the lounge chair, walked around the pool, and into the kitchen. Before she opened the lid on the large cooler, Bella noticed the distinctive short red hair. Christie was talking to the guy who greeted them when they arrived. Bella went to her friend. "When did you get here?"

"Fifteen, twenty minutes ago . . . enough time to knock one off with this fellow." He smiled proudly. "What's your name?"

"Jordie."

Christie extended her hand to the guy. "Nice to meet you, Jordie. I'm Christie. This is Bella." Jordie extended his right hand to Bella. She saw no reason not to shake his hand, so she did just that. "Thanks for the fuck, a worthy cock but a little quick on the trigger, I must say." Christie looked at Bella. "Did you do him too?"

"No. He offered it, but neither GG nor I took up his offer." Bella looked at Jordie. "You figure you'd ask every girl, and you'd find a few."

Jordie again smiled with pride in his eyes. "It works. My uncle told me it's called the Rasputin proposition."

"What does that mean?"

"Grigori Rasputin was some kind of mystic in Russia over a hundred years ago," Jordie responded. "According to Uncle Joe, Rasputin proclaimed that if you asked 100 women every night, you'll find one willing woman to go to bed with you."

"I guess you found your today's one then huh," Bella said and winked at Christie.

"Hey, he was a good ride. I don't care what you call it."

"How many have you had at this party?'

"Three so far. Do you want your turn?"

Bella smiled demurely. "No thanks. I'll pass."

"Where's GG?" asked Christie.

"She's outside waiting on me to bring her a soda."

"Well then, let's go. See'ya Jordie. Thanks for the poke."

Christie did not wait for a response and turned to the kitchen. Bella founded her friend. Christie stopped at the punch bowl and filled a red cup. Bella smiled to herself and felt no reason to tell Christie what she was thinking. She grabbed two Diet Cokes from the cooler. Christie did not take the open chair. Instead, she brushed Gretchen's legs apart, sat down between them, and leaned back against her friend's chest.

"Great to see you, Christie."

"Nice cushions, GG. How's it hangin'?"

Christie took the proffered soda can from Bella, opened it and took an initial swig. "Firm, and where they're supposed to be, since you asked." Bella sat beside them and swallowed some of her drink.

"I can feel that." They all laughed. "What's the topic this afternoon?" Christie asked

"We were talking about alcohol and tobacco before Bell got lost getting us a couple of drinks."

"No thanks to tobacco," Christie said rather matter-of-factly, "although I've smoked a joint or two when no other form was available. I don't much care for smoke. Burns my lungs and makes me cough. That THC inhaler they sell works wonders."

"Yeah, quicker than gummies and doesn't pollute your lungs," observed Bella. The girls watched the poolside players who were now showing obvious signs of intoxication. Several of the girls had already shed their bikini tops and appeared to be working toward discarding their bottoms as well. "Looks like things are going to get sporty."

"Yeah, this could get fun to watch," added Christie.

"You two," Gretchen said, pinching Christie gently, who jumped slightly, "are much more comfortable being naked in public."

"Not quite public, but point made," Christie said. "I see one erection already. It's only a matter of time before we witness tab 'A' in slot 'B.'"

"That's rather crude." Gretchen wrapped her arms around Christie's shoulders.

"I would say direct rather than crude. Plus, we've all done it. Heck, I had a decent romp when I got here."

Bella snickered at Christie's declaration. Gretchen had not been aware. "I presume the 'stiff dick' guy at the door," Gretchen said.

"Yep, that's the one," Bella replied before Christie added her giggling affirmation.

"Hey, the opportunity presented, and I'm glad I did it . . . a worthy cock, I must say." They watched. Sure enough, one couple began their coupling in the pool. They seemed oblivious to everyone else, or perhaps they just did not care. "And so it begins." Some of the others watched, but most of the people around the pool just ignored the sexual intercourse underway in the pool.

"Do you guys think that is alright?" Gretchen asked, gesturing to the pool.

"Sure," responded Christie rather strongly.

"Are they hurting anyone?" Bella asked.

"No," Gretchen answered.

"Exactly. If we're offended by people enjoying sex, then we've the choice to leave. They're not fucking in the town square or city hall. While my parents haven't explicitly taught me about freedom of choice, they certainly have left me with that belief. The whole drug thing is exactly that—freedom of choice."

"You think that is why the state passed the SCIP?" Christie asked.

"In part, yes. My Dad has the governor's commission meeting today. He says the evidence shows that legalization of drugs has reduced crime almost across the board. People no longer have to do illegal things to buy or sell that stuff. We can't go down to the store and buy them, but in a few more years, we can."

"Why can't we buy them?" Gretchen asked.

Bella chuckled. "I asked my Dad that very question the other day while we were talking about the commission conference. He said there were several reasons. We're young and still growing, and they don't know if some drugs might affect our growth. The law still considers us minors until we turn 18, so our parents are responsible for what we do."

"Then, freedom of choice belongs to our parents," Gretchen stated, "but not to us."

"Our freedom of choice belongs to our parents until we're considered adults under the law."

"At least your parents acknowledge there're things outside their bubble," Gretchen whispered, as the coupling pair in the water made sounds of climax.

"They're trying. I'm grateful. Yet, I still feel they don't appreciate what's going on around us."

"Speaking of that," Christie said, "do you guys remember Johnny 'O,' Johnny Oscarson?"

"Sure," Bella answered. "He was the quarterback of the football team last year."

"That's him. I ran into him the other day at the mall. He told me some of his teammates are havin' a party at the university . . . a closed sex party."

Gretchen gasped. "He knows *las tres amigas* enjoy a good time. We've talked about trying something like this for quite some time now. This looks like the perfect opportunity."

"Sounds a bit much," Bella said.

"Yeah," added Gretchen.

"Johnny told me they're all regularly tested, and they're disease free."

"So are we," Bella injected.

"Yeah. My point was or rather is that this party should be a safe place to try out the sex drugs we've talked about many times."

"I'm certainly not taking any of their drugs," Bella responded sharply. "I don't care how safe you or they think they are."

"Me either," Gretchen added.

"Sure, sure, you've been pretty clear about that for a long time."

"We can't just go to the store and buy those drugs," stated Bella.

"I think I've got a way to get high quality IDs we can use to buy what we want. We probably should use them at one of the small towns outside of the city like Minville."

"That's illegal," Bella pressed.

"The law hasn't caught up, Bell. You said you're for freedom of choice. We're just trying to exercise our choice."

"She does make sense, Bell."

"I've got to think about this."

"For God's sake, don't go talkin' to your parents and especially your Dad."

"I know, I know. I'd like to, but yeah, I know how they'd react, especially my Dad. That aside, I need time to think. Just so I understand our time window, when is this . . . this party supposed to take place?"

"In a couple of weeks . . . weekend after next. But, if we're going to get IDs, we need to decide fairly soon. I imagine they don't make those things overnight."

"Understood," Bella responded.

Christie moved to avoid pushing off on Gretchen and stood. "I'm hot. I'm going in the pool." She did not wait for an acknowledgment, took three quick steps, and jumped into the pool feet first. When she came up for air, her top was around her neck and shoulders. Christie looked down, saw her bare breasts, and simply removed her top to throw it toward Bella, landing short of the mark. Several girls including Molly along with two boys were completely nude.

"Looks like this party is on a roll," Gretchen observed.

"Looks like it. We might as well join 'em." Bella stood, removed her wrap, and then she removed her top and bottom.

"Wow!" exclaimed Gretchen. "You're going the whole enchilada."

"Might as well, looks like everyone else is, and I prefer naked."

"Alrighty then," Gretchen declared, "naked it is." She stood to remove her wrap, top and bottom. "When did you start removing your hair?"

"I started trimming shortly after my hair came in, and I started shaving her last summer. I really like the feeling. The skin is so soft. Do you want to feel?"

"Right here? Right now?"

"Sure, why not? They're fucking in the pool. What's wrong with a little touchy-feely?"

Gretchen did not answer and reached for Bella's groin. She stroked Bella's skin, felt her own, and then she reached back to Bella. "I see your point. I like that feel. I'm clearly the last one of *las tres amigas*," she said, glancing at Christie, who now without her bottoms as well, "to do so, huh."

Bella giggled softly. "Get with the program, girlfriend." Bella jumped into the pool and hugged Christie. Gretchen joined them, and *las tres amigas* embraced in a group hug. Several others already in the pool joined in the group hug. It was a happy day.

—

5

Their morning classes remained ordinary and uneventful. Christie and Bella attended the same 4th period American history class. They usually headed to the cafeteria together. Gretchen would join them there for lunch. Today was just like the previous days of school except for the clothes they wore. The girls deposited their backpacks and books in their lockers. They walked side-by-side offering words and phrases to friends in passing.

The lunch selection this day was rather narrow—sliced ham and peas, or macaroni & cheese with cooked carrots. Bella did not care for the carrots; they were always overcooked, but she truly loved the way the staff prepared the mac & cheese. There was something about the cheese they chose and used. Christie took the ham. They went to the table on the far side of the room they used most often. The two girls had just sat down when they noticed Gretchen enter the cafeteria. Christie and Bella took several bites of their lunch before Gretchen sat beside Christie.

"Mac & cheese . . . yum," pronounced Gretchen.

"Yeah," Bella added. "Love the stuff. I've tried to duplicate it with my Mom's help, but we've not broken the code, yet."

"Let me know when you do." Bella only nodded her agreement. "Hey, Bell, has your Dad told you anything about the commission conference?"

"Yeah, Mom and I asked him a bunch of questions at dinner. He said the preponderance of information was presented by a dozen experts, including my Dad . . ."

"What is your Dad an expert on for the conference," interrupted Christie.

"He was reporting on the crime statistics before and after the SCIP Act."

"So, what did he report?" Gretchen asked.

Bella swallowed another bite of her lunch. "He said they see the change in the drug laws as positive across the board—good for society. Not everything was positive, but it was generally positive. For example, he said they see more suicides than they used to before the change, but notably fewer deaths due to overdosing or contamination. He also said several of the experts reported on measures to improve mental health services."

"Are they going to keep the law 'as-is'?" asked Christie.

"Pretty much, apparently, although they identified a number of improvements like better mental health treatment. They had a long discussion about the indulgence camps we've been talking about for months."

"Yeah, free drugs," Christie interjected.

"I don't think that's the point."

"Then what is the point," pressed Christie.

"In short, to reduce drug related crime. Addicts can get the drugs they seek without resorting to crime to get them."

"Sounds like heaven on earth," Christie said.

"From what my Dad said, they're pretty austere places, basically a cot, a cafeteria, and a drug dispensary—nothing else."

"That doesn't sound very attractive," commented Gretchen.

"Ya got that right."

"Are you curious?" Gretchen asked.

"I'd do it in a heartbeat, if I could," suggested Christie.

"Kinda," Bella gave her answer and then continued, "I think it might answer some questions."

"Like what?" asked Gretchen.

"I talk about freedom of choice all the time, as you know, but how much freedom can we have with our patents looking over our shoulder? How much privacy do we have living in our parents' home?"

"Good point," Gretchen responded.

"Part of me wants to try it, to answer those questions, but the other part of me is scared. I know my parents are trying to protect me, to teach me, to help me learn to fly, but I also feel the blanket of their affection. I suppose my feelings about the indulgence camps is kinda like learning to ride a bike or drive a car—scary and yet exhilarating."

"Do you think your parents would ever let you do it? I know mine wouldn't." Gretchen leaned forward on both her elbows like she was really intent upon Bella's answer.

"Mine either," added Christie before Bella.

"I don't know. I've not asked them anything even remotely close to something that big or that serious."

"But you think they might?" Gretchen persisted.

"I wouldn't call my parents liberals, but they're sure more open-minded than most adults I know. They've allowed me to do things, sometimes even with them, that I never dreamed they'd allow me to do."

"Like get drunk."

"Damn, girl, really?" Christie said.

"Yeah, instead of telling me not to smoke tobacco or drink alcohol, they let me learn for myself with them watching over me. They helped me discover what I could handle and what I couldn't. They allowed me to experiment and find my limits as well as see the effects. Mom video'd me racing Dad on the iRacing game before, during and after drinking. It was crazy to watch, very graphic. My Dad bought a breathalyzer so I could see what a cop would see if I got stopped or arrested. I also learned what happens when you drink too much too fast."

"What?" asked Gretchen.

"You puke your guts out," Bella and Christie said in unison, causing all three of them to laugh hard and attracting the attention of other students around them. That observation made them laugh more. As they regained their composure, Bella whispered, "And I learned I don't want to do that again." More raucous laughter enveloped the girls. Bella waited for all three of them to recover, and then she added, "They also taught me how alcohol works and what it does to your body."

"So that's why you don't drink at parties?" asked Gretchen.

"Among many reasons. Like we talked at the pool party last weekend, I don't want to lose control or my awareness of what is around me. My Dad has told me too many stories from his job about girls drinking too much, losing control, or worse passing out, only to wake up in the morning with a very sore puss that was full of cum and even bloody. I like getting tipsy sometimes, but only with friends I trust with my life, as my Dad says. I didn't know most of those people at Molly's party, but they were a friendly bunch, weren't they?" All three of them laughed hard again as images of naked and copulating people danced in their minds. They finished what they wanted of their lunches.

"What else did you learn from talking to your father about the conference?" Gretchen returned them to the topic.

Bella smiled. "We'll probably have to wait for the report. We certainly couldn't cover a whole day's conference, but one curious item was what he called the black hole prison system."

"You mean like astronomy black holes?" Gretchen asked.

"Kinda, I suppose. He said something like what goes in doesn't come out."

"Wow! That sounds pretty harsh," observed Christie.

"Yeah, I guess it's supposed to be. But, he'd say, they created indulgence camps to keep addicts out of prison. They still have the regular prison system for those who don't respect others, and they created these black hole prisons for those few who choose to never learn . . . to never learn how to live peacefully in society."

"What's it like in one of those places?" Christie asked.

"He said he didn't know. He's never been to one of those places. But, he thought from the descriptions that it wasn't a nice place . . . kinda like law of the jungle stuff."

"What do those black hole places have to do with drug consumption?" Christie continued to ask.

"I don't know. I guess nothing, other than when they were changing the criminal justice system, they wanted to separate out the drug crimes from the regular crimes and focus the prison system on rehabilitation rather than just incarceration. It sounds like they put the really bad guys in those black hole places."

Christie nodded her head in recognition or agreement, stood, and took her lunch tray to the busing window. Gretchen and Bella followed suit.

Without speaking, *las tres amigas* made their way outside to one of the benches they liked to use under a large, mature, oak tree. The warm air and light breeze made the shade refreshingly cool. As they usually arranged things, Bella sat between her two friends.

"OK, truth or consequences time," Christie began. "What's the decision on the sex party?"

"Nothing quite like the direct approach, Christie," Bella responded. All three of them giggled a little.

"You said you wanted time to think, Bell. It's been two days. I really don't think it's that complicated."

"Would you do it if I said no?"

Without answering Bella, Christie leaned forward and looked into Gretchen's blue eyes. "Are you going?"

"I'm with Bell, Christie."

"Then my answer is no," Christie offered softly. "I may be brave, but I'm not that brave. I'm not going to a party like that alone. Why don't you want to go?" she asked Bella.

"I didn't say I didn't want to go. I asked a what if? Part of me wants to go. A good sex party would be fun, and it sounds like this party has the potential to be what we've talked about trying for months. But we probably don't know all these guys. We're trusting our safety to Johnny."

The three girls sat silently for a score of seconds and watched the other kids milling about or collected in clumps of gossipy chit-chat. The light breeze felt good and refreshing.

Bella broke the silence. "Why do we need fake IDs?"

Christie smiled. "Well, actually, a couple of reasons. One, Johnny said it was B-Y-O-D, and given your distrust of people you don't know . . ."

"It's not distrust," protested Bella. "It's wariness. There are untrustworthy people out there, Chris. Hell, there're bad people out there, even bad teenagers. It's not like we're asking for directions. We're talking about putting stuff into our bodies and fucking guys we don't know. Anything can happen, Chris. I know Johnny, but I don't know him well enough to trust him with my life."

"OK. OK. I'm sorry. I didn't mean to touch a nerve. I was just trying to answer your question. Johnny knows we are 15. The other guys probably don't know, and they might ask to see ID. Underage girls would be an instant turnoff for some guys."

"It's the law," Bella added.

"And do you agree with those laws, Bell?"

"No."

"Neither do I. All three of us have tits 'n pubic hair," Christie giggled, "well, at least those of us who don't shave," she added, looking directly at Gretchen, who only scoffed and shook her head. "We can have babies if we want. All of us have been fucking for several years now. We know what we are doing."

"True," Bella responded. "The law treats us like mindless innocents that don't know that sex is so much more than just procreation. Heck, we've all been on birth control since puberty. You know my thoughts on this stuff. I'm all in favor of freedom of choice—our choice, not someone else's. This is not some parental or legal decision. It is private choice. The law has been wrong for a very long time, and no one has the balls to change it. The law needs to grow up. So, I do see your point there."

"The other reason, I mentioned I see two, is we need to bring what we wish to consume and buying what we want in Minville before the party is the easiest way to avoid questions."

"Why not just one of us buying the stuff?" Gretchen asked.

"Don't you think one young woman going into a pharmacy seeking to buy a bunch of drugs would look suspicious? We're trying to avoid drawing any attention to ourselves."

"Good point," answered Gretchen.

"Just to be clear here, we're talking about doing a bunch of things that are currently against the law, even if we don't believe they should be."

"True," added Gretchen.

"Yep, and all of those laws are morality laws," objected Christie. "A bunch of old-fart, stick-in-the-mud, white guys decided many years ago that they had to tell us how to live, what choice we could and couldn't make. They didn't know us, and they didn't care. They just wanted everyone to live the way they wanted us to live, as if they knew best for everyone."

"I couldn't have said it better myself, Chris. I've often wondered how our parents would feel or think if these damn laws weren't what they are."

Gretchen giggled as if she was the only one to get the unrecognized joke. "Yeah, but your parents and ours," she said, gesturing with the thumb to

Christie. "Your parents have let you do stuff that our parents would never even discuss, let alone allow us to do."

"Perhaps."

"No perhaps about it, Bell. GG's right." The warning bell signaling the start of afternoon classes rang. Kids began to file into the school building. "OK, we probably can't finish this now. Let's meet back here after classes, before the bus leaves." They usually had about 20 minutes of wait time. They all agreed. "We need to decide one way or the other. We're running out to time."

Las tres amigas walked into the building and to their lockers together, and then they had to split since they did not share any afternoon classes. Bella struggled to keep her mind focused on the material in her classes, when her thoughts continued to return to the open question they left on the bench. She knew Christie was correct in at least the need to decide one way or the other. Bella managed to fake her way through her three afternoon classes.

As was her routine, Bella's last stop was her locker. She shuffled books to make sure she had the books she needed for her evening homework. Bella walked with the flow of teenagers until she was outside, and then she diverted to 'their' bench. She was the first to arrive and sat on the far end of the bench. People watching always remained entertaining. Gretchen was the first to appear from the main entrance, and she had not yet reached the bench when Christie burst through the open doors. Gretchen had barely sat on the opposite end of the bench from Bella when Christie leapt into the center seat with a thud.

"We don't have much time, so what is it to be, girls?" Christie asked directly.

"I think I'm as curious as you guys," Gretchen responded first, "but I'm more than a little apprehensive about breaking the law to feed my curiosity."

"Valid point, GG," Christie answered. "I suppose I'm a little less intimidated about defying the law because I believe these laws are wrong, well intentioned perhaps, but still just plain wrong. These morality laws, like we've discussed so many times, are just conservative attempts to control us all, to deny us freedom of choice."

"So, this is some civil disobedience event," Gretchen suggested. "You want to protest the law?"

"Kinda, but that is a supplemental element. I want to get laid. I've always wanted to try a gang-bang event. We've talked about this. None of this is anything new to any of us. Johnny's offer to us is like the perfect setup—a closed, control group of studs. I don't know why I'm the one pushing this. I'm not trying to force you to do anything we haven't talked about doing for a long time. You haven't said anything, Bell. What say you?"

"I think GG is just expressing the same apprehension I feel. I don't think either of us disagrees, Chris. Yes, we've talked about doing this for many months, and now, the time has come. I'll confess that my curiosity and desire exceed my caution. My father is a police detective in this city. The last thing I need or want is for him to be disappointed in me . . . or either of you, for that matter. How confident in the quality of these IDs are you?" Bella looked directly at and held Christie's eyes. They stared at each other, while Gretchen looked back and forth between her two friends.

"About as confident as anyone can be in anything. According to the guy I know, the fellow who makes them is the best."

"So, we're going to do it?" Gretchen asked.

"Yeah. Let's do it." Bella looked into Christie's eyes. "What do you need from us?"

"He said a passport photo, your information, you know, your address, birth date, well, revised birth date, so we're all just over 21 years old, and I'll need $50 each."

"A bit pricey for a little laminated card, doncha think?" observed Gretchen.

"Perhaps so, but it's the going rate from what I'm told. So are you in or not?"

"I sure hope you're correct on all this, Chris," Bella commented. "We'll never know if this is a good idea unless we try. So, I'm in."

Gretchen flashed a sharp glance of surprise and incredulity at Bella. She stared for several seconds. Bella did not flinch or look away. "OK . . . *las tres amigas* . . . all for one and one for all. I'm in, too."

Christie looked directly and intently into Gretchen's eyes. "Really? Are you sure?"

"Look, Chris, I've got my concerns and misgivings, and I think Bella has them, too. But, if we going to do this, then we might as well go all in for better or worse."

"Excellent. Think of this as our demonstration for freedom of choice," Christie added.

"Nice touch, Chris, but that's a bit of a stretch. As much as I agree with you, the law is the law, and if we truly believe what we say, then we must change the law to respect the rights of all citizens. Just because I'm thinking of it now, let me say, that the age of majority set by law at 18 years of age may have been appropriate and necessary a few decades ago. While my parents would caution us to not be over-confident, I think we're far more informed about our bodies, our surroundings, and life in general than kids our age were 20 or 30 years ago. The laws are no longer valid or even appropriate, and it's up to us to change them."

"Dear God, Bell, I just want to get laid. I'm not interested in a crusade," Christie protested.

They all laughed hard and uncontrollably, so much so that students leaving school for the day looked askance at the three girls on the bench under the oak tree.

As their raucous laughter subsided, Gretchen said, "Looks like the buses are getting ready to depart. We'd better get on board."

Las tres amigas gathered up their backpacks and belongings. They boarded their assigned bus. Their plan was set in motion.

All three of them provided the required materials and funds the next day. They had taken the next step.

—

6

The Uber ride out of the city took two plus hours, plenty of quiet time alone with her thoughts. For Kelly Joubert, the arid landscape and barren mountains offered no attraction. She was deeply preoccupied with what she was doing. Kelly had decided two days ago that she was leaving, and she was convinced this was the correct path for her. Blessedly, the driver was not the talkative type, leaving her to her thoughts, and she was quite content with that state.

When they crested the last ridgeline, she saw the sprawling camp in the middle of the flat valley. Kelly was quite surprised there were no buildings outside the square of the camp. She estimated the camp boundaries were perhaps a half-mile on each side. A half dozen larger buildings filled one side closest to the two-lane highway. Behind the larger buildings, rows of identical buildings arranged in five columns with five rows filled the remainder of the square. Half the roof of each building was blue. The other half was white.

Kelly realized the driver knew exactly where he was supposed to go. She surmised this was not his first trip to Indulgence Camp Number 12 (IC12). As they approached the camp, Kelly noticed the blue portions of the building roofs were solar arrays for electrical power. A smaller portion of the roof components had to be a solar hot water array.

"This is it," the driver announced as he came to a stop at what was clearly the front entrance, "Indulgence Camp Twelve."

Kelly handed the driver a $20 bill as a personal gratuity for the driver and a job well done. The fare was charged directly to the debit card to her private account, separate from her accounts with Raoul.

"When you're ready to go home, just ping us on-line. We'll come get you."

"Thank you." Kelly got out of the nice Ford SUV, donned her small backpack, and carried her small duffle bag to the front and perhaps only entrance. She understood why the instructions said bring only what you can carry. There were no porters, bellboys, or assistants standing by to help. Before she opened the door, Kelly turned to watch the car drive away. "This is really real," Kelly said aloud to herself. She stared at the rapidly retreating car until the vehicle disappeared over the ridgeline they had just passed. Kelly opened the door and stepped into a bright white, clean, large reception room. The room was empty of human beings except for an attractive young man sitting behind the reception desk.

"May I help you, Ma'am?" the man asked.

"I suppose so. I'm Kelly Henry. I called to check on space two days ago."

The man consulted his clipboard to check some kind of list. "Yes, Ma'am. Here you are. Welcome to IC12. We have you on the list and were expecting you. First order of business is your induction interview, briefing and examination."

"Yes, that's what the checklist stated."

"Please take a seat. The next slot opens in 20 minutes."

Kelly nodded her head in acknowledgment. She was the only other person in the lobby and took a comfortable looking overstuffed chair in the corner. Kelly looked at the magazines on the side table and nothing was interesting or intriguing. She laid her backpack against the chair and closed her eyes. To her surprise, she felt at peace and her mind was rested. Her slumber lasted an unrealized amount of time.

"Ms. Henry," a middle-aged, homely, brunette woman said a little more strongly than normal, probably because Kelly missed the first two calls. She was thankful she had used her family name for the call rather than her married name.

"Yes," she said as she shook her head. "Yes, that's me." Kelly stood, grabbed her bags, and followed the woman through the door, down a hallway and into a small room with a brass numeral '17' on the door. The woman opened the door and stood aside for Kelly to enter first.

The room had bright white walls like the reception room and nothing on the walls—no mirrors, pictures, photographs or certificates—nothing on the walls except one red sign with simple white letters.

Thoughts of

Self-Destruction

Call x999 immediately

A small rectangular table with two, simple, straight-back, wooden chairs—the only furniture—occupied the room. The woman gestured for Kelly to take the chair on the left and then she took the opposite chair.

"My name is Browning, Amy Browning. I'm the duty induction officer for IC12. This is your induction interview."

"Is this a test?"

"Yes . . . of sorts. I must assess and document your qualifications for entry."

"I have to qualify?"

"Yes, you do. We have all sorts of folks who attempt to take advantage of the generosity of this state's residents and taxpayers. This is not a hotel, a homeless shelter, a free supply source, or anything other than its intended function as a sanctuary for individuals who need or wish to consume psychotropic substances in a safe place without societal pressure. With that preface, why have you come here?"

"I'm addicted to benzos."

"Which one?" interjected Browning.

"I've done several—Valium, Ativan, Versed, but my preferred pill recently is Xanax," Kelly responded. "I've tried to decrease or eliminate my consumption with a doctor's assistance, but I could not do it. I needed Xanax to be stable, but my husband began to berate me for my consumption, and all that did was make it worse. I've tried personal counseling, addiction counseling, couples and marriage counseling. I've consulted several doctors. They keep telling me I'm OK. I'm not OK."

Browning nodded her head. "I'm obligated by recent revisions to the SCIP Act to ask certain specific administrative questions." Kelly nodded her agreement. "Your age?"

"Twenty-five."

"Your gender identity?"

"I've all female parts. I'm a woman."

"Are you married?"

"Yes."

"Your husband's name, age and employment?"

"Raoul Beauvis Joubert. He's 38. Does his employment really matter?"

"Yes, it does."

Kelly considered whether she should end the interview process right then and there. She was afraid of her husband's employment. Browning stared and waited. "He'd a lawyer, an assistant district attorney."

Browning nodded her head and wrote down the information in her notebook, but she did not convey any judgmental expression. "Are you a resident of this state?"

"Yes . . . since I was born."

"So," Amy interrupted Kelly, "your husband doesn't know you're here, does he?"

Kelly stared at Ms. Browning as if she had just shape-shifted into another creature. "I haven't mentioned that," Kelly protested softly.

"Mrs. Joubert, I've been doing this since IC12 opened. I rarely get surprised these days. I've seen this before. Your situation isn't new." Amy paused, raised her eyebrows and canted her head in a gesture for Kelly to answer the question.

"Please, Ms. Browning, I prefer not to use my married name. I don't know if we're headed to divorce, but I really don't want to be reminded of him. To answer your question, no. He doesn't, and I don't want him to know.

I want to be safe with my thoughts. To be blunt, I don't want to worry about life for now."

Browning stared at Kelly for several seconds without expression. "With that, I must ask, and you really must be honest here, are you suicidal? Have you had thoughts of suicide?"

It was now Kelly's turn to stare at Amy Browning, who waited patiently again without expression for a response. They held each other's eyes. "I'd be lying to you if I said no, but that's not why I'm here. I'm not here to end my life. I'm here to find enlightenment, to seek meaning to my life, to find my path forward. Where I came from was a dead-end. I had no future, and I didn't like my present. I hope that makes sense."

"That almost sounds like you are seeking a religious retreat."

"Perhaps so. I suppose there is that aspect, but religious retreats don't involve drugs."

"What do you hope to accomplish here, Ms. Henry?"

Kelly laughed softly. "Good question." She paused and held Browning's eyes. "I haven't thought about that. I suppose the simple answer is, to find myself. The path I'm on is a dead end as I said. I believe I need a safe environment."

"Are you a threat to yourself, to another human being, or to society in general?"

"No, but they are a threat to me." Kelly stopped, wanting her answer to stand, but Browning did not react in any form or fashion, and only stared back at Kelly, waiting for an explanation. "My husband, my family . . . my whole freakin' family on both sides, everyone except my best friend Laura."

"For the record, who is Laura?"

"We've been friends since elementary school. Her full name is Laura Lynn Simmons. She is a licensed professional prostitute and occasional, recreational, drug user. She's the only one who understands me. She's the only one who knows what I'm doing here. She's the only one I'll allow to see me here. Laura is my only friend."

"I'm glad that you have someone, but another drug user is probably not the best choice."

"You don't know her," Kelly protested rather strongly. "She has a big heart. She knows me and accepts me. And, for your record, Laura has repeatedly tried to convince me and help me to break my dependence on Xanax. She's a very good friend."

"My apologies, Ms. Henry, I was only speaking from general history and experience. Just to be clear, if you're admitted, you don't want any contact with your husband or your family, correct?"

"Correct," Kelly confirmed.

"Addictions to prescription medications are a wholly different problem from addiction to what we used to call illegal substances or street drugs. We've a medical staff and psychological counseling services for residents who seek change and treatment."

"I read the pamphlet. I don't know what specific services you provide."

"Do you want to be free of your dependence?"

"Yes. I don't like what benzos have done to my life, and yet, I've only found stability with the drugs, and I feel powerless to stop. After being challenged by Laura, I think life and society are as much the driver of my addiction as the physical effects of the drugs."

Amy Browning lapsed into protracted contemplation, alternating her sight from Kelly to her notebook. Kelly sat patiently. Amy eventually broke her concentration and jotted down a few notes in her notebook. Kelly could not read what Browning was writing, not even a hint. "Ms. Henry, to be frank, you're right at the threshold of qualification. You're a woman of means. You can afford the drugs you seek, and you're not a threat to your community or society. However, there are complications in your favor. The fact that my evaluation places you at the threshold leaves us with several options. One, our processes stipulate in such circumstances that we seek an evaluation of another induction officer, or a third, if we are tied. Or two, I can turn you away with instructions to solve your personal problems, to expunge your demons, outside the indulgence camp system. Or three, I can admit you."

"I opt for number three."

Browning chuckled. "I'm sure you do, or you wouldn't be here." Again, Amy held Kelly's eyes and retreated to her thoughts. "Very well. We'll accept your residency."

"Thank you very much, Ms. Browning."

"Now, we transition to the camp rules. You'll be asked to sign your voluntary consent to obey these rules. Your signature will be witnessed and notarized. Then, your belongings will be thoroughly searched, and you'll be given a medical examination including a cavity search."

"Why?"

"As you'll learn, we can't and won't tolerate smuggling of any kind by anyone for any reason. If you brought substances with you, you'll be given the opportunity to dispose of those substances before your examination. Once you sign the rules consent, any smuggling of any kind will result in your immediate and permanent expulsion from the indulgence camp system along with notification of law enforcement. 'I forgot about that one' is not a get-out-of-jail-free-card—zero tolerance. Do you understand these instructions?"

"Yes."

Browning placed a check mark in a book on a clipboard form. "Very well. So . . . to begin. The indulgence camp is a quasi-open facility. It's not a prison or jail. You're not confined here. You're free to leave at any time you wish. Once your belongings are inspected, you'll be allowed to enter. If you choose to leave, you'll depart with only what you entered with today. You'll be subject to another medical examination and cavity search to ensure compliance. You'll be given a tour of the facility and shown to your bunk. You've identified as a woman. You may choose a female building or a mixed building."

"Female," Kelly said without being asked.

Amy nodded her head and ticked off another box on her clipboard sheet. "While you're a resident here, you'll have free access to the dispensary to obtain your substances of choice. We've a fixed menu. There is no system to order anything not on the approved menu. As with community retail outlets, the quality and dosage are tightly regulated to ensure consistency. The standard dosage is provided with each substance. Before you access the dispensary, you'll be asked to sign or reject a do-not-resuscitate form. You'll wear a bracelet that fully identifies you and your wishes. We'll abide your wishes. In here, you're free to take whatever you wish and as much as you wish. We'll advise you of the consequences, as best we know them, but we'll not intervene out of respect for what you have left of your personal privacy.

"All laws apply here. You can't violate any laws—none—not even petty crime. You're being admitted to indulge your desire for one or more psychotropic substances and to ensure you don't harm anyone or anything else."

"I've not harmed anything or anyone," Kelly protested, "ever!"

"Our briefing is general and applies to everyone. Before this system was created, consumers, even those not yet addicted, committed all sorts of crimes to feed their demand for the substances they sought, from shoplifting to armed robbery, from assault and battery to murder."

"I'm not one of those."

"Maybe not . . . yet . . . but prohibition inevitably led consumers to crime of one form or another. We've broken that cycle. So perhaps you're one of the few who didn't commit any crimes to feed your habit, but my point is, the state has chosen to indulge your need for substances, and in return, you'll remain peaceful and law-abiding. If you don't, you'll be expelled permanently— no second chances. The state will keep its end of the bargain as long as you keep yours."

"Understood and agreed," Kelly said.

Amy Browning leafed through the papers on her clipboard to make sure all the proper papers were present, and then she pushed it across the table. "The clipboard contains a series of required forms. The first are the rules of the camp that you must read and consent to for entry. The second page is a "Do Not Resuscitate" (DNR) authorization form. It will need to be notarized as well. This is very important Miz Henry." Kelly noted the change in title and liked it better than the customary traditional title. "Part of the freedom of choice represented in this camp is that you also have the freedom to overdose or create a toxic mix of substances. We want to respect your freedom of choice; thus, this form. Accepting and signing this form means that we'll not medically intervene if you overdose, intentionally or accidently."

"Suicide?"

"We don't and can't condone such action. We have 24/7 active measures to prevent suicide. However, there's a very thin line between freedom of choice and self-destruction. You'll see signs in every building of this entire camp," Amy said and pointed to the red sign on the wall. "It's serious, so if those thoughts come to you, please heed the sign and call immediately any time day or night. We'll do our best to help you from making an irreversible mistake. If you don't sign this form, we'll do our best medically to resuscitate you. Further, if you choose that path and activate our intervention, you'll be given a warning and probation. Every resident in this camp is free to indulge their consumption as she or he chooses. But, the SCIP Act establishes limits to avoid abusing the generosity of the taxpayers of the state. If there is a second resuscitation episode, you'll be given a choice, either approve the DNR or leave the camp, in the latter case law enforcement will be notified of your failure to comply. Any questions so far?" Kelly shook her head in the negative. "The next sheet is your next-of-kin notification should you have a medical emergency or expire."

"That'll be Laura—no one else."

"That's your choice entirely. I must also inform you that if you pass away for any reason, we're obligated by law to inform your husband, as long as you remain legally married. As such, we'll need his contact information in the appropriate place on the form." Kelly nodded her head. "The last form is an explicit voluntary freedom of choice statement to ensure you're making these commitments to this camp by your free will." Again, Kelly nodded her head. "While you carefully read these forms, I'll fetch our notary. Please don't complete or sign these forms until we've an independent witness, a notary, present."

Kelly nodded her head in agreement and began reading. Amy left and returned a few minutes later with an older woman she did not introduce. "I agree," Kelly declared without being asked. "I'm ready to sign."

Amy said, "Very well," and then she pushed a pen across the table. The other woman placed her pen and self-inking notary stamp device on the table. Kelly signed her name and pushed the documents to the other woman. The notary signed and dated the documents, stamped her signatures, and then initialed each stamp. The two women exchanged no words. The notary passed the documents to Browning, then gathered her things and departed.

"OK. As I explained earlier, this next step is crucial. That slot over there," Amy pointed to a slot in the corner that Kelly had not noticed before, "is a no-questions-asked disposal bin. I'm going to step out. Take whatever time you need, but you must go through absolutely everything you brought in here. You must make absolutely certain there are no undeclared prescription medications and no psychotropic substances—no accidents, no 'it's not mine,' no 'I forgot,' nothing. When you're done, knock on the door, and we'll begin."

"OK."

Amy did as she said, stepped out and closed the door behind her. Kelly lifted her backpack and duffle bag onto the table. She reached for her prescription bottles for Xanax and Ativan, then dropped them in the slot. She carefully searched every piece of clothing, her toiletry bag, everything, including her duffle bag. She found a small wrapper of what had to be cocaine from a few years back, from before the SCIP Act, which she had forgotten about, but she quickly dropped it in the slot. The cocaine bothered her. She searched everything, again. Satisfied she was clean, Kelly knocked on the door.

Amy entered and immediately began thoroughly examining everything in Kelly's bags and including the bags themselves, and then she very carefully patted down every inch of Kelly's body and clothing including her hair. Satisfied, Browning gestured for Kelly to bring her bags. Kelly followed Ms. Browning up the stairs to the second floor and down a corridor to a door labeled: Induction Medical. "I'll come back to pick you up when you're complete." Amy walked away in the direction they had just come.

Kelly opened the door and entered what appeared to be a medical clinic reception room.

A young man behind the desk said, "You must be Miz Kelly Henry."

"Yes."

"Did Ms. Browning explain to you what was going to happen next?"

"Yes, she did."

"Are you ready to proceed?"

"Yes."

The man gestured for Kelly to follow him. At Exam Room No.3, he opened the door. "Please remove all of your clothing including your underwear and socks. There's a medical gown on the exam table if you wish. Doctor Wood and his nurse will be with you shortly."

Kelly did as she was instructed. She saw no reason for the gown since they were going to be probing every orifice of her body. She waited patiently, sitting on discardable paper of the examination table.

An attractive, middle-aged man in a white lab coat with a black stethoscope draped around his neck entered the room followed by an equally attractive young woman also attired in scrubs and a white lab coat. "I'm Doctor Wood and this is Nurse Jenkins. We're here to do your induction examination. Our purpose is to document your medical condition upon entry. We'll also perform a required cavity search to ensure you aren't attempting to smuggle anything into the camp."

"I understand."

The medical examination was performed quickly, efficiently, and professionally. As indicated, they probed and examined each of Kelly's orifices and body cavities.

"You're in good health," Doctor Wood pronounced. "You're medically cleared for entry. You may dress and wait in the reception room. We'll call Ms. Browning, and she'll come to fetch you."

"Thank you."

Kelly waited in the reception room for several minutes.

When Amy arrived, they deposited Kelly's bags in the original interview room. Amy took Kelly on a guided tour. The center building, where they started, was the induction center but predominately the administration building. Director Mike Duncan's office was on the top floor. The first building to the west was the medical services building that contained a basic trauma triage unit, various clinics and staff offices. The farthest building to the west was the psychological and psychiatric treatment building as well as the addiction treatment unit for those who sought treatment. The next building to the east of the administration building was the dining facility that had the capacity to feed half the residents at a time. The mess hall served two sittings for three meals every day. Kelly learned that about 30 percent of the population chose not to eat at any given sitting. The building farthest to the east housed the maintenance staff and services.

Browning explained, "The male buildings are 'A' and 'B.' The female buildings are 'D' and 'E.' The mixed buildings are 'C.' There are five buildings in each column. Each building has bunk spaces for 160 residents. Each building has a common toilet and shower room at each end. You may have noticed that each building has its own solar power unit and solar hot water generation capability. You're assigned to bunk 114 in building D-2, and your building has the second sitting for meals." They walked together. Amy showed Kelly the toilet room with a partition between each toilet and no doors on the stalls. The shower was a large, tiled room with 20 showerheads and no partitions. As they walked back down the center of the building, Kelly noted small partial partitions separating a single bed in each space with a small cabinet on each side of the bed for her storage. The bed was made with sheets and a blanket. Two sets of what appeared to be pink scrubs were laid out on the foot of the bed. Large numerals painted on the wall above the bed marked Kelly's assigned bunk—114. "Here we are," Amy announced. "This is your assigned bunk. The scrubs are provided for your use. As you know, you've limited clothing. You're free to use your clothing, but you'll have to wash them. The laundry is in the maintenance building. The staff washes the scrubs if they are deposited in the marked bin at the ends of the hall before nine in the morning. You'll settle into the routine quickly. Do you have any questions?"

"What are the hours of operation for medical, the laundry and the dispensary?"

"All of them are 24/7/365. There is always duty staff. Only the mess hall and some of the administrative staff have regular, established and posted hours."

"So, I can draw any substance on the menu at any time, day or night?"

"Yes. Your choice. I'll also add that you'll likely have future questions. You can ask any staff member, or resident for that matter. There are long-term residents in every building."

"One more question." Browning nodded her head patiently. "Can I move, if I need to do so?"

"We don't encourage moving, but we don't discourage movement either. The only two restrictions are you may not displace anyone else, and you can't move without the administration's approval. We must keep track of everyone in residency here."

"So, only open bunks?"

"Yes . . . well, and as you would expect, the male only buildings aren't an option either."

"Sure, sure, quite understandable."

"Anything else?"

"Not that I can think of so far. Thank you for your patience, Miz Browning."

"You're welcome. Now, let's go retrieve your bags. You've got a little over an hour to your lunch period."

The two women left Building D-2 and returned to the administration building. Kelly's bags were exactly where she left them. She thanked Amy Browning, again, and then she made her way back to D-2-114 with her bags.

Kelly sat on her bed. It was not the best quality bed she had slept on, but it was adequate. She looked around the long hall. Of those beds she could see, more than a few had people laying motionless, some on top of the blanket, most underneath. Only a handful of residents were sitting on their beds or standing nearby. No one appeared to be talking, and no conversations could be heard. To Kelly's surprise, an almost eerie quiet filled the hall—no music or sounds of life. The process of unpacking and stowing things took only a few minutes. She did not bring much. Kelly stood beside her bed and just stared out the window above the numerals. The plain, non-descript desert landscape with the rugged mountains beyond just disappeared to her thoughts. *Oh my God, I hope I've done the right thing. Everyone seems to stay to themselves. I'm so all alone in here, but at least I'm safe and free of Raoul . . . well, at least for now.* Kelly returned to the present. *Nice pinks. I hope they fit.* Kelly looked around the hall. Of the half dozen residents she could see, they were all wearing pink scrubs. She stripped off her T-shirt, doffed her jeans, and her shoes and socks. She considered losing her panties as well but left them on. She was not wearing a brassiere and saw no reason to wear one now. The scrubs were a little roomier than she would otherwise desire, but they were comfortable. Kelly laid down on her bed and tried to expunge her thoughts.

A soft buzzer brought her back to consciousness. Pink clad women were walking to her right. Only one woman was not dressed in pink scrubs, and she stood out in simple grey sweats. Kelly joined the tail end of the group. They were heading to the mess hall. *The buzzer must be the second sitting signal for meals.*

The interior of the building appeared to be much larger than the exterior. Kelly stopped inside the double set of double doors to absorb the scene. Rows and rows of tables filled the hall. The cacophony of hundreds of chairs moving and people taking seats made it hard to hear anything other than the noise. Each table had four seats on the long sides and two seats on the short sides. Two tables on each side of the building-long center corridor defined each row, and there must be something like 40 rows. Each table had a tall center post that contained two large signs that appeared to be assigned building numbers for each table and each sitting. A handful of tables into the hall Kelly noticed the table signs on both sides of the corridor.

A-2

D-2

Kelly stopped to observe others. Most of the women were taking the seats closest to the central corridor. She made her way to an outer table with only three other women. None of the women anywhere around her appeared to be talking. They seemed to be staying to themselves, so Kelly followed suit. Men in yellow scrubs and women in green scrubs began pulling trays of prepared plates from a large cart carrier along the outer half-wide corridor. Each woman at her table took a plate off the tray and began eating. Kelly did the same. She placed the plate in front of her and stared at it—a thick slice of meatloaf, mashed potatoes with an indentation of gravy and green beans. A pitcher of water was their only drink. *This is definitely not a 5-star cuisine, but it's probably edible. Not my choice, but I'd better eat.* The food was adequately prepared but rather non-descript.

Judging from the occupancy of the dining hall, about two-thirds of the seats were filled. The muffled sounds of utensils, plates and trays provided a soft white noise background. *Nobody is talking. There are no words between anyone that I can hear.* Kelly finished her meal but waited to see if they were supposed to buss their plates and utensils. She stared at her plate and stirred the residue of her meal. Kelly finally saw two of the women at her table place their plates and unfinished meals back on the tray with the untouched meals. She waited for the two women to depart, and then, Kelly placed her plate on the tray and departed.

A walk around the camp seemed like a worthy endeavor, although the air was a little warmer than she cared for, but still the sky was clear, and a slight breeze added some cooling. It was a pleasant walk. Everything was the same except for the building labels. *This is definitely not a resort in the desert.* Kelly made her way back to building D-2 and entered by the rear entrance.

Kelly grabbed her toiletry kit, brushed her teeth, and returned to her bunk. She laid down for a short doze. By the time she returned to consciousness, she felt the black wave descending over her. *I need my Xanax.* Kelly walked slowly, sort of meandering, to the dispensary. Once again, the room appeared larger than she expected. Ten windows with partitions between each window occupied the wall opposite the door. A clerk sat behind each window. Empty chairs lined the wall on either side of the door opposite the windows. Only four windows were busy. Large signs filled both short sides of the room and displayed the menu of substances dispensed, composition, and standard dosage, along with names, side effects and such. Kelly went to the farthest open window to the left.

"Name?" asked the female clerk.

"Kelly."

"Full name."

"Kelly Margaret Henry."

The woman typed Kelly's name into her computer terminal. "Ah, yes, here you are. Just checked in today."

"Yes."

"I suppose welcome is in order. I hope you find what you're looking for here. Your family name is Henry, correct?"

"Yes, that's me."

"How can I help you?"

"Xanax, please."

"We only have generic Benzodiazepine. You don't have a declared prescription for Xanax."

"No. I didn't declare it."

"What were you taking and when was you last dosage?" the clerk asked.

"I think I was taking 0.5 milligrams three times a day, and my last dose was this morning."

"What do you want to do?"

"I'd like to get off the stuff."

"You really should see the duty physician for detoxification. The rules are you can have what you want. So, do you want a 0.5 milligram dose?"

"Yes, please." Kelly thought for a moment, while the clerk pulled a single foil-wrapped dose. She scanned the UPC code for the computer record. "I'd also like a dose of heroin."

The clerk hesitated and stared at Kelly. "It's not advisable . . . to mix these two."

"I understand."

The clerk brought back a single dose inhaler, scanned it, and pushed it across the counter.

Kelly took the two drugs. "Thank you."

"You're welcome . . . I guess. Be safe."

Kelly left the dispensary and returned to her bunk, picking up a chilled plastic bottle of water from the no-fee machine by the entry door. She placed the water and both packets on her left side stand, then laid down to contemplate what she wished to do. *I want, no, I need to zone out for a period, to forget my situation.* Kelly reached for the single dose heroin inhaler and squeezed the mist into her right nostril. She shook her head with the initial sting to her nose and felt the warm blanket enveloping her. *Wow!* Kelly laid down to let oblivion swallow her consciousness.

—

7

"**H**ello," Laura said softly, answering her private simple flip phone. She used her only smartphone for strictly professional purposes since checking the weather and managing her expansive contract files were easier.

"Laura?"

She did not recognize the voice. It was distinctively male and seemed distantly familiar. "Yes."

"This is Raoul."

"Joubert?"

"Yes. How many Raouls do you know?"

Laura ignored the question. *If you only knew . . .* She wanted to scold him for using her private telephone, however he had acquired her number. She knew precisely that she had not given him her private number. *Is something wrong with Kelly? I haven't heard from her since the last time we saw each other.* But she decided against chastising him. *He probably got the number from Kelly.* "What's up?"

"I'm at the Regency in room 724. I'd like to talk to you—*vis-à-vis.*"

What the hell? He lives just down the road. Why does he want or need to meet me at a ritzy hotel? OMG, he can't be looking for a freebie with his wife indisposed. "Why a hotel, Raoul?"

"I need to talk to you, and I thought a neutral, private place would be best. I'd be honored to take you to dinner, if you would prefer."

Laura hesitated with her mind running through multiple potential scenarios. In the end, she did not feel threatened. "I only have a few hours before I'm scheduled to see clients."

"That should be sufficient."

"Very well. I'll be there in 20 minutes."

"Thank you, Laura."

"Sure."

Raoul hung up before her. Laura finished preparing her body for work and jumped into her car. The drive took not quite ten minutes. She parked in the multi-story garage and took the elevator to the seventh floor. The designated room stood at the end of the single hallway. Laura knocked softly on the door three times. Raoul answered the door promptly, dressed in a long-sleeve white shirt, no tie and medium grey trousers.

"Thank you for coming, Laura," he said and stood back allowing Laura to enter.

Laura stood just inside a small anteroom. The room occupied the entire end of the floor and was a large suite with a large living room, two bedroom-bathroom combinations, one on each side of the living room. She waited for Raoul to lead the way. He gestured to the U-shaped couch facing the floor-to-ceiling windows overlooking the city. He gestured to one leg of the 'U.' Laura sat.

"Would you care for anything to drink or a snack?"

"No, thank you."

"Would you mind if I partake?"

"No, of course not."

Raoul poured himself what appeared to be a scotch rocks, then sat down on the couch leg opposite Laura. "I believe you were the last one to see and talk to Kelly. Do you know where she is?"

Should I lie? No . . . fuck him. Plus, I don't know for absolute certain exactly where she is, but I probably have a better idea than him. "I don't know for sure."

"Then you have an idea."

"Raoul, we talked about a lot of things, all of them in confidence. I can't betray her trust in me."

"I'm her husband."

This is not going to go well. "I can't and won't get in the middle of your marriage. What's between the two of you must be dealt with and settled between you."

"How are we supposed to do that when she is *in absentia*?"

"She'll let you know when she's ready," Laura lied.

"Do you believe that?"

"Yes."

"She hasn't run away?"

"I have no idea," Laura lied, again. *Damn it all to hell. I really want to slap him in the face with exactly what she thinks of him.*

"She left four days ago. Have you heard from her since then?"

"No."

"Would you tell me if you did?"

"Only if she wanted me to inform you."

Raoul stared at Laura for several minutes. "Kelly always told me you were her best friend. Those damn drugs have made her a recluse. She stopped seeing people. She shunned her family and friends. She withdrew into her own little world. I tried to get her to stop, to bring her back to the present, but those damn drugs had more control of her than me or anyone else. I want her back, Laura. Despite those drugs, I love her. I want her back," Raoul repeated.

"I'm sure you do, but I'm not a marriage counselor."

"So, this is some kind of protest about our marriage?"

"I didn't say that Raoul. Clearly, there are tensions between the two of you. Professional assistance will help you resolve those tensions?"

"Really? We've tried that, and this is what it has come to for us."

"The reconciliation of any problems depends upon attitude and recognition that a problem exists."

"She must think there's a problem, but I don't see the problem," Raoul confided.

"Perhaps that's the issue."

"That sounds like more psychological mumbo-jumbo."

"Look, Raoul, as I said at the beginning of this chat, I can't and won't be in the middle of your marriage. Kelly and I have been friends since elementary school. To be direct and blunt, my loyalty lays with her."

"So, you do know more," protested Raoul more aggressively.

"Perhaps I've said too much already. I didn't intend to upset you."

Raoul held up both hands in surrender. "My apologies if I spoke too forcefully. I just want Kelly back."

"I don't know what the future holds," Laura said. "I don't know where Kelly is, or what she wants. The best I can say is, you must wait for her to figure things out for herself. If she does choose to contact me, I can assure you I'll pass along your feelings."

"I don't like it."

"You've made that point crystal clear."

Raoul nodded his head. "Based on what has happened so far, I suspect you're likely to hear from her before I do. Will you just let me know that she is OK?"

"Only if she wants me to do that."

"How do we know she wasn't kidnapped?"

"I don't think so, Raoul, but I don't know for sure."

Raoul visibly became more agitated. "I could find her no matter where she is hiding," he said with a growl.

"I would urge you not to do that. Using the instruments of state for such personal endeavors isn't right. We all know you've a lot of power as a district attorney, but Kelly has her right to privacy. I strongly urge you to respect her rights. She deserves her space to sort things out for herself."

His agitation persisted. He twitched and shook for several minutes. Raoul stopped, opened his mouth to speak several times, did not say a word, and retreated back into his thoughts.

"Perhaps I should go," Laura said.

His visible mood changed in a flash. "Please don't go," he said softly in contrast to his previous tone. Laura gestured her 'what for.' Raoul smiled mischievously. "I'd like to contract for your services."

"So, you know my business?"

"I'm an assistant district attorney for this county."

"I've broken no laws. I've never even had a traffic ticket."

"No, you haven't. I think Kelly told me."

"Nice try, Raoul. Normally, I'd say business is business, but in this case, I think our personal relationships, both of us on different sides of Kelly, would unnecessarily complicate things."

"Not for me."

"I'm sure."

"Kelly and I haven't had sex in years."

Oh, I would love to tell you what Kelly thinks of that. Laura nodded her head in acknowledgment without speaking. "Have you had sexual relations with anyone else—female or male?" Laura asked.

"Does that really matter?"

"Always. STDs are a risk in my line of work. In this instance, I think the question is more relevant because of our shared relationship with Kelly." She waited for his answer. His eyes were twitching and his lips were quivering ever so slightly. "Your answer?"

"No."

He's lying. I'd love to confront him. "You've had no sex?"

"No."

He's still lying.

"Well, just masturbation, if you define that as sex."

"I do, in fact, define that as sex."

"OK, then yes, but not with anyone else."

Damn it all to hell, he's still lying, and he's a terrible liar. You'd think a lawyer was far better at lying than most folks. No wonder Kelly doesn't trust him.

"So, does that mean you'll do me?" Raoul asked calmly. Laura did not react or respond. "I'll pay double your going rate." Laura still did not respond and just stared at him. "Triple."

"The issue for me is not money, Raoul. I'm just worried anything that might happen between us might compromise my relationship with Kelly."

"It won't."

"You don't know that. You can't predict Kelly's response, and neither can I."

"We won't tell her."

"The last time we talked, she asked me if I had done you. I told her no, because that is the truth. I won't lie to her . . . not for you, not for anyone."

"If she has already asked you, then maybe she won't ask again."

"Why are you so desperate to get laid?"

"I wouldn't use the word desperate. I've never been with a professional, and this seems like an appropriate time. I'm not asking you as a friend. I'm asking you as a customer."

I'm not your friend. I'm Laura's friend. Against my better judgment, business is business, and Kelly has already accepted this potential. But I'm not going to tell him any of that. "I'll accept your triple offer."

"Great. So, what is your hourly rate?"

"$500."

"That's $1500. Lawyers don't make that much."

"Lawyers don't have the skills I do."

He laughed. "I suppose not. So how does this work?"

Laura guided him through various stages. He was clearly a virile, responsive male who needed very little assistance. He was gentle, calm and measured through the first few stages. When they got to the fornication stage, Raoul's demeanor and tone changed like his earlier mood swing, but instead of bad to better, this shift was good to worse. He literally lifted Laura and threw her face down on the bed, and then he lifted her hips onto her knees and thrust into her. His penetration was not slow, subtle or gentle. He pounded hard, almost violently, into her to the point of pain. Raoul grabbed her hair and pulled like the reins of a horse. Her scalp hurt. He slapped her buttocks, hard, both cheeks, so hard that Laura cried out in pain. She wanted it to stop, but she instinctively knew the best course was to finish it as quickly as possible. She used her tricks to finish him off rapidly. The deep, guttural, verging upon demonic, groan or growl coupled with his noticeably spasmodic convulsions signaled his conclusion and the end of his aggressiveness.

Raoul decoupled as soon as he was finished and flopped onto his back next to her. His chest heaved sharply as his body struggled to regain his breath. Laura looked at him and fought to control her disgust. She shook her head without him noticing and rose from the bed. Laura went to the bathroom, cleaned herself thoroughly, and turned around to inspect her reddened buttocks in the mirror. *It still stings.*

He was still on the bed when she left the bathroom. His eyes were closed, and his breathing rate had slowed markedly. Laura dressed as swiftly and silently as she could.

"Where are you going?" Raoul asked with his eyes still closed.

"This session is over."

He glanced at the clock on the nightstand. "I've still got 20 minutes more. I can knock off another one before my time is up."

"There'll be no other one, Raoul."

He raised himself onto his left elbow. "Did I do something wrong?" he asked with surprising innocence.

"I've been doing this work for six plus years, and I've never been treated like that . . . ever."

"I thought I paid for you to do whatever I want."

"Wrong." *Asshole . . . and not the good kind.* "I'm a human being. I deserve to be treated with respect just as much as you do." Laura finished dressing. She smiled at him. "You got your pass at the prize. You failed, and I've done my work. I'm leaving. You're not likely to see me again. You, or anyone else who treats me that way, won't get a second chance."

"I'm sorry, Laura. I got carried away."

Laura squared up to Raoul who was still naked and on his right elbow on the bed. "I'd appreciate my fee now. I need to go. I have respectful customers I wish to tend to tonight, customers who appreciate my skills."

"I certainly appreciated you, Laura. I've always wanted sex like that. I'm sorry I offended you."

"Apology not accepted. My agreed to fee please," she said and extended her right hand, palm up.

Raoul got off the bed, went to his clothes, and placed $650 in Laura's hand.

"It's a bit short. It's all I've got."

"I don't take kindly to any dine-n-dash, Mister Joubert."

"You know what I do, don't you?" Laura smiled at him. "You know who you're dealing with here."

"Mister Joubert, you don't know who you're dealing with, apparently. So, one last time, you owe me $350, since I knocked off the 20 minutes you contracted for with me."

"You're a fucking prostitute."

"Yes, I am, and I'm proud of my profession . . . apparently far more so than you are proud of your profession."

Raoul shifted his weight from foot to foot as he contemplated the situation. He held up his hands in surrender. "I'm sorry our conversation went sideways. You may not accept my apology, but I apologize, nonetheless. There's a high-end ATM in the lobby. Let me get dressed, and we'll go down together. You deserve full payment. You're the best fuck I've had in my life."

Laura smiled but did not reply. She waited as he quickly dressed. He put on his tighty-whiteys, his white shirt and trouser and shoes without socks. *He's not leaving. He's going to stay in the hotel room rather than go home. Strange.* Raoul gestured toward the door.

Raoul started to open the door but stopped and turned to Laura. "We won't be able to talk in the lobby, so please allow me to apologize again for my getting carried away. Some women like it rough. I should've asked. I'm truly sorry." Laura nodded her head, not wanting to speak or encourage him anymore. "I hope after all this you'll still tell me if you hear from Kelly." Laura stared into his cold eyes, remained as expressionless as she possibly could, and did not speak. *If you only knew and felt the rage I feel for you right now.* "OK. Let's go get you paid in full." He opened the door, and Laura stepped out into the hallway.

Laura followed Raoul to the elevator. They did not speak or touch. Laura purposefully stayed behind him and several feet or so away from him.

Raoul inserted his debit card into the ATM, and punched in his numbers and instructions. Laura stood behind him to avoid compromising his privacy. He turned and discreetly handed a wad of $100 bills. It was a lot more than the $350 she was owed. Laura looked at him with a puzzled expression. "That's $2400," he whispered. "I paid you the agreed amount for the two hours you were with me. Thank you for your services."

"Thank you for honoring your commitment. I'll let you know if I hear from Kelly . . . if she says it's OK for me to do so."

"Thank you. Is she really that angry with me . . . that she would vanish *non communicado*?" he asked.

"No comment."

"OK. I'll wait. I hope to see you again."

Laura shook her head. "That's not going to happen, Raoul. Once burned, shame on you . . . There won't be a second burning."

"I'm truly sorry you feel that way . . . well, actually . . . that I made you feel that way."

"That's what all abusers say, and you should know that from your line of work."

"I'm sorry, Laura."

She only nodded her head. "Anything else? I really must be going." He shook his head in the negative. Laura waved in royal fashion, turned and walked away. As she approached the revolving door, Laura looked over her shoulder. He was still standing at the ATM watching her walk away.

Laura did not have much time until her first appointment this evening. She decided to go home and try her best to neutralize the effects in the time she had from her session with Raoul. *That is not going to happen again,* she told herself. *I hope none of my customers object to the marks he left on me.*

—

8

The drive home after a long workday for Detective-Sergeant Rod Ramirez had been longer than usual due to the dispatcher diverting him to assist in a particularly nasty traffic accident. He still expected to arrive home in time for supper with Marci and Bella, but just barely.

"There it is," Rod said aloud to himself as he turned the corner and saw their house. "Home," he added as if to reassure himself.

As he reached to switch the car off, Rod noticed the time—6:35 PM. He was an hour later than usual. The scene changed instantly as he entered the kitchen, Marci was sitting at the bar-height counter separating the dining table from the kitchen. The table was set for three as usual. Marci's expression was stern and not happy.

Rod immediately assumed his tardiness was the source of Marci's unhappiness. "I'm sorry, sweetness. I got an assistance call on the way home."

A small smile briefly softened Marci's expression and then vanished. "You're not the problem this time, Rod."

"OK. What's the problem, then?" Rod asked, as he loosened his necktie.

"Our daughter."

"Oh, oh! Where is she?" he asked, looking around as if she was hiding somewhere close.

"She's confined to her bedroom without her laptop or phone."

"Damn, what the hell did she do?"

"You probably should grab a beer or glass of wine and sit down."

"This sounds serious," he mumbled, as he took off his necktie and suit coat, then grabbed a beer from the refrigerator. He sat next to Marci at the counter. "Whas' up?"

"Bella cut school today with two of her friends. Someone, as yet unidentified, drove them to Minville. They were arrested attempting to buy various sex drugs and using fraudulent IDs. The other two girls were also arrested for fake IDs. The driver, and presumably owner of the car, managed to sneak away before the police learned the girls had a driver. He or she apparently violated no law, but they, the police, want to talk to the driver."

"What the hell, Marci."

"I know . . . very disappointing. Anyway, dinner is ready, keeping it warm in the oven. So, do you want to talk to her before or after supper?"

"My urge is to interrogate her straight away. We really need to find out what happened." Rod paused to think for a moment. "I'd suggest we act like nothing has happened, eat dinner in peace, and then after the dishes are done, we'll sit her down together, and I'll work my magic."

"Be gentle, Rod. She's only 15 years old."

"She apparently violated the law."

"Yeah, but they also know whose daughter she is and released her to my custody," Marci added.

"Did you pick her up? Did you talk to the officers involved?"

"Yes, and yes. I got a call here a little after noon from Lieutenant Johnson. The arresting officer was a patrolman by the name of Thomas."

"Why didn't he just call me?"

"He checked and knew you were on duty. He didn't want to interfere or impose. I told him tomorrow was your day off. He's expecting a call tomorrow morning."

"OK. I'll take care of it in the morning. So, do we have a plan for Bella?"

"Yes. She is probably expecting you to jump her."

"Exactly."

"Pretending nothing has happened may well destabilize her hardening position."

"Exactly."

Marci chuckled softly. "I've been around you too much," she said, stood and embraced her husband from behind. Marci kissed Rod on the cheek. He leaned his head back so she could kiss him on the lips. "Why don't you go get her and sound as cheery as you can? I'll get dinner on the table." Marci went to the kitchen.

Rod walked down the hallway to Bella's closed bedroom door. He knocked and heard her acknowledgment from inside. Rod opened the door to find her still fully dressed in her school clothes lying on top of her bed comforter. "Sorry I'm late, sweetie. Dinner's ready and Mom's waiting on us." Bella stared at her father like he was some alien. "Is something wrong, Bella?"

She shook her head and sat up on the edge of her bed. "Isn't there something you want to talk to me about?"

"Like what?"

"Oh, nothing, Dad."

"Mom's waiting on us," Rod said, bowed to his daughter, and gestured to the door for her to lead him to the dining room.

Bella looked to her Mom as she entered the dining room. Marci smiled warmly at their daughter. They sat in their usual places—Marci on Rod's left and Bella to the right. Bella began serving herself two good scoops of macaroni & cheese with hamburger blended in the mix. He pushed the casserole dish to her mother, and then she took a tong full of tossed green salad, depositing it on her salad plate. The ladies waited for Rod to serve himself.

When Rod finished, Bella said, "I'd like to say grace, Dad."

"I think it is Mom's turn, but I don't think she would object."

"Nope," Marci added.

They joined hands and bowed their heads. "Thank you, oh Lord, for the bounty before us and the blessings of loving parents whose hearts are filled with forgiveness." Rod smiled slightly, only to himself. "God bless this family and this meal. Amen."

"Amen," Marci and Rod said in unison.

"How was your day?" Rod asked his wife.

"A little unusual, but I got some writing done." Marci was writing her third romance novel. Her first two had sold surprisingly well with comparatively little advertising by a small press publisher.

"How far along are you?"

"I'm working on chapter 28 of 40 in my outline."

"Good progress."

"I think so. Ahead of plan I'd say."

"Excellent."

Rod ate a few bites, and then he looked at Bella. "How was your day, sweetie."

Again, Bella looked at her father like he was an alien. She glanced at Marci, who only smiled modestly, and then back at her father. "Have you talked to Mom?"

"I talk to Mom all the time. I love her and miss being with her all day while I'm at work."

"Great. I mean did Mom tell you?"

"Tell me what?" Rod finished his meal.

Bella finished her meal. "You're going to make me say it."

"Say what, sweetie?"

"Are you finished, Mom?" Bella asked, clearly wanting to change the subject.

"Yes. Thank you."

"I'll clear the table," Bella said and stood. She collected her parents' and her dishes, took them to the sink and got them soaking. She returned to retrieve the remainder of the casserole dish and salad bowl. Bella portioned the macaroni & cheese into individual containers for refrigeration. The small remainder of salad fit easily into a single, separate container. She filled the casserole dish with soapy water to soften things up for cleaning. Bella cleared the rest of the table and wiped it down. She also refilled her parents iced tea glasses and hers. Bella sat back down at the dining room table but did not speak.

"Where were we?" Marci asked.

"I do believe you were about to tell us something important," answered Rod without expression, looking directly at Bella.

Bella glanced at each of her parents several times, perhaps looking for a reprieve. "Mom had to drive out to Minville to pick me up."

"I thought today was a school day," Rod observed calmly.

"I cut school with Gretchen and Christie."

"We didn't get a notification of a missing student," said Rod innocently.

"I sent the school an eMail."

"So, if I understand you correctly, Bella Joy Ramirez, you fraudulently presented yourself as your mother."

"I would not say it like that," Bella protested.

"Very well, then, how would you say it?" Rod asked. Bella stared at her father for several seconds as she considered her words. "Well . . . I'm truly intrigued to hear your explanation, and I'm fairly certain your mother is as well."

"Absolutely," Marci added.

They both waited for their daughter's answer.

"We just wanted a day off," Bella finally said.

"We aren't yet to why, Bella, we're still stuck on fraudulent use," Rod responded, using his police shorthand jargon. He had more questioning for his daughter and her use of a false identification card for illegal purposes.

"I didn't think of it as fraud, Dad. I just needed an excuse, so I didn't show up on some truancy report. Christie and Gretchen did the same thing."

"So that made it OK," Marci challenged her.

"Because your two friends have lower moral values than you were raised with in life. How do you think the school will view any future eMail from your mother?"

"I hadn't thought of that. I just wanted a day off from school."

"You could have asked," said Marci.

"Would you have let me go?"

"We'll never know, but at least we would have talked about it."

"I know I screwed up, you guys. I'm sorry, truly sorry. It seemed like a good idea at the time."

"I'm sure it did, Bella, but it wasn't. It was a very foolish, selfish, and immoral thing to do. We'll come back to this element. Now, I want to hear all about your adventure in Minville. I want the truth, the whole truth, and nothing but the truth, Bella Joy. This isn't some youthful rebellion. The floor is yours."

Bella looked down at the table and shook her head. "You probably already know. You're a cop."

"I'm not just a cop. I am a detective-sergeant."

"I know, Dad."

"Well . . . the whole truth?"

"We went to Minville to buy some drugs for a party. We used fake IDs. The shop owner suspected we had fake IDs and somehow alerted the police. The Minville police officer showed up before we could pick up the drugs. We were arrested. They called Mom. She came down to pick me up. I still don't know what happened to Gretchen and Christie."

"How did you get there? None of you have a license or a car."

"A friend drove us."

"Who be that friend?" Rod asked in contemporary street-speak. Bella hesitated. She appeared to Rod to be more interested in protecting the driver. "The longer this goes to get to the truth, the worse it'll get, Bella Joy."

"What does it matter who drove us to Minville?"

"Well, Bella Joy, to be brutally blunt, he is an accessory to multiple crimes. Who is the driver?" Rod asked, again, more sternly this time.

"He didn't do anything wrong," Bella protested. "I made a mistake . . . ."

"Multiple mistakes, Bella . . . multiple crimes."

"Dad, please . . . I'm sorry. We were just trying to have some fun. I didn't mean for any of this to happen."

"I'm sure you didn't. We'll get to your motivations eventually, but you must tell me who the driver is, Bella. The sooner you tell me the truth, the sooner we move on. I can't help you without the truth."

"I don't want to get him in trouble, Dad."

"Too late, Bella. He was in trouble when he picked you girls up this morning." Rod did not press his interrogation and decided to give Bella a little breathing space to think.

Bella took a drink of iced tea. "It was Johnny Oscarson."

"Your school senior quarterback last year?"

"Yes."

"Well, that compounds the problem for him."

"Papa, please," she pleaded, almost crying. "He meant no harm."

"Drunk drivers don't intend to do any harm either, Bella, but they do enormous injury, and death to innocent people. Most criminals don't intend harm, but their actions do harm, nonetheless, usually considerable harm. Before we move to the next phase," Rod stated and looked at Marci, "do you have anything you want to say or ask at this point?"

"No, you're doing quite well, as always," answered Marci. "Proceed."

Rod looked directly at Bella and held her eyes. "I'd be lying if I tried to tell you I hadn't cut school when I was your age. That's an important but comparatively minor infraction. Running away with an adult as a minor child . . ."

"I didn't run away," Bella protested.

"The law sees it differently, my darling daughter. Yet, the real, root issue for me, for us, for your Mom and me is the drugs. The drugs are legal, now, except for minor children. Whether you like it or not, Bella Joy, you're still 15 years old, and the law defines you as a minor child. In fact, the law establishes your parents as responsible for your actions. This is the context in which we are having this discussion.

"My brothers in blue, if they knew how open we've been with you, wouldn't approve, and more than a few would condemn your mother and me as having lost our minds. We chose a different path with you. We didn't want your youthful curiosity to place you in a bad situation or cajole you into making terrible choices. And for all our efforts to raise you in a progressive, intellectual manner, we find ourselves in a very uncomfortable and precarious position. So, if you have any respect for either your mother or me, you'll tell us why."

"Why what?"

Rod took a deep breath and counted to ten softly. "This is no time to be coy or modest, Bella Joy."

"Gretchen, Christie and I have been talking about trying cocaine and ecstasy for months. The opportunity presented itself, and we took it."

"Opportunity for what?"

"You know," Bella quipped. Rod and Marci stared at Bella's eyes with intensity and as little emotion as they could not contain. "You really want me to say it?" Neither of her parents twitched. "We were going to Johnny's fraternity party."

"It was a class day for them, too, if he really is enrolled at the university. What you're describing, and especially with those two drugs, is a sex party."

"Papa!" protested Bella.

"Really?" Marci asked, adding to Bella's protest.

Rod looked at Marci, and then back at Bella. "This is not my first rodeo. You're a middling teenager, years past puberty. We collectively agreed to put you on birth control when you biologically became a woman, just to ensure you didn't have the burden of an unwanted pregnancy. We've tried to respect the growing sphere of your privacy as a human being and as a citizen. The law will consider you an adult in two plus years. Our job as parents has been and continues to be your preparation for adulthood and citizenship. Are you maintaining your birth control?"

"Yes!" Bella protested, again.

Rod looked directly at Marci. "Out of respect for our daughter's privacy, we don't need to know if she is sexually active. However, presuming she is, she really needs to have the HPV vaccine."

"Really, Rod," Marci said with irritation in her voice. "I thought we were talking about her cutting school, using a fake ID and illegally buying drugs."

"Ecstasy, more precisely called MDMA, is a sex drug. Cocaine is used for many reasons, but one of the principal uses is sexual enhancement. Let's not kid ourselves here."

Marci shook her head, as if in disbelief, and then nodded her head several times. She looked at Bella. "Are you sexually active, Bella?"

Their daughter stared intensely at her mother. "Yes."

"Are you using protection?"

"Yes. Condoms."

"They fail," interjected Rod. "We'll come back to birth control. I want to go back to the primary matter at hand here. Was this your first time using a fake ID to purchase any psychotropic substances?"

"What is that . . . psychotropic?"

"Drugs that affect a person's mental state."

"Yes."

"Have you used any of these drugs before?"

"Yes . . . but not combined with sex."

"So, you've not used a fake ID to buy drugs prior to this afternoon?"

"No."

"How long have you been doing this?"

"Doing what exactly?"

"You've become quite the street lawyer, haven't you?" Rod paused to allow her to answer, but Bella just stared at her father with a smug expression. ". . . using drugs."

"A few years."

"What drugs have you bought and tried?"

"We've not bought drugs ourselves before. This was our first attempt. We've tried just about all of them. We all have."

"I'm not particularly interested in the others, at this point, and you say 'just about all of them.' What exactly does that mean?"

"We've tried most of them. The only ones we haven't tried are heroin, benzos and mushrooms."

"Oh, Bella," Marci reacted, verging upon crying. "Why? Why?"

"They're legal . . . ."

"Not for minor children," Rod corrected her rather sternly.

"I'm not a child."

"According to the law, you're a child until you turn 18 years of age."

"That's bullshit."

"Bella Joy!" exclaimed Marci.

"Sorry, Mom . . . Dad. It's just I don't feel like a child. The law is wrong. We've not hurting anyone. We've not broken any laws."

"You have, Bella. The SCIP Act specifically excludes children under 18 years of age without parental guidance, permission and supervision. To my knowledge," Rod paused to glance at Marci, who shook her head in the negative, anticipating his implicit question, "we've not given our permission for you to consume these drugs, which means you're in violation of state law and subject to punishment."

"Dad!" Bella protested.

"The law is the law, Bella . . . change it, don't violate it."

"OK. I get it. I understand. I don't agree, but I accept it. So, are you going to send me to court and jail for this?"

Rod thought for a moment. "I'll call Lieutenant Johnson in the morning and see where he's at, and then we can go from there."

"Daddy, I don't want to go to jail or even juvie," Bella said softly, like the daughter she used to be.

"You violated the law, Bella Joy. I don't know if I can fix this one. The state went to extraordinary lengths at considerable risk to make psychotropic substances safe for those so inclined to consume them. The state specifically sought to avoid just this situation. When news of these arrests become publicly known, as they most assuredly will, the forces of regression will seize upon this incident as justification to return to the bad old days of prohibition. These are the consequences of your actions, Bella. You think you're no longer a child. Welcome to adulthood. We don't know how this is going to play out. Until we know otherwise, you should prepare yourself for paying the price for violating the law."

"I made the mistakes. I'll pay the price." Bella paused and looked down at the table for several seconds, and then she looked back at her father. "When you talk to Lieutenant Johnson, would you please ask about Gretchen and Christie. I don't want any special treatment different from them."

"A noble gesture," Rod responded, "but, some of that will depend upon their parents and their lawyers if they engage them. The best I can promise is to do the best I can with the circumstances."

"Thank you, Papa."

Rod nodded his head in acknowledgment. "So, Bella, my darling juvenile delinquent, until we sort this out for you and your friends, the restrictions imposed by your mother shall stand. Understood?"

"Yes sir."

"Do you want to add anything, Mom?"

"Nope. I'm good."

Rod looked at Bella. "Thank you for being our daughter and clearing the table. Now, no dessert for you . . . off to your room for contemplation."

"Can I have my phone?"

"No!" exclaimed Rod and Marci in unison and with emphasis.

Bella chuckled. "Like you always say, we never know unless we ask."

"Valiant try. Off you go.

Bella rose from the table, kissed Marci and Rod on the cheeks, and then headed off to her room. They heard her bedroom door close.

Rod took a good swallow of his iced tea, and then looked at Marci. "What do you think?"

"I believe she got the message," Marci responded. "We'll have to check in with her in a few days. Let's give her that time to process what you told her."

"Good idea. I agree. What happens next depends in large measure upon what the Minville Police and the assigned prosecutor, if it has gone that far, decide to do with this. We should avoid talking to the other girls' parents until we know what the full situation is here."

"Makes sense." Marci smiled. "You want some ice cream?"

"What do you have?"

"Butter Pecan."

"Works for me," Rod said.

They took turns checking on Bella. Her bedroom door remained closed, and her room remained quiet. They left her alone with her thoughts.

Mid-morning, the following day, Rod called Minville Police Lieutenant Brad Johnson.

"I've been anticipating your call," Johnson said.

"Well, not exactly the context I'd prefer for a professional introduction. Here I am. What can you tell me?"

"I surmise you're generally aware of the details."

"From my daughter's perspective only."

"I imagine her rendition is generally correct. Three minor females were arrested in our jurisdiction for violation of provisions of the SCIP Act, namely the attempted purchase of regulated substances, and violation of the fake ID statutes. In their favor, they didn't resist or give us any problems. Among your list of questions is probably the status of your daughter's two companions."

"Yes, that's on my list."

"Their parents were notified as was your wife. The other two remain in custody. Both their parents rejected custodial release."

"Well, that answers that," Rod said matter-of-factly. "Have you notified the prosecutors?"

"No. I was waiting to talk to you." Rod shrugged his shoulders reflexively, expecting Johnson to continue. "Allow me to ask you a rather personal and direct question." This time, Rod gestured impatiently with his hand to come on, as if Johnson could see him. "Do you think you can handle your daughter's education, so that she does not repeat this mistake?"

Rod chuckled softly. "My guess is, you don't have any teenage children and especially a teenage daughter." Johnson hesitated, probably contemplating whether to respond. "We had a long chat with Bella last night. Both Marci and I believe she got the message. Her curiosity overran her common sense. To be forthright, this wasn't the first offense for any of the three."

"No record."

"Sure, they weren't caught, but she confessed to the previous events of drug use, but this was apparently their first attempt at direct purchase. You've been open with me. I'll share what I learned from last night's interrogation. If you need it, the driver was a 19-year-old, reportedly a college freshman, by the name of Oscarson, Johnny Oscarson."

"Thank you. That saves us a step. We'll check it out . . . just for closure."

"Understood."

Johnson did not speak for several seconds, probably thinking about what to say next. "It was an attempt. We're prepared to not file charges." Rod nodded his head, again, to himself. "But . . ." Johnson paused for emphasis, ". . . the IDs were high quality. The forger duplicated three of the five security marks. We really want the forger. I suspect the bastard is more likely located in your jurisdiction rather than ours. So, I propose we work a joint operation to snatch the forger. Further, your daughter may well be the key, and if you agree, I'd like you to lead the joint operation for your jurisdiction."

"I'll need to clear a joint op with my captain."

"Understood and agreed."

"Then, we've a provisional deal."

"Excellent. We'll not charge the girls, and we'll release the other two to your custody and return them to their parents. How you sequence things is your business. I only ask that you keep me informed. Once we have a lead, we'll frame our plan. I've confidence in your relationship with your daughter. The girls may not have known what they had in their hands, but those IDs were probably why they didn't get caught until yesterday." Rod saw no reason to correct Brad's misconception. "The shopkeeper had all of the check tools. It points to the need for the state to deploy that equipment to all distribution and retail locations. Three of five is just too close."

"You got that right."

Lieutenant Johnson handled the telephone calls to Gretchen and Christie's parents for permission to transport their daughters while Rod drove to Minville. As they agreed, Marci called the school without disclosing to the administration the reason, to keep Bella home for the impending interrogation continuation.

Johnson and Ramirez went through the procedural steps for Rod to temporarily take custody of the two detainees. He chose not to talk to the girls, and they did not speak to him, other than to thank him for facilitating their release and transporting them home. Rod tried hard to minimize the conversation with both sets of parents.

Rod carefully worked his way through the interrogation. The process took three days and through the weekend. He called Lieutenant Johnson several times each day to keep him informed of the progress. Rod eventually learned that Christie contacted a nefarious middleman to acquire the forged, laminated, driver's license cards. In collaboration, Ramirez and Johnson coordinated the acquisition of multi-jurisdictional warrants to surveil the middleman and eventually gain the connection to the source. Two and a half weeks after becoming aware of the forged ID cards, they arrested the source forger as well as a good portion of his distribution network. In the search of the man's workshop, they discovered currency plates and immediately notified the U.S. Department of the Treasury for federal investigation and prosecution. The forger had produced a wide variety of high-quality fake documents including passports, diplomas, and even marriage and divorce documents.

Rod Ramirez made sure to compliment his daughter's forthrightness and the assistance of her friends for the pivotal if not vital help in cracking a major forgery system. The investigation and prosecutorial actions spurred the state to carry out wider deployment of the security devices to read numerous important identification documents. Bella even received a letter of gratitude from Lieutenant Johnson and the Minville Police Department.

—

9

Rod Ramirez had easily and swiftly reached the threshold of 'beyond a reasonable doubt' for notification of the district attorney's office. He had been waiting an hour for an assigned prosecutor to arrive and participate in the final interrogation. The details of this particular case had been transmitted to the district attorney's office first thing this morning.

Rod remained convinced Maxim Jurgensen amply met the criteria for designation as a habitual criminal who had not responded to the layered and escalated rehabilitation provisions of the law. Jurgensen was a 47-year-old man born to a seriously broken family and bounced around the foster-care system until he took the path of crime. His first arrest and conviction came at age 12 when he was caught shoplifting US$500 plus worth of goods from two stores. As a middle-aged adult, Jurgensen had a long record of arrests, convictions, and punishment at every level except one, and that was the objective of this morning's meeting. His list of crimes ranged from his initial but not only shoplifting event to armed robbery, and included violent crimes from reckless endangerment to assault & battery with serious injury. He had killed two and seriously injured a half dozen other people for which he was convicted of vehicular manslaughter under the influence of multiple intoxicants. Many of his adult crimes involved intoxication of various forms from alcohol to methamphetamine and phencyclidine (PCP).

The telephone on his desk rang. The duty desk sergeant informed Rod that Assistant District Attorney Joubert was on his way up. Rod closed the folder of evidence collected on Jurgensen from various local, state and federal agencies. He activated the Sleep mode on his desktop computer. As he looked up, Joubert walked across the squad room toward Rod's desk.

Rod stood and extended his right hand to Joubert. "Good morning, Raoul."

They shook hands, and then Joubert responded, "If you say so."

"Bad day?" Rod gestured to the padded straight back chair beside his desk.

As he sat, Raoul said, "Every day is bad these days."

"You want to talk about it?"

"No." Joubert opened his leather case, extracted a file that was much thinner than Rod's folder, and then placed his case on the floor beside him. "I've reviewed your charging evidence several times and conferred with the DA. We also had a conference call yesterday afternoon with the state's attorney general.

We all agree with your assessment. The Jurgensen case looks ripe to be our first Black Hole prosecution.

"Jurgensen has a very long rap sheet, longer than most, I must say. He qualifies by the definition as a habitual criminal. He has failed the SCIP Act indulgence camps, twice, and served three stints in prison, the last one concluded just five months ago. His latest arrest was three days ago for armed robbery with meth intoxication."

"Exactly. Do you have the tox-screen?"

"Yes. Blood level three times over standard dosage levels and that was an hour after his arrest."

"Correct."

"He just doesn't get it, does he?" Raoul asked, more as a statement than a query.

"Nope. Have you seen the security video from the store?"

"Yes. Thank you for that. He made it easy, didn't he?"

"He certainly did. My interpretation tells me he didn't care. By the way, you may not be aware, but we ran the vid clip through the FBI's facial recognition system—positive with level one certainty."

"Doesn't get any higher than that."

"Nope."

"Where's the perp now?"

"Locked in Interrogation Room Number 4 with his public defender. They're waiting on us."

Joubert stood. "Then, let's not keep them waiting any longer. We're going to press for a fast-track prosecution."

"Seems appropriate to me," Rod commented.

The two men left the squad room, walked down the hallway to the last interrogation room with a two-foot-high numeral '4' painted on the door below the reinforced window. Rod disengaged the lever lock door handle and entered first, holding the door open for Joubert.

"It's about time," protested Public Defender Henry 'Hank' Houseman.

"Sorry about that, Hank. We're here now, and I think we can make quick work of this, so you can get back to your busy day."

"Not so fast," Houseman objected. "We haven't seen the charging document. How the hell are we going to have a pre-trial hearing day after tomorrow?"

"We're fast-tracking this one."

"What about bail?"

Joubert smiled. No one else did. "You're kidding, yes?" Houseman did not respond in any manner and just stared at Joubert. "No bail."

"Why?"

Joubert smiled tolerantly. "The state intends to try Mister Jurgensen here as a habitual criminal and declare him unredeemable."

"You can't do that," protested Houseman.

Again, Joubert smiled, this time with far less tolerance. "Yes, we can, and we most assuredly will."

"Then, why are you here?"

"Hank, you have copies of the evidence, including a copy disk with the security video from the store he robbed at gunpoint. We added in the extra clip of the FBI's facial recognition software at work along with the result. If you don't have his rap sheet, I suggest you do your homework. The bottom line is, Mister Jurgensen has exhausted his options and the patience of the state. The state intends to press for conviction and Black Hole confinement."

"That is unconstitutional!" Houseman objected loudly.

"Not yet, Hank. We're quite aware that the Black Hole provisions are under challenge in and under review by the Judiciary. As of yesterday, the attorney general feels the state's argument is sound and will be upheld by the Supreme Court. Until then, the Black Hole confinement facilities are open and accepting qualified inmates. Your client here," Raoul said, pointing at Jurgensen, "is the textbook case for the legal provisions of Black Hole incarceration."

Houseman shook his head with visible agitation. "Once again, why are we here?"

"We wanted to ensure you're properly informed and offer your client the opportunity to plead guilty and get on with his life."

"In a Black Hole," Houseman nearly screamed.

"Yes."

"There's no fucking way. You're going to have to prove your case before a jury. And further, I'll ensure the inhumanity of those miserable prisons are presented in evidence for the jury to consider."

Joubert smiled at Houseman, and then he looked directly at Jurgensen. "Well, Maxim, the decision belongs to you, not to your counsel. Do you just want to get on with things?" Jurgensen shook his head in the negative. "Does that mean you refuse the opportunity presented?" Jurgensen nodded his head in the affirmative. "Last chance."

"I don't want to go to that place they call the Black Hole."

Raoul smiled broadly and nodded his head. "Oh my, I can certainly understand that Maxim. May I call you Maxim?" Joubert did not wait for a response. "Do you know why they call it the Black Hole?" Jurgensen shook his head no. "It's named after the astronomical term for a massive and dense celestial object that possesses such enormous gravity that not even light can escape. You literally can't see it. We know it's there because of what it does to the surrounding space. In our particular terrestrial case, it's where we send habitual criminals, such as yourself, never to be seen in law-abiding public again. Your days of exploiting and terrorizing our peaceful, law-abiding citizens are over. Our community will soon be rid of you. I hope and trust your days of abusing this community, any community, like a schoolyard bully, were worth it to you, because you've had your last bite of the apple. Once we're done with you in court, after you receive the due process granted to you by the constitution and you denied to your victims, you'll face whatever life you have left immersed with your kind. With that little soliloquy complete, we're done here."

Joubert stood, followed by Ramirez.

"Wait, wait . . . allow me to confer with my client," Houseman said.

Raoul looked at Rod. "Are you OK with the continued occupancy of one of your precious interrogation rooms?"

"Sure . . . for now."

"Very well, counselor. You may use the state's property to confer with your miserable client until we need this room. After that, we may have to move you to the jail where you can chat with your client to your heart's content."

Ramirez and Joubert left the room. Rod locked the door. They returned to Rod's desk. Raoul sat, and Rod swiveled his chair so that they were both facing the interrogation room. Rod watched the window intently.

"This is my first Black Hole case," Rod said without looking at Raoul.

"Mine, too. First for the county."

Rod glanced quickly at Raoul. "Do you really think the Black Hole prisons are going to stand up to 8th Amendment scrutiny?"

"None of us can ever predict how the courts are going to rule on any particular case. Attorney General Smithson believes the case law supports the process. I haven't reviewed their citations or arguments, but I've worked with John Smithson for many years. He tends toward the conservative end of the spectrum, and I trust his judgment. From what I know of these Black Hole prisons, they are brutal, or at least can be. The arguments against them as 'cruel and unusual punishment' are compelling and can't be ignored. However, the state's tolerance of habitual criminals has boundaries."

"Why not just regular prisons or even super-max prisons like we used to have?"

"Part of the criminal code reform carried out in conjunction with the SCIP Act changes involved restructuring the penal system to amplify the rehabilitation aspects of punishment. The state has chosen to extend itself in treatment, retraining, and rehabilitation, but we also drew the line for the boundary of magnanimity for our citizens and taxpayers. I've not been to one of the Black Holes, but from what I know, they're like Animal Farm on steroids."

"Yeah. I've not seen one either," Rod said, as he continued to watch the door. "I've not seen the inside of one. Yet, I briefed the governor's commission a few weeks back. I felt a little awkward. I know the streets, but those Black Holes are challenging my imagination. On their face, they make sense. There're really bad men out there, and they deserve to sort things out the way they do."

"There are limits to treatment of the recalcitrant individuals like Jurgensen. I think what has swayed the lower courts so far is the reorientation of prisons at the lower level. Every effort has been and is being made to redeem a lost soul. Our state's recidivism rate has been and remains the lowest in the nation since we implemented these changes. That fact alone speaks volumes. The new system seems to act like a beneficial filter. We save as many as we can, but there are limits . . . and, we don't have the death penalty anymore."

Rod noticed Houseman at the window waving his arm. He pointed to the door and said, "Looks like Houseman is done."

They both stood and went to the door. Houseman gestured for them to come in. Joubert shook his head and waved his hand for Houseman to come out. Rod unlocked and opened the door. After Houseman stepped out, Rod closed and locked the door.

"What's up?" Raoul asked.

"My client would like to offer a deal."

"No deals," Joubert responded swiftly and matter-of-factly.

"You haven't even heard the offer."

"I don't need to hear anything from him. He's going to disappear, and we'll be done with him."

"Wait a second, now. He's offering to give you the perpetrators in several of your unsolved crimes."

"What does he want in return?" Joubert asked, knowing the answer that was coming.

"Conventional prison without parole."

"No deal, Counselor."

"You can solve other crimes."

"The days of warehouse prisons are over, Hank. We'll likely solve whatever crimes he is referring to without his assistance. The state has made every possible effort to rehabilitate your client. He has summarily rejected every generous opportunity extended to him. He has crossed the threshold of tolerance defined by the law. These are the consequences."

"Excuse me, Mister Joubert," interjected Rod Ramirez. "May I have a word, please?" He stepped back five good paces from Houseman and turned to face the advancing Joubert. Raoul was a good four inches taller, so his back would block both of them. Raoul signaled with his eyes—what is it? Rod whispered, "On the street side, I think we should at least hear what crimes he is referring to before we dismiss his offer."

"Really? You want to let this cretin off the hook?" Raoul whispered back with a pronounced tone of irritation.

"It doesn't cost us anything to listen."

"Other than it gives the perp a ray of hope."

Rod offered a facial expression of: is that so bad?

"OK. OK," Raoul responded. "We'll listen. I recommend we let him talk. No questions. No discussion. No negotiations. If you think something is worth more, tap the table with your left index finger. At that point, we'll take a break to discuss your assessment. Is that agreed?"

"Yes," Rod whispered.

Joubert turned and walked back to Houseman. Ramirez followed.

"We'll listen to what your client has to offer. There'll be no negotiations. He's a habitual criminal destined for the Black Hole, as it should be. Are we clear?"

"Yes . . . crystal . . ." Houseman turned and led them back to the interrogation room.

Rod unlocked the door and opened it for Raoul and Hank. Houseman sat next to his client and whispered something to Jurgensen. Raoul and Rod waited patiently without expression. After several minutes, Hank sat back and gestured to Jurgensen to make his pitch.

Maxim Jurgensen spoke freely, voluntarily, and confidently. He declared that he had personal, direct knowledge of the perpetrators of an automobile theft ring, an armed bank robbery five years ago, a rape four years ago, and another bank robbery in the planning stage. Rod did not tap his finger. He did think he should offer his assessment to Raoul before a final decision was rendered. Rod looked at Raoul and nodded his head to the door.

"Excuse us please," he said as he stood, not waiting for a response.

Rod joined Raoul in the hallway, away from the door window, so they could talk freely. "Without more details, it's impossible to judge whether his information has any value. I think I know the status of two of the cases. The investigations are active and not stalled. The rape could be helpful if he truly knows the rapist. The robbery in planning would be beneficial to get ahead of, but there are no guarantees because whatever information he has would be a snapshot from a few days ago at best. The planners could change directions for myriad reasons, and if he was a direct party, his arrest may well spook the planners."

"So, what are you saying? Do we deal or not?"

"To be frank, I think that decision is above my paygrade. Other detectives are involved. None of those cases, if my judgment is correct, are in my basket. I should at least talk to my captain, if not the chief."

"Should we do that together? I mean, from my perspective, I doubt the veracity of his words. He's desperate to avoid the Black Hole."

"Your choice. Do you need to check with the DA?"

"Good point. I probably should as well. This has become a high-profile case because it is our first Black Hole prosecution. Since you've got the lock, why don't you inform Houseman and Jurgensen that we need a few minutes to an hour to respond."

"OK," Rod responded. Joubert went to the open office allocated to visiting lawyers for the district attorney's department that they maintained at the police station for just this purpose. Rod informed Hank Houseman and left him with his client in the locked room. Rod briefed his captain, and as expected, they called the chief to brief him. The police supervisors were intrigued and tempted, but ultimately declined the offer.

When Rod left the captain's office, Raoul was sitting next to his desk. Before he sat down, Rod noticed Houseman standing at the door window. He held up his right index finger. Hank nodded his acknowledgment and stayed at the window. Rod looked at Raoul and said, "They were no help. Both my captain and the chief ultimately said the decision is up to you. As I suspected, they are tempted, as a shortcut, but they're sufficiently comfortable with where we are in these open investigations . . . so, over to you, mister district attorney."

Raoul chuckled softly, more visible than audible. "Oddly, I got the same thing from the DA. With all that, I don't see sufficient evidence to justify taking the deal. Judging on past experience, I think we'll both agree that our perp will likely try to add more. I'm good with your investigative work here, Rod. We've ample hard evidence well beyond probable cause and also beyond reasonable doubt. So, we're agreed?"

"Yes."

"Very well, let's get this done. We both have other work to do," Joubert said and stood.

As Raoul and Rod approached the interrogation room, Hank left the window. When they reached the room, Houseman was standing behind Jurgensen with his hands on his client's shoulders.

Raoul did not feel the need for a summary preface. "No deal. See you in court." Raoul turned, and Rod followed.

"Wait! I've got more," Jurgensen shouted.

"Not interested," Raoul responded without turning around.

"How about a drug smuggling network and a murderer?"

Raoul Joubert stopped and faced Jurgensen. "I understand and appreciate you're desperate to avoid the Black Hole. I know I would be, if I was in your shoes. You've had your chance at redemption. You were given more than sufficient, verging upon excessive, opportunities to become a peaceful, law-abiding, productive, member of society. You chose to reject every single opportunity. We'll do just fine with our investigations and prosecutions of criminals. We don't need or want your help. This state doesn't have the death penalty. You'll die a natural death for your kind. The state will soon be satisfied." Joubert looked directly at Houseman. "Your client is going to be returned to his jail cell. If you want to continue your important discussions with your client, I must ask you to move to the jail's legal support facilities."

Hank Houseman did not speak, patted Jurgensen on the shoulder, and gathered his possessions. He departed without further exchange. Raoul followed Hank, and Rod followed Joubert.

"I've got more to offer," Jurgensen said loudly.

"Too late," Raoul stated emphatically without looking around.

Rod closed the door with Jurgensen still shouting things that everyone ignored. He gestured for the duty police officer to remove Jurgensen and return him to his holding cell for transfer to the jail.

Joubert started to leave but turned to face Rod. "We're good. Unless something changes, I'd like to see you in court day after tomorrow for Jurgensen's pre-trial hearing."

"Should be no problem for me. If you don't hear from me, I'll be there. Just tell me the court room and the time you need me there."

"OK. Thanks for your help this morning. Rod. Well done."

Joubert turned. "Wait a sec," Rod said. Raoul turned back around. "Unrelated . . . different case . . . what's happening on the Baxter and Ignatius fraud case?"

"Interesting that you asked. Earlier this week, the feds invoked their primacy since their evidence demonstrated far greater interstate fraud than was involved at the state level. Baxter has been transferred to federal custody. They're now arguing among themselves where to file charges. My guess is, they'll file in the Southern District of New York. Ignatius remains in our custody for the moment. His bail was denied as a serious flight risk. Just this morning before I came here, the U.S. attorney called to inform me that new evidence acquired by the FBI and SEC indicates he may have been more involved in Baxter's scheme than previously appreciated. Until the feds take over, we'll continue to prepare for trial on perjury and false statements charges. We can't predict how a jury is going to respond, but every jury I'm aware of in trials for financial crimes since the Great Recession of '08 has been resoundingly unsympathetic to the shenanigans of bankers and money managers. I suspect Baxter and Ignatius are headed toward long-term incarcerations as guests of the federal government."

"Thanks for the update. I was the arresting officer under a no-knock warrant we executed several weeks back."

"Oh yeah. I forgot about that aspect. The whole case has been saturated with tables, graphs, and accounting data. If I remember the arrest report, you and your colleagues caught up with them at the end of a sex party."

"Yep. Three men . . . Baxter, Ignatius and the bank's lawyer Ted Graves along with three prostitutes."

"Laura Simmons among them?"

"Yes, as I recall . . . three very proper, licensed ladies . . . not particularly bashful or modest, I must say. All of them were stoned on heroin. We had to Narcan them all to bring 'em around."

"What did you think of Simmons?"

"She was fully legal—current license and medical certificate. Rather classy, I must say. She impressed me with her knowledge of current events—quite articulate and refined. Quite the contrast with the streetwalkers we had to deal with before legalization and regulation. She knew nothing of Baxter's activities. Once we completed our interviews, she was released. Why do you ask . . . if I may inquire?"

"Oh, nothing official. She is a friend of my wife. They've known each other since elementary school."

"Small world."

"Quite so. I've met her a few times. I was impressed as well."

"She's very comfortable and confident with her body, and an exquisite body, if I do say so myself. She clearly takes good care of herself and seems to be proud of her profession."

"Thanks. I was just curious."

"Sure, anytime, Counselor."

"Thanks, Rod. OK, see'ya Friday. I'll let you know the precise details when I get back to the office."

"I'll be ready."

"Great," Raoul said and departed.

—

10

The tinkling ringtone of Laura Simmons' private flip phone nearly timed out when she finally hit the answer button and fumbled for the speaker button. Laura was bone-numbing tired from last night's pleasure. She opened one eye briefly to see the time on the large digital clock on her nightstand—7:47 AM . . . it was light outside beyond her bedroom curtains. Laura mumbled something unintelligible.

"Hello . . . hello," came Kelly Henry's distant voice. "Are you there, Laura?"

"Yeah, I'm here," Laura responded weakly without opening her eyes.

"Late night?"

"Yeah. I've only gotten four hours sleep so far. Is everything OK?"

"Couldn't be better, which is why I called. I've adjusted to my new life here. I really would like to see you. I've been here almost three weeks and not seen or talked to anyone. You're my only friend, Laura. Can you come see me?"

"Today?"

"Yes, if you can."

Laura blinked her eyes open, rolled on her back, and stared at the ceiling. She was awake now. "I need to wake up. Didn't you take an Uber out there?"

"Yes . . . worked fine."

"OK. I'll take an Uber so I can sleep a little more on the way rather than drive. I've appointments tonight, so I won't be able to stay all day."

"No problem. I'm only asking for a few hours of your time . . . just to catch up."

"OK. I can handle that, I think."

"Has Raoul contacted you?"

"Yes."

"Good. We can talk about that, too. When can you get here?"

Laura rose her torso onto her right elbow to look squarely at the clock. "I collapsed into bed a few hours ago. I need to clean up from last night. I won't do any other prep. I'll throw on a T-shirt and jeans to save time. It's a couple of hours drive. I'd say about 11 or 12, how's that?"

"Perfect. The food here is pretty ordinary. Plus, you're not allowed inside. Could you stop in Morristown, that's the last town before you turn east into the desert. Grab a couple of Subway sandwiches. They have soda, water and stuff to drink here."

"Sure. What do you want?"

"After weeks of this food, anything would be great. Just get me another one of whatever you choose. I'll reimburse you."

"No need. OK. We've a plan. Can I bring you anything else?"

"Nope. Just your lovely self . . . oh yeah, and on the Subway sandwich, please make mine a foot long. I'll gorge myself."

Laura laughed, imagining the cafeteria serving them simple porridge and bread. "Will do. Let me go so I can jump into the shower."

"OK, Laura. Thank you so much. I'm sorry I interrupted your sleep but thank you for coming."

"You bet. See you soon."

They terminated the call. Laura ordered an Uber for 30 minutes hence using her professional smartphone application, then she went directly to the shower. The warm water felt so good and refreshing. She toweled dried her hair and brushed it out, flossed and brushed her teeth, and added some underarm deodorant. Laura did not feel the need to wear any underwear, so she donned her jeans and a solid pink T-shirt. She put her small shoulder bag over her shoulder and chose her darkest sunglasses.

The driver woke Laura as he pulled into a parking lot clearly in the desert. The large sign said:

Indulgence Camp

No. 12

Laura noticed immediately that the buildings were not constructed for architectural aesthetics. She shook her head as the high-end SUV came to a stop. She was not here for the buildings or the facility. Laura thanked the driver and gave him a $40 cash tip. She grabbed the Subway bag.

The middle-aged female receptionist checked Laura's name against some list on her computer screen. Laura was not aware that access authorization was necessary, but that is what this felt like.

"You are here to visit Kelly Henry?"

"Yes."

"Please take a seat. I will notify her that you are here."

"Thank you."

The receptionist texted something, and then she made a land-line telephone call. Laura could not tell whether the two actions were related, but it did not really matter. She did not have to wait long, perhaps five minutes or so.

Kelly appeared in the lobby dressed in light green scrubs like some medical professional. Upon seeing Laura, she bounded to her friend, embraced her tightly, and then kissed her on the lips. "It's so great to see you again, Laura.

You're a sight for sore eyes." Kelly noticed the sandwich bag on the chair next to where Laura was sitting. "Fantastic! You brought sandwiches."

"Turkey breast, I hope that's OK. I got a foot-long as you requested." Laura purchased a six-incher for herself.

"Perfect! We've a visitor's dayroom that is passable. It's a little too hot outside for the patio."

They passed through a side room, and then into a comparatively large room with a couple of dozen picnic tables. There were seats for perhaps 200 people, but less than ten people were in the dayroom with only two of that number in colored scrubs. Kelly chose a table near the window looking out on the desert valley and away from the other people.

"What would you like to drink?" Kelly asked.

"Iced tea if they have it."

"Sure do." Kelly went to a bank of vending machines and obtained a bottle of iced tea for Laura and water for herself. Laura noted that no money was required. "Here ya go."

"Thanks."

Kelly was most intent upon the sandwich. She moaned audibly as she took her first bite and tasted the sandwich. "The simple pleasures," Kelly mumbled as she continued to chew her large bite.

Laura did the same.

After several more bites, Kelly put the first half of her sandwich back down on the open wrapper, took a drink of water, and then looked at Laura.

"How've you been?" Kelly asked.

"Great, actually. Business is good."

"Do you still like it?"

"Sure do . . . for the most part. I get paid handsomely for pleasure. What's not to love." Laura thought for a moment. "I do get a bad apple every now and then . . . bad guys who think they can manhandle me because they are paying me. I've gotten pretty good at dealing with them. I've only contacted the police once since I've been doing this line of work."

"Great. You're so lucky. It sounds like you're happy."

"I am, but more importantly, how are you?"

Kelly smiled broadly. "I'm so glad I did this, Laura. I feel free for the first time in my adult life. This place is no resort, but it is adequate—livable. Most folks are here for their own reasons and not particularly outgoing, so it tends to be a little lonely."

"You sound happier and more upbeat than the last time we talked."

"I am . . . I'm most definitely happier. There are things about this place that I wish were different, but most are a small price to pay for the freedom I feel."

"Like what, if I may ask?"

"Well, one immediate point, after we're done here, I'll have to strip down to my skin and be cavity searched."

"Oh my . . . why?"

"They've very strict rules about smuggling. I'm fairly certain they'll thoroughly inspect whatever is left of my sandwich."

"That's pretty intrusive."

"Yes, but like I said, it's a small price to pay. The techs are respectful, and I've never heard of anyone being abused. Even the men keep their distance and respect our space. Really nice, actually."

Laura took another bite of her sandwich as she thought about what Kelly was saying. She took a drink. "Why would anyone need to smuggle stuff in here when you can get whatever you want for free?"

"Well, some out here are more particular than others. For example, they don't offer any of the synthetic opiates like oxycodone or fentanyl. They don't even offer higher or lower derivatives of opium other than heroin—no opium, no morphine, *et cetera*. In my case, they only offer generic benzodiazepine rather than my preferred prescriptive version—Xanax. The doctors helped me adjust to the generic and weened me off the stuff. I haven't taken a benzo for several days now, and I feel great."

"Then why are you still here?"

"To be frank, I'm hiding."

"From what?"

"From Raoul. From life. Like I said, for the first time in my life, I feel free."

"What about the other drugs?"

"As advertised, I can get whatever I want. I think you described it to me like heaven on earth, and I could not agree more. That's how I feel. I've tried a little of all of them . . . well, except PCP. That stuff scares me. There are few in here who take that stuff—all men. It makes them crazy. Since I've been here, a couple of them got violent. They called the police. I was told they were arrested and taken directly to prison."

"Without a trial?"

"Small print. We had to sign a document of the rules to enter. One of those rules is consent to consequences for violations. I witnessed one of those guys come unglued in the cafeteria. It took six techs to subdue the man; he truly went crazy. I'm told other men handle the stuff properly, but a few don't."

"So, you've done cocaine, LSD and Ecstasy?"

"Yep, I don't do most of it regularly. Once I got off the benzos, I seem to prefer THC . . . the inhaler makes it very easy and comparatively quick, like smoke but without the smoke. Really nice, easy to dose. The high is really mellow."

"You don't need to be here for that, Kelly," Laura offered.

"No, sure, you're right, but I feel safe here, as I said." They both consumed another bite of their sandwiches. "You said you talked to Raoul. How's he dealing with my disappearance?"

"He was pretty upset. He really jumped me hard. He was sure I was an accomplice and knew where you were."

"Did you tell him?"

"Nope. I told him nothing about your plan or where you are. He wants me to tell him when I hear from you . . . just to make sure you're safe and OK, according to him. At first, he thought you might've been kidnapped."

"Are you going to tell him about seeing me today?" Kelly asked with concern.

"Only if you want me to tell him, or anyone else for that matter." Laura thought about how much she should confide in Kelly. She decided to let Kelly determine how much she wanted to know. "He asked me to meet him at the Regent Hotel."

"I know what he wanted," Kelly said with a chuckle. "Did you give it to him?"

"Do you want to know?"

"Yes."

"He paid me, so yes, I did him, but that was the last and only time?"

"Why? He's got a healthy libido."

"Way too rough for me."

"Oh yeah, I've seen that part of him more often than not. I never liked it, but for all I knew, it was just the way things were. He's a man. I'm a woman."

"You need to experience a decent lover, Kelly. Most of my clients are gentle, respectful, kind and generous."

"Raoul is not one of those."

Laura giggled softly. "No, he's not. He had his one shot, and he failed . . . although I must say he was generous. He paid me more than he had to, given the circumstances."

"Thank you for enduring that. I don't want any more of it either. I'm glad he paid you more than necessary."

Laura finished her six-incher. Kelly finished half of her sandwich and wrapped up the remainder for later consumption.

"I hope none of that offended you, Kelly. I struggled with that decision. I didn't want to violate our friendship, even though it was business, not personal or for pleasure."

"Nope, not offended whatsoever. I couldn't care less. When I leave here, it'll be to divorce him. I suspect it's more likely he'll divorce me for what used to be called abandonment . . . or perhaps denial of conjugal or spousal services." Kelly chuckled softly.

"I take it from your words that you don't want me to tell him anything."

"Frankly, I don't care . . . except, knowing him, he'll likely show up here with his credentials or even with a couple of police officers to reclaim his property."

"OK."

"I'm not interested in being anyone's property anymore."

"Can't blame you there," added Laura.

"But I'm not going to put this one on you, my friend. Let's see if this is acceptable to you. You can tell him you've talked to me. Please don't tell him you visited me or know where I am. I simply have no interest in seeing him or even hearing his voice. You can tell him I'm safe, healthy, and no longer addicted to benzos. I'd prefer you don't share my indulgence with other substances. He'd only use it as leverage against me."

"No problem, Kell. If it's OK with you, I'll avoid contacting him, unless you want me to do so. I'm not particularly interested in hearing his voice either. If he does call me, I'll tell him the bare minimum, as you suggest, to avoid disclosing any details to him."

"That should be fine. I really don't care beyond anything that might inspire him to chase me or track me down. If he asks you about divorce, tell him to just do it. I don't want anything. I don't expect anything from him."

"You're entitled by law to half of whatever you accumulated together," Laura stated.

"I know, but I don't want any contest. I don't want to face him, to see him, ever again."

"When . . . if it ever comes to that, let your attorney handle the negotiations and details."

"Sure."

"Tell me a little about living here," Laura requested, wanting to change the subject.

Kelly laughed softly. "Not much to tell, actually. As I said earlier, this is no resort—minimal services, just enough to keep people alive, if they wish to stay alive."

"Are there many suicides . . . or deaths in general?"

"There are some. I've seen three, one in my building, since I've been here, but beyond that, I'd have to ask the administration. They're required to record such statistics. People don't talk much in this place, but I've overheard a few conversations. My guess is some people come here to die. Others just don't want to live. They're content to zone out until the time they don't wake up."

"Does anyone recover and leave?"

"Sure. Again, I don't know how many, but my guess is around half voluntarily leave. Again, I'd have to ask about the numbers, but that's my observation since I've been here."

"How many times can you come and go?"

Kelly thought about Laura's question for a few seconds. "I've not heard anyone speak of limits like that. There's nothing I can remember in the entry documents about limits. I'm not particularly interested in finding out the answer."

"Which group are you in, Kell?"

"Well now, isn't that the profound query." She took another sip of water, not quite finishing the bottle. "The truth is, I don't know. I have my moments."

"Moments of what?"

"I have highs and lows."

"Tell me about the lows . . . if you don't mind."

"I'll be honest and candid with you, Laura . . . maybe even a bit blunt. I'd be lying if I claimed to never have had thoughts of ending it all."

"Kelly!"

"It's OK. They're less frequent these days. Based on my feelings since I've been here, I'd say it's possible that those moments might actually disappear."

"That's good, isn't it?"

"I suppose. I don't think much about it. It's an important question." Kelly lapsed into contemplation and stared out the window at nothing in particular. Laura chose not to disturb her thoughts. Neither one of them cared much about the time, although Laura caught herself glancing at the clock and calculating her threshold for notifying her clients and offering them a substitute—one of her friends and colleagues. Laura returned to the present, first.

"Can I see your room?" asked Laura.

Kelly blinked a few times and laughed loudly. "Guess I flew away there, huh?"

"Yeah, ya did. I didn't want to intrude upon your thoughts."

"Sorry about that. I wish I could show you my little space, but the rules are only residents past the reception area. My space is not much . . . more like a cubbyhole than a room. There are only slanted half side barriers, not really walls, on the side and nothing at the foot."

"Not much privacy."

"Nope. Hard to masturbate like that."

They both laughed at the thought or image.

"Anyway, I suppose I should think about your question," Kelly said.

"Which one?"

Again, they laughed together.

"I guess I've been a little drifty this afternoon. The question, at least as I interpreted it, about what group I'm in, which is another way of asking what do I want to accomplish? What do I want to do with my life?" Laura simply nodded her head slightly and did not reply. "I was so focused on getting away from Raoul and just not thinking or feeling for a while to clear my mind." Again, Laura just nodded. "Right now, to this moment, I can't see beyond this phase, this place. The residents and techs leave us alone, so I've not really devoted any time to thinking about the future. To be frank, I don't yet see a future."

"Oh Kell . . ."

"Naw, not to worry. I think it'll come to me in time. The future will appear to me . . . probably like a vision. They've specialists here to help us find that future, but I've not sought them out, yet."

"Maybe you should just open the door and see what happens. From what you've told me, it doesn't sound like there is any pressure from any direction, so it would not cost you anything, except a little time."

"Good point. To tell you the truth, the only thing that has intrigued me, that has tickled my imagination, is your profession."

"I enjoy it," Laura responded. "But it's not for everyone."

"Are there men who do it?"

"Yes, of course. Most customers for both male and female prostitutes are men, but there are more than a few female customers . . . just mostly men . . . and, there are plenty of gays out there, male and female."

"What would you say is the ultimate requirement for your line of work?"

"Good question. Let me offer an answer in a roundabout way. Underlying everything is compassion—feelings for other people. Prostitution is more than just the mechanics of sex. Oh sure, there are some men who are just what we call 'cum & go' guys. They just want someone to get them off as quickly as possible without any fluff. But many others want a human connection. Yet, if I had to boil it all down to one element, I'd say sexual orientation or preference. I've no official study or such, but I think most really successful prostitutes are evolved pansexuals."

"What on earth does that mean?"

"To my thinking, a pansexual doesn't care about the package as much as the contents. They enjoy sex with anyone with a good attitude—man, woman, transgender, gender ambiguous—doesn't matter."

"I've no idea what most of that is all about."

"On top of that, you really need to enjoy sex. Biologically, sex is for procreation. However, there's a reason both men and women feel pleasure. The French refer to an orgasm as *la petite mort*—the little death, because the sensations are often so intense it feels like you'll explode."

"I've felt a few of those . . . all with masturbation. Raoul never much cared about my pleasure."

"I did note that reality, Kell."

They both laughed.

"I don't know if I can do that," Kelly said.

"Then it's probably not for you. Except for the 'cum & go' guys, customers feel your attitude. They sense your mood, and they play off your feelings. If your heart is not in it, they detect it, and for many of them, it becomes a real turn off, and thus dissatisfying. It seems like it's a delicate balance, but it's much more natural if your heart is in it."

"I just don't know . . ."

"Then let go of the notion, Kell. Trust your gut feelings. Your gut is telling you no. I knew I wanted to do this kind of work since my teenage years. Many people say the ideal is to work your passion. Not everyone can find that state. You seem to be in a safe place for now. Take the time you need. Enjoy your newfound freedom. Your future will come to you in time."

"I sure hope so."

"It will. I have faith."

"Thanks, Laura. You've been so kind and generous. I've occupied three hours of your time already. I'm sorry I woke you up this morning. When I woke up this morning, I felt I really needed to talk to you. Thank you so much for coming all the way out here. You've a two-hour drive back. They've a special Uber number to get a quick response . . . well, as quick as possible way out here."

"You're most welcome, Kell. Anytime. Call me whenever you feel the urge. I'll do my best to give you whatever time you need. It'll be so good to get you back to life."

"You're so generous and such a good friend. Now, let's get you on your way. You've got fucking to do."

They both laughed. The two women stood, deposited their bottles in the recycle bin, and disposed of their trash. Kelly carried the remainder of her sandwich to consume later. In the lobby, the duty receptionist, now an attractive young man, helped Laura call a special Uber vehicle. Kelly remained with Laura in the lobby. They talked about odds and ends like the flora and fauna outside the fence, and even the ever-present weather. Kelly had experienced her first dust storm—strong winds that kicked up great clouds of dirt. The dust storm she endured enveloped the whole camp and reduced visibility to near zero. She missed dinner that day. Most of the residents did not venture outside even for the short distance to the cafeteria. None of them wanted to be sandblasted.

It took only 20 minutes for the van to arrive. Kelly and Laura hugged and kissed before Laura got into the van. They waved to each other as the vehicle drove away. Once out of sight of the camp, Laura reclined her seat, left her seatbelt fastened, and quickly drifted off to sleep for the two-hour drive back to the city.

—

11

Detective-Sergeant Rod Ramirez appreciated the comparatively quiet morning that allowed him to catch up on his paperwork. When his desk telephone rang, he wondered if that quiet period was ending.

"Ramirez," he said succinctly when he put the handset to his ear.

"Good morning, Rod. This is Brad Johnson from Minville."

"Great to hear from you, Brad. What can I do'ya for?"

"We tracked down Johnny Oscarson in the fake ID case. He's in your jurisdiction. If you have the time, I'd like to interview him with you at his apartment. He has no classes after lunch before his football practice. I'd like to meet with you in say an hour or two at your office, so I can update you on what we know so far, and what we're missing. Then, I'd like to drive over to his apartment to get there around one this afternoon. The interview should go quickly . . . unless he decides to be a stick in the mud. How does that sound?"

"Should be no problem for me. I'll make sure my captain knows you'll be here on a cross-jurisdictional investigation."

"Excellent. See'ya in an hour or so."

Rod hung up the telephone and went directly to brief his captain on the Minville initiative. The captain gave his consent along with the incessant encouragement to keep him informed.

Ramirez returned to his desk and logged into the department network. He wanted to read up on the object of the investigation before Johnson arrived. The city, state and national databases contained very little information. "Looks like the kid has kept his nose clean," Rod said quietly to himself. He had been finger-printed for a background investigation related to the purchase of a Walther PPK 32-caliber semi-automatic pistol a year ago, when he turned 18 years of age. "Nice choice," he said again to himself. Johnny successfully completed the state sanctioned firearms training course. His only noted violations of law were two traffic tickets, one for speeding (12 mph over the local speed limit) two years ago, and a parking ticket last year. Based on what he saw on this computer screen, Rod felt Johnny Oscarson would be a fairly easy interview and would not present a problem . . . well, other than they would need to localize that pistol before jumping into the investigation. Rod also noted that Minville had not submitted an under-investigation report to the database.

Out of related curiosity, Rod checked the system for information on the three girls, including his daughter. Fortunately, Bella Ramirez was clean. Their arrest was not noted, yet. Rod jotted down a quick note in his pocket notepad to ask Lieutenant Johnson if they had or would submit the arrest report. Normally, such arrests would be recorded in the database and would be searchable. Gretchen Hessian was likewise comparatively clean with only one traffic ticket for failure to yield six months ago. Christie Theriot's record proved to be a little more problematic.

Christie had two separate arrests for shoplifting. Her parents paid the fines and restitution. She was also arrested for turnstile jumping, plead *nolo contendere*, and was sentenced to four days in juvenile detention with one year of probation, which had not expired by the time of their fake ID arrest. Depending upon how Minville decided to handle the case, her probation violation might prove to be far more serious for Christie. Rod wrote another query in his notepad to ask Johnson regarding Christie's background contributing factors. She was also the subject of a missing person report, having apparently run away from home two years ago. More troubling for young Christie, her father had two arrests for domestic violence. The second one resulting in a conviction at trial and a 30-day jail sentence along with two years of probation that he was still under, at least for another five months.

Lieutenant Brad Johnson arrived and introduced himself. Rod suggested they use an interview room for their discussions to avoid the cacophony of the squad bay.

"Thanks for helping, Rod," Johnson began.

"Sure."

"We're reaching the end of our investigation and just need to cross the 't's and dot the 'i's before we close this bugger. As I indicated on one of our previous telecons, the Secret Service and Treasury Department have taken over the investigation and prosecution of the forger. The last information report from the Secret Service indicated our link to the forger was an important element for their prosecution of a larger nationwide network. The middleman given to us by Christie Theriot has been turned over to the district attorney's office in our county. Looks like he'll be doing some hard time . . . not his only transgression. That brings us to the three girls. You probably checked the database."

"Yep."

"Then you've seen the backgrounds. The only one in this affair we've not talked to is Oscarson, which is exactly why we want to tie up that loose end."

"Quite understandable."

"As you probably already know, your daughter Bella and Gretchen Hessian have clean records—Christie Theriot . . . not so much."

"Troubled childhood," commented Rod.

". . . to say the least. Having seen too many similar cases, I suspect there's much more to that part of the story than we know."

"Agreed."

"You're probably wondering where we're going with this," Johnson said.

"Yep," Rod responded and tapped his closed notepad with his left index finger.

"I don't expect any problems with Oscarson, but our department's action … my action … will depend upon whether his part of the story matches up with what we already know. If it does, then I'm prepared to close the investigation and not register their arrests, since the Secret Service has picked up the evidence chain and indicated they don't need us. If his story doesn't match, then we've a different problem that may dictate submission of our arrest report. If everything connects, we'll pass on this event."

"That answers one of my questions."

"We should probably discuss any potential mitigation actions we might take in the Theriot part of this case after we have talked to Oscarson."

"That works for me and was my second question."

"Excellent. Then do we have a plan?"

"Yes."

"The clock is ticking. Shall we get on with it?"

The two law enforcement officers left the interview room and took Rod's official vehicle since it had all the local jurisdictional equipment and connectivity. The drive took all of 25 minutes with comparatively light traffic for the middle of a workday. Rod parked on the street with a clear view of Oscarson's apartment. They both relooked at his most recent photograph for recognition, and they waited with very little talking. They did not have to wait long.

Johnny Oscarson appeared from the far corner of the building, went directly to his apartment door, unlocked it, and entered, closing the door behind him. He only had a moderately full backpack with his hands free. The two officers noticed no additional bulges. Rod knew and told Brad there was no back door to these apartments.

Rod and Brad exited the vehicle and walked directly to the apartment door. Rod instinctively checked his shoulder holster under his suit jacket … just to make sure. He knocked on the door and noticed the peephole change colors, but nothing happened. Rod waited a few more seconds, and then said, "Johnny, please don't make this more difficult than it already is. Open the door. We just need to talk." Rod waited a score of seconds. "The longer you wait the worse this situation will get, Johnny. I strongly suggest you open the door, now." They heard the lock release and the door opened. Rod presented his credentials. Brad did the same. "I am Detective-Sergeant Ramirez. This is Lieutenant Johnson of the Minville Police. We've a few questions. May we come in, or would you prefer to come out?" Oscarson opened the door wider and stood back. Rod and Brad entered. Oscarson gestured to the couch in the living room, and he pulled up a small chair to sit across from the two officers. The apartment was surprisingly well kept and orderly, especially for three college guys.

"Just for the record here, what is your full name?" asked Rod.

"John Robert Oscarson."

"You go by Johnny?"

"Yes, since I was an infant."

"This is your residence?"

"Yes."

"Do you have any roommates?"

"Yes. Two."

"Are either of them in this apartment now?"

"No. They won't be here until later this afternoon. I get out of classes early to rest up and relax before football practice each afternoon. They have regular afternoon classes."

"Do you have any weapons in this apartment?"

"Yes. I have a pistol for self-protection."

"Please retrieve that pistol holding the barrel and place it on the kitchen table," Rod calmly commanded.

Johnny went to his bedroom. Rod instinctively stood and moved to the wall farthest from the table . . . again, just in case. Johnny appeared a short time later holding a Walther PPK pistol by the barrel. He placed the weapon on the kitchen table and looked from Johnson to Ramirez. Rod gestured for Johnny to be seated again. Rod quickly scanned the pistol. The serial number had not been altered and matched the state records. The safety was engaged. He removed the clip—full—and drew the slide back to eject a live round from the chamber, catching it midair. Rod checked the chamber to ensure it was empty and then released the slide. He placed the pistol, magazine and ejected round on the table, and then he joined Brad on the couch.

"Thank you. We're just being safe for all of us. We appreciate your forthrightness here." Oscarson nodded. "Please tell us what you know about events in Minville on Wednesday last week."

"Minville?"

"Yes."

"I don't . . . ," Oscarson paused immediately when Johnson held up his right hand to stop.

"Mister Oscarson," Brad began, "that was not a worthy start. We aren't your parents, and you're no longer considered by law to be a child. I suggest your attempts to deny, obfuscate, hide, or outright lie will only dig the hole you're in deeper—much deeper. Do you understand?"

"Yes sir."

"You may assume we know more about this issue than you think we do," Johnson added.

Oscarson oddly shook and then nodded his head several times in sequence.

Johnson continued, "The only thing that will save you is the truth, the whole truth, and nothing but the truth."

Again, Johnny alternately shook and nodded his head, again. Brad and Rod waited for Oscarson to silently evaluate his situation.

"Maybe I should get a lawyer," Johnny said submissively.

"You're entitled to seek legal counsel anytime you wish," Rod declared. "Before we suspend this interview to await your lawyer, we've not charged you. You aren't under arrest or even detention. We're simply trying to gather the facts on an incident that occurred a week ago Wednesday in Minville."

"I got a call from Christie Theriot. She had heard that a fraternity at the university was having an open party on Wednesday."

"A weekday?" Brad asked.

"Yes. It's not unusual."

"You live here, which suggests you aren't a member of the fraternity."

"I know guys who are."

"When was this call?"

"Monday evening. She asked me to pick her up along with two of her friends. I thought why not, so I picked all three of them up just after noon on Wednesday. When we got to Minville, they said they needed to stop at the pharmacy, which we did."

"Did they say why?" Rod asked.

"No. I just assumed it was for breath mints or deodorant, or something like that. I didn't ask, and they didn't tell me."

"Did you think it was appropriate for three high school girls to be going to a party in a different town on a school day?" Johnson asked.

"We'd done it before, so no, I didn't think it was unusual."

"How old are the girls?" Brad pressed the questioning.

"Seventeen."

"They are 15 years old . . . all three of them."

"Oh shit!"

"Why did you leave them in Minville?"

"I was waiting outside since they said it wouldn't take long. Several minutes later, a police car arrived. I moved to avoid interfering and kept an eye on the door. When Christie came out with the other two in handcuffs behind their back, they were clearly under arrest for some reason, and there was not much I could do, so I left."

"Do you know why they were arrested?"

"At the time, I assumed it was for shoplifting. A few days later, I learned it was for using fake IDs to buy party drugs."

"Who told you?"

"Christie."

"Did you meet with her?"

"No. I was at the university. I had classes. I only talked to her on the phone."

"So," Johnson said and paused, "if I understand your statement, you claimed you didn't know they were underage, and you didn't know they were going to use forged state driver's licenses to illegally buy controlled drugs prohibited to underage people."

Oscarson bowed his head. "Yes."

Johnson stood. "Excuse us for a moment," he said to Oscarson, who nodded his consent. "Please remain seated." Again, Oscarson nodded. Johnson moved around the table to the far corner of the room behind Oscarson, so they could keep an eye on the young man and the pistol still on the table. Brad leaned forward to whisper in Rod's left ear. "So far, his story matches our information, some of which he couldn't have collaborated with Theriot or the other girls. We could probe deeper, but I'm inclined to close this case here."

"Agreed. Statutory rape is not the object of this investigation, but I'm very curious . . . not just for my daughter."

"Understood. As we discussed earlier, I'm reluctant to go too deep . . . for your daughter and the other girl, Gretchen."

"Agreed, Lieutenant. I support your decision."

"OK. I'm going to conclude here with a little fear-of-God speech to this kid."

"Works for me."

Brad nodded his head once and headed back to the couch. Rod followed.

"Thank you for your honesty and candor with us, Mister Oscarson. We've what we need. We'll conclude our investigation."

Johnny sighed deeply and said, "Thank you, sir."

"Before we leave you to the rest of your day, your practice and your studies, I feel compelled to tell you off the record that you came very close to serious violations of law. I must remind you that sexual relations between a 19-year-old male and a 15-year-old female is statutory rape by law in this state. Transporting underage girls without parental permission can be charged as kidnapping. Aiding and abetting the use of forged identification cards by minor children for felonious acquisition of controlled substances is itself a felony under the law." Shock appeared in Johnny's eyes and color drained from his face leaving him with a grey pallor. "Lastly, as I suspect you're unaware, one of those girls—Bella . . . Bella Ramirez—is the daughter of Detective-Sergeant Ramirez," he announced and directed his thumb to Rod. The expression instantly changed from shock to mortal fear. Johnny appeared to be on the verge of passing out. "Detective Ramirez has shown extraordinary restraint during this interview, which is a tribute to his professionalism. That said, Mister Oscarson, we leave you this afternoon with one overriding thought for your consideration and memory. You're extraordinarily lucky in this incident. This could've easily been much worse for you. As such, I strongly suggest you modify your behavior to avoid such events in the future."

"Oh God, yes. Thank you, sir." Johnny quickly looked at both police officers several times. "I'm truly sorry I made those mistakes last week. I can assure you it'll never happen again. I'm so sorry."

"Very well. Thank you, again." Johnson stood and did not wait for an answer. Rod followed Johnson out the door and to the car.

Rod started the car's engine for the air conditioning, but he did not take the car out of Park. "I so wanted to jump him about rape."

"I'm sure you did. I know I would if I'd been in your shoes, but I meant what I said. Thank you for your restraint, Rod. I'm comfortable closing this case without charges or report submittal. Your daughter and Miss Hessian are the beneficiaries."

"Thank you, Lieutenant."

"Please, Brad is sufficient. Now, one last thing before I head home, if you have the time."

"Sure."

"I'd like to stop by the Theriot house. Christie is or should be at school still, and I'd like to catch the mother. We'll call it a show the flag effort, to see if we can help the daughter get on the correct track."

"I'm game." Rod started the car, put the vehicle in Drive, and headed to the Theriot house. He remembered the location from dropping off their daughter.

The drive took just 20 minutes. Rod parked in front of the Theriot house. As he got out of the car, Rod noticed the wife and mother in the living room window. She quickly ducked back away from the window. The two officers walked calmly and casually to the front door of an above average home built in Spanish ranch style with expertly maintained hedges, flower beds and lawn. The large brass door knocker announced their arrival quite well.

The door opened with Mrs. Theriot dressed in jeans, a modest loose-fitting T-shirt and bare feet. "Good afternoon, Detective Ramirez. Who is your friend?"

"Good afternoon to you, Mrs. Theriot. This is Lieutenant Johnson of the Minville Police."

"Oh, oh!" she exclaimed and shook hands with both police officers.

"May we come in?" Rod asked.

"Am I in trouble? Do I need to ask if you have a warrant?"

Rod chuckled. "No. We're only here in an advisory capacity at the moment."

"Then by all means, please do come in."

Barbara Theriot invited the two officers into her living room and asked if they wanted anything to drink or some cookies. Neither man did.

"What brings you to our home this afternoon?" Theriot asked.

"We wanted to update you on our investigation," answered Rod and looked at Brad to pick up the discussion.

"We've completed our investigation. We've agreed to not file charges or file an arrest report."

"Whew! Thank you for that. On behalf of my daughter and my husband, thank you very much."

"Christie is an extraordinarily lucky young woman, Mrs. Theriot. She was the central instigator in the whole episode. Your daughter was surprisingly close to a major Secret Service counterfeiting operation . . . probably far closer than she knows or could ever imagine. Her situation and the others involved might have been markedly different if that duty pharmacist hadn't sounded the alarm at the stage they were at last Wednesday. We thought we might find you for a quiet frank chat."

"What about?" Barbara asked with an odd air of naïveté.

"Your daughter is struggling, Mrs. Theriot," Brad continued. "She's on a path that will take her to a very dark place. Based on the evidence we have, she needs help to change the course of her life. I imagine you know the truth in my statement." Brad paused for a response, but none came or appeared on her face. "Further, your husband's conduct is not helping."

"There are numerous programs to help women in your situation, Barbara," Rod added.

"How dare you both for attacking my family," Theriot growled rather harshly and jumped to her feet.

Rod gestured for her to stop. "That's not the response we expected," he said. "If that's how you see our extended outreach effort to help you and your daughter, then our initiative is for naught, and we're wasting your precious time." Rod stood. Brad joined him. "We'll be going, and we'll leave you to the fate you face. Have a good day," he said and turned to the door.

"Wait! I'm sorry I overreacted," Barbara said in a far more subdued tone. "Please, don't go. I need to hear what you have to say. I'm truly sorry for my kneejerk reaction. Please be seated." Both men and Barbara did as she suggested.

"Lieutenant Johnson and I," Rod began, "are from different jurisdictions. We've different experiences. We didn't know each other until this episode broke last week. My daughter is involved in this. And yet, our views of this incident have brought us both," Rod said, gesturing to Brad and himself, "to the same conclusion. We've seen these things before. You're not the first and won't be the last, Barbara. Christie is also not the first child to suffer from a troubled childhood."

"But . . . ," she stopped when Rod raised his hand.

"We're not here to insult you, to hurt you, to cause you discomfort. We're only here as concerned, knowledgeable observers. As I said, we've seen these signs before."

"I'd like to add," interjected Brad, "my words may have been too frank, but that is who I am—Detective Friday, 'Just the facts, ma'am.' We just want to do our moral duty as concerned citizens to intercede in what appears to be a tragic sequence of events along a very dark path."

"What can I do?" Theriot asked demurely. "I've talked to Christie so many times. She no longer listens to either of us. She's afraid of her father, so that's some degree of control; but she's not afraid of me."

"Neither of us is a professional psychologist or psychiatrist," Rod offered. "Decisions in your life and your family are yours alone. We've no place injecting ourselves into your family. We're only giving you the extra benefit of our experience. Brad said it precisely and succinctly. You must decide what to do with the information. Our daughters and the young man who drove them to Minville came dreadfully close to very serious crimes that would have altered their lives perhaps permanently. You don't have much time left to change the path Christie is on to this point. An abusive marital relationship is never beneficial to anyone except the perpetrator, and especially for minor children who are still in their formative years. Christie is near the end of that phase, which is precisely why we offer our observations."

"What have you done with Bella?" Barbara asked.

"We've talked to her with the facts . . . not just in their transgression but with similar events."

"I don't know about any of those things."

"You know about respecting other citizens and about obeying the law. I think both of us," Rod said, again gesturing to Brad and himself, "chose to come here, to take a chance, to give you information to consider in your decision-making process. You must decide what is best for you and your daughter. We're incapable of making that decision for you. I suspect in your heart you know what you should do. Comparatively few men appear on any police blotter for domestic violence. Your husband has appeared twice. Whether your daughter's criminal conduct can be attributed to her father's conduct is not our call . . . but the experience Lieutenant Johnson and I have and are sharing with you tells us your situation is quite similar to other women in abusive relationships along with the consequences for the children."

"Detective Ramirez stated the situation perfectly," Brad added. "The choice is yours."

"He's a good man. He provides for us quite well," she said, waving her arm around the room.

"And yet, his police record is irrevocable and undeniable. We've seen this too many times, Barbara," Rod indicated. "One incident is one too many. You're seeing . . . we're seeing," Rod said, again gesturing to Brad, "the consequences. Your daughter has a growing juvenile police record. She can learn from her negative experience so far. You must decide what's best for you and your daughter, but we'll say that professional counseling can and often is very helpful at assisting individuals to see the dark path they're on in life."

"Exactly," Brad said.

"I wish this was easy," she nearly whispered.

"Life is not easy, never has been, never will be," said Brad.

"I'll think about what you've told me. I don't know what I'll do or can do, but I'll think about it. I can't talk to my husband about any of this. He'd not react well."

"That observation speaks volumes to us . . . and should to you as well," Brad said.

"I know," Theriot again spoke demurely. "I'll talk to Christie when she gets home." Barbara stared at Rod for several seconds. "May I call you some time for your experience?"

"Any time you wish, Barbara. Lieutenant Johnson and I are public servants. We'll do our best, or at least what we can, to help you and your daughter. You can call me anytime the urge strikes you."

"Thank you very much, Rod. I've got a lot to think about."

Rod nodded his head in agreement. "Now, I think it best if we're not here when your daughter and husband arrive home."

"It's nearly that time, isn't it?"

Both men stood. Barbara stood as well and extended her right hand to both men. They went to the front door. Barbara opened the door. Brad exited first. Rod stepped to the door and turned to say to Theriot, "Good luck, Barbara. God be with you."

"Thank you, Rod."

Neither man spoke as they drove back to his station and Brad's car. Several miles into the transit, Rod said, "I don't envy her position."

"No . . . tough spot. We did what we could."

"Ya got that right. From here, we can only hope."

"Yeah. It didn't start well, but I think she finally got the message."

"I agree. For her daughter's sake, I hope she can find the courage to do the correct thing."

"Leave him."

"Yes, exactly," Rod said. "I suspect we've both seen positives and negatives."

"Quite true. In all of my examples . . . the only solution is separation, sole custody, and a court protection order. It's not stopped bad men in every circumstance, but it has worked more often than not."

"Agreed. My experience as well. Although we couldn't say that to her."

"Right on."

They both lapsed into contemplation for the remainder of the drive. Traffic was already building toward rush hour. Rod did not envy Brad's drive back out of the city to Minville, but Johnson did not complain. They congratulated each other for a productive afternoon, while they stood in the parking lot. They shook hands and promised to stay in touch. Rod Ramirez stood where he was until Brad Johnson's car disappeared. He committed to himself to talk frankly with Marci and Bella when he got home. It was quittin' time, but he needed to report to his captain and close out his workstation.

—

12

Assistant District Attorney Raoul Joubert requested a pre-pre-trial meeting. Rod found Client Conference Room number 9 in the city's justice building. He knocked on the door and heard a muffled 'enter' before he opened the door. The two greeted each other, shook hands, and sat down on opposite sides of the six-place table.

"Thanks for showing up early, Rod. I don't anticipate needing you at this stage, but better safe than sorry I always say."

"No problem. The sooner we get this slime ball put away the better."

"You got that right."

The Jurgensen arraignment had gone smoothly and quickly. He pled not guilty to the array of charges. District Court Judge Harold Michaels set Jurgensen's bail at $500,000, as an on-going threat to society. He was not able to come up with the ten percent surety deposit for bond and had remained in jail.

"I'll present the physical evidence your team has collected. I expect that evidence to be more than sufficient for probable cause . . . and beyond reasonable doubt for that matter. These hearings aren't always predictable. Sometimes the judge wants to test both the prosecution and the defense, but our objective is to convince the judge there is sufficient evidence for trial, and we're likely to prevail. From what we know of Houseman's intentions, he is probably going to attempt to convince the judge that sufficient justification exists to force further efforts at a plea deal to preclude trial. Our argument will be to deny that effort, if he chooses to exercise it. This is where the potential of your participation comes into play. The judge may want to hear about the details of Jurgensen's arrest, and possibly any previous experience you've had with the defendant."

"OK. I'm prepared. I reviewed his file and our work-up, so I think I'm ready."

"Good. Again, based on Houseman's prior statements regarding this case, he may try to make the Black Hole prison system the issue at trial. Judge Michaels is not likely to tolerate the move at deflection, but it's probably a step we must go through to protect the defense prerogative. Any questions?"

"Nope. I'm ready if you need me," Rod stated.

"Excellent." Raoul collected his papers and put them in his leather case. "We're a little early, but as you know, we need to be in the courtroom before the judge."

The two men walked to the elevator and took the lift to the third floor. They turned right down a short wide hallway to a set of double doors. Beside the doors, a large brass card holder held a black print on white sign indicating the courtroom was assigned to District Judge Harold Michaels. The courtroom was empty—not a single soul, yet. Rod took a seat in the gallery halfway back on the right behind the prosecution table. Raoul continued to the prosecution table, stood as he removed the papers he needed, and then he sat at the table to scan his documents one more time. Ten minutes later, single individuals began to trickle into the courtroom. Two deputy bailiffs brought Jurgensen in cuffed and shackled in an orange jumpsuit with **JAIL** in big block letter stenciled to the back of his jumpsuit. They stood him between the table and chair, and removed the chain connected handcuffs and ankle shackles. They pushed the chair up and sat him at the table. The rather massive man with dark skin pigmentation dwarfed his companion, a diminutive, young, blond woman with her hair drawn up on her head in a tight bun. Hank Houseman arrived just ahead of the judge—just barely, and he did not acknowledge anyone, not even Raoul Joubert or his client. Houseman was still standing when the senior bailiff announced in a strong masculine voice, "All Rise . . . for Judge Harold Michaels." Everyone stood.

Before he reached his plush leather swivel chair, Michaels commanded, "Please be seated."

Once the shuffling sounds ceased, the senior bailiff announced the case before the court.

"Is the prosecution ready?" Judge Michaels asked directly of Raoul Joubert.

"Yes, your honor. Assistant District Attorney Raoul Joubert for the people."

"Is the defense ready?"

"Yes, your honor. Public Defender Hank Houseman for the defense. I'd like to offer a motion to dismiss before we begin."

"A little out of the ordinary, Mister Houseman. On what basis, may I ask?"

"The state has been unwilling to negotiate in good faith and insists . . ."

"Stop, Counselor. The state has presented nothing, yet. Don't you think it would be wise to hear what the state has to say before you offer motions?"

"He's going to insist upon the so-called Black Hole punishment, if convicted."

"I've not heard him say anything of the kind. Now, I'll indulge you for a moment, Counselor, since I know these Black Hole prisons are quite sensitive to some citizens, and they're under judicial review in higher courts. However, this isn't the time for such a motion. Your attempt is tabled for now."

"Your honor, I don't want to offend the court . . ."

"But you are."

"My apologies, your honor, but these Black Hole prisons are worse than the death penalty and leaving that punishment on the table at the outset is not worthy of a modern judicial system."

"I appreciate your opinion, Mister Houseman. However, I've ruled on your suggestion. So, unless you wish to arouse a contempt citation, I recommend you table your argument and let's get on with this pre-trial hearing."

"Yes, your honor," Hank said in a more subdued voice. Judge Michaels watched Houseman for a few seconds, and then he looked directly at Raoul. "Mister Joubert, you may proceed."

Raoul stood. "Thank you, your honor. This case is straightforward, and the physical evidence is irrefutable and compelling. Mister Jurgensen committed multiple felonious crimes including armed robbery, possession and use of a firearm by a convicted felon, burglary, and intoxication by methamphetamine in the commission of these crimes. The prosecution will present validated video recordings from multiple sources of the defendant in the commission of these crimes. Further, an independent assessment by the FBI with their facial recognition application positively identified the defendant in those videos. With a court warrant, a blood sample was taken by the police department two hours, forty-three minutes after the defendant committed these crimes and yielded methamphetamine at 3.2 times the state's threshold for intoxication. In addition, he had trace levels of tetrahydracannabinol, cocaine, alcohol, nicotine, and phencyclidine below the state's threshold intoxication levels in his system when he committed these crimes.

"Of particular note in this case, the defendant has amply met the established criteria for designation as a habitual and recalcitrant criminal who continues to present a persistent and on-going threat to the safety and well-being of our community. The state has extended itself well beyond any reasonable measure to rehabilitate Mister Jurgensen and enable him to be a peaceful, law-abiding, productive citizen. He has summarily rejected all attempts to help him. I am compelled to note that he was twice given the opportunity to seek his desired intoxicants at Indulgence Camp Number 12 in accordance with the SCIP Act. The first time he chose to leave voluntarily from the generosity of the state's taxpayers. The second time he became violent under serious phencyclidine intoxication, and again in accordance with the SCIP Act, he was expelled from IC12 and rendered to state prison. In IC12, he had access to all the psychotropic substances his heart desired, and yet he rejected every single attempt to help him.

"As Mister Houseman preempted, the state intends to convict the defendant of his latest crimes, present the full body of evidence to designate him as a habitual serious felonious criminal, and seek sentencing of the defendant to a Black Hole prison for the rest of his natural life."

"Thank you, Mister Joubert," Judge Michaels acknowledged, and then he looked directly at Hank Houseman. "The defense may proceed."

Houseman stood. "Thank you, your honor. The defense's argument rests upon the state's unreasonable insistence upon a cruel and unusual punishment for a crime that injured no one."

"Isn't that the prosecution's prerogative, Mister Houseman?"

"Yes . . . yes, it is, your honor."

"Continue."

"The defendant repeatedly offered to help resolve numerous unsolved crimes, to provide direct information on the perpetrators of other crimes he was directly aware of, and the prosecution rejected Mister Jurgensen's offers offhand."

"So, now, you seek to convince the court that your client, the defendant, has miraculously found a sliver of conscience and will do his civic duty. Is that correct?"

"I wouldn't say it that way," Houseman responded with a diminished tone.

Michaels smiled. "Now, I'm truly curious, so I'll continue, for now, to indulge your deviation from proper judicial protocol. How would you say it?"

"I'm trying to reach a deal with the prosecution prior to trial."

". . . to avoid trial?" Judge Michaels said more as a statement but with a hint of query.

"Yes. My client is prepared to plead to a lesser crime and a lesser punishment in exchange for essential information on the actual perpetrators regarding six unsolved crimes."

"Well, I'll be," the judge said with unbridled sarcasm, "that sounds like an extraordinarily generous offer, but before I address my query to the state's attorney, I'm compelled to ask, do any of these unsolved crimes your client is referring to involve Mister Jurgensen in any form?"

Houseman and Jurgensen leaned toward each other. The attorney used a notepad to shield their whispered exchange that lasted several minutes.

"Mister Houseman," Judge Michaels said, with some frustration, "I appreciate your need to talk to your client. Would you like a 15-minute recess to confer with your client?"

"Sorry, your honor. Yes, the defense asks for a 15-minute recess."

The judge adjourned the hearing and departed the courtroom. Houseman and Jurgensen left the courtroom as well, undoubtedly finding an open conference room for their discussions. Two deputies trailed Jurgensen, not allowing him out of their sight and reach.

Joubert remained at his table. Rod took the opportunity for a comfort break and returned to the courtroom before the others. The senior bailiff checked the courtroom several times with progressively more irritation that the defense had not returned. On his third check, he walked through the courtroom and signaled to the deputies standing guard to retrieve the now tardy defense attorney and his client. Once they were back at their table, the senior bailiff disappeared out the back door and returned a few seconds later to announce the judge.

"Are you prepared to proceed, Mister Houseman?" Judge Michaels asked.

"Yes, your honor," Hank stated and stood. "Against my judgement and counsel, my client wishes to speak for himself."

Michaels looked directly and sternly at Maxim Jurgensen. "You have the right to speak, Mister Jurgensen, but I'm obliged to add my counsel to that of your attorney. As with your Miranda rights read to you by the police upon your arrest, anything you say in this courtroom can be used against you. Do you understand these rights?"

Jurgensen stood, "Yes, your honor."

"Very well, then. You may proceed."

"I don't want to go to the Black Hole prison."

"Mister Jurgensen, I do believe that point is well understood and is not the object of the current motion presented by your attorney. Please confine your remarks to the subject at hand." Confusion bloomed across Jurgensen's face. The judge picked up the point. "What is your proposal to the district attorney? And specifically, my query, are you involved in any fashion, directly or indirectly, in any of these crimes you offer to help solve for the state?"

Jurgensen nodded his head. "Mister Houseman repeatedly told me that if I answered yes to your question that I'd be admitting I was at least an accomplice in those crimes."

"Your attorney is correct, Mister Jurgensen. I strongly advise caution on your part."

"I understand, but I'll answer those questions truthfully if the prosecutor agrees to allow me to plead to a lesser charge in exchange for regular prison rather than the Black Hole."

"That is hardly a proper motion here, however, I shall allow it for now. Over to you, Mister Joubert."

Jurgensen joined his attorney in their seats. Raoul stood.

"The prosecution is not interested in any deal. With the police department, we assessed the potential of any information the defendant might provide. We mutually decided the need to remove him from the community outweighed any potential benefit he might offer. The police reviewed their open cases and felt they were making good progress without the defendant's alleged information. Bottom line, your honor, the defendant is a perfect example of why the legislature established the Black Hole prison system. The defendant has shown no willingness to reform his behavior, to rehabilitate himself."

"I object," shouted Jurgensen.

Judge Michaels quickly banged his gavel. "Quiet! Mister Houseman, I strongly suggest you advise your client to keep his mouth shut until it's his time to speak."

Houseman grabbed Jurgensen's arm and whispered instructions to him.

"We've no interest in hearing the defendant or negotiating a plea deal."

"That's a rather strong position, Mister Joubert. Are you sure your position is in the best interests of the state and jurisprudence?"

"Yes, your honor. As I stated for the record, the defendant has exhausted the state's generously offered opportunities to amend his behavior. His crime, after all the state has done to help him, was violent and injurious to society. He terrorized the people involved. It's the district attorney's office assessment that he deserves his fate."

Judge Michaels stared at Raoul Joubert for more than a few seconds as he considered what had been said. He then looked directly at Jurgensen. "I'm generally in favor of plea deals to avoid the extraordinary cost of jury trials that are never predictable, case in point, the O.J. Simpson criminal trial decades ago. However, I'm not compelled to direct the prosecution to negotiate. The district attorney has made his position quite clear. So, I'm going to table the defense request until after we complete the evidentiary phase of this hearing. At that point, if I feel the state doesn't possess sufficient evidence beyond a reasonable doubt, thus without a clear path to prevail at trial, then I'm prepared to rule on the defense request to negotiate a mutually acceptable plea deal."

"Thank you, your honor, for leaving the question open," Houseman said.

"I'd not advise holding onto hope here, Mister Houseman. I want to see the state's evidence before I conclude this discussion. That said," Judge Michaels offered and looked directly at Raoul, "please proceed with your presentation, Mister Joubert."

"Thank you, your honor, by all means."

Over the next nearly one hour, Assistant District Attorney Raoul Joubert presented the physical evidence collected in the Jurgensen case before the court. Raoul carefully and meticulously presented the video validation and chain of custody information in accordance with the state's established judicial procedures.

Rod Ramirez had seen and studied the videos dozens of times, both before and after the validation process was completed. They had seven different videos of the crime scene with date-time annotated that showed the commission of the crime—before, during, and after. The one common fact that still amazed and baffled Rod in every video clip was Jurgensen's identification. To Rod, it appeared like he intentionally and purposefully wanted to be identified, looking directly or nearly directly at the camera. Three of the surveillance cameras were camouflaged and unrecognizable as cameras. The clear face shots made the facial recognition process easy on the scale for such things. Each vid clip also had a date-time noted video of the FBI's facial recognition and identification actions. Each identification search took from 11 seconds to three minutes and 20 seconds depending upon the quality of the video and the angles involved. In each surveillance scene evaluation, the same name appeared on the screen—Maxim Georgi Jurgensen. As a collateral display, the FBI's action page also brought up a summary to Jurgensen's arrest and conviction record contained in the national database.

Joubert also presented the fingerprint identification data from the store's door handle, inside and outside, along with a clear, high quality, set of prints off the store counter. Raoul made sure each fingerprint location was carefully annotated on a still image from the appropriate video. Again, the FBI's identification process was video recorded and shown in the courtroom. The pistol he used and had been recovered during his arrest was meticulously identified in the images as well as the national database.

The next segment detailed the defendant's record of criminal activity since adulthood. Each arrest, charging, trial conviction and punishment were covered in excruciating detail. Joubert also carefully described each and every attempt at treatment for his drug use and addictions, as well as his illegal activities associated with distribution and sale of illegal substances. Raoul kept his tone measured, calm and clinical to remove any hint of emotion in his words.

"That concludes the state's evidentiary presentation, your honor," Raoul said.

"No witnesses?" asked Judge Michaels.

"I think we can all see from the physical evidence we hold overwhelming evidence of the defendant's culpability in the charged crimes. The state is prepared to call the arresting detective as a witness; however, we do not believe that is necessary given the preponderance of physical evidence. The state concludes its presentation."

"Very well. Mister Houseman, your turn," Judge Michaels stated.

"Thank you, your honor," Houseman said as he stood. "The defense disputes each and every one of the so-called items of evidence presented by the prosecution. I will note specifically that the FBI's screen presentation in each video assessment shown by the prosecution displayed less than 100% accuracy—the FBI's own data. My client is not the subject in those videos. As such, I am compelled to submit a motion to dismiss those items of video evidence. My client visits that particular store on a regular basis, so of course, his fingerprints appear on various surfaces in and around the store. We do not dispute the presence of my client's fingerprints in that store. Lastly, the pistol found at the time of my client's arrest was planted by the police to frame my client. My client plead at arraignment not guilty. He is innocent of these charges. The defense concludes."

"Any rebuttal?" the judge asked looking first to Joubert and then to Houseman. Neither attorney chose to offer rebuttal.

"Very well," Judge Michaels began. "On the defense motion to dismiss and suppress the video evidence, I say denied. The state has followed established judicial procedures to ensure the unadulterated recording of surveillance camera data. I find the defense's argument to reject the fingerprint data uncompelling *prima facie*, as the state went to considerable effort to correlate the fingerprint examples with the surveillance video data. Whether the video conclusively identifies the client can and should be established and judged before a jury.

"Now is the time to return to the defense's objection at the outset," continued the judge, "to impose an arbitration regarding the potential of the Black Hole punishment provisions of the Judicial Process Reform Act. I certainly appreciate the apprehension associated with the so-called end-of-the-road punishment imposed in the form of the Black Hole prison system. I cannot imagine facing that punishment. Further, I will note for the record the multiple challenges to the Black Hole provisions at various stages of judicial review. I am unaware of any injunctive or other preemptive action by any court. In fact, several courts have summarily rejected injunctive motions. Until there is an obstacle of some form, this court shall abide the law as written and interpreted to date. The available judicial review information to this point in time suggests the challenges to the Black Hole prison system in operation within this state are not likely to prevail under judicial scrutiny. That said, I do not see sufficient evidence to impose arbitration with respect to any plea deal. The district attorney has presented ample evidence on record to qualify for the defendant's categorization as a habitual criminal. I can find no reason to intrude upon or interfere with the criminal trial process and the potential for sentencing to the Black Hole prison system."

"Your honor," protested Hank, "that is unfair and opens these proceedings to appeal."

"Mister Houseman, I shall not take the bait as I suspect you are rapidly heading toward contempt of court. So, out of respect for your exceptional work as a public defender, I wish to intercede in perhaps a lame attempt to help you avoid such a charge from the bench. With that preface, do you have anything else you would like to say?"

"No, your honor."

"You will retain your rights under the law and may challenge on appeal for cause any and all segments of this trial." Judge Michaels paused and looked down, presumably at his judicial calendar. "The trial in this case will begin three weeks hence with jury selection. Do I hear any objections?"

"No, your honor," Joubert and Houseman said in unison.

"Very well, gentlemen. See you then. We are adjourned," Michaels said and banged his gavel.

"All rise," commanded the senior bailiff. Everyone in the courtroom stood as the judge departed, followed by the bailiff. The deputies chained Jurgensen and led him away to his jail cell.

Raoul Joubert filed his papers in his leather case. As he passed Ramirez, Raoul gestured for Rod to follow him. They went to the conference room. Raoul closed the door behind them but did not sit. "We're in good shape for trial. We're ready to go. My concern now is the defense may, out of desperation, try to compromise the investigatory evidence by making various pretrial demands for very specific video and recording details that may lead to manipulation. The defense has copies of everything we've provided through discovery. Their requests for precise analytical information regarding the recordings and other forensic data should come through me or my office, but in this case, I suspect Houseman and/or his agents may try to circumvent the normal communications process in an effort to compromise the evidence. You may well be aware of such conduct . . ."

"I am," Rod interjected.

". . . but, I just need to say it aloud between us. I sense a level of desperation I rarely witness, and as such, I urge caution. Better safe than sorry," Raoul repeated.

"As soon as I get back to the station, I'll make sure the evidence cage takes one more scrub of our holdings to ensure everything even remotely related to the Jurgensen case has been custodially transferred to your office."

"That works for me. Some may complain we're interfering with normal evidence assessment, but we can't tolerate any compromise of that data in this case. We need to stay in closer communications for the next few weeks to deal with whatever Houseman may attempt. I hope I'm just being overly cautious, but I'd not put anything past him."

"Sure, no problem, Raoul. We'll get attentive and suspicious as well."

"Good. Let's get this done."

"You betcha."

The two men shook hands and went their separate ways.

Rod returned to the office, briefed his captain when the opportunity presented, and then he went to the basement evidence cage. The supervising sergeant's office was more like an extension of the cage than it was a proper office, but it worked. Rod briefed the sergeant on the problem and the district attorney's instructions. He understood and acknowledged the instructions. The sergeant pulled a large sheet of pre-printed, red, special handling labels from his office supplies shelf. In big bold letters added by a large, black Sharpie, he wrote 'open by Det-Sgt Ramirez only.' The man said, "Come with me."

Rod followed the sergeant to the controlled counter for the cage. Both men had to present their ID badges, which were electronically scanned before the electronic locks were disengaged. They followed the officer to the designated box. The sergeant, witnessed by the duty officer, pulled the box out partially and lifted the half lid. Rod examined the contents. They appeared to be exactly as he had left them. Satisfied, Rod nodded his head in consent. The sergeant applied the adhesive-back labels to the box with the largest one across the half lid, sealing the box with a clear identification that no one was to access the evidence box without Rod's expressed consent.

The special procedures had worked properly in other sensitive cases, and Rod had no doubt they would work in this case as well.

Rod returned to his desk, his computer, and his other work. *Another step down*, he told himself.

—

13

Laura truly appreciated and looked forward to the collective sex parties that booked her for the whole evening. They were so much easier—no travel from appointment to appointment, less repetitive clean-up and preparation, less dressing and undressing. The avoidance of a schedule made relaxation and enjoyment far more attainable than individual customers.

This particular evening involved a recurrent group of lawyers, mostly in private practice, but off and on they also had a few public service attorneys. They tried to tell them beforehand how many would attend and partake, so that they could have sufficient professionals present, but the number who actually showed up was rarely precise with this group. The host usually made the arrangements and requests. This particular event portended the unusual category in that two of the wives would be joining in the festivities. Couples did not happen often, but they did occur.

Juli and Sandi had been invited, so Laura eagerly anticipated reconnecting with her colleagues and friends. Laura had heard of the other two female professionals, but not yet met them. She knew them by secondhand reputation only, so far. Laura was encouraged to hear that the male professional was none other than Kodi Hansen; she had known him since high school, and they had been intimate more than a few times back in those days. She always liked working with him.

Laura had a good sleep and a simple but delicious salad lunch. She had decided to pick up her substances for the party before she needed to prepare herself for the party, just in case she might have to go elsewhere for the items she sought. For this task, she donned modest shorts, a T-shirt, and flip-flops.

The three-mile drive did not take long. Traffic was not yet a problem. The Walgreens drug store she commonly used sat on the southwest corner of two major streets. Only a half dozen automobiles and one motorcycle were parked in front of the store, which meant the store would not be too busy. Laura parked away from the other cars and walked inside directly through the aisles to the back-corner pharmacy counter. She was pleased to see they were not busy; she hated standing in line for anything. An elderly woman, perhaps in her early 80s, waited in one of four chairs. Laura recognized both the counter-clerk and the pharmacist.

"Good afternoon, Carly," Laura greeted the clerk.

"Good afternoon to you, Laura. Working tonight? How can I help you?"

"The usual . . . some controlled substances."

Carly nodded her head and looked over her left shoulder to the duty pharmacist, "Doctor James, customer for controls," she said loudly in their shorthand.

Laura had known Doctor Bradley 'Brad' James, PharmD, for a dozen years, her early teen years when she picked up prescriptions for her parents. He was a very attractive, middle-aged, happily married man who had never been a customer of Laura's, but who was well aware of her profession.

"What's your druthers this fine afternoon, Laura?" he asked.

"Good afternoon to you, Brad," Laura said. He nodded his acknowledgment. "A dose of MDMA, an Amyl Nitrite inhaler and a box of Silk Skin condoms."

"Party tonight?" he asked, as he turned to retrieve the order.

"Yep. Should be fun."

"Condoms are on the rack," Carly said, as if Laura did not know where they were, and pointed to the small shelf to the right of and below the counter.

Laura retrieved the small box of six Silk Skin condoms and placed them on the counter. A few minutes later, Brad returned with a single foil wrapped tablet clearly labeled in large, black, block letters **MDMA**. The small inhaler had a similar label, **AN**. Laura already had her driver's license out.

"ID?" Doctor James asked, as he always did, even though he knew Laura Simmons well. He had told her years ago that he continued to ask every customer for their identification to maintain consistency in dispensing over-the-counter controlled substances. Just nine months earlier, the pharmacy implemented state-sanctioned scanners. He inserted Laura's license. The scanner performed its validation process, beeped, and displayed a large green light. Brad then scanned the Universal Product Code (UPC) digital barcodes into the device. "Anything else?"

"Nope. Thank you. That should do it for tonight."

James pushed the drugs with the box of condoms to Carly, standing to his right. Carly rang up the purchase. James looked directly into Laura's eyes and said, "We started a new service for prostitutes, which you might wish to register."

"Do tell?"

"We get a lot of questions for licensed professionals and referrals— changing times. We have a form you can fill out to register, or you can do it on-line, if you wish."

Laura looked at the wall clock. She had plenty of time. Laura gestured for the form. She quickly scanned it—pretty simple and straightforward. "Sure. I'll do it."

Laura took a pin from the small cup on the counter and began filling out the registration form. It asked for her full name, any alias or trade names she used, her license number and expiration date, and medical certificate number and expiration date. Just then, Laura noticed the elderly lady was standing next to her and staring at her. No one had been called for an order being ready. She looked to her left and gestured with her eyes, as if the woman might have something to say.

"Are you a prostitute, dear?" the lady asked rather boldly.

"Yes, ma'am. Do you need my services?" Laura asked in all sincerity and an air of levity.

"How dare you? I don't need the services of a whore, and no one else does either."

Laura turned and faced the woman. "Easy now, lady. Not everyone agrees with you. I've done nothing to offend you."

"Just your existence offends me. You're a sinner in the eyes of the Lord. You've abused the Lord's body and insulted all of us pure women, and our duty to birth the next generation."

"I'm sorry my profession offends you, ma'am. But I enjoy what I do, and I'm proud of my profession. I respect your right to believe as you wish, but you've no right to condemn me for my choices."

"Oh, sure I do. The Lord gives me that right. You're a heathen and sinner before God."

"That is between me and God, isn't it, not between you and me."

"But I am God's agent."

Laura smiled and turned back to completing the form.

"You've no right to contaminate this place," the woman continued. Laura tried to ignore the old woman. "You're the lowest of society and deserve to be cast out never to return. You're the wicked of Sodom and Gomorrah, and deserve to be struck down by the Lord's terrible swift sword."

"Ma'am," interjected Carly Brown, "this is our place of business. I must ask you not to harass our patrons."

"Patrons!" the old woman shouted, almost screaming, as she shook like she was having a seizure. "This . . . this . . . this creature is Satan's spawn and evil among us."

"Ma'am, please," Carly tried to calm the woman, as Laura continued to complete the form.

Brad James joined the fracas. "Mrs. Kerry, please calm yourself, or I shall have to ask you to leave this store."

Laura tried very hard to ignore the old woman and focus on the registration form. The surprisingly frank questions impressed Laura. *Is the social conservative American culture really changing faster than I realize?*

"She doesn't deserve to be in decent society," Mrs. Kerry continued to shout even though she stood within arm's reach of Laura. "She contaminates everything and everyone."

"Mrs. Kerry!" Brad protested.

For the first time since the old woman's tirade began, she turned her wrath on Doctor James. "Do not prostitute thy daughter, to cause her to be a whore; lest the land fall to whoredom, and the land become full of wickedness."

Laura could not pass up the opening. "Let's try a scripture citation a little more current. 'Let he who is without sin cast the first stone.'"

The vehemence, verging upon violence, flared brilliantly in the old woman's eyes scaring Laura and causing her to step back out of striking distance. *This is hardly Christian behavior.* The old woman opened her mouth and raised her fist but stopped when she noticed a uniformed police officer advancing rapidly toward the pharmacy. Brad must have tripped some silent alarm signaling his need for immediate assistance.

"What seems to be the problem?" the officer asked loudly and firmly.

"This woman is a prostitute," the old woman said, pointing her shaking left index finger at Laura.

The officer smiled and tried to appear as friendly and unthreateningly as he could. "Ma'am, prostitution is legal in this state."

"It's a sin against God," Mrs. Kerry growled.

"You're entitled to believe as you wish, as your beliefs dictate. But you can't impose your beliefs on other citizens or cause a public disturbance that interferes with commerce."

"She is a heretic. She is Satan's bastard stepchild."

"Ma'am, that's enough," the officer cautioned. "You can leave the premises of this store, now, or I can arrest you for disturbing the peace. What is your choice?"

The old woman seemed to calm herself. "I will take the Lord's work outside, officer." Mrs. Kerry shook her right index finger this time at Laura, but she did not speak.

The police officer waited until he saw the old woman exit the store, then he turned to Laura and asked, "Are you a professional?"

"Yes," Laura answered.

"I am Officer Adams, Badge no.18752. May I see your license and medical certificate?"

"Certainly." Laura opened the pouch of her across the shoulder wallet. She handed both cards to the officer. The officer examined them and returned the cards to Laura. "I'm sorry for the disturbance and intrusion upon your day, Miz Simmons." The officer turned to Doctor James. "Are there any other problems here?"

"No sir. That was it. She went high and right in an instant."

"She's from a different era, I guess. What's her name . . . for my report?" Adams asked.

"Kerry, Mabel Kerry," Brad responded. "I can get you an address, if that would be helpful."

"Sure, yes, please."

Brad James tapped on his computer screen. "Here it is: Mabel June Kerry, 1345 South Henry Street, 83 years of age."

"Thank you, Doctor James."

"Thank you for responding so quickly, Officer Adams."

"The alarm system worked as intended this time. Don't forget to reset the lever."

Brad James looked and slipped the red lever back to the right, turning the light from red to green. "Done. Thanks for the reminder."

"Alrighty then. Have a great day," Officer Adams said, then turned and departed the store.

Brad watched the officer leave the store, then looked at Laura. "On behalf of our store, Miz Simmons, I apologize for this incident."

"It's OK, Brad," Laura offered calmly. "I was old enough to know what society was like before prostitution was legalized and regulated. She's of that generation. It's not the first time I've faced that kind of prejudice, and I'm fairly certain it won't be my last."

"Things will change. Give it time."

"Oh, I will."

"So, after all that, do you have your completed registration form?"

"Yes," Laura answered and pushed the form across the counter to Brad. As he read the inserted details, Laura gathered up her purchases and placed them in her small pouch.

"Looks good. I'll get this entered today. Thank you for your patronage, Miz Simmons. Good luck."

Laura returned home, determined to shake off the distasteful incident. She took a nice warm shower and enjoyed the warmth washing over her body from top to bottom. Laura kept to her routine to ensure every element of preparation was fulfilled. She decided on a simple, floral print, spaghetti strap, summer dress without underwear since she knew it was going to be shucked in short order upon arrival. Laura had plenty of time before she needed to leave, so she made herself a nice cup of Earl Grey tea to relax before departure. She swallowed her MDMA dose with the last gulp of tea. As was her practice, Laura planned to arrive slightly before on-time. The tea was perfect and did the trick for her. Her thoughts of the drug store incident were rapidly becoming less frequent, but they still popped into her consciousness. Laura tried to focus her thoughts on the pending pleasure, sure to envelope her in less than an hour or so.

The drive to her single appointment for the night proved easy and comparatively effortless with most of the traffic lights going her way. Other cars were parked in the driveway and on the street along the property. The house belonged to Joan and Carl Cambridge, both prominent lawyers in the community, and the property and multi-level home appeared stately, well maintained, and typical for a well-to-do family.

Laura pushed the doorbell button to the right of the door and was treated to a melodious and distinct multiple bell tone more like a cathedral rather than a residence. The large oak door opened to reveal a blond woman who was completely naked except for elegant slip-on sandals on her feet.

"You must be Laura Simmons," the woman announced in an infectiously jovial voice and advanced toward Laura, who nodded her head in acknowledgment. She extended her arms intent upon a hug. "I'm Joan Cambridge," added the woman as the two women embraced and then declutched. Joan held Laura at arm's length by the shoulders, showing no signs whatsoever of modesty or concern for public exposure. "My husband Carl and others speak very highly of you as a person, a human being, and of course as a skilled professional. Thank you for coming to our little *soirée*, Laura." Joan released Laura's shoulders and opened the door wider. "Please," Joan added as she swept her left arm in a large arc toward the interior as part of a curtsey, "do come in and join the party."

"Thank you very much, Joan."

Before they reached the living room, Joan pointed down the left hallway and said, "Clothes are optional. Entirely your choice. Clothes room is all the way back on the left."

Laura did not hesitate and lifted her thin dress over her shoulders and head, revealing her naked body.

"My, my, my, you have quite the package, my dear," Joan said, as she exaggerated her visual examination of Laura's nude form. "You can put your dress and purse on the bed," she added, pointing to the back room designated as the clothes room.

Laura deposited her purse, covered it with her dress, and removed her shoes. As she entered the living room, Joan shouted boldly, "Hey everyone, this lovely lady is Laura Simmons." Joan introduced everyone, but Laura could not register all of the names. To her surprise, Brad James sat at the end of the pass-through, bar height counter. She waved, and he returned the wave. One couple and one man remained dressed for some reason. Everyone else were either naked or in various stages of undress. An older woman wore an odd, black leather, dominatrix outfit that left her breasts and genitalia exposed. *That woman has to be Sweet Thomas.*

Juli Mason was bent over a chair and was already servicing a man Laura did not recognize. She waved to Laura as the man continued to copulate with her.

Sandi put her drink on the kitchen counter pass-through and walked swiftly toward Laura with her arms extended and her breasts swaying rhythmically. Her warm flesh felt so soft and smooth. They kissed and separated. Sandi returned to chatting with Brad.

Carl Cambridge came over with his maleness at full attention. He hugged Laura and whispered in her ear, "Thanks for coming, Laura."

"My pleasure," Laura whispered back. She wondered if his embrace signaled an early coupling, but the thought passed quickly when he turned to tend to some other social duties.

Laura poured a bottle of sparkling water—*acqua frizzante* in Italian—into a glass. She stood alone at the edge of the living room, watching the people. Laura could feel the MDMA kicking in and amplifying her natural urges. She was ready, but she continued to watch. The party seemed to be in the social stage as people were getting to know each other. Of course, there was touching and fondling, but Juli and her penetrator were the only two coupling so far that she could see, and that activity reached its inevitable conclusion. The sounds of slapping flesh with the deep satisfying groans terminated their coupling.

As Juli and the man were finishing up, Laura contained her electrifying shock when Raoul Joubert appeared from the right hallway with a young, petite, blond woman with her hair gathered up in a now somewhat disheveled bun on her head. Raoul saw Laura and smiled. He placed his right hand on the small of the young woman's back and guided her toward Laura.

"Great to see you, Laura," Raoul said. "Do you know 'Blondie'?" he asked, nodding slightly toward the shorter young woman.

"I've heard a lot about you, Laura," Karen 'Blondie' Baker declared. "Great to meet you," she said and extended her right hand. The two women shook hands.

"Nice to meet you, Blondie," said Laura. She could not resist, and she reached for and gently rolled Blondie's unusually long left nipple between her thumb and index finger. "Great nipples."

Blondie smiled. "Thanks . . . one of my attractive features."

"Yes, they are," Raoul added.

"Thank you, darling," Blondie said with a giggle.

Raoul looked directly at Laura as he held onto Blondie. "Perhaps we can do a threesome," he said with an inquisitive expression.

Laura smiled politely and responded, "Not going to happen, Raoul."

"Why?" Blondie asked sharply. "I was really looking forward to playing with you, and he's got a great cock."

"I've no problem playing with you, Karen, but Raoul and I have history. He knows the facts, and he knows how I feel."

Baker displayed an odd mixture of surprise, shock, disappointment and confusion.

"It's history," Laura contributed, "best left in the past." Laura stared sternly into Raoul's eyes. "You've got ample women to choose from here tonight. You don't need me."

"But I want you. I want to show you that the last time was a mistake."

"Once burned, shame on you. Twice burned shame on me. We passed the first stage. We aren't going to the second."

Raoul grinned with a twinge of irritation. "You're getting paid well for servicing the guests at tonight's party."

"And I'm open for business . . . except for you."

Raoul turned and stormed off, heading outside to the patio and backyard.

"What did he do?" Karen asked, with genuine curiosity.

"I'm not into pain, and rough sex usually involves pain."

"Yeah. He can be a little rough, but that's our job, isn't it?"

"Do you enjoy pain?"

"No.

"Some people do. 'Sweet' Thomas is probably here tonight for that purpose," stated Laura, referring to Mary 'Sweet' Thomas, a 47-year-old female prostitute, who had been in the business for 25 years. She was reputed to be very skilled; often taught others, and was considered a BDSM expert—Bondage, Discipline, dominance and submission, Sadism and Masochism, and other related interpersonal sexual dynamics.

"I've heard of her work as I've heard of yours. I prefer yours, but I was taught to give the customer what he . . . or she wants. Raoul apparently likes to give it rough for his turn-on."

Laura studied Karen's yearning eyes. "There are plenty of professionals who believe as you do, Blondie. I'm not one of those individuals. I have my limits, my boundaries—no pain, no excrement, no humiliation, and no sub-dom stuff . . . just not into it. I want to be respected for what I do. If a client isn't willing to respect me as a human being and a professional, then I no longer have any interest in them or their money."

"That sounds like a lot of exclusions."

"Your choice, Blondie. You must decide what you're willing to do with your body, and most importantly, to enforce those boundaries. The days of prostitutes being considered third rate refuse of society are over. As a matter of fact, I had a confrontation with an older woman at the drug store this afternoon that illustrates my point. She said all kinds of nasty things about me and my profession, but a police officer arrived and ordered her out of the store. She was of that generation who were taught that prostitution is nasty, dirty, and a sin against God."

"I've never encountered someone like that," stated Karen.

"If you stay in the profession, you probably will eventually, and I'd encourage you to be prepared. My counsel . . . try to avoid the confrontation. They're entitled to believe whatever they wish to believe for whatever reasons they wish. But the zealous believers may not back off, as the old woman did in my case, and then you need to be prepared for how you wish to handle it. We've nothing to be ashamed of anymore, and those old folks will eventually die off for a more enlightened tomorrow. Just be proud of who and what you are."

"My parents aren't very supportive," Karen confessed.

"Mine are. The best I can say is, do what you can to teach them, to help them understand and appreciate that you're happy doing what you want to do. It took a few years and standing my ground for my parents to adjust to my life choices."

"Maybe you can talk to my parents," Karen said.

Laura chuckled softly and took another sip of her carbonated water. "You know what, I'd be happy to do that. Let's just work out a time and place."

"Thank you so much, Laura. You really make sense to me. My parents might actually listen to you."

"I can't promise anything, Blondie, but I believe in our profession, and I'm willing to give it a go."

Karen looked over Laura's shoulder. "Wow! You don't see that every day."

Laura took another sip of her water and turned around to see a markedly different scene. A man was kneeling in front of Kodi Hansen, the lean, well-muscled, 27-year-old male pansexual prostitute, whom Laura had known since long before turning professional.

"We didn't use to see 'M' to 'M' sex at hetero events like this, but we are seeing more as they gain confidence. This guy clearly feels safe and comfortable, which is a really good thing it seems to me."

"Kinda fun to watch, actually."

But it was Sweet Thomas getting her groove on in a dominatrix roll with a male submissive Laura recognized as Boris Mikalenko, who had been dressed along with his wife Talia when Laura arrived. He was no longer dressed, and neither was Talia, who was now helping Mary. The two women were whipping Boris's buttocks in between squeezing his scrotum and kicking him in the groin. It was too much for Laura.

"Excuse me," Laura announced, "I can't watch that shit." She turned to the observers who were not yet participating and said firmly, "Who wants some of this?" Laura raised her hands above her head and pointed down at herself as she sauntered slowly to the left hallway.

"I do," Joan shouted joyously, as she jumped up, pulling up Carl behind her. She waved with her free hand to Laura to follow them down the right hallway. In what was clearly their bedroom, Joan literally jumped on Laura.

Before the two women got deeply involved, Carl asked, "May I take pictures?"

Joan stopped long enough to gesture with her eyes that it was up to Laura.

"Sure. Snap away."

Carl remained uninvolved directly and seemed content to take pictures both broad and close. The two women had satisfied each other several times before Carl gave into his natural urges and copulated with both women in various mutual positions for the three of them to enjoy. When the three of them were sated, at least for the moment, Carl laid on his back with one woman cuddled into each shoulder.

"You were right, Carl," Joan said somewhat breathlessly, "she is everything you claimed."

Carl smiled but did not speak.

"Thank you for the compliment," Laura responded.

"Justly deserved," Joan added.

"If I may ask, who was the man on Kodi?"

"Pretty hot huh," Joan said. "That man is Roger Zemanski, a partner in the same law firm with Boris Mikalenko. He's pretty comfortable with his sexuality."

"A good thing," Laura added.

"Quite so. He's probably taking the first of several deposits by now."

Laura understood the meaning but felt the need to provide a different comment. "I just couldn't stand watching Sweet do her thing."

"Each to his own," Carl said.

"I've gotten kind of used to it," added Joan, "but it can be a bit much."

"Too much for me. Just not my thing."

By the time Joan, Carl and Laura returned to the living room, Sweet had moved her show outside. Over the next few hours, Laura took care of most of the men in one form or another. They all managed to talk in between the sex and truly enjoyed themselves.

Well after midnight, the activity seemed to be slowing. Juli found Laura in the kitchen.

"Great party," Juli said.

"You got that right," Laura commented.

"Is it horse time?" asked Juli, using the old street slang for heroin.

"Up to you," answered Laura, "just not for me tonight . . . or rather this morning."

"Suit yourself. Joan said it was OK to crash on the couch."

"Enjoy, Juli. See you next time."

"Sure thing."

Laura felt some folks had either retired to the bedrooms or had left. As etiquette dictated, she sought Joan or Carl, and found Carl first. "Are we done for the evening?"

"I think so, Laura. Several have left already." Carl held up his left index finger for her to wait. He went to the credenza, pulled open one of the drawers, and removed a rather thick appearing white letter envelope. Carl handed it to Laura and said, "Thank you very much, Laura. We genuinely appreciate your enthusiasm and expertise. Hopefully, you will agree to future engagements."

"I enjoyed it, Carl. Please thank Joan for me. She's a rare gem."

"Don't I know it. I was blessed to find her all those years ago."

Laura hugged Carl, kissed him, and went to the clothes room. Some clothes were missing, indicating the owners had indeed departed. She put the envelope in her small purse, quickly slipped her dress over her head and shoulders, and then smoothed the dress against her body. Laura put the long purse strap over her head and across her right shoulder.

To her surprise, Joan seemed to be waiting for her at the entryway. Joan extended her arms. The two women hugged tightly. Joan kissed Laura passionately, and then held Laura's head and said softly, "You're a treasure, my dear. Thank you for coming. I truly and eagerly look forward to our next meeting."

"Thank you, Joan."

Laura felt the usual warmth of satisfaction on her drive home. As was her normal practice, she made herself a cup of tea to relax. She also counted her proceeds—30 fresh, crisp, $100 bills. She also prepared her deposit slip and bank envelope for depositing at her bank later today. Laura had a quarterly tax payment due to the Internal Revenue Service in the next two weeks. After making her accounting records entries in her desktop computer, Laura finished her tea. She took a quick shower since she did not need to wash her hair. Laura smiled to herself. She was ready for a good night's sleep and off she went.

———

14

Marci and Rod Ramirez had struggled with their discussions swirling around their daughter's brush with the law several weeks ago. They both knew and admitted their initial response had been inadequate. They had consulted other friends who were parents, some of whom had dealt with and were still dealing with similar issues. They searched online with numerous different keywords and read every article or document that seemed relevant. Several drug treatment specialists Rod knew from work proved quite helpful in assisting them in forming their opinion. They still did not have the answers they wanted, but the tick-tock of the clock since Bella's incident progressively added apprehension. The balance point mutually arrived two days ago. Saturday afternoon, the designated time was upon them. Bella knew 'the talk' was pending, although she had hoped it would just go away. No such luck.

After a together lunch, the Ramirez family gathered in the living room. Bella and Marci sat on the couch. Rod turned his plush recliner toward the couch.

Rod opened the talk. "Mom and I have been discussing your choices and the consequences surrounding your violations of the law."

"We've been over this," Bella protested.

"Only the surface aspects—the law, your crimes, and potential charges. We haven't discussed the underlying root causes."

"What does that mean?"

"There are reasons you did what you did, and understanding those reasons is critical to amending your behavior."

"Look, Papa, I know you're a police officer and steeped in the law. We didn't consider the law. We talked about it a little, but we considered it more as a nuisance rather than an obstacle. We made a mistake—a serious mistake—and each of us has apologized for that mistake. Like you told me weeks ago, the information provided by Christie helped you break a major counterfeiting network."

"Bella, those are the surface things I mentioned—the public elements. Mom and I are far more concerned with what's inside you. Why did you do those things?"

"I told you. It was just curiosity. We wanted to try something different."

"Let me try to crack this open," interjected Marci. "We, your Dad and I, agreed before you were born that we would be open, frank, and direct with you as you grew up. We both felt far too many children grow up in ignorance about all sorts of life forces—not just sex and drugs, but also alcohol, tobacco, gambling, relationships, diseases, all of it. We've tried to give you the information before you were confronted with those life choices. I'll say directly and emphatically that Dad and I feel like we failed you. Somehow we didn't teach you properly."

"Momma, please, don't be the martyrs here. You didn't fail me. I've been extraordinarily appreciative, although I may not have always shown it, for what you and Papa have done for me. I'm grateful—truly."

"Bella, you need to listen to us," Marci continued. "Now is not the time to be defensive. We're not asking you to defend your choices. We're only asking you to be open, truthful and expansive with us."

"I am, Momma."

"Respectfully, Bella, you're not."

"From our perspective," Rod picked up the dialogue, "you are, or were, heading down a dangerous and potentially heartbreaking path. We're seriously concerned for your safety."

"Nothing is going to happen to me."

Rod laughed loudly. "Sorry," he said, as he fought to suppress his laugh. Marci looked at her husband with a confused and questioning expression. "That's exactly what young people your age believe. Bella Joy, my darling daughter, despite what you may think, you're not invulnerable. The drugs you're experimenting with, that you are curious about, are serious substances. There were very real reasons why they were classified as controlled substances and prohibited from consumption. Our state chose to make these substances, or at least the generic version of these drugs, legal and regulated to reduce quality and dosage overdose deaths and contaminant toxicity. The state didn't say they're safe for anyone to take them, which is exactly why these substances are still prohibited for children under 18 years of age."

"Do you know what addiction is?" Marci asked.

"Yes, Momma," replied Bella with some irritation. Marci gestured with her facial expression—well? "Addiction is dependency."

"It's much more than that, Bella," said Marci. "These substances can alter your body chemistry such that your body demands a steady and often escalating supply of the substance. These things are especially active in young bodies still maturing. For example, fetal alcohol syndrome wasn't understood until 1973, when research documented birth defects and growth abnormalities associated directly with the mother's consumption of alcohol during pregnancy. Even a small amount of alcohol that makes it through a pregnant mother's blood and the umbilicus to the fetus can cause damage that lasts a lifetime."

"I'll add," Rod interjected, "that's precisely why the laws against consumption by children of alcohol, tobacco and other psychotropic substances were put in place. Further, most parents don't teach their children how to responsibly deal with the effects of these substances. They pretend alcohol doesn't exist or isn't an issue for the education of children. We tried to not be those parents. We agreed to teach you what we thought was a more progressive path. So, I suppose this discussion is more about you than it is about us. To that end, that is why we are asking you to help us understand . . . why?"

"I told you, Papa, we were just curious."

"OK . . . about what?"

"I don't know . . . just curious."

"Look, Bella," Marci jumped in, "you really must articulate your feelings and your thoughts. We're concerned . . . no . . . no . . . we're worried about where you're headed with this apparent attraction to controlled substances."

"I'm grateful both of you are concerned about my safety, but I'm not going to do anything stupid."

"How will you know? These things can go too far very quickly. These are powerful substances that by their very name alter your mental, emotional and physical processes. So, we need you to tell us exactly what you were thinking, or you are thinking to this point."

"The public information says there are safe levels."

"Yes, there are," Rod responded. "Derivatives of opium have been used for pain for many decades. Heck, during the evacuation of Saigon at the end of the Vietnam War, Navy corpsmen gave methamphetamine pills to the Marine helicopter pilots to keep them in their machines for more than 24 hours without a break. The problems are rarely the substances themselves, but the abuse of those substances. And, the line between therapeutic and abusive use can be very thin and misty. You don't know those lines. That is exactly our fear."

"Do you know those lines?" Bella asked innocently.

Rod smiled. "Nice one. No, I've never done those drugs. I've not experimented with dosage to determine those thresholds for me. But, I know they're out there."

"How do you know?"

"Because many experts who have done that kind of research have told me."

Bella looked down at her knees and lapsed into contemplation, which seemed like a good sign to her parents. Rod and Marci glanced at each other several times, as they watched their daughter thinking, and neither of them chose to disturb Bella's thoughts. Several minutes passed in silence.

"OK. At the risk of saying too much, I'll level with you," Bella said and paused. Neither of her parents reacted or interfered with their daughter's thought processes. "We had heard that cocaine and ecstasy enhanced sexual sensations and pleasure. We also had heard that the fraternity that some of Johnny's football buddies belong to were going to have a sex party. We wanted to see if the rumors were true, and we wanted to try it all." Bella paused, again, to allow for her parents to react. They simply stared intently at their daughter. "It was probably a bit much."

"Ya think?" Rod asked rhetorically.

"We felt that Johnny would be sufficient protection, if things started to get carried away."

"He might have been directly involved with whatever they had planned for you three, Bella," Marci said. "Parties like that, especially those where you don't know and trust every single person in the house, not just the room—the house—things can get unstoppably out of control in a heartbeat. Even if Johnny had done what he said he would do, he might have been overwhelmed along with you three girls."

"We've seen it more than a few times in my line of work," Rod added.

"I can see that now, but we were excited about the plan."

"You, and here I mean all three of you, were lucky. That party might have gone down as you dreamt it might, but odds are it would have evolved as other such parties evolve. You have only to look at the Brett Kavanaugh confirmation hearings to see the reality of this phenomenon. I can't tell you how many unreported rapes have occurred at such parties. In law enforcement, we usually see the aftermath years later when it is often too late to try and punish the perpetrators. Guys in those circumstances depend upon the incapacitation of their victims. Young women often lose consciousness, and by the time they regain awareness of their circumstances, they realize they have sometimes, seriously abused genitalia."

"I wasn't going to let that happen," Bella claimed.

"You most likely wouldn't have had that choice, Bella. The common law enforcement slang term we use is a Mickey—adding a psychoactive or incapacitating agent to a drink without the consumer's knowledge. It was a technique used by a bar owner in Chicago, more than a century ago, who dropped an incapacitating agent like chloral hydrate into a person's drink. Once unconscious, the victim was robbed of his money and valuables, and dumped in the gutter. The criminal's name was Michael 'Mickey' Finn. He was eventually caught, prosecuted and punished. The technique became widely known, and it was only a matter of time before sexual predators figured out they could use the same technique with different substances like variants of benzodiazepine, rohypnol, known by its street name roofy, and other so-called date rape drugs. By the time the victim detects something was wrong, it was too late. I may not have told you the history of all that, but we certainly taught you not to take intoxicants in any form—alcohol, marijuana, opiates, all kinds of things—in any situation where you can't trust your life to every single person in the room, house or building. You were taught that years ago."

"Yes, I was."

"Then why, Bella?" Marci asked.

"The excitement of trying something new overrode what you taught me."

"And that is exactly what worries us the most."

"How am I supposed to learn? How am I supposed to spread my wings and fly on my own? You can't keep me locked in my room."

"No, no, no . . . ," Marci protested.

"We're not trying to lock you up, Bella Joy," Rod added his protest. "We've been trying our best to give you the tools to make safe and proper life choices. We emphatically don't want to shield you from life. We want you to not just survive in life but to thrive."

"Really, Dad! This isn't life or death."

Rod smiled. "How do you know that? How can you be so sure? Did you know every single person—male or female—who was at or going to be at that party?"

"No, of course not."

"I rest my case."

"Papa, everyone is not a criminal out there. You've even been on the evening news telling everyone that the crime rates continue to decrease."

"Yes, I have, because that is what the data show us. But in group gatherings, it only takes one bad man to put his sights on you."

"Then back to my earlier question. How am I supposed to learn?"

"Bella Joy, my darling and beautiful daughter, do you remember how we taught you about alcohol?"

"Yes."

"Tell me."

"You had me drink some wine or beer, then gave me a breathalyzer test. We did that until I couldn't pass one of your field-sobriety tests."

"What did you learn?"

"I learned I could only handle a glass of wine, maybe a little more, or three beers, before I showed signs of incapacitation."

"You also learned when you began to feel effects. Your Mom and I do enjoy a glass of wine or a couple of beers. We've never denied you in joining us with that enjoyment. But I'll ask you again, as I have so many times, when was the last time you saw us drunk—staggering, slurring my speech, losing coordination, any of the symptoms?"

"Never . . . to my knowledge."

"Exactly. There is a reason for that. We know and respect our limits."

"So, you're telling me I should go find a boy to fuck me and try those drugs for sexual enhancement?"

"Bella!" Marci objected.

"Sorry, Momma. You said be frank and open."

"You've words, Bella. You don't need profanity to convey your thoughts."

"Well?" Bella said in an emphatic questioning tone.

"There are less dangerous, or exposed, ways of experimenting, Bella."

"Like what?"

"Masturbation," Marci contributed. "You can experiment in your room. If you do, just let us know, just in case something goes wrong."

"Masturbation is not sex. I mean sexual intercourse," Bella said, winking at Marci.

"That depends upon how you define sex," said Rod. "Sex can and should be defined as any touching for pleasure. It is much more than just penile-vaginal intercourse."

"So, a hug or a kiss is sex?"

"Depends upon the hug, but yes, they are or can be. There are plenty of men who are being charged with sexual assault for giving an unwanted or a little too intimate hug. Anyway, for the purposes of this discussion, yes, masturbation is sex and would serve your purposes for experimentation."

"What about sexual intercourse?"

"Bella, sex is no different from drugs in this context," Marci responded. "We hopefully taught you not just the mechanics of sex in various forms, but we also tried very hard to teach you to respect procreation, the biological function of sex, as well as the responsible enjoyment of sexual pleasure. We wanted you to be informed. We didn't want you to be experimenting in ignorance. Perhaps, we taught you more than we should've done, but we did the best we could. We did what we thought was right. Both of us," Marci said, glancing at Rod, "did not want you to learn about sex the way we did. Our parents tried to ignore sex, like it didn't exist. We were lucky as teenagers. Many others were not."

"I may not always show it, Momma, but I'm truly grateful for your teaching me the facts of life, and I'm very proud of you both as parents. Heck, as my friends would tell you, I praise you guys so much my friends tell me to shut up." They all laughed. "But, back to my question."

Marci and Rod looked at each other, as if they were non-verbally debating who should or how to respond. Neither of them jumped at the opportunity.

Marci broke the stall. "You can handle this one, hon."

"Thanks, dear," Rod responded. "Both of us knew this day would eventually be upon us, but neither of us wanted this day to come." Rod paused and kept his gaze on Bella, who did not budge or twitch. "We knew it would, but we just didn't want it to come." Again, he paused. "You'll be 16 next month. Do you recall or know what statutory rape is?"

"Yes, Papa. You taught me."

"Please tell me in your words."

"It is sexual relations with an underage person, especially with an older person."

"That's close enough. The law changes when you turn 16 years of age and disappears entirely when you turn 18 years of age—the age of majority, as the law says. The laws were created under the premise that children, anyone under the age of 18 weren't mature enough to make an informed choice regarding sex. I'll add here, until a few years ago, sex in this context was vaginal intercourse. All other forms of penetrative sex were considered sodomy and activated a different set of prohibitive laws." Rod paused, and Bella nodded her head with an inquisitive expression, as she was wondering where her father was headed. "As you informed us earlier, you're sexually active, which is your choice. We'll not intrude upon your privacy, although my inclination as a law enforcement officer pushes me to investigate this matter vigorously. I apologize for this circuitous answer, but I needed to say these things. At the bottom line," Rod said and glanced at Marci, who nodded her head slightly, "we would much rather you do your desired experimentation in the safety of our home. If something goes wrong, we will be here to help."

"So, you're telling me that it is acceptable for me to have sex—penetrative sex as you call it—in my room, and I can try those drugs to see how they affect me."

Rod grimaced noticeably. "I bite my lip when I say it, but yes . . . at least you'll be safe."

"Really?" Bella asked, looking directly at Marci. She wanted Mom's consent, too.

"Yes, Bella," answered Marci. "You're biologically a woman. You're fully capable of becoming pregnant. We believe that you understand the precautions and dangers you must continually assess. Although you made a serious mistake weeks ago and that mistake has shaken our confidence in your judgment, we believe you have the tools to make the correct decisions for yourself."

"Since I can't legally buy the drugs, you'll buy them for me?" Bella asked.

"Yes."

"I'd be lying," Rod added, "if I said I'm not reluctant to do so, but we have to believe in you. Now, before we go much farther down that path, I must urge caution. These are powerful substances. None of us knows how we'll react to these materials."

"Would you try them with me?"

Rod chuckled nervously. "I'd like to say yes, but I work in a profession that doesn't tolerate intoxication at any level, and they still test us even though these substances are legal."

"We're making an enormous compromise here, Bella," Marci said. "You're not yet an adult although you may feel like you are. The law says you're not allowed to purchase any one or combinations of these drugs, which means the responsibility rests squarely upon us. Your Father and I are prepared to respect your choices, your desire to learn about life around you, but we must impress upon you the risk we're taking in allowing your experimentation."

"I do, Momma."

"I sure hope so, Bella," Rod interjected.

"We're prepared," Marci contributed, "to support your experimentation as long as you do it here, in our home, so we're available to help, if needed, and you respect our concerns. You can't be providing these drugs to any of your friends. You simply can't. What they consume is the responsibility of their parents, not you, and certainly not us. Violations of these constraints will place us directly in legal jeopardy, and you've no right to do that."

"That is the paramount point, Bella. As a minor child under the law, your choices can and will likely affect us in one form or another. We've gained confidence in the quality and dosage of these substances. We believe you can safely assess the effects for you. I don't know firsthand, but I've read enough to believe there are positive effects as long as they are used responsibly and not abused. Mom and I grew up in a world that tried mightily to put the fear of God into us regarding these drugs; those laws sought to keep us ignorant. We don't want you to be ignorant. We want you to be informed, to make informed choices, for your safety and for your pleasure. That said, you must understand and remember, so much of this scares the hell out of us. You're about to venture out onto ice that we've not tested, that is totally unfamiliar to us. We're resisting our reluctance, to enable you to learn better than we were allowed to learn at your age. We're taking a helluva risk to allow you to learn."

"I can't promise to not make mistakes, Papa. I'll inadvertently or unintentionally cross the line. I'll sincerely try not to do so, but I can't find the boundaries without trial. However, I think I'm aware enough to recognize and appreciate what you're doing for me."

"Just talk to us, Bella. The more you can share with us, the more confidence we'll gain, and the less apprehension we'll feel. Just talk to us."

"I will, Momma. Some of this is not so easy to do, but I can promise to try."

"OK," Marci said. "We can ask no more."

Bella glanced repeatedly at both her parents, as she considered whether or what to say. "I'm going to take another risk and share a related matter," Bella said and paused, presumably to allow a response. She received none. "I've thought about the indulgence camp."

"How so?" Rod quickly asked.

"I've thought about trying it."

"Why?"

"It seems like an easy environment without risk to either of you."

"I'm not sure I see the attraction," Marci said.

"The indulgence camp system is not some drug resort, Bella Joy," added Rod. "Those camps are meant to get addicts off the streets and out of the public domain for public safety. They're intended to respect the individual addict's right to privacy and freedom of choice without endangering innocent members of the public. To our knowledge, you're not an addict. Are you? Are you taking anything that you're taking regularly?"

"No. It's not so easy to acquire drugs."

". . . as intended."

Bella nodded her head. "I'm just curious."

"Curiosity killed the cat, as the old saying goes," responded Rod. "First, you don't qualify. By your admission, you're not addicted to any of these substances. Second, you've means, we've opened the means, for you to acquire any of these substances . . . in moderation. Third, you're underage. You must be 18 to enter one of those camps."

"Would you give me permission, if I asked?"

"The best we can say," Marci answered, "we'll talk about it . . . if the question ever comes."

"Do you feel the urge for steady or regular consumption?" asked Rod.

"No, but I can imagine that potential."

"Oh, Bella," Marci said, almost crying. She wiped away a few tears as they descended her cheeks.

"If those urges are that close, we'd be foolish to feed that potential," said Rod.

"Damn it! I knew I shouldn't have opened that up."

"Bella Joy, what do you expect. Addiction to anything, not just these drugs, but any obsessive behavior is ultimately injurious to your body, mind and soul. Why should we ever feed that potential?"

"Because I shared and asked."

"So, if you ask to slash your wrists or jump off a cliff, we should just stand by and watch? Or worse, you want us to be complicit in your self-destruction?"

"I'm not suicidal."

"Perhaps not outright, Bella," Rod responded, "but that is exactly how it sounds to us. If you're having those feelings, we really should seek professional evaluation and counselling before stepping off that step."

"I'm not crazy, Papa. I'm not suicidal," she repeated.

"Then what would drive your curiosity. The indulgence camps are not some joyride. They're serious places for a very real, societal purpose. They're not," he said with emphasis, "for curious children. Let me ask you, what do you think is offered inside those camps that you can't get out here."

"Unlimited drugs . . . and no judgmental parents."

"Well, maybe we're getting to the root of the matter," Rod said. "What is it about our words that led you to feel we're judgmental?"

"You don't approve of my choices."

"Which brings us back to jumping off a cliff. We aren't that complacent or uncaring, Bella Joy. What you may feel is our judgment is in fact serious concern for the welfare and safety of our only child. We can't and won't stand by idly and witness your destruction . . . not by your hand or anyone else's involvement. We love you, want you to be safe and healthy, and it'll be like this until we're gone. Get used to it. What on earth would you think of us if we just sat back and said who the fuck cares?"

"Rodrigo!" Marci shouted in protest. Rod nodded his head in recognition and held up his left hand palm out. "I can't chastise our daughter for profanity when you use it."

"My apologies."

Bella smiled with an expression of vindication or satisfaction. "It's just a thought, Papa."

"A very dangerous thought, it seems to me."

"Perhaps, but it's still just a thought."

"Let me ask you a couple of questions," Marci said. Bella nodded her consent. "Do you think you need, or it might be helpful for you to talk to a professional counsellor?"

"No. It's just a thought."

"OK. We'll table this discussion for now, as long as you promise us both that you'll talk to us before you do anything and especially if those thoughts return to you. We only want you to be safe and healthy."

"OK."

"No, I want to hear you and see you promise both of us."

"I promise," Bella said, looking softly at each of her parents.

"Promise what?" Marci pressed.

"I promise to talk to you before I do anything or have those thoughts."

"Very well." Marci looked at Rod. "Are we done?"

"Yes . . . for now."

"Then we're done for this afternoon. Don't forget your promise."

"I won't."

"Then," Marci announced, "we're done. I'd like you to help me get supper ready."

"Sure, Mom. I'd be glad to help as always."

"Good. Thank you for taking the time to talk with us, Bella. Thank you very much for trusting us with your thoughts and feelings."

"I'll add my appreciation as well," Rod added. "We know these topics aren't easy to talk about, especially with your parents, but these are vital moments in your maturing process."

"Understood, Papa. You two are the best."

"We don't always feel that way, but thank you for that, Bella Joy."

They broke up their little clutch and returned to their daily chores.

—

15

Judge Michaels brought the courtroom to order.

The trial in the case of The People versus Maxim Georgi Jurgensen had taken not quite three weeks. The jury took less than four hours to convict Jurgensen on all criminal counts and rendered their judgment that the defendant met the criteria as a habitual criminal in accordance with the Judicial Process Reform Act. The preliminary hearing had forecast the content of the trial. Comparatively little time was spent challenging the evidence. Public Defender Hank Houseman tested Judge Michaels' patience and tolerance repeatedly during the trial as he persistently challenged the law and the applicability of the law to his client. The defense attorney had been threatened with contempt of court charges a handful of times over the course of the trial. At the end, the jury was not persuaded by Houseman's arguments. The evidence was simply too compelling.

"We will proceed with the sentencing phase in the case of The People versus Maxim Georgi Jurgensen."

"Your honor," Houseman boldly spoke as he stood, "the defense offers a motion for your consideration."

"Of course, you do, Mister Houseman," the judge responded, and then he offered a hand gesture for him to proceed.

"The defense offers a motion to suspend the sentencing phase of this trial until the United States Court of Appeals for the Ninth Circuit has rendered judgment in the pending case of The People versus Armstrong."

"You are running out of opportunities to derail these proceedings, Mister Houseman. Please present your argument."

"Gladly, your honor. Mister Jurgensen remains in custody and presents no threat to public safety or peace. Arguments before the three-judge panel of the Ninth Circuit are scheduled for next week. There would be no harm in postponing Mister Jurgensen's sentencing until after we know the latest judicial position regarding the 8th Amendment challenge to a growing number of cases potentially affected by the court's judgment."

"First, Mister Houseman, the defendant has presented his defense. The jury has rendered judgment. Sentencing in any criminal case is not dependent or affected by other pending cases before this or any other court. Second, should the Ninth Circuit render judgment in your client's favor, appropriate adjustments will be made, as they always are. Third, the matter of the 8th Amendment challenge to the Black Hole incarceration provisions of the Judicial Process

Reform Act are such that they are likely to be appealed to the Supreme Court of the United States, and thus we shall not have judicial pronouncement for months, if not years. Depending upon the judgment of the Ninth Circuit, the Supreme Court may choose to allow the appeals court decision to stand. The outcome of judicial review is not predictable. Motion denied."

Michaels looked down, presumably at papers before him. After a score of seconds, the judge looked up and announced. "The defendant will rise." Jurgensen stood in his orange jump suit. Houseman stood with his client. "Mister Jurgensen, you have been found guilty by a jury of your peers on all criminal counts in this case. Further, the jury judged your history of crime, your repeated injury to public safety and peace, and your refusal to respond to all of the state's attempts to aid your rehabilitation thus classify you as a habitual criminal. I see no reason in any form, or from any aspect to question the jury's judgment. As a consequence, you are hereby identified for the public record as an unredeemable habitual criminal, and I sentence you to incarceration in the Black Hole prison system for the remainder of your natural life. May God help your soul." Judge Michaels banged his gavel.

"That is not fair!" Jurgensen raised his fists and shouted at the judge. Houseman tried to restrain his client, who was visibly agitated and shaking. "You can't do this. That damn place is worse than the death sentence. Just fuckin' shoot me now!"

Judge Michaels banged his gavel hard several times, again. "Mister Houseman, please advise your client to restrain himself.

"No! You aren't going to muzzle me. You don't know what the fuck you're doing. You can't punish me any worse than you have, so what the fuck do I have to lose."

"You may well be correct, Mister Jurgensen. Yet, the jury and this court have rendered judgment. The deputies are instructed to remove the convict."

Jurgensen resisted, struggling to prevent the two deputies from attaching the handcuffs and shackles. Four additional deputies appeared. Jurgensen screamed his defiance and resistance as he fought the deputies. He even bit the arms and legs of several deputies. They applied a face mask to prevent further assaults on the deputies. The five men and one woman finally got him secured and immobilized. His muffled protestations could still be heard, and the deputies carried Jurgensen out of the courtroom. Muffled conversations were audible but not discernible as observers left the courtroom. Rod Ramirez remained seated. Hank Houseman held a very stern expression and did not even recognize Rod's presence as he passed. Raoul Joubert was one of the last to leave, and as soon as he turned toward the rear double doors, he saw Rod and nodded his head. Dressed in a modest business suit without his badge or pistol visible, Rod remained seated. Raoul joined him one chair away and placed his briefcase on the chair between them.

"Well, that is that," Raoul said.

"Yeah, I guess Max was not happy about going to the Black Hole."

They both laughed heartily.

"Nope."

"I asked for permission to be on the transport detail," Rod announced. "His transfer will be processed tomorrow, and he is scheduled for transport day after tomorrow. I also coordinated with the captain of the guard at Black Hole Confinement Number Seven for a familiarization tour of his facility."

"Should be interesting."

"Yeah. Hopefully, I can get some questions answered that have been bouncing around my thoughts for a while. I didn't know those places don't have wardens in the traditional sense. They're like a security detachment to ensure no one leaves except in a body bag, and even that is temporary from what I'm told."

"Temporary?"

"Most bodies aren't claimed by family. In those cases, the bodies are cremated, and their ashes scattered outside the prison walls."

"That is the life they chose."

"Quite so. Max's little outrage display has heightened my curiosity. Beyond the fact that I want to see how those facilities work, now, I really want to get a feel for Max's fear with the Black Hole."

"Now that you mention it, I suppose I'm kind of interested in that place as well. But my workload would not permit a day trip like that."

"Just as well, counsellor. I'm told you wouldn't be permitted in unless you're trained and armed."

Raoul chuckled. "No time for that either. Perhaps we can have lunch after your familiarization tour, and you can educate me. My treat."

"Hey, who can turn down a free lunch."

Raoul pulled a leather-bound booklet out of his inside jacket pocket, leafed through the pocket calendar to the correct page, and took out a pen. "Looks like my Friday lunch is open. That OK for you?"

"Yes. I don't have the dance card you do."

They both chuckled. "Excellent. How about *Ristorante de Paolo* on Grand Street?"

"Never been there. I hear good things, so that should be fine. What time?"

Again, Raoul consulted his pocket calendar. "What about 12:30? I'll have my assistant ensure we have a reservation . . . just the two of us."

"Works for me."

Raoul stood but did not step away. "Done. Anything else?"

"If you have a few minutes . . ."

"Sure," Raoul answered and sat back down.

"The last time we talked, y'all had transferred Baxter to federal custody."

"Well, the cogs of justice continue to turn. An array of charges has been filed in the Southern District of New York. He remains and will remain in custody until his trial is completed. The feds have uncovered additional malfeasance. Baxter's crimes aren't on the scale of Bernie Madoff, but they're very serious, and at his age, he's likely to spend the rest of his life in prison."

"Too bad he doesn't qualify for the Black Hole."

They both had a short laugh. "Yeah," Raoul said. "He would be a ripe, fat pig in a den of wolves in one of those prisons."

"Just deserts, it seems to me."

"Ya got that right. Unfortunately, the feds don't have that punishment in the sentencing guidelines for federal felonious crimes."

"What about Ignatius?"

"As I think I may have briefed you last time, the FBI and SEC collected up additional evidence against Ignatius. He was much more involved than we originally thought. He was transferred to the feds and transported to New York City. He was charged at the end of last week. Ignatius also faces additional charges of perjury and obstruction. From what we see and know, they are both likely to be guests of Uncle Sam for quite some time."

"Good. Thanks for the info."

"Sure. Any time, Rod. By the way, I sat in the DA's weekly video conference call with the attorney general. Smithson informed us that more than a dozen states and even a congressional committee are interested in and requesting detailed information on our drug treatment and legal reforms. Our successes are beginning to get attention elsewhere."

"That's encouraging."

"None too soon from a law enforcement perspective. Smithson is keenly aware of the burden on our state by the lack of similar support programs in at least neighboring states. He chose to recount one particular case of an addict and criminal from Alabama who sought entry into IC9. The case instigated a policy debate in the governor's office regarding measures to reduce or preclude out-of-state pressure on our state. The governor has had a number of meetings with the governors of adjacent states, and he's even raised the issue as an agenda item at the last meeting of the National Governors Association. According to Smithson, the governor feels the tide is finally turning like it did when Colorado led the nation in reforming marijuana laws. Although Colorado chose not to enforce marijuana laws as early as 1975, the state did not change the law until

2000 with medical use and further in 2012 with recreational use. From what I hear, Colorado is likely to be the next state to follow us. Similar legislation to the SCIP Act has been introduced in the Colorado Senate."

"None too soon, indeed. We don't see those problems in our department, but we're certainly aware of them, especially as reported to the Governor's Drug Policy Commission a few months back."

"Oh yeah, I forgot you're a member of that commission. How did that go?"

"Pretty well, from my perspective. Since our last conference meeting, we had a conference call to discuss progress and recent changes. One of those new items was Judge Kendall's request for our concurrence in recommending a proactive campaign to be initiated to so-call 'sell' the SCIP Act to other states in a more aggressive manner to relieve the pressure on our state."

"Wow! Now that would be a switch."

"Yeah, I thought so, too. We're all convinced the feds aren't going to lead, so it's up to us to collect the states and educate them on what we've learned in the last handful of years."

"It sounds like the commission is reacting to these changes. Anyway, the vote of the commission was unanimous. Everyone seems to agree that the SCIP Act changes are having a very positive effect on our communities, but the pressures from other states is excessive and debilitating. Our citizens are paying for the treatment of out-of-state residents. It's not fair."

"So, the commission voted for a proactive campaign. What'll happen next?"

"Above my pay grade, I'm afraid. I'm just reporting what Judge Kendall put before the commission members. As is his practice, I believe the judge will inform us at the appropriate time."

"As the Chinese philosopher Lao Tzu said, 'The journey of a thousand miles begins with one step.'"

Rod smiled at Raoul's philosophical incantation. "If the Colorado experience with just marijuana is the metric, we're on a very long journey—a very, very, long journey. By your own recounting of the milestones, Colorado took 12 years, arguably 37 years to reach a more rational position. It took our ancestors 14 long years to recognize the folly of alcohol prohibition in a free society. We've been at this war on drugs for three quarters of a century, and we still have only scratched the surface with the SCIP Act. That was six years ago, and we are still alone."

"That was quite a speech, Rod."

"Sorry. I get carried away. My job is arresting bad guys . . . enforcing the law. My job doesn't render me ignorant regarding the consequences of these laws. The governor, God bless him, and the legislature are trying to do the right thing. The SCIP Act is making our state safer, more peaceful, and a better place to live and raise our children."

"I agree, Rod. I agree. We're doing our part."

"I suppose. But there is so much more to be done."

"You got that right," Raoul said. Several silent seconds passed. "Now, as much as I would like to continue this discussion, I really must be going. I've got another case this afternoon."

"Sure, sure, sorry to take up so much time with my rant," Rod said.

"No problem." Raoul stood. Rod did the same and walked out of the empty courtroom with the assistant district attorney. They took the elevator with other people to the first floor. The covered but open walkway took them to the parking garage. Raoul pushed 'L2." Rod pushed 'L4.' The one floor ride took just a few seconds. The doors opened.

Raoul said, "Oh wait! Could you step off a second?"

"Sure."

The empty elevator doors closed, and the car continued up two floors. "I meant to ask you after trial for a favor." Rod nodded his head. "I know this is a bit out there, but I'll confide in confidence to you and trust you to be discreet." A puzzled expression bloomed across Rod's face. "My wife, Kelly, has been missing for many weeks."

"Did you report her disappearance? Has a BOLO been issued?"

"No to both."

"Why not?"

"I've reason to believe she has run away."

"That's abandonment."

"Not a high yield accusation and a bit antiquated these days."

"You want me to find her?"

"I know this is rather far out there, but it would be way too obvious if I initiated a search."

"You got that right. The courts don't look kindly upon us using the instruments of state for personal reasons."

"You're precisely correct, which is exactly why I can't do it myself."

"Hire a private investigator. They're pretty good at finding people."

"Appropriate recommendation. Can you recommend one who you have confidence in for a matter like this?"

"No."

"Me either."

"Before we go too much farther down this road, have you checked your credit cards and bank accounts?"

"Yes. Nothing."

"Your phone records?"

"Yes. Again, nothing."

"How about a Google search or some other public search engine?"

"Yes. Numerous times. Nothing."

"I guess she really doesn't want to be found."

"So, it would seem."

Rod held Raoul's eyes as he considered his response. "OK, Raoul. I'll see what I can find with our network. I won't initiate a formal search unless you make a declared complaint. Who knows, something might pop up without a record of a formal search."

"Thanks, Rod. I can't and won't ask for more. I just need a little distance. You might check with her best friend Laura Simmons. You might get more from her than me."

"Understood. I'll see what I can do . . . as a favor to you."

"Thanks, Rod," Raoul repeated, and then he pushed the up arrow on the elevator. "See ya on Friday."

The elevator doors opened. Rod stepped in the elevator car. "You betcha," Rod responded as the doors closed.

Rod's thoughts were dominated by Raoul's favor request. It was always a misty but red line in such circumstances. He needed a plausible reason for the searches, just in case he was challenged. No reason came to him. *When in doubt, tell the truth.*

On his way back to the office, Rod hit the In-N-Out Burger joint and grabbed a cheeseburger, fries and a large unsweetened iced tea he would eat at his desk while he checked his messages, eMail, and open cases. He had only arrived at his desk and not sat down, when he saw his captain's gesture to come hither.

"Whacha need, Cap."

"So, the judge sent your perp to the Black Hole."

"Yep, but not without a fight. The convict didn't like his sentence, and he decided to let the judge and all the rest of us know how he felt. It took six deputies to restrain the bastard, and they had to put a face mask on him after he bit two of them."

"You don't see that every day."

"Nope.

"The sheriff's office called 30 minutes ago to inform me and you that the departure time on Thursday is 08:00 from the county jail."

"Excellent. After Jurgensen's performance in the courtroom, I'm even more curious to get a good look-see at that place."

"He's going to BHC7 in case you didn't know."

"That's my understanding. I've had several conversations with Captain Sullivan, Tim Sullivan, who will be the duty captain of the guard for our arrival on Thursday. I'm all set up to get the cook's tour of the place."

"I wish I could go with you. I've been curious about those Black Holes since their inception."

"At our last commission meeting, the fellow who came up with the idea of those facilities claimed the name from the astronomical term, in other words, nothing escapes the gravity of a black hole. They tell me there are no interior guards or service personnel. It is literally survival of the fittest inside the walls."

"Doesn't sound very friendly, especially when we consider the assholes in those facilities are cutthroat men who've no respect for other people or even human life."

"Yeah. What Jurgensen is learning the hard way, the Black Hole prisons aren't for common criminals. Once you become designated a habitual criminal, the gates open to the Black Holes."

"That's an important distinction. OK, enough of the social hour, what do you have on your plate?"

"Just the usual, Cap. I need to get caught up on communications, and I'm collecting evidence on two open cases. Forensics is still processing their take. I've got one other unknown that's still with the medical examiner; he may have called by now for a witness; I'll see."

"Nothing that would preclude your day out on the transport task?"

"Not that I can see at the moment. They don't need me. I'm just an add on."

"Not anymore. I didn't mention it earlier, sorry, but the sheriff's transport officer pulled one of his deputies for the detail, so now you're an essential. If something comes up, we'll need to give them a head's up as soon as possible."

"Sure. No problem."

"OK. Back to work," the captain said and added a shoo gesture.

Rod returned to his desk and cold hamburger. He punched in his bilateral password, called up his communications page, and did a quick scan. No voice mails. Only two eMails. Rod emptied his lunch bag, unwrapped his hamburger, and took a healthy bite—*barely warm but still good*. Neither eMail offered any relevant additional information. Rod left the communications window open and then clicked the additional buttons to open the network search window. He took another bite of his hamburger, leaned back in his ergonomic chair, and casually looked around the squad room. Most of his shift colleagues were out of the office. Only two off-duty officers in the squad bay at their desks and working intently on whatever it was they were working on at the moment. Rod took a few good sips of his unsweetened iced tea.

Satisfied he was clear, Rod typed 'Kelly Joubert' in the subject field on the top-level search screen and hit ENTER.

The other associated fields filled in with related data—Margaret, her given middle name; Henry, her childhood familial surname; marriage to Raoul, address and such. Rod scanned the remainder of information. He nodded his head when he scanned the priors' section—no felonies, no misdemeanors, no arrests or even suspicions. She only had two traffic tickets since she obtained her first license at 16 years of age—both for speeding, one for 10 mph over the posted limit, the other for 14 mph over. The juvenile problems box was not ticked. Even if it had been, he would have needed a court warrant to examine that section. Fortunately, it was not ticked, so that potential did not have to be considered. *Kelly is refreshingly clean.* He scanned the second page that contained known employment, volunteer work and such. The second page on most citizens was usually sparse. It was often empty for citizens who resorted to criminal conduct. The third page miscellaneous section recorded that she had voluntarily answered questions regarding an immigration control inquiry with respect to her gardener a few years ago. She also had several witness statements that offered nothing. There was another page, so he hit the NEXT button.

The red colored font caught his attention immediately. Honor Hospital had filed a POTENTIAL DOMESTIC ABUSE report required by law. The attached photographs displayed various views of serious contusions and one laceration on her left cheek that required six stiches to close. Kelly refused to file charges or even answer questions regarding the incident. *This is not good.* Whether Raoul was involved, or the perpetrator, was not indicated, and there was no sign of any follow-up investigation that suggests the assigned detective intentionally decided not to probe farther into the case.

The FBI National Crime Information Center (NCIC) yielded nothing beyond a sliver of what was contained in the department database.

Rod could not find clues as to where Kelly Joubert might be. *She may have just vanished off the grid to avoid her husband.* If that was the case, Rod resolved to not disclose her location, even if he did find it. His curiosity was now piqued. Rod ate the last bite of his burger as well as the last few sticks of his French-fried potatoes, and then leaned back in this chair to contemplate this particular situation and his next steps.

I can't count how many of these database scans I've done in the course of investigations. It's not every day I see the red colored font regarding potential domestic abuse accusations. My instincts tell me this is not a simple missing spouse issue. There is not enough to confront Raoul Joubert. He has to know I would see this. Damn it all to hell, why did he put me in this position?

Rod's curiosity pushed him to expand his search horizon. *Raoul mentioned Laura Simmons. I remember that name. The prostitute I questioned when Baxter the banker was arrested. This is getting curiouser and curiouser.* Rod thought about his approach to the call, found Simmons' private phone number, and tapped the numbers into his personal smart phone.

"Hello," the soft female voice answered.

"Miz Simmons?"

"Yes."

"This is Detective-Sergeant Ramirez."

"Ah. I remember you . . . the Baxter case."

"Yes. Good memory."

"How can I help you detective?"

"If I'm informed correctly, you're friends with Kelly Joubert."

"Did something happen?" she asked in a quivery tone, clearly disturbed by his query. "Is she OK? What happened?"

"No, no, Miz Simmons. I have no information regarding Miz Joubert's status, which is precisely why I'm calling. I just want to ascertain her condition and location."

Laura's tone changed in an instant. "Why are you asking?"

"Her husband is concerned about her welfare."

"Yeah, he is the problem."

Damn, that's not a good sign. Now I'm in the middle of a domestic dispute with a powerful state attorney who is apparently an abusive husband. This isn't going to end well.

"Do you know her location?"

"Yes."

"Is she OK?"

"Yes, to my knowledge. I visited her a few weeks ago. She was just fine. She's where she wants to be."

"I don't want to inject myself into a domestic quarrel."

"You got that right. Me either."

"So, from your responses, you don't want to disclose her location?"

"She asked me not to betray her, and unless you have some serious criminal investigatory reason for demanding that information, I shall respect her fundamental right to privacy."

Well, that settles that. "Thank you very much, Miz Simmons. Nothing more. Have a great day."

They disengaged. Rod leaned back in his chair, again. *She said visited that suggests she is in a hospital, drug treatment facility, or some other established organization. Hospitals or drug treatment units were less likely since they were temporary, and Simmons stated she was fine.* His curiosity drove him to answer the question. Whether he disclosed his findings to Joubert was yet to be decided. On a gut hunch, Rod called the IC12 administrative office.

"IC12," a male voice answered.

"This is Detective-Sergeant Ramirez. I've a simple question. Is Miz Kelly Joubert a resident at your facility?"

"Just a sec . . ."

Rod waited patiently for the administrative receptionist to answer. Several minutes passed, and then a female voice came on the line.

"This is Carly Korber, director of operations for this facility." Rod reintroduced himself. "Is your inquiry part of any official investigation, Detective?"

"No."

"Then, I'm afraid this conversation is concluded. We've a responsibility to respect the privacy of our residents."

"I'm only unofficially inquiring as to her location and status."

"I can neither confirm nor deny her presence at our facility."

Well, that likely answers my question. If she was not there, she would probably have said no. But she was also warning me off, and I'd best not press that point. "Thank you very much for your time, Miz Korber. Have a great day."

Kelly Joubert is most probably a resident of IC12 for some substance consumption reason. And she was likely in stable condition; healthy or not was a point of definition.

Now, the salient question was, should he disclose his findings and opinion to Raoul Joubert. Those red font words in the department network database drew Rod up short. He felt no reason to open a formal investigation, although his gut told him there was probable cause. Rod had seen those signs before. There was consistency in the broad, general indications. *I had no idea that Raoul might be one of those.* Rod felt his anger rising. *There is no freakin' way I'm going to tell him where she likely is. So, what do I tell him? My call to IC12 was a hunch. I don't have to disclose that to him. I'll just tell him I found nothing in the department database or NCIC files. Damn, I really thought he was a good guy. I wish I hadn't agreed to do him a favor. I really would've preferred not to know any of this.*

—

16

This was Christie's first day back in school since the ID incident. Neither Gretchen nor Bella had seen her or talked to her since the incident. Her parents had told them she was in good health but not in school. One of their joint teachers indicated Christie had been keeping up with remote learning procedures, but she refused to offer any more information.

Gretchen and Bella sat at their usual table in their usual positions for lunch—a ham & cheese sandwich with potato chips—not a gourmet meal but adequate. They had each taken a few bites, when Gretchen announced softly, verging upon a whisper, "There she is."

Bella turned her head to see Christie collecting her meal at the service line. Both girls watched their friend carry her lunch tray and take her seat next to Gretchen. "Welcome back, Chris."

"Thanks."

"Where've you been?" Bella asked.

Christie shook her head. "I don't want to talk about any of that in here."

"Outside?"

"Yes."

"OK. We'll wait. We've been very worried about you."

"Thanks. I'm fine. I'm not and wasn't ever sick, and we'll talk about this later."

"Sure," Bella responded.

Gretchen put her arm around Christie's shoulders, drew her close, and kissed her cheek. "We're just happy to have you back."

"I'm glad to be back, not so much for school, but especially to finally be back together."

"Let's eat," Bella declared. "My curiosity is killing me."

All three of them laughed. While they did not wolf down their lunches, they focused on finishing what they had before them and deferred their conversation. Christie was the last to finish. Without speaking, *las tres amigas* rose, bussed their trays, and walked together outside. Someone they did not recognize occupied their bench. They decided to use the athletic field bleachers for their discussion. The highest bench seats seemed most appropriate to give them the most privacy plus give them at least a quasi-backrest. They sat with Christie in the middle.

"Spill your guts, girlfriend," Gretchen commanded.

Christie smiled. "Where to begin?" The other two did not react or speak, giving their reunited friend the space she probably needed. "You may not know," she began glancing at Bella, "your dad and an officer from Minville visited my Mom at home a couple of days after our arrest. A bunch of things began to happen at the same time after my Mom's conversation with your Dad. She turned off my phone and locked it up, and then she switched and only allowed me on it when she could watch me do my online homework."

"Why was she so hard on you?" Bella asked.

"Well, it turns out our little adventure and Mom's chat with your Dad convinced her she had enough of my Dad's crap. We went to court and obtained a court order to kick my Dad out of the house. She also went with me to a specialist psychiatrist every day for a couple of weeks and a couple of times twice a day." Christie looked directly at and held Bella's eyes. "It seems your father convinced her that my Dad's abuse was the source of her unhappiness and my acting out."

"Wow!" Gretchen exclaimed.

"Yeah, it's been a lot. As part of my recovery process, which is still ongoing, I want to genuinely and sincerely apologize to both of you for getting you into trouble. I understand what we did was wrong and has consequences. One of those consequences is I guess I'm headed to a broken home, and my parents are going to divorce. My Mom has been working very hard to stabilize things as quickly as possible and help me get on the correct path, as she calls it."

"There's no need to apologize," Bella said. "We talked about what we're going to do. We agreed—all three of us. It was not your fault. You didn't make us do anything."

"My Mom and our therapist convinced me that I instigated it all because I had the contact with Johnny, and I got the IDs."

"That's not fair, Chris," Bella interjected. Christie started to audibly and physically sob. Bella and Gretchen simultaneously wrapped their arms around Christie, which only made her cry harder. No one spoke. Tears descended Bella's cheeks. She glanced at Gretchen and noticed tears descending her cheeks as well. "Let it go," Bella said louder than she wanted to get past the sounds of Christie's remorse and relief. She was now doubled over with the head on her knees, crying hard, as her body convulsed in sorrow. Bella and Gretchen looked at each other over Christie's back and shook their heads together as they continued to sooth their comrade. Christie's crying slowly began to diminish. The girls let their friend proceed at her own pace.

As her sobbing stopped, Christie wiped her face and sat up. "Now, I've made my jeans all wet." All three of them erupted in raucous laughter that took several minutes to subside. "Thank you for being my friends," she said, patting the knees of her friends and looking into the eyes of both girls. "This has been a very hard couple of weeks. I know better. The therapist helped me see and realize my anger. I'm feeling better, and I'm very proud of Mom. She took massively huge steps toward helping me and herself. I never realized directly how abusive my father was, and my Mom has done a lot of crying through these therapy sessions. We talked for several days about whether I was ready to return to school, and . . . well . . . here I am."

"We're glad to have you back," Gretchen said.

"Yeah, exactly," added Bella.

"You know, Bell, I really must thank your father. If it hadn't been for him, I'd probably be in juvvie. Until I can thank him personally, please tell him for me."

"I'll do that."

"So, what's happened while I was gone?"

"Before we get to that," Gretchen jumped in directly, "do you have your phone back?"

"No. I've got another couple of weeks to go. I suspect my Mom will tire of not being able to text or talk to me whenever she wants. I'm not going to press her."

"We'll wait it out, too," Bella added. "We're just glad you're back with us."

"Thanks, guys. So, back to my question."

"Let me tell you," Gretchen said with an almost giddy tone. "Bell's parents want her to fuck in their house, and they'll supply the drugs."

"W-T-F?"

"Whoa, that's not what they said."

"Well, then, what exactly did they say?" Christie asked.

"We talked several times over several days about why we, or rather I did what we did. I told them my thinking. They were far more concerned about my safety than about the drugs or sex."

"My Mom is probably closer," Christie said, "than my father ever was or ever would be. But, there's no way I can bring that up with her until we get to a more stable position with therapy." Christie looked deeply into Bella's eyes without a blink. "So your parents will let you try MDMA and coke with sex in your house."

"Yes, although I'm not eager to test the new rules."

"My parents are a long way, a very long way, from that kind of permission," Gretchen contributed.

"At least, I know, or I think, it's possible."

"They also told her she could try the indulgence camp."

"GG," protested Bella, "that is not what they said. I raised the question we've talked about numerous times. Initially, they didn't react well. As we talked, they softened. The best I could get was a 'we'll-talk' condition if I ever get to that stage."

"Which is parental-speak for no," Christie added, inducing laughter among the girls.

"Perhaps. We may never know. My question to them was figurative. I think they were more shocked than anything and didn't want to admit it."

"Maybe," Gretchen said and paused, "we can do the drug-enhanced, gang-bang party at your house since we never made to the university party."

"Ah, no!" Bella objected. "Ain't gonna happen."

"Why? You said they said it was OK."

"My parents may be more liberal than most parents, but there is no way I'm going to take advantage of their generosity and understanding. Further, as my Dad likes to remind me, we are all still minors under the law. There is no way I'd even ask them such a thing. And, I must remind you both that you can't talk to anyone about this stuff. These're very private discussions within my family. I share with you because you're my best-ies and have been for years. I trust you."

"We love you too, Bell," Christie said.

"Exactly," Gretchen added.

"Thanks, girls. To change the topic, has anyone heard from Johnny?"

"Yeah," Christie responded. "I talked to him a couple of times after that day. He was pissed that we got him in trouble and got visited by your Dad," she said, looking directly at Bella, "and another officer. They scared the hell out of him. But, he was angrier that we spoiled the party. The guys wound up doing a circle jerk." All three girls laughed hard for several seconds.

"Poor boys," Gretchen offered between laughs.

"Ultimately, nothing happened to Johnny or any of the other guys," Christie continued. "He said your Dad told him that if we had gone through with the party, they could've been charged with statutory rape."

"Now that pisses me off," Bella said. Gretchen and Christie looked at Bella with confused expressions. "We've talked about this before. Those damn laws treat us like we have no brains, no knowledge, no means to make rational decisions. We knew what that party was about. We discussed the ramifications for several days. We knew what we were doing, and it's not like we were seven years old and ignorant. Hell, all three of us have been enjoying sex in one form or another for years. We're far better informed and taught than kids our age might have been a hundred years ago. Those damn laws have got to be changed."

"You really should run for Congress and even for president," announced Gretchen, "so you can change the laws." They laughed. "Heck, we'll help you." They laughed harder and longer.

"Nice thought, GG, but first we're all too young. You have to be 25 for the House and 30 for the Senate. You've got to be 35 years old for president."

"Then you've got a few years to prepare," Christie said. "I think GG is on to something here."

"You've been talking about freedom of choice and our right to privacy for a long time. You guys have always agreed and contributed. You guys should run."

"We don't have the passion you do, Bell," Gretchen responded.

"Sure, you do," Bella said. "Anyway, it doesn't much matter since we're at least ten years from being in a position to change laws."

"Write the law, Bell," Christie added, "and send it to the Legislature, to Congress, oh hell, send it to everyone. Who knows what might take root? Heck, Bell, you could become the Johnny Appleseed of privacy and choice." They all laughed. "It's a bit far out there, but we never know unless we try. It's just like sex and drugs, or any other part of life."

"True," Bella answered. "It's a lot to think about in all this." *Las tres amigas* sat silently and stared out across the track and field to the thick tree line beyond the athletic complex. Each of them alone with their thoughts. Bella was the first to break the silence. "You know, guys, I think that is one of the reasons I want to try the indulgence camps, to see for myself whether they do what they say they do. From what I hear from my Dad, those camps seem to be the key to improving our relationship with drugs. My Dad also says our experience with the SCIP Act is not likely to change the Controlled Substance Act at the federal level . . . well, at least until enough states pass similar laws."

"Don't you have to be addicted to one or more drugs to get into an indulgence camp?" asked Gretchen.

"Yes, that is my understanding."

"Then, are you planning to get addicted?" Christie asked.

"I haven't figure that out, yet. Addiction has never seemed like a good idea or an attraction." Bella paused for several seconds to think. "I just think knowing firsthand is far more enlightened than hearing someone else's stories."

"Yeah," Christie and Gretchen added together.

"Anyway, we're a long way away from any indulgence camp experience," said Bella.

"Since we're talkin' about these things, are you curious about what your Dad calls Black Hole prisons?" asked Gretchen.

"Jeez, GG, it's a freakin' prison. The extent of my curiosity about prisons from juvvie to those Black Holes is served by *Orange is the New Black*." They all laughed, again. "Indulgence camps are not prisons. From what I know, I think the best descriptor would be sanctuary. They seem like sanctuaries for those in need. And like my Dad says, those camps break the chain that often led to crimes. All I know, or at least I think, is prohibition is never the answer. My parents, well all of our parents, are free to buy and use these drugs, but do they? No. They choose not to use any of the stuff."

"We've tried some of them," Christie observed.

"Yeah, we have," replied Bella. "And we've learned that what our parents were told was wrong. They were lied to by the government. First, none of the controlled drugs cause addiction, if they're used properly. Second, they have positive uses despite the fact that the federal law says there are no proper uses. At least our state is trying to take a more progressive approach to drugs." Bella looked at her two friends, as if to open the conversation to their opinions. The fifth period alert bell rang. "Well, that settles that. Time to get back inside."

Las tres amigas descended the bleacher steps and made their way back inside. They stopped at their lockers to collect their afternoon textbooks and materials. They said goodbye and then split to attend their separate afternoon classes. They all felt they had more to discuss, but the exigencies of their daily, or at least school day daily, routine interceded. They would meet back up when the school day was done.

—

17

The drive out of town to Black Hole Confinement camp number 7 (BHC7) took 2 1/2 hours. The disruptions of convict Jurgenson made the journey much longer than a normal hour and 45 minutes. The driver-deputy had to stop the armored van several times to deal with Jurgensen, who persisted in being unruly. In the first instance, Rod and the other security deputy had to fight a thrashing Jurgensen with a combination muzzle and spit mask. Jurgensen remained chained hand and foot, connected with a conventional steel chain through a wide leather belt around his waist and a reinforced deck ring on the floor, between his feet. The mask and chains proved insufficient to restrain the convict. Jurgensen started banging his head against the steel walls of the interior holding cell. Jurgensen rendered himself unconscious once. He picked up his self-harm conduct as soon as he regained consciousness, opening up a wound on the back of his skull and bloodying himself and the van interior. With blood present, Rod and the guard had to take potential pathogen precautions that required a second roadside stop. They made no attempt to bandage the wound, and again, they fought with a thrashing convict to place and strap down a full helmet on Jurgensen's head. The convict could only mumble now, and no one could understand what he was trying to say. Rod and the deputies no longer cared. Jurgensen had exhausted their patience, indulgence, and tolerance. At least their efforts had silenced Jurgensen except for a few more episodes of banging his helmeted head against the van wall.

When BHC7 first came into sight, the deputies were not particularly impressed. *This was not their first trip to BHC7, even though we are transporting our first BHC convict. They must've done a good route reconnaissance—a Google Maps and Google Earth study of the roadway, turns, bridges, and the approach to the facility.* For Rod Ramirez, his initial sighting surprised him and defied his imagination. It was a large block in the middle of a comparatively flat valley, like a fat monolith. There were very few distinctive features—most notable among those few . . . the building was light grey, not black. The walls had no apparent openings—no windows, no doors, nothing, just blank concrete walls. The structure had four square holes in the roof about a third of the size of the outer walls. Four small parapets, barely discernible from a distance, stood at the four corners. The exception to the stark exterior was a small building of similar construction attached to one side facing the roadway approach. The small building had two rows of vertical slit windows. As they got closer, Rod saw a modest size parking lot half full with what appeared to be private automobiles and pick-up trucks—probably belonging to the staff. As they got closer, Rod noted additional details. The walls were bare, solid concrete, perhaps heavily reinforced with steel reinforcing bars. The mazes of reinforced fencing around the small, attached building indicated the structure was the only entry and exit to the facility.

The driver knew precisely where to go. At the guard salient next to the large, see-through, entry gate, an extendible drawer emerged from the reinforced structure. The driver deposited his clipboard of associated papers. The drawer retracted. Several minutes passed before the gate slid open slowly. Once open sufficiently, the van entered a holding section.

"We stay here until the guards signal us to exit," the guard deputy announced.

Rod did not move.

The gate closed behind them. Two armed guards emerged from the side door of the entry control structure—one armed with an assault rifle and the other armed with a shoulder-strapped shotgun. The assault-rifle guard inspected the vehicle, top, and bottom. Satisfied with the van's condition, he signaled for them to open the doors.

"OK. Time to transfer the convict," the guard-deputy said. He opened the door for himself and Rod, then opened the sliding door to the confinement cell. That action caused Jurgensen to start thrashing again.

The three men stood and observed Jurgensen's antics.

The assault rifle guard eventually said with a humorous tone, "We see this behavior more often than not. We'll give him a few minutes to work it out," the man said more loudly than necessary, probably more for Jurgensen than them. "If he doesn't calm down, we'll incapacitate him."

After about five minutes, Jurgensen continued to thrash against his chains. The assault rifle guard dropped his weapon on its shoulder strap, removed his TASER, displayed it just a few seconds for Jurgensen to recognize what was coming, and deployed the TASER shot. Jurgensen stiffened and convulsed. The guard-deputy opened the floor lock. The two prison guards dragged Jurgensen out of the van, to and through a small sliding gate that opened upon command from somewhere else. The two guards dragged Jurgensen down an enclosed corridor. The first gate closed before another barrier in the side of the admissions building opened on command. Once all the gates closed, the door to the entry structure opened. A uniformed captain emerged.

"Welcome to Number Seven. I'm Captain Tim Sullivan, duty captain of the guard for this facility."

Rod stepped toward him and extended his right hand. "I'm Detective-Sergeant Rod Ramirez."

The two men shook hands. "May I see your badge and ID card, please?"

Rod displayed his badge and presented his ID card. Sullivan carefully examined them, looking several times between the ID card and Rod. "You need to update your photograph, Sergeant."

Rod chuckled and responded, "Yeah, probably so. It's probably ten years old." Rod looked over his shoulder at the two deputies. "Are you guys going to join us for the tour."

"Nope," the security deputy said. "Been there, done that, for both of us," he added, gesturing with his thumb over his shoulder to the driver. "We're going back into town for lunch. You want us to pick something up for you."

"We've no food facilities here," Sullivan volunteered.

"No, thanks. I'm good without . . ."

"When do you want us back here to pick you up?"

Rod looked at Sullivan.

"The cook's tour takes about an hour. There's not that much to see. However, I suspect you'll have questions. Say . . . give us another hour or two. That should be sufficient."

Rod traded cellphone numbers with the deputies, just in case. Satisfied they had recorded the numbers and names correctly, the two deputies departed. With a signal from Sullivan, the entry gate opened, the van backed out, and the gate closed and locked.

Ramirez turned to face Sullivan. "I'm all yours."

"Before we get started, a few questions if you don't mind."

"Shoot."

"Why are you here?"

"What do you mean?"

"Is your request official or personal?"

Rod thought for a few seconds how he wanted to answer. "A little bit of both, I suppose. I was the investigating officer in the Jurgensen case. I supported the effort to charge him and identify him as a habitual criminal. During his trial, he went into meltdown at even the thought of being sentenced to this place. I could certainly sense a mortal fear within him. That suggested he knew more about this place than I did."

"You're a member of the Governor's policy commission."

"Yes, I am. This visit is not directly or indirectly related to my work on the commission."

"Knowing who you are, I had to inform my superiors of your request. They, in turn, informed me of their concerns for the consequences."

The words induced a definite irritation in Rod. He fought to suppress any emotion he felt and keep his facial expression neutral. He knew he had to be very careful with his words. "I'm not here on behalf of the commission or any other governmental institution. My work as a line detective, as well as with the commission, have heightened my curiosity about these facilities. My request was simply to that end, satisfy my curiosity. To say that what I may learn here won't affect my professional efforts would be a falsehood. I expect that this visit may alter my view of things."

"We don't do public tours," Sullivan said. "This is a serious and brutal place . . . by design. We're neither advocates for nor detractors from these prisons. There are genuine reasons the public doesn't have access to these places," he added, gesturing with his thumb over his shoulder at the high concrete walls.

"How did Jurgensen develop such a fear of this place?"

"I've no idea. My guess is, bleeding-heart lawyers who are trying desperately to get the courts to declare these prisons as cruel and unusual punishment."

"Well, there is that."

"Those lawyers have probably spread the word among their scum-bag clients."

"Jurgensen had a public defender by the name of Houseman," Rod said and paused to allow Sullivan to comment. Tim only shook his head in the negative. "Jurgensen got the word from somewhere else. Nonetheless, he acted out at his sentencing and during his transport out here. Their resistance— Jurgensen and Houseman—to the Black Hole system was strong, consistent, and adamant, from the preliminary hearing to the ride out here."

"I think the legislature intended this punishment to be relevant, appropriate, and fearsome. If that was the intent of the government, they definitely accomplished their objective. I doubt we will ever allow public access. This place is pure Darwinian survival of the fittest. Most inmates don't last long here. Not one inmate has survived more than five years. They come here to die alone . . . well except with their kind. There are no visitors."

"Their kind?"

"Habitual criminals. They all share that one common point."

"What's the usual cause of death?"

"Blunt force trauma. There are very few shivs here, not zero but few. The last time we had a stabbing death was three years ago. They usually beat themselves to death. By the way, I must say the data suggests the violence inside is diminishing. As you'll see, the inmates are left to their own processes."

"Have I satisfied your concerns?" asked Rod.

"Yes. I'll only add, between professionals, they call this place a Black Hole for a reason. You're being given extraordinary access. We can't and won't constrain your recounting of what you'll see today, but we'd prefer no information regarding what you see and hear today reach the public domain. Our objective isn't secrecy, after all this is a state and thus public facility. Citizens can easily read the law and establish what this place is based on, and generally how it operates. We believe this place should be a Black Hole for information as well, not just residents. We seek some degree of mysticism."

"Understood. I've no reason or inclination to discuss this place in public."

"One last item, our guards are for external security only. Our security processes are highly classified and segmented for a reason. Naturally, I won't be able to discuss some of our security measures with you. In fact, I'm the only member of my shift who knows all of the systems and protections we've in place to ensure this facility remains secure, and no one leaves this place alive. As a consequence, I'll simply ask you to respect that underlying principle."

"Agreed," responded Rod. "I can live with that constraint."

"Very well, then let's get started. First off, before we leave this area," Sullivan said, swinging his arms around the fencing, "this is the only way into or out of the facility. There are no other access points. The gates and such are all double actioned in that it takes two separated officers to agree on opening a particular gate. As you probably noted on your entry, only one gate can be opened at a time. We've multiple checkpoints in plain view from multiple directions to make it through the access point."

They moved through a series of gates, using a different corridor than Jurgensen was taken into the prison. A separate locked door gave them entry into the attached building after the last passage gate locked behind them. The small lobby was strictly utilitarian. The light greenish-yellow walls had no artwork or even photographs of the president or governor. Only one other solid, metallic door opposite the entry door undoubtedly led to the interior. A small window that appeared to be very thick, laminated, polycarbonate with no direct openings provided access control. A single, circular, wireless, combination speaker/microphone in the middle of the window offered the only means of communication. A uniformed officer sat behind the protector. Tim inserted his ID badge in a protected card reader.

The guard said in a very tinny voice, "Captain Sullivan recognized."

"I have Rodrigo José 'Rod' Ramirez for approved entry," Sullivan announced, as if he did not know the man on the other side of the window.

Rod noted that the captain did not use his police title rank. A drawer extended from below the window. "ID and badge, please, Mister Ramirez." The guard knew what Rod did.

Rod complied, depositing his police ID and badge, as well as his state driver's license into the drawer that retracted into the wall. Rod watched as the man carefully examined the provided identification and made several entries into his computer screen.

"Rodrigo José 'Rod' Ramirez identified. Mister Ramirez, please look at the blue dot," he said and pointed at a blue dot above the communicator.

For the first time, Rod saw the blue dot above the communications circle. There were no wires. Probably a camera.

"Thank you. Please place your right thumb on the print scanner and do not move," commanded the guard. Rod again complied. The guard observed as a green light illuminated the underside of Rod's thumb. "Thank you." The guard did his work in silence. After several minutes, the wall drawer extended. A large, red, ID badge on a blue, sturdy, neckband joined his identification items. "Please wear the facility ID badge at all times. You'll be required to surrender the badge on your departure."

Rod placed the badge neckband over his head. The red card had 'VISITOR' in bold, white, plain letters. His photograph, clearly just taken, appeared below the label with an adjacent Datamatrix digital code square. Hard plastic sealed the badge. Rod returned his ID items to their proper place.

When the guard observed that Rod was ready to enter, he said, "Please insert your ID badge in the reader." Rod inserted his new badge. "Detective-Sergeant Ramirez recognized. You may proceed."

Sullivan touched Rod's right shoulder and gestured to the other door. As Tim reached for the simple, vertical, bar handle, the electronic locks audibly released. He pulled the door toward him and motioned for Rod to precede him inside. A moderately wide hallway extended away from the door. There was a crossing hallway that was lighted but with no signs. Three closed doors on each side of the hallway in each section before and after the cross-hallway. Once the door closed behind them, Tim said, "We'll take the second door on the left."

Rod stood beside the door and waited for Tim to lead the way. The moderately sized room appeared to be a conference or training room with a long table with four chairs on each side and a single chair at the head with a large television or computer screen at the other end of the table. Tim patted the chair just to the left of his chair, signaling for Rod to sit. Tim took the chair at the head of the table and retrieved a wireless keyboard.

"I thought it best to go through a little general briefing and orientation. Ask any questions you wish at any time you wish. Don't worry about interrupting me. I may not be able to answer any specific questions, but if so, I'll tell you. Please don't hesitate to ask." Rod nodded his head in acknowledgment. Tim initiated a PowerPoint presentation that apparently was used for many purposes beyond briefing visitors. He flashed through several introductory slides that he apparently thought were not necessary. Tim stopped on the layout of the facility. Using a high-end LASER pointer, he began briefing Rod. "We use this room for many purposes including team meetings, training, visiting dignitaries such as yourself . . . ." Rod laughed audibly. ". . . and for video conference calls. So, to begin . . .

"By the time we get to the control room, your prisoner should be finishing up his induction process. He was brought in through the receiving door." He aimed the pointer at the screen and illuminated several connected chambers. "We're here." The red light showed the room they were in at the moment. Tim circled the upper two-thirds of the administrative building. "These are the operational and administrative offices."

"The warden?" asked Rod.

"We've no warden. These offices and rooms are mostly for the duty guard sections. We do have some support offices like finance, human resources, and mental health professionals, but it's for the guards."

"If it isn't sensitive, how are your guards organized?"

"We've four teams led by a captain. My team is on duty today, and we're Team Three. Each has four operators. We might otherwise call them guards, but as you'll see, there is not much to guard anymore, at least not at a facility like this. Each team has a larger reaction team that is more like a tactical unit. Cross-trained individuals can and often do shift from element to element. Each team is on duty here for 24 hours, then off for three days. We maintain a watch at night when the interior lights go off."

"So, you've infrared to keep track of things during lights out periods?" Rod asked.

Sullivan smiled. "We've many sensor media, including visual and infrared, to keep track of things on the inside. The developers of these facilities were quite serious in their efforts to ensure we maintain the inhabitants on the inside."

"Has there ever been an escape?'

"No."

"Attempts?"

"Yes."

"How many?"

Again, Sullivan smiled. "A few is as far as I'll go on that question, and I won't discuss the means used in any attempt. The bottom line remains . . . no successful escape, and we're going to do our best to keep it that way."

Rod nodded his head. "Just curious."

"Understood. As they say, the only foolish question is the one not asked. I've a greater obligation that I'm sure you recognize."

"I do."

"The capacity of the facility is established by the residential rooms—only one resident per room. We've not yet reached our capacity, but if we did, a new resident might have to be transferred to one of the other BHC facilities." Sullivan pointed at several rooms. "As you'll note, a resident can close his room door and lock it for some degree of protection. Every door can be opened remotely, should the need arise.

"There are four quads," he said, pointing to the four quarters, "two floors each, with an open quad, so they can get some sun and rain when it comes. Each room has heating and cooling with the room door closed. It shuts off if the door opens."

"How do you keep track of what happens in a closed room?"

"Save that question for the control room. I think the answer will be clear."

Rod nodded his head. He stood and walked to the screen for a closer inspection of the floor plan. "How do you get residents, as you call them, into their assigned quad?"

Sullivan pointed at a diamond shaped space in the junction of the four quads. "A closed tunnel goes from the admin building," he said, placing the LASER spot on where they were now, "to this access lobby. You'll see it on the screen in the control room. The tunnel is the only direct access point to the quads, so it is not accessible from the outside, except by the tunnel. You'll also note small compartments beside each access door. These are the access locks. Through these compartments, food is delivered to each quad, and the dead are removed via these lockout chambers."

"Wow! What about medical treatment?"

"There is none—no medicines, drugs, or treatment. They're left to natural causes, and sometimes not so natural, which is more than they allowed their victims."

"So, if a resident is beaten and bloodied, he's left to self-healing?"

"For the most part, yes. Again, this is more than they allowed their victims. We do see other residents helping as best they can, but we've no medical treatment facilities."

"I thought you said earlier that you had mental health professionals."

"That capacity is for the operators. We learned early on that some residents of these facilities didn't act like human beings. The stress on the operators led to early difficulties. Since we provided mental health care, those problems vanished."

"What if one of your men is injured?"

"We've women operators here, too."

"Sorry . . . your people."

"Each team has two medics or EMTs. They generally stabilize any injured person. If the injury is serious, then they are medevac'd to the hospital at Springerville. I might add that the Springerville Police Department is augmented by the state to maintain a SWAT force that is twice the size their city warrants. They're our designated back-up. They train out here at least once monthly to maintain proficiency with our security procedures and provisions."

"Very impressive, Captain."

"Thank you. The designers and engineers did a magnificent job—not perfect—but still magnificent."

"Do they have a kitchen for food preparation?"

"Nope. We can't allow utensils or cooking provisions. They get military-grade MREs—Meals Ready to Eat."

"I'm familiar."

"Army?"

"No. Marine."

"Semper Fi," Sullivan said proudly and fist-bumped Rod.

"What do they eat with?"

"A rather ingenious invention, a specifically designed plastic spork that literally disintegrates within days of exposure to saliva or water. Years ago, we had several residents try to use the sporks as a weapon, but they quickly figured out they had a choice, eat or try to make a shiv quickly enough to be useful. Eating won out."

Rod chuckled at the image of such disappointment.

"I might add here that the lessons we've learned in the Black Holes have apparently changed meal procedures at the conventional prisons as well. I'm not sure, but I've been told."

"Then, do they have hot water?"

"Not hot, but warm . . . yes, they do. The temperature is maintained well below the scolding threshold, but it does give them comparatively hot water for their meals and washing."

"I presume the separate building," Rod said and pointed to a much smaller square building behind the main building, "is your maintenance and services building?"

"Yes, exactly. We've sophisticated purification provisions for our water supply that we get from Springerville. We get our power off the grid, but we also have 100% back-up power independent from the grid. We also have well provisions as a back-up to our normal water supply. We try not to tap that because the capacity is limited out here."

"Have you ever had a riot?"

"Yes. The quad system confines violence to a particular quad. Our first position is to watch. If it's just a fistfight, we let them work things out, which they usually do—cuts and bruises but not much more. Occasionally, fights escalate to more serious affairs. We've a water jet suspended in the middle of each quad . . . rather ingenious. The device has an effective aiming system that calculates the ballistic drop of the water stream. Works like water on a dog fight; they stop. They're generally left to their own devices, but we're obligated to remove the dead."

"How do you do that?"

"Remove the dead?"

"Yes."

Sullivan put his pointer red dot on one of the lockout chambers. "We send our tactical team in via the lockout chamber. They retrieve the body in a body bag and depart by reversing their route out of the quad."

"Ambush?"

"Always a potential in such an operation. The team is armed. All members carry lethal pistols. Half the team is armed with lethal automatic weapons, and the other half with non-lethal shotguns with bean bag shots alternated with a rather fancy paintball—knocks you down, leaves a persistent blue splat, and a helluva bruise. The water cannon helps. The operators have become quite proficient in using the device."

"Have you used lethal force?'

"Yes . . . twice since I've been here. The tactical teams are very carefully trained, and currency maintained. We've a realistic training room in the support building, and we reinforce the rules of engagement often," Tim said, pointing at the building in back. "Collective memory of the residents seems to be sufficient to avoid such encounters, although we suspect through turnover, we'll likely face those events periodically over time. I should say here that we're prepared to deal with every potential even inside or outside, and we maintain contingency plans for each type of event. Yet, the whole of the Black Hole, all four quadrants, remain peaceful, routine, and boring frankly. Flare-ups are comparatively rare. For the last four years, we average 5.6 events per year, with 1.2 of those reaching our intervention threshold. These are bad men, but they seem to develop their own order for surviving."

"You mentioned exterior protection," Rod noted.

"The designers and engineers studied period external escape efforts, both successful and not, and hypothesized the potential modes, as best they could imagine. They built those lessons learned into the design of this place. There are limits, of course. I mean, you and I both know we would not stand much of a chance against a company of Marines. Fortunately, that potential is highly unlikely. Even if something of that magnitude should occur, the best we can do is slow them down, to buy time, for the cavalry to arrive. I can only cover so much of the details, but that's probably best covered during our tour of the control room. I can access all of the cameras from here, but I think it's important for you to see for yourself."

"OK. I look forward to it."

Sullivan paused and held Rod's eyes for a handful of seconds. "Any more questions at this stage?"

Rod shook his head and then said, "Tons, but none that pop into my head just yet. I'll probably have many more as I absorb what I see and hear today."

"No worries, Rod. You're welcome to call or eMail me with any questions that come to you in the future. I'll say that the content of my response will be more constrained in open media." Tim looked at his watch. "Your prisoner Jurgensen should be finished with his induction. It would be a good time to head to the control room so that you can observe his installment."

"Sure. Good idea."

Sullivan secured the computer and video screen. "Follow me." He stood, exited the conference room, turned left, and then Tim went down the right hallway. Two closed doors on the right. A security door of apparent heavy metallic construction, a badge reader and keypad on the wall beside the handle, and heavy covers over the seams and hinges. Only one closed door occupied the left wall. Sullivan stopped at the left door and pointed to the security door at the end of the hallway. "That door accesses the resident induction area and is the only access to the resident areas from these administrative offices." Sullivan pointed at the door next to where they were standing. "This is the control room. The ambient light level is kept low, so we'll take a few seconds once inside to let our eyes adjust." Rod nodded his acknowledgment. The door had the same badge reader and keypad as the security door. "Insert your badge, do not remove it, and key in '9999.' It tells the tracking system you are a visitor without routine unescorted access."

Rod did as he had been instructed. After he pushed enter, a green light illuminated the badge reader. "You can remove your badge now." Sullivan inserted his badge, left it in the reader, and keyed in his PIN. The electronic lock released, and Tim removed his badge. He opened the door. Rod stepped inside and waited for the captain to join him and close the door. They stood next to each other without words as their eyes adjusted to the dim light. Two operators sat at what appeared to be identical workstations with three large video screens in front of them arranged in a quasi-arc with a larger than normal keyboard with two blocks of keys, one on each side of the QWERTY key array and an adjacent number pad. Each operator had multiple windows open on each screen, with about half of the windows cycling between many different camera views. A very large, wall-mounted, video screen occupied the space at the top of the wall above the workstations.

Sullivan tapped Rod on the left shoulder and gestured for him to follow. He stepped up three steps and entered into a glass-enclosed booth facing the operators. The door damper closed the door behind them.

"This is the duty captain's workstation," Sullivan said, "in the event of an incident or some special situation." Pointing to the identical swivel chair next to the captain's workstation, he said, "Have a seat." Tim entered his password, and a control screen appeared on his display. He keyed in some commands. Several surveillance camera views appeared on his screen. He picked two and put them on the big screen. The left one showed a long square tube that had to be the tunnel leading into the quad. Two men in black uniforms were pushing a rather large wheelchair with the form of a limp man in orange clothing in the chair. "Well, now, we don't get to see that every day," Tim began. "It seems your boy got a little carried away with his resistance. Per our rules, a medic administered a short-term sedative to quell his resistance. Per the rules, they'll enter the lockout chamber, deposit him on the floor, and then administer the antidote. They'll observe him from an outside monitor, as will we. Once he has regained his coordination and is standing, the operators here will unlock and open the inner door."

"He's been doing this since his preliminary hearing and demonstrated his displeasure with the judge's sentence," added Rod.

"My guess, he'll try to stay in the lockout chamber. The residents of that quad will tolerate that only so far since as long as he remains in there, that lockout chamber is disabled—no food, nothing. The residents won't take kindly to that interference."

Rod noticed for the first time a large map of the facility. A small LED light in the Quad Three lockout chamber shown red. A green light remained illuminated in the middle of the access tunnel. "Are the guards standing by outside?" Rod asked.

Sullivan punched several keys, and another camera view replaced the tunnel image. Both guards stood to the right of the large door with an enormous '3' on it. They were watching the associated monitor.

Rod quickly glanced at the wall map. A green light illuminated across the lobby square, indicating the camera now showing the guards.

Jurgensen began to stir, and then in an instant, he jumped to his feet, staggered a few times as he regained his balance, and then he backed away from the open door toward the surveillance camera above him. Several orange attired residents looked into the chamber, apparently out of curiosity. Others cycled through to observe their newest member. Jurgensen was leaning against the outer door, as far away from the inner door as possible in the lockout chamber. After a few minutes, a rather smallish, slight resident entered the chamber by several steps with two larger residents in the doorway. The man seemed to be talking to Jurgensen.

"Can you listen?"

"Sure." Sullivan punched two control buttons.

". . . can't stay," the small man said.

"I don't belong here," Maxim protested.

All three of the other men laughed hard. "Dude," the small man said, as he regained his composure, "this is not the way you want to start your residency with us."

"Fuck you!"

"Look, dude, I don't know you from Adam. But, dude, let me 'splain somethin' to you. This chamber is how this quad receives our food. As long as you stay in here, we don't get no food. Ya hearin' me, dude?"

"Fuck you!"

"OK. If that's the way you want it, stay in here. Ain't nuthin' goin' ta change 'cep you're goin' ta piss off the entire quad, and that ain't gonna be pretty." The small man turned to leave, and the two observers left. As he reached the door, the small man turned and said, "There is a meal out here for you this afternoon. It'll be gone in a few hours. And one last thing, if you stay in here until the alarm sounds in the morning, you'll be removed forcefully and these fellas, who by that time will be very pissed off, won't be gentle. Your choice, dude." The man did not wait for a response.

They continued to watch for several minutes. Jurgensen began to pace back and forth, mumbling something unintelligible to himself.

"I've not seen one this bad before," Sullivan observed. "None of them wants to enter, but I've never seen one so resistant that he's willing to anger the entire quad of bad men."

"What is the alarm the small man mentioned?" Rod asked.

"It's a klaxon type sound within that quad to alert the residents that the lockout chamber is blocked. It means nothing can come in or go out. Years ago, before I joined the team, I heard the residents tried to block the lockout chamber. A dead body remained in there for nearly four days. The stench and no food finally convinced them to comply."

"Amazing how survival works."

"Exactly."

"I imagine you've cameras everywhere?"

"Yes, we do. I can't possibly show them all."

"You mentioned infrared earlier. Can you show me?"

"Sure." Sullivan made several more keyboard entries. He moved a small boom microphone to a few inches from his mouth. Tim keyed a button, a red ring appeared around the end of the boom mic, and then he said, "Lights out test." Both guards raised a thumb without speaking. Sullivan hit another button, and the lobby square went dark. He keyed another couple of buttons, and the two guards reappeared in clear, crisp, infrared showing the thermal contrast in the lobby. "Test complete," Tim announced. The white-hot hands with thumbs raised appeared sharper than the regular light image. Sullivan turned the lights back on in the lobby.

"Damn, that's high-quality imagery," observed Rod.

"Yeah, state-of-the-art stuff from the military. They spent a lot of money on our surveillance tools and saved a lot more money by not needing interior guards and support facilities."

"You said you have cameras in several cells, or rather resident rooms."

"Right." Sullivan scanned several screens, found what he wanted, and made the appropriate commands on the keyboard. An infrared image appeared of a man lying on his back in a darkened cell. "This fellow sleeps a lot. They can request lights out in the rooms. He always locks the door from the inside when he's sleeping." The man was not moving other than his chest rising and falling. The man's body was noticeably cooler than the two guards. Then, he noticed a brighter spot at the junction of his legs.

"Damn! Is that what I think it is?"

"Yep, quite common, actually. If he still has it when he wakes up, he'll probably jack it."

"Intercourse?"

"Yeah, that too, from time to time."

"It's allowed?"

Sullivan chuckled softly. "We don't interfere. They do what they want to do in there."

"Force? Rape?"

"It happens. My guess is, if your man Jurgensen persists in blocking the lockout chamber until tomorrow morning when the food delivery is made, he'll be treated to a thorough thumping, and then forcibly raped by whoever wishes to have a go at him inside that quad."

"That's a crime. You don't stop them?" Rod asked.

"Nope. Them's the rules. Given the warning he received this afternoon, he might not survive it, depends on how tough this guy is."

"He's a pretty nasty character—no respect for anyone else and rather dispassionate for others."

"Well, he's heading toward a very harsh lesson."

"And you don't interfere?"

"Nope."

"Wow!"

"Yeah, it's a bit much, especially for street law enforcement officers such as yourself. The rules are different in there. After observing their behavior for years now, I must say they've a set of collective rules that just evolved, to the best of my knowledge, that established an odd order to things inside. They enforce those rules with ruthless brutality. Most residents learn quickly, or he'll probably die a hard premature death."

"No wonder they call it the Black Hole and Jurgensen was so, and still is, resistant. I'm not sure how he would know what goes on in here, but he apparently had a pretty good idea."

"And he instinctively knows he's no longer at the top of the food chain no matter how bad he was. Things are different in there. He could be the strongest, meanest guy in the quad, but the collective is far, far stronger . . . and more ruthless. The longer his resistance goes on, the more severe his life-lesson will be."

"That brings me to a question that has stuck with me since Jurgensen learned the prosecution would seek his designation as a habitual criminal with a sentence to the Black Hole. He clearly knew what this place was." Rod paused to think about how he wanted to ask the question. "As I mentioned earlier, Jurgensen knew what this place is about, and it was more than the simple description offered to the public. What means of communications outside the walls do the residents have available to them?"

"None. There are no telephones, no computers, no mail service, nothing. Every day, we receive letters and packages for one of the residents or another. We've a big red stamp that says, 'Not deliverable.' The Postal Service letter carrier or delivery service leave with the item. It's here for a few seconds at best. People have tried all sorts of ingenious techniques like marriage proposals, mother's funeral, terminally ill sister, all sorts of things. They're all responded to in the same manner."

"Not deliverable."

"Yep."

"No one has ever left this place?"

"Not alive."

"Faked death?"

Sullivan laughed. "They're photographed and fingerprinted where they fall. The recovery team places them in a body bag and removes them from the quad. The bag goes directly to our internal crematorium. The last thing that happens before he goes into the furnace is one more photograph of the man's face—often not in good shape, I must say, and then the bag and body are reduced to ash. The residue is swept up, taken outside on the grounds, and widely scattered inside the wire. So, no, no fake deaths."

"He knew some details that I haven't even seen or heard today," Rod mused.

"The only access are lawyers."

"Lawyers?"

"Every resident is still a citizen . . . with minimal remaining rights. One of those rights is the right to counsel for appeals. The attorney general must certify the attorney. We don't get that many . . . a visit on average about every two to three months. There was a third, but he died, and his case died with him. As I imagine you're aware, two cases are working their way through the judicial appeal process. I've not read the court documents, but I imagine some details appear in those legal documents."

"Have the lawyers been able to exert discovery in those cases?"

"No, and that is one of the points of contention in at least one of the cases."

"Do you think your secrecy will hold up?"

"I've no idea, but I sure hope so. We don't need bleeding heart liberals baying about the dignity of man. Every single one of our residents has exhausted multiple attempts to reform their behavior and repeatedly refused to obey the law. These fellows are truly habitual criminals who show no respect for other citizens or property. The number of bastards who qualify for this place is a tiny fraction of one percent of the incarcerated populations. They deserve what they get here."

Rod contemplated Tim's words for several seconds and decided to move on. "You mentioned exterior surveil . . ." Rod's cellphone ringtone announced an incoming call. He looked at his smartphone screen. *It's the transport deputies.* "Excuse me."

"Sure."

Rod took the call. It was one of the deputies checking to see if he was ready to be picked up. He had already taken more time than planned. Rod answered in the affirmative and was told it would take about 20 minutes for them to arrive. He thanked them and said he would be ready. After he disconnected, Rod looked at Tim, "My transportation will be here in 20 minutes, so I'd like to take our remaining time to hear a little about your exterior surveillance. I mean, what if some cohorts of these inmates . . . er . . . residents decide to attack the facility with helicopters and RPGs to blow a hole in the wall to free their *jefe*?"

"I won't be so foolish to claim we can stop anything as I said earlier, a company of Marines would give us a go. That said, we have sophisticated provisions." Sullivan made more keyboard comments. A series of various size arcs appeared on the wall. All of them were green except for one smaller, yellow one off the northwest order. He seemed to key up that yellow camera. Rod saw a video image appear on Sullivan's screen, and a tracking bracket appeared. Sullivan hit a key. The tracking bracket centered on the image. He zoomed in.

A Jeep appeared along the inner of two tall perimeter fences. A man had dismounted and was checking something along the fence. Rod glanced at the wall. The yellow arc had moved and narrowed to indicate the camera's field of view.

"Fence patrol . . . checking something . . . not sure what. He'll report if he finds anything unusual. I can talk to him directly, if necessary."

A larger corner arc turned yellow and caught their attention. Sullivan commanded the appropriate camera. He waited for the tracking bracket to find its target. "The system identified movement in the northeast sector as a coyote." Tim repeated his command. When he zoomed in, sure enough, a coyote was trotting across the terrain a half-mile beyond the outer fence.

"Man oh man, that is impressive," Rod exclaimed.

"Never ceases to amaze me, and I've been at this for a while."

"Skipper," a female voice came over an intercom, "looks like the inductee is finally recognizing reality."

"Thanks, Barb." Tim keyed the Quad Three lockout chamber just in time to see Jurgensen leave the chamber, and the door closed.

Rod could not hear the lock, but the indicator light turned from yellow to green, and the lights went out. The guards tapped the external monitor off and departed. "You mentioned helicopters. Do you scan the airspace?"

"Yes, although I can't show you that one. Let it suffice to say we can pick up anything from a small remote-controlled drone to a jet. We often pick up hawks or vultures that the system is fairly good at identifying—not perfect but pretty good."

"Defensive measures?"

"I can't discuss those, I'm afraid. Let me say that we've a variety of defensive and offensive means to deal with what comes our way."

"Tell me you can't shoot down a drone or a helicopter?"

"I can't tell you either way. I'll say the airspace within a five-mile radius and up to 10,000 feet is a declared, permanent, prohibited zone with appropriate warnings to violators of our exclusion zone."

Rod checked his watch. "I'm afraid my time is up."

"Let's get you out to the entrance." Captain Tim Sullivan logged off and secured his workstation, stood, and gestured to the door.

The brightness of the hallway lights hurt his eyes, but they adjusted quickly as they walked. As they made their way out of the admin building, the sunlight was even brighter, causing another jolt of pain.

"I hope I was able to give you a good feel for this place," Sullivan said.

"Yes, absolutely . . . in spades. It's an awful lot to absorb."

"Yeah, I felt the same when I reported here for duty. Like I said earlier," Sullivan said, "when new questions arise, just contact me. I'll do my best to answer within our constraints." They stopped at the backside of the guard station and stood in the shade. Rod's ride was not here yet.

"Let me ask you a summary question."

"Sure. Shoot."

"Do you think this place is serving its function?"

Sullivan smiled. "Depends upon your point of view, I suppose. This place wasn't cheap to build. I couldn't show you all of our capabilities, but I think you got a good feel. Just one closing thought, for now, I think most of us truly believe the Black Hole facilities are fulfilling exactly what the state intended in building this place and the others."

"I'd agree." The transport van arrived. "Thank you for spending the time with me. You've answered my questions. I wish you the best of luck, and I can assure you, I'll do my part. I'm a believer."

"Thanks, Rod. Safe journey home."

The two men shook hands. Rod saluted, and Tim returned the salute. The guards let him out the pedestrian gate.

Once they were out of the valley, out of sight of the Black Hole facility, the deputies tried to question Rod about his experience and Black Hole tour. Rod answered a few of the simple, public-type questions but avoided the detail questions. He explained that he was sworn to maintain the secrets of the place—a little of an overstatement but not much over. During most of the drive back into the city, Rod was left with his thoughts. *All in all, that place is much more than I ever imagined. I really need to talk to Raoul Joubert about the legal aspects of the lawyer disclosures. The Black Hole prisons are doing precisely what they were intended to do—permanently remove habitual criminals from society. I'd sure hate to see those places irrevocably altered. Time shall tell the tale.*

—

18

As the appointed invitation time approached, Laura's sense of trepidation grew exponentially. She thought about the pre-meeting telephone call with Karen 'Blondie' Baker two days ago. First and foremost, the meeting was still on. *It would've been so much better if they or she had canceled the meeting, but no such luck. I can't do it now.*

According to Karen's words, her mother, Jean Baker née Turing, was more sympathetic but still against her chosen profession. Her mother did volunteer work with several community agencies—hospital reception, food bank, and church mental health services. Jean was a year younger than her husband and the mother of three grown children—Blondie was the youngest with an older brother and a sister who was the oldest of the siblings. Her father, Jordan 'Jordie' Baker, was 43 years old and the sole owner of a very successful plumbing business—Baker's Plumbing Company. Karen described her father as a strict traditionalist, who tolerated his wife's volunteer work only after the children were grown and out of the nest. Both of her parents were high school graduates but attended no college-level classes.

Karen had told Laura that her mother was amenable to hearing from Laura, but she had to beg her father to listen, to open his mind, and to think about what Laura would tell him. She had also cautioned Laura that her father might storm out, but if he did, she expected him to calm down and return. Karen believed deep down that he wanted to learn, to understand, but his upbringing largely dictated his attitude toward most political or social issues. *I sure hope Blondie hasn't placed too much hope on my ability to educate her father and help him understand our chosen profession.*

The Baker family lived in a gated, upscale neighborhood. Laura pushed the large, blue, access button on the keypad code box at the gate.

Blondie's voice came through the less-than-optimal audio feature. "Is that you, Laura?"

"Yes ma'am."

"Great."

The portal slowly swung open. Laura drove through and stopped just beyond the threshold to observe the gate close behind her. The provided house address was down the third street to the right and the fourth house on the left of the *cul-de-sac* street. She did not have to search for the house numbers. Blondie was standing outside on the front porch dressed in modest khaki, knee-length shorts, and light yellow, feminine blouse. Laura turned around and parked correctly in front of a single-story, well kept, above-average house. The lawn and various hedges, bushes, flowers, and trees were all very well maintained.

Blondie was standing in front of the driver's door when Laura switched off her car and grabbed her small, over-the-shoulder purse. Laura locked her vehicle as a matter of routine. Blondie hugged Laura tightly and whispered in her left ear, "Thank you so much for coming, Laura." Karen kissed Laura on the left cheek and released her. "I hope this goes well, but I'm a realist."

"I don't want you to get your hopes up too much."

"Oh, I won't."

"I should've asked when we talked. So, I don't screw up, how do you want me to refer to you?"

"The whore would be fine." They both laughed hard for quite a long time, playing off each other. Once their laughter began to subside, Blondie answered, "Karen is fine. My parents have never liked my nickname. I've had it since junior high, but they say it reminds them too much of the Blondie comic strip character."

"It matches your hair."

"Always has, but they are what they are, so I try to avoid reminding them. I've no idea whether they know my nickname is my professional name, and I don't want to remind them of that either."

"Understood."

"Anything else before we go inside?"

"Nope. Let's git 'er done." They both giggled at the phrase made popular by Larry the Cable Guy.

The two walked up to the front door. Karen opened and led Laura inside. She turned right, and Laura followed. Jean and Jordan Baker were standing.

"Mom, Dad, I'm honored to introduce my friend Laura Simmons," Karen announced.

They shook hands. Jean offered drinks, although no one accepted the offer. Karen and Laura sat on the couch with their backs to the large window, and Jean and Jordan sat in separate chairs facing the sofa.

"Welcome to our home, Laura," Jean said.

"Thank you.

"Karen tells us you wanted to talk to us."

Laura chuckled nervously. "I'm afraid your daughter may have misstated things a little. These little chats aren't something I enjoy or look forward to in any form. Karen asked me to speak to you about my profession, our," Laura paused to look at and gesture to Karen, "profession." Laura tried not to look at Jordan, but she could not ignore the scowl and lowered chin like a bull ready to charge. "In conversations like this, the risk of TMI—Too Much Information—is quite high. So, perhaps, the best way to approach this is for me to answer any questions you have, anything you wish to discuss. I must say at the outset that I'm very open, not particularly modest, and I'm very proud of what I do for a living. As such, I'll answer whatever questions you wish to ask to the best of my ability. I'd also like to preface this discussion with an acknowledgment that Karen hasn't given me any coaching. She only asked me to talk to you about what I do. That said, I'm ready to answer whatever you wish to know." Jean nodded her head in agreement. Laura glanced at Jordan, who remained inanimate and intimidating, but she returned her focus to Jean.

"I'm a bit nervous about all this, Laura. I'm definitely not comfortable talking about sex, and for most of my life, the profession of sex was prohibited by law. Jordan and I grew up with prostitutes . . . wait . . . I guess the first question is, how do you refer to yourself?"

"Citizen."

Jean giggled very nervously and uncomfortably. "I mean your profession?"

"I'm not particularly attracted to labels or titles. I've been called a lot of things. I'll generally answer to whatever descriptor you choose to use. If you need a label, I suggest prostitute is adequate."

"Disgusting!" Jordan exclaimed. "The Church condemns it no matter what you call it and regardless of these damn liberal laws."

Laura did not take the bait. She smiled at Jean and then looked directly at Jordan. "You're welcome to use whatever label you wish, Mister Baker."

"How about whore or cunt!"

"Daddy!" "Jordan!" Karen and Jean protested simultaneously. Jordan waved his hand dismissively and returned to his silent scowl.

"Your choice, Mister Baker. I'll not object. I've heard those words and worse in my profession. You're entitled to speak your mind . . . as am I."

An awkward silence gripped all four of them. Laura was not going to break that silence. It served no purpose to risk antagonizing him any further.

"Daddy," Karen began, "I want you to listen. Laura has been in the profession longer than I have. She is a consummate professional. What she does has been legal for almost eight years now. You really need to listen if we are to have any hope of repairing our relationship." She paused and stared at her father. He simply nodded his head once. "To get to the point and break the ice crust here, I'll ask, please tell my parents why you do what you do?"

Laura nodded her head and then shrugged her shoulders. "Simply put, I love sex. I truly enjoy the pleasure of it. Even bad sex is good sex to me . . . well, up to a point."

"Is that how you feel?" Jean asked her daughter.

"Yes, for the most part, Mom. I've tried to have this conversation many times, to help you both understand. Laura is highly respected in our profession. I felt she might be better at helping you both since she has no vested interest here."

Jean held Karen's anticipatory eyes. "Sweetie, I know you want us to accept your . . . your . . . your profession, but you're asking us to undo a lifetime of training, education, and indoctrination. The Church is very clear. I . . . we . . . can't see the path to acceptance."

"If I may, Mrs. Baker," Laura interjected and waited for Jean's consenting nod. "First, I laud Karen's initiative. She clearly loves you both, and I know she is trying not to disappoint either of you. She is going the extra mile in her effort to preserve her family. Karen asked me to speak with you to that end. Second, I try very hard to avoid placing myself within relationships of any kind, which makes this meeting very difficult for me. Third, and I say this with the utmost respect for each of you for your religious beliefs, and your personal choices and opinions, but the world and this country are changing. Prostitution has been part of society since recorded history began six millennia ago. I think it safe to say the process has been in demand across all those years and remains in demand today. I make a great living doing what I do. I pay my taxes. I'm saving for retirement. I'm doing all the normal things a professional should do. Lastly, I agreed with Karen's request because I went through the same, shall we say, convulsions with my parents."

"Are you implying that your parents accept your business now?"

Laura smiled and answered, "Well, I can't say they're standing on the corner shouting 'my daughter's a prostitute, and I'm proud of her,' but they have accepted what I've chosen to do. Growing up, they always told me to choose my path to find my happiness in labor. We're not quite to the stage of them asking how my day of work was, but we do talk about elements or aspects, and we joke about things now."

"How did you get to that point?" Jean asked.

"Talking."

"I can't talk," interjected Jordan, "about our daughter, our youngest child, fucking strange men."

"I do women, too," added Karen with some surprising frivolity and flippancy.

"Damn it, Karen," protested Jordan, "this isn't a joke. God sanctified your body to bear children for future generations. You've shit in the temple."

"I'm sorry you feel that way, Daddy," Karen responded with solemnity. "I respect my body, and I think Laura does as well."

"I do."

"But the Bible says it is a sin."

"And Jesus said, 'let he who is without sin cast the first stone,'" said Karen.

"Don't be smart with me, young lady . . . wait, you're not a lady; you're a whore, selling access to your precious body. You're intentionally choosing to sin every single day."

"It's not a sin, Daddy,"

"Yes, it is," objected Jordan strongly, nearly shouting.

"The Bible also says it is a mortal sin to touch a pigskin—a football," Laura added.

Jordon snapped his head to Laura, giving her an icy, angry glare. "You're not going to change my mind. There isn't anything I need to know from a whore," he growled, stood, and stomped out of the room in a huff.

"I apologize for my husband's petulance, Laura. This is a very sensitive issue for him for a host of reasons."

Laura nodded and waved her hand dismissively. "Long journeys begin with small steps. So much of this reaction, at least from my perspective, stems from unquestioning submission to *dicta* derived centuries ago. We could get into the sociological aspects of society's past prohibitions on prostitution, but I'm not sure how productive that would be other than to reminisce about history. The bottom line, it seems to me, is the prohibition of anything, prostitution, drugs, gambling, anything, is not viable in a free society."

"So, is anything permissible then?" Jean asked.

"As long as no one is injured or property damaged, yes, I'd say so. The state hasn't yet gone that far. The legislature has taken a huge step toward that state with the legalization and regulation of prostitution, and now drugs as well."

"Do you take drugs too?"

"Yes, recreationally. I occasionally consume psychotropic substances in my work; rarely otherwise. I do enjoy a glass of wine from time to time."

"Aren't they dangerous?"

"Before legalization, yes. You never knew what was in the stuff—the cutting substances, contaminants, dosage, and such. Since the state started regulating production and sale, the drugs are high quality, consistent, standard dosage, and with defined effects. If you take any of the substances in the recommended dosage, there is minimal risk of overdosing or collateral poisoning. There are, and probably always will be, individuals who take too much for whatever reasons they chose; but that is the point. It is their choice entirely."

"But drugs have been illegal for so long."

"Alcohol was illegal a century ago."

"Good point." Jean lapsed into thought. Neither Karen nor Laura chose to intrude upon her thoughts. "Do you ever run into bad men that you would rather . . . rather . . ."

". . . not service?"

Jean giggled softly. "Yes, that you would rather not service?"

"Yes, it happens, but those men only get one pass. I won't give them another chance. I've run into a few customers who were not respectful. They don't get another opportunity, and I share such information with my colleagues for their protection."

"Is there anything you won't do?" Jean asked.

"Yes. I don't do pain, excrement, and as I mentioned, no disrespect. Sexual pleasure is a great big, beautiful array of sensations, feelings, emotions, and attitudes. I find my profession very rewarding in many ways."

"What if you aren't attracted to the person?"

Laura giggled softly. "Interesting question . . . that has a complex answer. First and foremost, as many athletes claim, performance is so dependent upon attitude. Sex is no different. I know many people are visual; in other words, their involvement and pleasure are directly dependent upon appearance. There are more than a few men who achieve a full erection just seeing an attractive, fully clothed woman . . . or man for those so inclined. To be candid, that is precisely why I work hard to maintain my body and appearance. I'm not one of those. As I mentioned earlier, I can't find much affinity with labels; yet, I acknowledge that descriptors are often useful or effective. When necessary, I identify as pansexual."

"Pan . . . what?" asked Jean.

"Pansexual. It is a descriptive word that means I'm attracted to all genders, all sexual identities . . ."

"All genders?" Jean interjected. "Are there more than two?"

Laura smiled. "This is not a topic most conventional, heterosexual people think about or are even aware of, so quite understandable, Mrs. Baker."

"Please . . . Jean. I'm not much on formality or hierarchy."

Laura nodded her head in acknowledgment. "Most folks believe gender is binary, male or female, penis and testicles or vagina. That simple binary perspective doesn't recognize a spectrum of 'tweeners as I call them: hermaphrodites, ambiguous genitalia, altered genitalia, and even no genitalia. I can't claim to have experienced all possible combinations, but I've enjoyed more than a few. I've been with a few that are regular customers who are 'tweeners. One has a penis and vagina, but no testicles. You might say she just had a large clitoris like some women, but her urethra is part of her penis, not below her clitoris like most women. Anyway, my point is I could not care less what any one customer has between her or his legs. I'm far more attracted to a positive attitude regardless of how they're equipped or the package they come in for our playtime. To me, attitude is everything. People of any gender or sexual identity who don't believe in themselves, who are self-conscious about their bodies, are an instant turn off for me."

"I see," Jean said and lapsed into her thoughts. "What about diseases? We've always been taught that prostitutes are prone to sexually transmitted infections."

"Another conservative myth that is simply not true. STDs are always a risk, but so is influenza or the common cold—the rhinovirus. When the state legalized and regulated prostitution a few years back, prostitutes like me came out of the dark. Prostitutes don't create or generate any disease. Infections do happen, just like they happen with all human beings. From my perspective and from my colleagues to the best of my knowledge, our regular medical check-ups catch infections earlier, and contact tracing as they use with influenza outbreaks are very effective in stopping infections."

"Have you had an STD? What about HIV-AIDS?"

"Yes. I have. Once. It came from an out-of-state trucker. I was treated quickly and effectively. They also found that trucker and treated him effectively, so I was told. My medical certificate is current, as of last week, and I remain in good health. I'm happy. I enjoy my work, and I make a very good living doing what I do.

"Oh, you also asked about HIV. The risk today is not what it was in the 1980s when we didn't know much about it. Centuries ago, syphilis was a death sentence, just like HIV was in the 1980s. A century ago, Spanish flu and the 1918 pandemic killed millions worldwide. We've dealt with swine flu, avian flu, and the coronavirus pandemics. HIV was no different in a general sense. We've effective treatments. Broad screening and contact tracing have dramatically reduced infections and transmissivity. What I've learned from all this is, the best approach to dealing with diseases is illumination; knowledge is better than ignorance. HIV spread undetected within the male homosexual community that had been kept in the dark for so long and is not significantly different from how prostitutes were treated in those days."

Jean Baker shook her head. "This is so much to absorb and reconcile. We fear for our youngest daughter's safety, for her acceptance in what is predominantly our conservative society. There is so damn much I don't understand. We just want her to be safe, happy, and successful."

"I've not had children, but I do believe all parents, no matter what your nationality, religion, language, education, or such, want the same thing for their children. It is natural and normal."

Jordan Baker walked back into their living room and asked before he sat down, "What is natural and normal? Certainly not prostitution."

Laura ignored the gibe and considered whether or how to respond. Mister Baker's expression was demonstrably different. *What transformed his mental and emotional state?*

Jean beat her to a response. "Parents want their children to be safe and happy, to have a better life than they had."

"I'd agree with that," Jordan said. "Where this discussion goes sideways is prostitution can't possibly be a part of that happiness."

"Why not, Daddy?"

"Because it is wrong and a . . . ," he stopped and took in a deep cleansing breath, and then slowly and audibly let it out. "I'm trying to understand." Jordan looked directly at Laura. "I apologize for my hostility regarding your chosen profession, Miz Simmons. I just hold this mortal fear my . . . our youngest daughter is running full speed into the abyss."

"Answer my question, Daddy," Karen demanded.

Jordan turned his gaze on his daughter. "To be blunt, I grew up with the knowledge, some might call it parochial indoctrination, that prostitutes, addicts, homosexuals, and other aberrant behaviors don't conform with society's standards of normality."

"The world is changing," added Karen calmly.

"Not to my liking," answered Jordan.

"So, freedom of choice only applies to choices that you and others decide are acceptable. That hardly sounds like freedom."

"There must be standards. Morality is vital to a healthy society."

"What you seem to be missing, Jordie," said Jean, "is morality is what we do when no one is watching. Morality is very personal."

Jordan waved his right hand like he was shooing a fly. "What good does prostitution do for society?"

"Well . . ."

"Let me answer that one, Laura," Jean interrupted forcefully. "Just in the short time Laura has bravely spent with us, I've learned a lot. She's a knowledgeable, articulate, caring woman. I'd say she has educated me, and I surmise she's educated many more around us."

Jordan's angry expression returned. "Surely, you've not changed your commitments to God's teaching."

"Don't do that, Jordie," Jean admonished her husband. "The Church and religion in the main haven't been and aren't flawless. They're human beings—flawed human beings like all the rest of us. They're not God. Just a few centuries ago, the Church tortured innocent people and burned others at the stake simply because they weren't believers or didn't believe as the Church wanted them to believe. Just a mere few decades ago, the Church prohibited the use of birth control measures or even teaching girls about their menstrual cycle and fertility. There are many reasons the Church chose to do what it did in the past, but even the Church is changing. Jesus taught us to love our fellow man. We've struggled with accepting that lesson." Jean leaned forward, resting her elbows on her knees, and looked directly at Karen. "I'd like to hear your answer to your father's question."

"I will try."

"Don't try, do!" Jordan chided.

"You've always said that. I respect Laura. Many others respect her as well. But, I'm not as experienced or polished as her. To me, we provide a service that many people demand. The law says it is legal."

"The law is wrong," Jordan interjected.

"Why? Why do you say that Daddy?"

"There is . . . there are genuine reasons the law was the law, and now this liberal legislature has thrown it all away."

"We could argue that point all day long," Jean said. "You're entitled to your opinions, Jordie. It seems that if you were to have your way, we would never improve. We would always just stay as we are at any particular moment."

"It's not that way at all," Jordan protested.

"It sure seems so," Jean mumbled.

"Let's go back to the question. If we assume for the moment that prostitution is an improvement, as you suggest, what good does it do for society?"

All three of the Bakers looked at Laura. "The answer depends upon your perspective." Laura picked up the lance. "For example, if you believe that sex is only for procreation in a monogamous for life, heterosexual marriage, then prostitution serves no purpose whatsoever."

"What's wrong with that?" Jordan asked.

"Nothing, but that is your choice," responded Laura. "I certainly believe you've every right to make that choice with your partner for your family. However, I must ask, what gives you the right to impose your choices on everyone else?"

Jordan jumped to his feet as if he was going to storm out, again, but this time he huffed and puffed, pacing back and forth behind his chair. The three women watched him for what seemed like several minutes. He eventually stopped and placed his hands on the back of his chair. "You still haven't answered my question. I haven't seen or heard a reason for changing the laws."

"Let me try this, and I hope this is not too graphic," Laura began. "A few nights ago, I worked a party hosted by a small group of lawyers. They're swingers. I'd done that group a handful of times."

"Swingers?" Jean asked.

"It's a name adopted by people who enjoy sex for pleasure and share within the group."

"Share?"

"Yes. They're broadly married couples who enjoy sex with others in many forms outside their marriages."

"Oh!"

"This particular group usually engages prostitutes like me from time to time for new sensations, new pleasures. One of the invitees at that party was a lawyer on my no-fly list," Laura said, and quickly glanced at Karen and winked. "The point is, there are many productive citizens in good standing who don't subscribe to the monogamous-for-life, heterosexual, sex-for-procreation-only standard enforced by socially conservative citizens and believers."

"They should," Jordan said forcefully.

Laura giggled softly and smiled. "Of course, that's your opinion. That's the choice you and Jean decided was best for you."

"We didn't decide," Jean exclaimed with emphasis on the verb. "We never discussed such things. We just accepted that standard because that was the way it was. There is so much about life that we just never knew. No one ever talked to us. We never talked about such things."

"Exactly my point, Jean," Laura said. "Ignorance was the norm back in those days. Society is learning about homosexuality, about transsexuals, about alternative lifestyles, and so much more."

"Maybe ignorance is better," Jordan said rather meekly.

"No, it's not, Jordie! Ignorance is never, ever better. The doctors like to tell us about informed consent. We should have informed consent for everything—all the morality issues like gambling, birth control, drugs, prostitution, *et al.* Maybe, just maybe, Laura and our youngest daughter are in the vanguard of that societal change. Perhaps, we should be talking to our daughter about her happiness, rather than trying to impose our constraints on her."

"Jean, surely you can't be serious. You're giving up so easily."

"Yes, Jordie, I'm deadly serious. Well, that may not be the best choice of adjective, but that is how I feel."

All four of them remained silent for several minutes, confined to their thoughts and feelings. Laura knew she could not speak, although she had more, she wanted to say. This was not her forum. She was a guest and had been invited into their home to answer questions. They all waited.

Jordan was the first to speak. "If I may," he said with a normal conversational tone, "you're espousing a universal, anything-goes policy to public behavior."

"I wouldn't say that," Laura responded.

"Then, how would you say it?"

"We needed a different approach than prohibition to morality issues. We learned that lesson a hundred years ago with alcohol, and to a certain degree with tobacco, but we failed, until recently, to learn that lesson with drugs and prostitution. Prohibition is rarely an effective choice in a free society, but prohibition is the antithesis of freedom—the government dictates behavior to the people. The changes in the law, at least within this state, recognize our freedom of choice, for both customers and providers, and takes a more informed path to deal with societal risks. To be brutally blunt, just a couple of decades ago, any bodily penetration other than vaginal was considered by law to be sodomy—a serious felonious crime. Masturbation was considered a sin against God. We were taught that smoking one joint led automatically to harder drugs and addiction—a so-called gateway drug. We were told by Congress that there was no societal value to drugs like marijuana, cocaine, or heroin. It was all false, all based on seriously erroneous assumptions. What Congress reacted to was the symptoms or consequences of abuse. Yes, there were bad aspects. The same was true of prostitution. Through education and experience, we've seen substantial value, at least to some folks. The state now regulates the quality of all psychotropic substances . . ."

"Sorry," Jean interrupted, "my ignorance is showing again. I'm not familiar with the term—psycho-something. What is that?"

"It's the word the scientists apply to an array of substances that affect mental activity, behavior, emotions, or perception, like mood-altering drugs." Jean nodded her head somewhat tentatively. Laura chose not to delve deeper into the definition. "Anyway, we've found that many of the problems were a direct result of contaminants used in diluting the psychoactive material or taking too much. Case in point, methamphetamine has been used successfully for many years when used properly with the correct dosage; and yet, we have seen very erratic, often violent, behavior when an individual took too much, usually without knowing. We use derivatives of opium to this very day to treat pain successfully. None of those drugs become addictive until they're abused—too much for too long. I've tried just about all of the stuff on the approved list at one time or another, since legalization and regulation, and I'm not addicted to anything . . . well, except pleasure, perhaps." Everyone chuckled, even Jordan Baker. "What we've witnessed and are living today is the value of education and informed consent. From my perspective, all of these morality issues—gambling, drugs, prostitution, abortion, alcohol, tobacco, and so many more—should be dealt with in the same manner—education, knowledge, and respect."

"Are you telling me you've taken heroin and cocaine, and stuff like that?" Jordan asked.

"Yes."

"Damn, this is crazy."

"Why so, Mister Baker?"

"They're dangerous drugs. They lead to addiction and dependence."

"I'm testament to the fallacy of your statement. I don't take heroin often, just on occasions when I just want to zone out. I don't take it regularly, maybe a couple of times a year. Perhaps, I'm the exception, but I don't think so. Others in my profession have used those drugs. I don't know anyone who is addicted—a steady, regular consumer. A very good friend of mine, from elementary school, checked into one of the indulgence camps, more to escape than anything else. She has access to all the drugs she wants with no cost other than the rules of the camp. To my knowledge, she's not addicted to anything, other than perhaps the peace she feels at that place."

"I've heard of those places on the news," commented Jean.

"This is all knowledge, information to help us better understand. The government has reported significant drops in overdoses, in crime, in death, in addiction, in just about every aspect of our society. We're much better off respecting freedom of choice. It's who we are as a people, as a society. The same is true in my profession. It's much harder for bad people to traffic in children. We see far less violence and crime that used to be associated with the criminal subculture that fed off illegal prostitution. I've only been in the business since about the time the law changed, but one of my friends, who's still in the business, began 20 years before the law changed. She's the one who should be talking to you. She knows firsthand what it was like before the law changed. There is no question we're all better off—less disease, less violence, less abuse, less crime, every metric I can think of to measure." Laura paused and looked at Karen. "Your daughter is trying a profession she thinks is right for her. From talking with her, I'm not sure she's convinced that it's right for her, but there's no doubt that it's her free choice. No one is pressuring her. She's new and still learning, but I must say she has a great attitude. Whether she stays in the profession and makes a career of it will and should depend upon her experiences and choices."

"Do you agree with that?" Jordan asked his daughter.

"Yes, Daddy, I do. Laura says it far better than me, but that's how I feel."

Jordan shook his head, perhaps more in disappointment than rejection. He looked back at Laura. "Where do you draw the line? We've all heard what I'd call horror stories of prostitutes being made to do unspeakable things. Where do you draw the line?"

"In today's world, prostitution is no different from the law, medicine, a pilot, or a shop keeper. They retain the right to refuse service."

"She's exactly right," Karen interjected. "I was one of the women working that party Laura mentioned earlier. I wound up doing the guy Laura mentioned who was on her no-fly list, as she calls it. I learned. I'll not be doing him ever again."

"What did he do?" Jean asked. "What made you feel that way?"

Karen glanced at Laura and smiled. "Let's just say he's not gentle."

"Oh, Karen," Jean exclaimed.

"No, no, Momma, no need to worry or fret. He didn't hurt me in any way. He broke no laws that I'm aware of that night."

"That man is a lawyer, a powerful lawyer," Laura added. "He's also the husband of my friend, who is in an indulgence camp."

"Maybe he deserves a little of his own medicine," suggested Jordan.

"Now, Jordie, don't go all macho on us," Jean admonished.

"As Karen accurately stated, I do believe, he broke no laws. He's done nothing wrong. From my perspective, he just doesn't know how to be respectful, or perhaps he never learned to respect women."

"And he's a lawyer, you say."

"Yes, but that doesn't make him better or worse, just not acceptable to me . . . and now to Karen. That said, I wanted to finish answering your question. Each of us must establish our boundaries, what matters to us. I'm quite comfortable with my boundaries, and I enforce them—my no-fly list. Once burned, shame on them; twice burned, shame on me. Now, today, I've the law on my side, and most bad guys know that fact. In my years in the profession, I've only had to report two men—both for assault and battery. And the important fact is, the law prosecuted and punished those men for their crimes. I've not had to do that in many years, and it seems to be happening less these days. So, hopefully, Karen doesn't have to experience that extreme, but it should be encouraging to her and presumably to you as her parents that those days are largely behind us."

"Aren't there women who like it rough?" Jordan asked.

"Yes, the older gal I mentioned is one of those . . . her specialty, actually. She's been at it for nearly 30 years, so she clearly enjoys what she does. It's just not for me."

"Nor me," added Karen.

Jordan Baker smiled at his daughter. "Like I said, I've learned a lot. Thank you, Laura, for taking the time with us . . . and being patient with my obstinance." He looked at Karen and held her eyes for several seconds before he spoke. "Are you really happy doing this? I mean, after all, it's not something you learned from us, or we even discussed."

"Yes, I am. Laura's perception as she stated it was correct; I'm not sure I want to do this for the rest of my life, but I'm enjoying what I'm doing now."

Jordan stood, extended his arms, and went to his daughter. They embraced and held each other. Karen nodded her head several times, so her father was apparently whispering words to her. Tears were easily discernible streaming down her cheeks. She nodded her head several times, while still nuzzled into her father's shoulder. Jordan drew back just enough to kiss his daughter's cheek and wipe away the tears.

When Jordan and Karen finally declutched, Jean stood and embraced her daughter. Jordan extended his right hand to Laura, who rose to shake his proffered right hand.

"Thank you again for your time and patience."

"You're most welcome, Mister Baker."

"Jordan or Jordie, please, Laura. You've earned it."

"Thank you, Jordan."

The Bakers invited Laura to stay for dinner, but she had clients scheduled for the evening. They offered a raincheck at her convenience that Laura accepted. *I don't know when or if I'll ever use the raincheck, but the gesture is certainly appreciated.*

Karen walked Laura outside to her car. They stopped at the sidewalk adjacent to the residential street. "I can't thank you enough, Laura," Karen said. "I really never thought my father would come around, but you helped him make a start of it."

"I noticed tears in your eyes when he hugged you."

"Yeah, definitely brought tears to my eyes. He told me he loved me. He promised to work on being proud of me, but he loved me. He also said he'd respect my choices as long as I'm happy doing what I'm doing."

"Sounds like a big step forward."

Karen laughed hard. "You've no idea. Before this afternoon, I believed I was on the verge of losing my parents forever. It was heartbreaking. Not so much my mother, but she was following him. Knowing them, I'll betcha they're talking about all this right now, and that's a very good thing. I think it safe to say you've changed my life, although that was probably not your intent."

"No, it was definitely not my intent. I was really reluctant to do this. I hate getting into the middle of anyone else's relationships, especially families. But I felt I could help, and I do believe what I said this afternoon."

"Yeah, you can tell. I'll probably find out more as I talk with my parents, but at first blush, I think that's probably what swayed my father. I imagine he could sense your sincerity and commitment despite his antics." They laughed together. Karen extended her arms, and they hugged for several seconds. Karen released Laura. She reached and grasped Laura's head, and then she kissed Laura. Just a peck at first, and then she kissed her passionately. Laura returned the passion. When she stopped, Karen continued holding the sides of Laura's head and said, "You're an extraordinary woman. I can't possibly repay you for what you've done this afternoon. I can only hope we become fast friends for life, Laura. You're so special," she repeated.

"Well, that was quite a display of gratitude."

"Justly deserved."

They hugged and kissed again. Laura got into her car, buckled her seatbelt, started the engine, and waved good-bye to Karen. *That was sure an interesting afternoon*, Laura thought as she drove away. Her thoughts lingered longer than expected, as she struggled to shift gears and get her mind on her upcoming work. She had plenty of time to get ready. For this night's work, she needed to get in the mood and mindset to perform appropriately. Laura was confident she would get there, but the words of the afternoon kept coming back to her. *That felt good, but it's not something I want to do on a regular basis.*

—

19

The previous two days loomed like dark storm clouds over Rod's thoughts, so much so, that for the first time in his life, before or after marriage, he was not eager to arrive at home. Marci was not perfect, but neither was he. Rod always considered himself a realist—a pragmatic realist, which made his job easier to tolerate. But his self-image was being utterly tested. The very nature of his post-military profession brought him into direct, often intimate, contact with the dregs of society. Over his years of service, Rod felt his home was a sanctuary—a place of rest and disengagement. He rarely saw the good in humanity in his line of work, so he relished his time with his wife and daughter. Yet, this serious dust-up with Marci sprang from a conversation between Marci and Bella before Rod arrived home from duty two days ago. He had spent the last two nights on the couch, so he had not had a good night's sleep since this whole flare-up had begun. Rod knew Bella was growing up fast, too fast for his liking, but he wrote that off as common father-daughter tension. He had always seen her as intelligent, insightful, broadly aware of society, custom, and history, but his view of their daughter had been under significant challenge since her arrest months ago.

The conversation in question turned out to be a calculated tactic by Bella Joy to align her mother and achieve the immediate objective she sought. Two days ago, Bella asked her mother for parental consent to enter Indulgence Camp Number 12. She apparently held little hope of convincing her father. Although Rod strongly disagreed with and disapproved of Bella's foolish request, oddly, he respected the judgment and perception of the inherent divide between her parents. To her credit, Marci was not supportive or in favor of their daughter's request from a personal perspective, but she took a more matter-of-fact assessment.

The mood in the Ramirez household had been decidedly chilly since their blow-up argument that night two days ago. Rod had not been able to talk to either his wife or their daughter. The anger and sense of betrayal he felt were not subsiding. Rod regretted even saying he would consider such a move when Bella first brought it up months ago. He wanted to believe in their daughter, but his primal fear overrode everything else. He truly feared what might happen should Bella cross that bridge.

Rod stopped his unmarked department automobile at the last corner. He stared at the modest but beautiful house. He smiled briefly, but then the darkness returned. Rod hated, truly hated, the dark thoughts and that dread dominated his thoughts. He knew down to his bones that Bella's request was wrong in every possible aspect, and he felt impotent to impress upon their daughter and her accomplice, her mother, that IC12 was intended for hardcore addicts, not for some teenage experimentation. Bella had never been abused. She had no underlying reason to seek oblivion, even temporarily. Even worse, why had Marci sided with Bella and rejected his arguments? The situation remained baffling to him.

Rod took in a deep cleansing breath and slowly exhaled, and then said aloud to himself, "Best get on with it. Nothing is going to change out here."

He drove up to the driveway and backed into the drive, just in case he needed to leave in a hurry, not so much from the dark storm clouds, but if the department called him out with an urgent situation, he might have to leave quickly. Rod used his pocket fob to open the garage door. As he walked into the kitchen, the most distinctive sense was the lack of any smells of Marci's cooking. The kitchen table was clear, with only a vase of not so fresh flowers in the center. He looked around. Marci was leaning against the counter next to the sink with her arms folded across her chest. She held a rather stern expression. They stood staring silently at each other for several seconds, then Marci unfolded her arms and pointed to the living room. Rod knew what she intended, and he was not eager for this conversation, but he knew it had to happen.

Rod jumped in first. "Where's Bella?"

"In her room."

"So, no supper tonight?"

"You can make whatever you want after we're done, but no, I've not made dinner tonight. I've had enough of this icy silence and separation. We're going to sit here and starve until we get this resolved in one way or another." Rod nodded his head acquiescently and without words. They sat across from each other. "Have you had any change of heart?"

"No."

"Then, we're going to proceed without you."

"Why, Marci? Why?"

"We taught our daughter to think for herself, to weigh her options and risks. She's done what we taught her to do. I've talked to her numerous times since this all began. I know she is sincere, and to the best of my limited knowledge, she knows exactly what she's doing."

"She doesn't, Marci, and neither do you. IC12 is not some spa or vacation resort. It's a serious place for addicts who can't control their urges. The state created those camps to get addicts off the street and reduce crime. They're rather stark places with the barest of essentials."

"She knows that."

"How? How on God's little green earth could she possibly know?"

"She's afraid to talk to you, Rodrigo. You've made her afraid."

"I want her to be fearful of things. There are many things in life to be fearful of around us. Our daughter seems to have developed an unexplainable attraction or fascination with these drugs. Addiction is not some game or youthful challenge. Help me understand. Help me understand why she's so determined to do this? Perhaps, we've been too lenient and accommodating to her whims, Marci. We've bent over backward to feed her curiosity, but this is one of those things that could easily and irreparably alter her life. If she does this, she could very well be closing many doors of opportunity for the future and her entire life. To me, this is no different from her wanting to jump off a cliff to see what it feels like to hit bottom. She is asking us to stand by and watch her jump."

"You can't be serious, Rodrigo."

"I'm deadly serious, Marcella Christina Velazquez."

"So now we're not even married!" Marci protested.

"Don't do that," objected Rod, as he held up his left ring finger to display the wedding band he had worn since their wedding day. "We've given in to her every whim. We agreed to let her experiment with drugs and fornicate in our home, but that's not lenient or progressive enough for her. Where do we draw the line, Marci? We clearly have allowed her to go too far."

"She's nearly an adult."

"She's not quite sixteen freakin' years old, Marci. She apparently thinks she's already an adult and able to make adult decisions, but she's not. She's still a minor under the law, and that will be true no matter how lenient we are or become. She's only finished nearly two years of high school. She still has two years to go, set aside college, professional training, whatever she decides to do with her life. Going to an indulgence camp is not the way to go. This is us watching her jump off the cliff. Are you happy with that? She might survive; she might not. Are you happy watching our daughter risk the rest of her life like this?"

"This isn't what I wanted for her either, Rodrigo. I've tried to deflect her . . . I have. But she's very determined."

"I'm determined, too. I'm determined as hell not to stand by and watch our daughter commit suicide. These drugs are not playthings for children to dabble with, Marci. They're dangerous substances."

"Being melodramatic in this discussion isn't helpful."

"Melodramatic!" Rod shouted, nearly screamed.

"You've told us," Marci responded as calmly as she could, "that the changes in the drug laws were intended to reduce the risk of overdosing, of becoming addicted, of being poisoned by collateral substances. You've told us the government sought to reduce the risk of injury or addiction."

"Yes, I have. That's my understanding."

"Then shouldn't we believe."

"Marci, please," Rod said with his hands clasped together in front of him, as if in prayer. "She's fifteen years old. She's not 25. You know, just yesterday, we arrested a girl Bella's age. She was jacked up on meth and was caught stealing a bunch of candy from Walgreens that she intended to sell to other kids to buy drugs. Worse, she wasn't buying the legal, controlled version. She was buying the illegal stuff. Fifteen years old! I interviewed her more out of curiosity since this was the day after our argument. She was like a caged and wounded animal chained to the interrogation room table. She had never heard of the indulgence camps or the changes in drug laws. She started using after the SCIP Act took effect. She was ignorant, and she was deeply addicted. She was going through withdrawal in that room as I was talking to her. She would've done anything to get just one more fix, and I do mean anything. She literally offered to give me a blowjob right there in the room if I'd just give her one more fix. It was tragic, Marci. Fifteen years old! I tried but couldn't determine how she got that bad, but I imagine her parents had a lot to do with it—both are criminals, the mother is a junkie as well. No matter how hard the state tries to reduce the death and destruction of drug abuse, we still see cases like this girl. Much less than we used to, but still, one case like this one is too many. We can't allow our daughter to be just another statistic of failure."

Tears descended Marci's cheeks. She could only stare at her husband. With shaky, stammering words, Marci said, "I could not forgive myself if something like that happened to Bella."

"Then, we must say no. Bella can't get in that place without parental or custodial guardian consent."

"What about the arrested girl?"

"What about her?"

"What's going to happen to her?"

"Her case is made worse by the reality that we've been unable to find her parents, either one of them. I've not talked to the DA, yet, so I don't know what they intend to do. In other similar cases involving minor children, the parents authorized admission to the indulgence camp. In this instance, the DA might seek state guardianship by abandonment, and the guardian will likely authorize her admission. This girl, although way too young for this kind of thing, is what the indulgence camps were built for in all this. That girl is dreadfully close to far more serious crimes to feed her habit. When I informed her of what the indulgence camp was, she was perceptive enough to recognize what it meant to her. Whether she can be saved is anybody's guess."

"That's tragic, Rod."

"Yes, it is, and that's exactly the path our daughter is running headlong down . . . running, Marci. Our permissiveness is not good enough for her. She wants unfettered access to these drugs without condition or constraint."

"I don't think it's that bad, Rod. I don't think she's seeking addiction. She's seeking knowledge. There still is no science to answer her questions. I'm afraid of what she might do if we don't recognize her curiosity. I fear that threshold is closer than we think, closer than Bella is aware of or capable of appreciating."

"Exactly!"

"Something is driving her," Marci said.

"Bella needs to understand that force. As parents of a minor child under the law, we must also understand, and up to this point, I do NOT understand. I can't and won't consent to her admission without understanding what we're doing."

Marci stared at Rod. She appeared to be contemplating how she wanted to say what she wanted to say. "This discussion is between you and me," Marci said. "As I told you two nights ago, she's convinced me, and the form says parental consent singular, not plural."

"You would really do that?"

"Let me put it very simply, directly and plainly. I'm far more concerned about my relationship, our relationship with her than I am about our marriage. I'm worried about losing her. I'm not worried about losing you."

"Really? Perhaps you should be."

"Rod!" Marci protested.

"The cliff is right there, Marci. How far are we going to allow our daughter to go down that dangerous path."

"You're sending enormously conflicting messages. On the one hand, you talk about danger and death, and on the other hand, you claim the indulgence camps are supposed to make us safer. What am I supposed to believe?"

"The changes in the drug laws were intended to deal with a broad, general problem that has plagued our society for decades. The law wasn't intended to deal with our daughter. That responsibility belongs to us and us alone."

"This is all so confusing."

"One more thing, IC12 might not accept our daughter, even if we do consent to her entry."

"I hadn't thought of that. I thought you said they accepted anyone in need."

"I did say that, but there have been abuses, and the entry requirements have applied screening rules. To my knowledge, they don't have a children's facility or section, but they do accept qualified minor children. There must be some layered threshold for acceptance. In essence, there are older teenage children who are treated as adults in the camp. Unfortunately, there are more than a few teenage addicts. At 15 plus years of age, I think Bella is in the window, but that does not make it right for her. There is no guarantee she'd be accepted even if we both authorize her admission."

"She might well press this until she can be admitted without our consent," Marci added.

"Why? What on earth is driving her to take this risk? I've seen no signs of addiction in her. From my perspective, she's curious and wants to learn more, so she figured she would immerse herself in consumption and experimentation."

"So, you're prepared to accept the risk of forcing her to become that girl arrested yesterday?"

"Hell no! I want to stop her."

"What are you prepared to do, lock her up until she is 18?"

"Marci, you're being ridiculous."

"No more so than you are, Rodrigo. One more time, I'm compelled to state emphatically that I'd prefer she left this phase of her life behind her, that she found some other focus for her curiosity. I've tried to coax her to change from the path she's on, but I don't see this as demonstrably different from allowing her to date, or obtain a driver's license, or engage in unprotected sex. She is a woman biologically. She is also intelligent, articulate, perceptive, and inquisitive. Bella's exploring the world around her. She's exposed to pornography, to morally challenging behavior, to all sorts of difficult matters. She's learning to evaluate and decide. There comes the point that we must trust her to make the correct decision for herself . . . as we've taught her to do."

"We didn't teach her to become an addict."

"No, we didn't. The difference here is that I respect our daughter's strength of character. I've talked with her many times since her arrest. I'm convinced she knows what she's dealing with in this issue. She's not ignorant or jumping blindly. She knows what she is doing and wants to do. She knows more than we do about some of these things. She's got firsthand experience. We don't. We've got to give her credit here, Rod. She's an intelligent, perceptive, and inquisitive young woman who's driven to learn more, to educate herself beyond schoolwork. We've got to learn to respect her individuality. We've got to trust her, Rod."

"What is that exactly, Marci? What is her objective? What is she trying to accomplish?"

"Maybe you should talk to her, Rod. I have!"

"Fine. Let's get her out here."

Marci gestured with her head toward Bella's room. Rod stared at Marci for several seconds, as if to assess her sincerity. He nodded his head and stood. Marci tracked him with her eyes but offered no further indications. Rod walked down the hallway. Bella's room door was closed. He knocked but got no response. He knocked again and said, "Bella, may I come in?" No response. He slowly turned the door handle and opened the door. Bella sat at her small desk with her full headphones on and concentrating on her laptop. Rod touched her on the shoulder, startling her to such an extent that she nearly fell off her chair.

Bella ripped off her headphones. "You scared me, Dad!"

"Sorry. I knocked, but you couldn't hear me. Mom and I would like to talk to you in the living room."

"What about?"

"I think you know perfectly well, so please join us in the living room." Rod did not wait for a response and returned to Marci. He sat, and they waited.

"Is she coming?" asked Marci with some impatience.

Rod barely had time to nod his head when Bella appeared.

"Where do you want me?" Bella asked.

"Wherever you want," Rod responded quickly, "in this room." Bella giggled, but neither Marci nor Rod did so. She chose a single chair separate from Marci and Rod.

"What's up?"

"You tell us," Rod said.

Bella looked directly and intently at her father. "Have you talked to Mom?"

"Bella Joy, this isn't some video game or school play. This is life. You know damn well I've been talking to Mom."

"Rodrigo!" Marci protested.

Rod nodded his head. "Your mother and I have been at odds since your little request. We're trying to reconnect and get back to normal, but you're in the middle of this. You've seriously divided your mother and me for the first time since we've known each other."

"That was not my intention, Dad."

"Then what was your intention?"

"I need to explore that option."

"Do you need to explore death and rape."

"Dad, that's not fair."

"Life is not fair. There are many things that I think would be interesting to explore, but the risks are too great."

"Like what?"

"This conversation is not about me, Bella Joy. It's all about you and your choices. Let's stick to the topic."

"Like what?" Bella repeated and ignored her father's direction.

Rod glanced at Marci and got a 'well' expression on her face. He shook his head. "Like climbing Mount Everest, or going to the South Pole, or venturing to the moon. There are tons of things I'd like to do but never will because the risk vastly outweighs the reward."

"So, you're telling me the indulgence camp is riskier than climbing Mount Everest?"

"No, I'm not, but the indulgence camp is not without risk."

"Dad, from my perspective, I think you're mixing the way drugs used to be with the way drugs are today."

"Perhaps. I grew up with public, general condemnation of drugs, and incessant stories of death and destruction induced by illegal drugs."

"You've also told us," she said, glancing at her mother, "that the changes in the law were making our community safer, including for addicts."

"Is that your aspiration, Bella Joy? Do you want to become an addict?"

"Daddy!" protested Bella. "Of course not."

"Then why are you hell-bent on taking this risk?"

"I don't know. I just do."

"That's not good enough, Bella. Whether you like it or not, you're still a minor child under the law, which means we, your Mom and I, are responsible for your actions. You've apparently convinced your mother, but you've not convinced me."

"I don't need you . . ."

"Oh, that's rich, Bella Joy. I didn't birth you, but I was an essential contributor to your very existence. You don't need me? Really?"

"If you hadn't interrupted me, I was going to add that I only need Mom's signature. I only need one parent to approve entry, not two."

"That statement hardly alters anything. What you're also saying is you're apparently comfortable dividing Mom and me, pitting us against each other. Is this really how you want it?"

"No, Daddy, that's not how I want it. I'd prefer us to be together as we always have been, but you're the one who refuses to be with us for some old-time, long gone reason."

Rod thought about Bella's pronouncement. His daughter just stared at him. He decided to take a different tack. "Do you see or feel any risk in playing with these drugs?"

"Yes, I do. There's risk in everything we do . . . driving a car, walking down the street, going to school, everything. From everything I have learned, the risks of these drugs aren't what they used to be when they were illegal. Am I wrong?"

Rod opened his mouth and started to respond but stopped before a word came out. He thought carefully, exactly how he wanted to answer his daughter's challenge. "Bella, none of us can predict how anyone is going to react to any one or combination of the designated substances. I freely admit that my opinions regarding you specifically are colored by my life experience. Yes, the new laws are making our communities safer. The drugs themselves are safer, but they can be easily abused, leading to addiction.

"That said," Rod continued, "neither of us," gesturing to Marci, "have veto authority. I won't stand in the way of you doing what you think is best for you," Rod paused and held Bella's eyes. "However, if you've any respect for me as your father, you'll help me understand what you're trying to accomplish. Just because you can do something doesn't mean you should do that thing. I've every right to try or consume any of the designated substances legally, but I see no reason to do so. That observation returns me to my earlier question, Bella Joy. Why? What are you trying to accomplish? Why is this important to your growing into useful adulthood? I see this fascination you apparently have with drugs has no way forward to productive citizenship. Our job as parents is to teach you, to help you grow into being a productive, contributive citizen. I see this moment in your growth as verging upon failure. I can't see the way forward for you. These drugs are a dead end. So, I return to that one simple question, why?"

"I just want to try it," Bella said.

"Not good enough. Why? What purpose does this fascination of yours serve?"

"I don't know, Papa. It's just something I need to do."

"Bella Joy, you've got to search your thoughts, your feelings, your opinions, whatever it is that has you focused on entering an indulgence camp. You know, I suspect there are many parents out there who'd look upon what we've done with you so far as coddling you, pampering you, as giving into your youthful whims, and very wrong from the get-go. They'd quite likely accuse us of being too lenient, too permissive with you, to being delinquent parents. We've allowed you to experiment here at home where we can help you, if necessary. We've given into your curiosity. You've yet to help us understand why we should give in to your curiosity again. What is different? What do you see as available in the indulgence camp that you don't have here? Why Bella . . . why?'

"You're not there!"

Rod took the slap in the face and tried hard to hide his shock. He opened his mouth to speak several times, but he couldn't make any words come out. Rod struggled to conceal the sharp pain he felt. He also looked to Marci with a quizzical expression, as if asking her to help. She only shook her head ever so slightly. Rod was used to combative responses from suspects under interrogation. He was usually very quick with his response, but he instinctively knew his daughter wasn't a suspect under interrogation.

Bella must have sensed the wounding of her words. She stood, circled her chair, and sat back down. "Mom, Dad," she began looking at both of them, "I love you both. I recognize and acknowledge all you've done for me, to teach me. I'm a very lucky girl to have you as parents. I know you've tried very hard to teach me, to help me understand things in life. I believe I understand better than you give me credit for here. Neither of you have been exposed to what is around us all the time these days. You didn't grow up with these things."

Rod leaned forward and started to respond, but he held up when Marci shook her head and nodded toward Bella. She was signaling him to listen.

"You're judging me by the only means your experience gives you. I feel like you see me in those terms. I think the term was once a junkie, always a junkie. I'm not a junkie or an addict. My generation sees these substances as not particularly different from alcohol or tobacco. You've allowed me to have wine or beer when you do, but I don't partake all the time. I don't hit the liquor cabinet when you're not home, although I could easily do so. As I understand what you've told me and what I've learned, you believe the designated substances, as you call them, are worthless—a dead-end road, as you say. I believe you feel there is no useful purpose, and one thing leads to another. I think there is too much evidence that says such thinking is not accurate. History tells us that the law classified marijuana, meaning everything, THC, CBD, and all of its component derivatives, as a gateway drug and of no value. I don't know who determined that, but it's in the congressional record, and it's clearly false. Those old laws were based on a lie, perhaps many lies. THC has been proven to be very useful in easing the symptoms of some chronic illnesses and severe treatments like chemotherapy. We also know that opium and its derivatives have highly beneficial effects on pain reduction. Even LSD has a therapeutic value at the proper dosage. I've taken advantage of your permission to experiment. I see and have felt value to some of these substances. I've tried others and don't feel any benefit to me, although I know other people do find value in some substances that I don't. I like wine, but I don't feel the need to drink it all the time or drink it to incapacitation. I feel exactly the same with some of those designated substances. I feel you watching me. I feel it's kind of like you watching me enjoy sex—a very personal endeavor. I don't feel free to find my way. I think the indulgence camp will give me that freedom. I'm only asking you to trust me, to trust your teaching of me."

"Very well said," Marci added.

"Yes, I agree with Mom."

"Then you'll give me permission?" Bella jumped in quickly.

"You're asking way too much from me, Bella Joy. I've seen far too much of what drugs have done to people. We arrested a girl about your age for stealing a large amount of candy to sell in order to feed her dependence on methamphetamine. That's the image in my mind when you ask me to consent to your admission to an indulgence camp. That's exactly what I've a mortal fear of happening to you, our only child and daughter."

"I can't promise that won't happen, Papa, but that's certainly not my intent. I can't predict the future any better than you can. I genuinely understand and appreciate your fear in this. I truly do, but I feel it's something I need to do."

"OK, then why is it something you 'need' to do?"

Bella looked at her mother as if seeking guidance.

Marci said, "Tell him exactly how you feel, Bella. He deserves to hear your feelings in your words, not mine. Tell him what you told me."

Bella stared at Marci, nodding her head several times. Rod kept his eyes on Bella's eyes but glanced with disbelief at Marci several times as he waited for Bella's statement.

Bella took a deep breath, and exhaled slowly and audibly. "First, Papa, I don't want to hurt your feelings. I love you very much, and I'm very proud of who you are and what you do . . . for me, for Mom, and for our community. But . . . there is always a 'but' it seems." Bella paused and searched her father's eyes for some sort of reaction. She received none. Rod held his emotionless interrogation expression. "I say this with the greatest love . . . you intimidate the hell out of me, Papa. I've lived all of my conscious life in a kind of fear of disappointing you. Your strength of character has driven me to focus and do the best I possibly can in anything I've ever done. This particular topic is no different. I believe you've been very straight, direct, and candid with me. I've not been able to do the same with you . . . out of my fear of disappointing you. I've been most grateful that both of you have tolerated my curiosity. I recognize that each of you has had to overcome your experiences, your indoctrination, your learning, and your biases with this topic. I've done a lot of extracurricular homework on this matter. I've thought about this request for months. I've tried to figure out how to do what I think I need to do without disappointing you. I chose to talk to Mom first because I couldn't figure out how to accomplish that objective. I knew this conversation was coming because Momma has been very clear that she wasn't comfortable giving me permission alone. So here we are.

"I've tried as best I can to avoid your root question. I owe you the best answer I can give you. From everything I've read and heard, the indulgence camp will give me the freest and most independent view of what consumption means to me. They don't have a children's wing or segregated facility. They'll treat me just as any other resident. I'll have to make decisions on my own without your supervision. I think and feel that experience will give me everything I need to know and perhaps want to know. I think I'll be better prepared to become an adult and consume responsibly, if I should so choose. I've tried very hard to use what you've taught me and to learn for myself. I may well be the best-informed 15-year-old on the planet." Marci was the first to chuckle softly, followed in short order by Rod and eventually Bella. "I think the indulgence camp is the freest of all possible situations for what I need to do," Bella said and stopped without taking her eyes off her father.

"Well, with a speech like that, how could I possibly say no."

"Thank you, Papa," Bella gushed with a heavy tone of relief.

"Wait. I didn't finish what I wanted to say. I'm impressed by the extra mile you've gone with this request of yours. I think I finally understand what you're trying to achieve. I'm not a pilot, but I imagine this is what a father-pilot feels when he sends his daughter up on her first solo flight. We could talk for hours about so many aspects of this issue, but I think you've said what you needed to say, and I am grateful that you finally trusted me with your candor." Rod looked directly at Marci and held her eyes. "So, you're convinced? You want to do this?"

"She convinced me two days ago," Marci answered, "which is precisely why I raised the issue with you. To answer your second question, no, I don't want her to do this. I'd prefer this whole matter just disappear, but that doesn't acknowledge our daughter's rapidly growing maturity. It sounded funny when she said it, and I think you will agree, she is far better informed than either of us was at her age, and maybe even at our age now. That said, I decided two days ago that the dreaded day had arrived. We must let her fly."

Rod nodded, thought for a few seconds, and then looked at Marci. "Thank you, my darling, for seeing the proper path and forcing this family discussion. Once again, you've demonstrated your wisdom. To be honest, I was not happy with the rift between us over the last few days. I'll be candid, I'm still not comfortable doing this, but I'm far more fearful of splitting on this decision. So, if this is what you need to do," he said, looking at Bella, "then we will take this risk together. I'm convinced you've devoted considerable effort to this question. I don't want you ever to be afraid of talking to me or to either of us. We must trust each other."

"Thank you, Papa. I'll do my best not to disappoint you."

"Don't worry about that, Bella. The important lesson from all this is that we must talk with each other freely, openly, and in the best candor we can muster up."

"Agreed," Bella responded. "I'm sorry I couldn't do that earlier."

Rod nodded his head and waved his hand dismissively. "Now, some sobriety. Regardless of how we feel or our permission, the indulgence camp has no obligation to accept your entry. You need to be prepared for that possibility."

"I am, and I understand."

"Very well, then we're agreed. I shall have to suppress my personal fear, and we'll do this together as a family. I shall do my best to contribute to your experience and investigation. And I'll hope and pray that you come out the other side a better person with all the answers you seek."

"Thank you so much, Papa . . . and Momma."

"OK," Marci pronounced, "for better or worse that is decided. Now, we've a more immediate task. We need to get this family fed."

"How about some good old-fashioned heritage food?" Rod suggested.

"Works for me," Bella responded.

"Me as well," added Marci.

They took the family automobile rather than his department vehicle, even though the rules encouraged him to do so. Their favorite heritage cuisine, as Rod liked to call it, was offered at *Restaurante de Pequeño Guadalajara*. It was not the closest, but it was their preferred restaurant, plus they knew the owner.

Rod ordered frozen margaritas and a bowl of the house guacamole for all three of them. It was not until their meals had been placed before them, and they had taken a few bites that Rod returned them to the topic of the evening. "So, now that we've passed the hard part, when are you thinking about executing your request?"

Bella finished her mouthful. "There are only ten days to the end of the school semester. I was thinking a couple of days after that."

Rod looked at Marci and received a confirmatory head nod. "That'll work. I'll get the day off for whatever date you choose. We'll drive out together."

"Please don't do anything special, Daddy. I want to stand on my own. If they disapprove me, then that's what was meant to be."

"That sounds reasonable. We've a date. I shall pray this turns out correctly."

Their discussions transitioned to lighter, more entertaining topics that produced laughter and lighthearted jabs. They each enjoyed their meals and a nice, fried ice cream dessert.

It had been a very long couple of days. Rod felt better than he did when he arrived home but suppressing his fear would be his own silent struggle until this phase of Bella Joy's young life was behind them. *God help us all.*

—

20

$\mathbf{M}$axim Jurgensen had waited not so patiently for this moment. His first beating at the hands of other residents had occurred 10 days after he entered Quad Three of BHC7, which had been the precipitant for his request to Hank Houseman. They had discussed the possibility before his trial, but they had not talked; more accurately, they had not been able to speak with each other since his trial. Since his initial request, Maxim had been thrashed two more times. He renewed his request after each incident.

The intercom broadcast for him to proceed to the lockout chamber was his first encouraging sign. Once in the transfer space and the door behind him locked, the entry door opened, and two very serious-looking men dressed in full-up black tactical gear entered with weapons drawn. They were wholly covered; no skin was observable. They had plates of presumable armor of some form all over them. The two men looked like a black version of Star Wars stormtroopers.

"Turn around and put your hands on the wall and spread your legs," the lead guard commanded.

Maxim did as he was instructed. The other guard stood to the side with his weapon raised with an unobstructed line of sight. The lead guard frisked every inch of his body as if Maxim might be hiding some hidden weapon. Once satisfied, the lead guard hooked the leg shackles and wrist cuffs, all connected by a common chain to a thick waist belt buckled in the small of his back. The guard then installed a bite/spit mask.

"I don't need that," Maxim said.

"Shut the fuck up," the lead guard commanded harshly. "You have a history, and those are the orders. Get used to it. This is your attire outside Quad Three for the rest of your miserable life."

With the restraints satisfactorily in place, the covering guard went through the security procedures to open the door to the lobby. The lead guard tightly held the back handles as they moved through the opening. They waited until the door locks reengaged and then checked the door.

Maxim waddled along with the clattering of his chains, led by the lead guard down into the tunnel and back to the administration building. He had not seen these places since his arrival.

The three men slowly made their way to one of six secure, small conference rooms. Each room had a thick, polycarbonate window that also attenuated any interior sound but allowed continuous observation. The guard placed Maxim in the room with a large painted '2' on the door. Using a permanently installed heavy chain on the table that was bolted to the floor, the guard locked Maxim's restraint chains to the table chain, and then pushed him into the straight back metal chair facing the door.

"Ready on two," the cover guard said aloud, using an apparent wearable communications device inside his helmet and mask.

A third guard similarly attired brought Hank Housemen from outside the conference room area to Conference Room Two. As they approached, the lead guard opened the door inward.

As soon as Houseman saw his client, he turned to the guard and said, "Is all that really necessary?"

The lead guard responded, "The resident has no communicable diseases. He's a spit risk, but that's your choice."

"Please remove the mask."

The guard did so.

"Now, please remove the restraints," Houseman commanded.

"Ain't gonna happen, counselor. We'll be watching. You can signal us when you're ready to depart."

Houseman nodded his head and entered the room. The door closed and locked behind him. Before he sat down, he stared at Maxim's face and said, "What the hell happened to you?"

"Had the shit beat outta me three times since I've been here."

"Have they done anything to protect you?"

Maxim laughed loudly. "That doesn't happen here."

"I really need to get some pictures of your injuries."

"You can ask, but I doubt that'll happen."

Houseman stood, went to the window, and gestured as if he had a camera. The lead guard shook his head in the negative and then drew his right hand across his neck. Hank pointed at Maxim's face and then looked back at the guard. Again, the lead guard shook his head. Houseman returned to his chair and wrote some notes on his yellow legal paper tablet.

Hank finally looked at Maxim. "What can I do for you?"

"You gotta get me outta here. These crazies are going to kill me."

"Our appeals were all rejected. I've exhausted my tool kit."

"What about my constitutional rights? What about cruel and unusual punishment?"

"First," Houseman said and paused, "I'm a public defender. I'm here today on my vacation time. I can't take on a constitutional challenge. That's beyond my capacity. However, since we've discussed this potential before your trial, I've taken the liberty of contacting several defense and constitutional attorney friends of mine. Several have declined to represent you. Two haven't responded yet, so I assume they're considering the potential. Frankly, you're not a good case for such a challenge. I also contacted the lead attorneys on two of the cases within the court system to see if they would add you to their petition. It's a long shot, but we'll see what plays out."

"Look at me," Maxim said, drawing his wrist restraint chains taut. "This isn't supposed to be part of my punishment."

"How many have been beaten like you?"

"Me and another guy are all I've seen.

"That's all?"

"That's more than enough. This isn't part of my punishment, and I'm afraid they're going to kill me."

"What did you do to instigate these beatings?"

"Nothing."

"It had to be something, Mister Jurgensen. Otherwise, there would be more injured inmates."

Maxim thought about what he wanted to say. "I just wanted to be respected."

"You mean like your victims?"

"Whose side are you on?"

"Mister Jurgensen, let's not beat around the bush. You've been duly convicted in a court of law and designated a habitual criminal. This is the state's intended punishment for habitual criminals."

Maxim sharply drew all of his chains taut in a very loud display. His movement induced prepared alertness with the guards outside. He eventually relaxed. "I know what the courts did to me."

"The courts didn't do anything to you, Mister Jurgensen. Your conduct produced this. It's not like you weren't given ample warning of the consequences. But, enough of that, let me ask you a few questions." Maxim nodded his head. "First, did anyone intervene to stop the other inmates beating you?"

"No. That's not how things work in here."

"Did you receive any medical treatment for your injuries?"

"Again, not how things work."

"Do you get exercise?"

"Whatever I can do in my cell or the commons, but I don't do that very often. I'm afraid of them getting to me again."

"So, you're afraid of injury or for your life?"

"Yes! Absolutely! It's not safe in there."

"To take an argumentative tact, given the court documents available so far, safety belongs to you. If you find a way not to offend and get along with the other inmates, you would not likely be in danger."

"You're telling me that survival of the fittest is acceptable."

"No, I'm not. I'm only reflecting what some of the court filings state."

"Easy to say; not so easy to do."

"Do you have any friends in your quadrant?"

"Not really. There's a couple of fellas I talk to now and then, but I still don't trust them."

"It would seem the best course given the exigent circumstances . . ."

"The what?"

"The current circumstances . . . is to develop some friendships with others you can rely on for protection. Banding together might be the only way, at least until conditions change. Going it alone doesn't seem like a wise choice. Anyway, the choice is yours. You're the only one of us who lives here."

"Live is a rather loose term, don't'cha think?"

"Quite so. Next question." Maxim nodded his consent. "How is the food and living support?"

"The food is better than regular prison. We get military, freeze-dried meals. We get warm water, not hot water, but the meals are pretty good. We get a silly little spork that dissolves after use in a few days."

"Without supervision, is there any hoarding or fighting over food?"

"No. None that I've seen. Sometimes there is a little selection dispute. One person wants a particular meal type that someone else has. But it usually gets worked out. The administration threatened to supply only one meal type if it remained a problem. I'm not sure what you meant about living support?"

"Stuff like soap, toothpaste, toilet paper, and such."

Maxim laughed. "We seem to have plenty of toilet paper, although I heard stories about a protest years ago where the residents of the day used toilet paper and cloth to plug up the toilets. They stopped supplying toilet paper, and the residents sat in sewage and filth for several months. We don't get soap."

"Why not?"

Maxim smiled. "You clearly haven't seen what a bar of soap in a sock can do to a human body. No, we don't get soap—the best we can do is rinse off. We have plenty of water, although the hot water is not hot. It's only warm, not hot enough to burn. We do get small tubes of toothpaste but no toothbrushes. Again, the handle can make a good shiv. The living conditions are quite basic, and some might say inhumane."

"Do you have any entertainment?"

Maxim laughed so hard he could not answer, although he tried several times.

"Television, books, newspapers, videos, and such," Houseman added.

Jurgensen continued to laugh. Houseman waited for Maxim to regain calm and tried to remain expressionless and patient. Maxim took a couple of deep breaths and then answered. "Nothing. We've no contact with the outside world, past, present, or future, or in any form. The only entertainment we have is masturbation. Well, some folks are fucking. I've seen 'em, but that is not for me . . . either way."

Houseman wrote more notes. "Is there anything you'd like to tell me about this place and your incarceration in this place?"

"Get me outta here. They're going to kill me," Jurgensen repeated.

"Who is they?"

"Other inmates. There's a handful of 'em in my Quad. They don't like me for some reason."

"Could it be that you antagonize them?"

"What does that mean?"

"Perhaps you irritate them in some way, and you could just amend your behavior."

"Easier said than done."

"Can you or would you name these antagonists, you mention?"

Maxim grinned broadly at Hank. "Names are not common in the Quad. I only know two men, and even at that, I only know their first names, Ben and Paul. Neither of them is against me. I don't know the names of the guys who are against me."

"Anything else?"

"I guess not. So, what's next?"

Houseman put his pen and notepad back in his briefcase. "As I said early on, I'm reaching out for you to find a constitutional attorney who is willing to take on your challenge on a *pro bono* basis. I've got several feelers still outstanding."

"I've heard that term, *pro bono*. What does that mean?"

"It is Latin that means, for good. The legal meaning is they're willing to work without billing you."

"That's good cuz I've got no money to pay you or pay them. When can we get an appeal to the Supreme Court?"

Houseman immediately held up his left hand, palm forward. "Whoa, now. You jumped quite a few necessary steps on that journey. First and foremost, as I said, I can't do it. I'm here on my vacation time out of courtesy to you. Unless we can find an attorney to represent you, I'm afraid it's don't pass go, don't collect $200. So, first things first. Whoever represents you must go through the district court, the appeals court, and then get accepted by the Supreme Court, and even if you make it to that stage, there is no guarantee the justices will accept your argument. They've already denied one similar appeal, leaving the lower court ruling in place and valid. I hope to hear something, either way, in a few weeks. I'll get a message to you as soon as I know something." He gathered up his papers, put them in his briefcase and stood. Hank extended his right hand across the table, and before they could shake hands, he heard a loud knock on the window behind him. He looked over his shoulder to see the lead guard waving his gloved right index finger, signaling no touching. Hank withdrew his hand. "I'll be in touch as soon as I've something to report. Please be patient and try to stay away from your antagonists."

Maxim Jurgensen nodded his head but did not reply. He remained seated, manacled to the anchored table, awaiting the guards.

The electronic locks audibly released. The guard pushed the door open. Houseman stepped out into the hallway. The door closed and locked. Houseman turned to the lead guard. "Are you just going to leave him in there?"

"First, not your problem. Second, no, we've got to get you outta here before we move him. He sits until we're ready."

"Very well. I need to see the superintendent, warden, director, or whatever you call the person in charge."

"That would be the captain of the guard."

"No . . . his boss."

"I've no idea whether the director is present, and he doesn't see anyone without an appointment," the guard announced. "The captain is the man in charge."

"How about this. Let's go to the office and find out, shall we?"

"As you wish, counselor." The lead guard motioned for the escort guard to take Houseman out of the operational spaces to the administration office.

Once the two doors to exit the operational area closed and locked in sequence, the lead guard motioned for his partner to prepare the resident for movement back to his Quad. The process stepped through the sequence in reverse. Once inside the lockout chamber of Quad Three, the lead guard raised his rifle and placed the red LASER spot directly over Jurgensen's heart as his partner removed the cuffs and shackles from Maxim's wrists and ankles. "Don't move until the interior door unlocks. Do you understand?"

"Yes."

The two guards backed out and checked to make sure the exit door was locked.

Once the exit door locked, the interior door unlocked. Maxim stepped to and pulled the door open. The resident he knew as Paul was waiting just inside.

"How did it go?" asked Paul, as the door locked automatically.

"Not perfect, but better than I expected." Paul gestured for Maxim to continue. "He can't do it, but he's looking for another lawyer who will do it for free. He said he would let me know as soon as he finds someone who's willing to do the work."

"Well, I guess that is better than nothing. What did he say about the beatings?"

Maxim chuckled softly and started walking to the stairs leading to his cell. Paul stayed with him. "He actually said he'd talk to the director, as if that might change things." Maxim laughed hard. "He's no clue how this place works. He told me to keep my head down." He laughed more.

"Not so easy in here," Paul added. "Do you think it's going to work."

"I've no idea. My guess, it's a long shot. He's a public defender, so not at the top of the food chain, but hey, at least he's trying." They reached Maxim's cell. A quick scan indicated his cell had not been disturbed. They sat on what served as his bed. "He told me he is contacting the lawyers that are farther along in the courts to join those cases. I've no clue how that might work, but that's what he said. Who knows how this will play out?"

"So, I guess we're still on our own."

"Yeah . . . seems so." Maxim lapsed into thought. Paul started to hum some non-descript song. Maxim shook his head, and then he looked out the high, barred, polycarbonate window. "We've got a couple of hours before evening meal gets here. I'm going to take a nap."

Paul stood and said, "OK, buddy. See'ya later." He departed and closed the cell door behind him.

Maxim rose to lock the door. It was the only way he could sleep. He laid down, thought about the afternoon's discussion, but did not last long, as he lapsed into sleep for a nap before evening meal.

Hank Houseman waited in the plain, minimalist lobby. An officer in black attire and captain's bars on his open collar points approached. Hank stood.

"Good afternoon, Mister Houseman," the captain said, extending his right hand. They shook hands. "How may I help you?"

"I need to talk to the man in charge of this place."

"I'm the duty captain."

"No. I need to talk to your boss, whomever you report to here."

"The director asked me to assist you. That's what I'm trying to do. How may I help you?" Sullivan repeated.

"With all respect, Captain, I don't have much time, and I don't need a filter."

Sullivan took a moment to consider his response. He could simply stonewall the attorney, but the director did not want any conflict. Sullivan raised his right index finger, gesturing for a minute, then turned and departed. The captain returned in a few minutes. "Please follow me, Mister Houseman."

The electronic lock door clanked. Sullivan pulled the door open and led Houseman down a narrow hallway with no side doors or windows, just overhead fluorescent lights and another locked door at the far end. A well-hidden camera must have shown their approach to a controller since the electronic lock released just before Sullivan reached for the handle. The captain pulled the heavy door open and again led Hank into a closed stairwell. Stairs only went up, so up they went. They turned at a mid-flight landing. The stairs continue to another level, but they exited at the second floor. The exit door made no sound. A wider corridor went left and right, and had doors on both sides, some open, some closed. They took the left portion to the end. A middle-aged, modest, female receptionist or secretary nodded to Captain Sullivan as they entered the room. Sullivan went to the door opposite the entry door, knocked twice, and opened the door.

A surprisingly young man, perhaps in his late 30s or early 40s, stood and came around the desk. He was dressed in a light grey business suit, light blue shirt, and no tie. The man extended his right hand. "Good afternoon, Mister Houseman." They shook hands. "I'm Director Willis. I understand you need to see me." Willis gestured to the four chairs around a circular table. Hank sat across from Willis. Sullivan between them.

"Yes. I'm the public defender who represented Maxim Jurgensen."

"A public defender, ay. We don't see much of those out here."

"Yes, well, I told Mister Jurgensen I would follow-up on his request for legal support. We intend, well, not me, but someone else will file an 8th Amendment constitutional challenge on his behalf."

"Good luck with that."

Houseman did not know quite how to take that comment, but he chose to ignore it. "I need to file a formal complaint."

"About what, pray tell?"

"Mister Jurgensen sustained serious wounds, and those were just the ones I could see, from three beatings according to him that he received at the hands of other prisoners in his area. You're obligated to protect him from such assault and battery episodes. I want to know what you're going to do to protect my client?"

"My, my, counselor, that's quite an aggressive demand."

"Well?" Hank said with demonstrable impatience.

"First, we've no such obligation under the law."

"Other prisons do," interjected Hank with pronounced anger.

"This facility is not like other prisons, counselor," Willis stated. "The rules are different here. Your client knows that, and I dare say you know that. The men confined in this facility didn't respect other peaceful citizens.

They were given multiple opportunities to reform their behavior and become peaceful, contributory individuals. They repeatedly rejected every attempt by the state to help them. So, now, the state has acknowledged their choices in life and allowed them to live as they choose for their kind. They chose not to live by society's rules. Now, they get the opportunity to make up their own rules without injury to innocent citizens. The fact that your client can't figure out how to get along with other residents like him speaks directly to his anti-social attitude. He apparently can't get along with other men just like him."

"Protect him!"

"How would you propose we do that?"

"Put him in isolation. Move him to another block. Do something."

"First, we've no such capability. Second, there are men just like him in the other three quadrants and moving him won't likely change anything. Third, we aren't here to serve those residents. They made their bed. Now, they lay in it."

"What about medical treatment for his wounds?"

"Not our problem. They fend for themselves. Our sole job here is to secure the walls to prevent any escape and thwart any attempt to penetrate. We're doing our jobs to the fullest."

"You're the warden."

Willis held up his right hand for Houseman to stop. "There's no such position here, or at any Black Hole Confinement facility. My job as the director is simply to ensure that duty captains," Willis said, nodding to Sullivan, "have the personnel, equipment, and support they need to perform our function. If your client doesn't want wounds he can't treat properly, then he had better figure out how to get along with the other residents in his quad. Like it or not, they're his family now. The state's policy is the removal of habitual criminals from society and containment of those individuals for the rest of whatever life they have left. The purpose here is to protect society, not these men."

"That's not acceptable," Hank said emphatically.

Willis chuckled softly. "I'm afraid you've no say in any of this. If you choose to file legal action on behalf of your client, that's your choice. That's your right under the law. Until the law is changed and the policy amended, we'll continue to do our jobs to the best of our ability under the law."

"Fuck the law!" Houseman shouted and banged his fists on the table. "I'm only asking for compassion for our fellow man."

"Compassion, ay. You mean like your client showed to his victims?"

"I . . . I . . . I . . . ," stammered Houseman, "I can't believe you're so heartless. They're human beings."

Willis smiled. "That last point is debatable, counsellor. Society has declared them *persona non grata*, but we can't deport them. The state has decided this is the best and most appropriate treatment for those who choose to violate the peace and the rights of others. You can huff and puff all you wish, Mister Houseman, but nothing is going to change, unless, or rather if, the Supreme Court sees the 8th Amendment differently than the state does. Until then, your client must find his place in his new family or suffer the consequences as they decide.

"Now, I've listened, and I've tried to explain. I wish to offer an observation in closing this impromptu meeting. I recognize and acknowledge that this facility, and its sister units, appears to be very harsh, but it's only a reflection of the harshness inflicted upon peaceful citizens by these men. They're getting what they gave. It's as simple as that. I'm a believer that this is the proper way to deal with men like these. I'd only say, get used to it. We are protecting you."

"Wha . . . I . . . na . . . ya . . . ," Houseman stammered again. Whatever it was that he was thinking or wanted to say, he gave it up. "Thank you for your time," Hank said in a calm, soft voice. He stood and extended his hand to both Willis and Sullivan.

No more words were exchanged as Captain Sullivan escorted Hank Houseman out of the BHC7 facility. Hank tried to void his troubled thoughts for the long drive back. He was quite late to his plan for the day and would not arrive back in the city until after dusk. It has been a long day. He wanted it to end.

—

21

The last week had been terribly hard on both Marci and Rod. Bella had held up her end of the unholy bargain and completed her sophomore year of high school. The three-month summer break had begun. For several days, Rod considered not joining his wife and daughter for the trip out of town, but when the day arrived, he decided doing it as a family was more important than his misgivings. His moments of regret continued to percolate up into his consciousness, and he fought those thoughts with his recognition of preconception. Rod had grown up in the old world and struggled with adjusting to the new way of looking at things. He knew the data supported the progressive approach, but now, the issue had become very personal. He worried terribly about their daughter. His job was to keep her safe and teach her how to be a happy, productive citizen who respected others.

Bella was now a resident at IC12, and their first contact had come in the form of a text message. She indicated she was doing well but missed her parents. Her message asked them to visit her. Marci agreed without talking to Rod, and this was the agreed to Saturday.

The first 45 minutes of the drive had gone smoothly but without words between them. Marci was the first to break the silence finally. "What do you think we're going to find?"

"I've no idea."

"Do you think we've lost her?"

Rod quickly glanced at Marci, and he returned his attention to the roadway and traffic ahead of them. "My dear God, Marci, I sure as hell hope not . . . but I'd be lying if I denied the potential."

"I sure hope not as well. I pray this is just a short phase she must pass through in her long life."

"Me too, Marci. Me too."

They drove several more miles with moderate traffic that did not bother Rod much. Only once did he reach for the police light switch, but he thought twice and just backed off to change lanes.

"Do you think she could get sucked in and stuck there?" asked Marci.

"Little late for that 'Q,' I'm afraid." Marci did not respond or even twitch. "Of course, it's possible. More than a few people have become addicted."

"But I thought you said the changes in the state's drug laws were intended to avoid addiction."

"That's exactly what I said, and that's what I believe. However, there's nothing in the law or the application of the law at IC12 that precludes individuals from taking more than the recommended dose of any substance. Addictive thresholds are defined by concentration and frequency, what the experts call dose density and duration. One dose doesn't do it—no poof, you're addicted. We've no idea what she's done out there."

"I guess we're going to find out," Marci mumbled.

Rod did not respond and lapsed into his thoughts. *We could find anything between she's had enough to she never wants to leave. We've got to be prepared for any of that and everything in between. She's done and is doing what she's intent upon doing, and we must prepare ourselves mentally and emotionally for whatever that outcome might be. I just hope Marci will be able to handle whatever that outcome happens to be.*

A cumulonimbus cloud structure billowed up to the southwest and attracted Rod's attention. The mental calculations rumbling through his brain sought to estimate whether the potential thunderstorm might be a problem for their return to the city later this afternoon. "Looks like a big thunderstorm brewing to the southwest. I don't think it'll affect us for the trip home, but we need to keep an eye on it."

"I'm worried, Rod."

"About what?"

"About our daughter, you ninny."

"Yes, well, so am I. We need to be prepared for the worst. The potential is very real." Marci only nodded her head and held a somber expression. "The die is cast. What will be will be, and it's largely out of our control. Our daughter, and only child, is growing up so fast."

"Do you think we did the correct thing allowing her to do this?"

"I've had my doubts since before we agreed to her request. I've seen what drugs can do to a human being. I know what they can do. Sure, most of my experience is before the law changed, but we still see it." They rode along in silence for a few miles. "Regardless of what we face out there, Marci, we must stay together and support each other. We've nearly finished raising our daughter. Well, hell, she may have already flown the coop. If so, I didn't expect it so soon and certainly not to this degree, but this is life. Sometimes the eagle chick falls out of the nest before she can fly and doesn't survive. This is what we signed up for, Marci. We must stand by our decision and do our best to support our daughter as she sets her course in life. Whatever Bella Joy decides for her life, we must support her and guide her as she will allow us. We must not allow her choices to divide us."

"I know, Rod. I love you."

"I love you very much, Marcella Christina, more than you may ever realize." Rod slowed and pulled well off the roadway, to the edge of the available shoulder. He placed the car in park and turned to face Marci directly. Rod reached for and grasped her left hand in both of his hands. "Whatever we find out there, we're a couple, bonded together for life. We've done the best we can. We have to believe we've taught Bella Joy to make the best decisions for her life. She's going to make mistakes. She's going to skin her knees. We must let her live her life. If we believe what we've taught her properly, she'll make us proud. We must first believe in ourselves, in our relationship, and we must also believe in her."

"I sure hope so."

They picked up three Subway six-inch sandwiches in Springerville, the last town before they reached IC12. Bella had asked for a Club sandwich. Bella had told Marci they had no food services near the facility. They were now well outside of the populated area. Only a few cars swiftly passed by them as they sat on the roadway shoulder. "Believe, Marci. I imagine you've got misgivings as I do, but we did the best we could. We've tried to be more progressive and informed than our parents were with us. We've done the best we can."

Marci leaned toward her husband and kissed him. "Thank you for that, Rodrigo. I needed that. Now, this milestone isn't getting any closer sitting here on the side of the highway."

Rod smiled, kissed Marci one more time, and shifted back to his driver task. They traversed the remaining 20 minutes of their outbound journey without incident or words. He parked the car in a wide-open space at the back of the lot, even though he could have parked upfront with the vehicle's government plate. Rod left the engine running to keep the air conditioning working for their comfort, unbuckled his seatbelt, and turned to Marci one more time. He gently grasped Marci's left arm just below her elbow. Looking calmly and sincerely into Marci's golden-brown eyes, Rod said, "No matter what we find inside, we go in and come out together""

"Together!" Marci exclaimed with feeling.

"Let's go see our daughter."

Rod put the sun shield across the front windscreen and locked the car. They walked across the parking lot hand-in-hand and into the administration building. The receptionist recorded their identities and the purpose of their visit, and then she directed them to the visitor's lounge. A quarter of the tables were occupied with an even smaller fraction of chairs filled. The residents were readily identifiable in solid, medium tone, medical-type scrubs in various colors. They moved to a table by the exterior windows, the farthest from the other visitors. He placed the bag of sandwiches in the middle of their selected table. Rod had expected Bella to be waiting for them, but it was only mildly disconcerting that they were waiting for her. *But I suppose that makes sense. After all, we are the visitors.*

"Maybe she forgot we were coming today," Rod mumbled.

"She'll be here. She's probably waiting for our arrival notice."

"I hope so."

"She sounded genuinely excited to see us when I talked to her on the phone. She'll be here."

"Hmmph." Rod went to the vending machine and was surprised to see no payment was necessary. He retrieved an ice-cold Orange Crush for Marci and a Diet Coke for himself. Rod had no sooner sat down and popped the tops on the soda cans for Marci and himself, when Bella appeared and took a second to scan the room. Bella ran across the room, weaving past the intervening tables like a football running back, and leaped into Rod's outstretched arms. She wrapped her arms and legs around Rod's torso like she had become part of him. Rod could feel her chest convulsing as she sobbed softly with her face buried in the crook of his neck. With her soft convulsive breathing and the grip her body held on him as signs of life, Rod whispered, "It's OK, sweetie. I've got you." He repeated his words several more times before Bella began to release her grip on Rod.

Bella lowered herself to the floor and turned to her mother. "Oh, Momma," she cried, as she embraced Marci. Bella eventually settled and disengaged. Without words, she went to the vending machines and selected a Fanta Grape for herself. "So, tell me, how have you been?" Bella said, glancing at her mother and father several times.

"We're not here to report on our relationship," Marci said. "We're here to find out about how our daughter has been. So tell us already."

"Wait!" interjected Rod. "Are you coming home?"

Bella smiled at both her parents. "Not yet."

"OK?"

"You'll never guess whom I met in here." Marci and Rod stared at Bella. Marci eventually shrugged her shoulders as if to gesture, are you going to tell us or not? "Mrs. Joubert, Kelly Joubert, actually, she goes by her original name Henry, now, the wife of Assistant District Attorney Joubert."

I'll be damned. That's quite a little news flash—confirmation of what I suspected earlier. I'll have to think about whether to share that bit of information with Raoul Joubert, but not now. "I know who she is married to, Bella," Rod responded. "Why is that relevant to how you're doing? We've been on pins and needles since we dropped you off."

"I just think it's weird," Bella added. "She's rich. She has a powerful husband. And she's in here with me."

"OK, Bella Joy, we can talk about all that and everyone else, but we'd like to establish your health and well-being first."

"Let's step back a few steps," Marci jumped in before Bella could react. "We're desperate to know how you feel? How you're doing? What you're thinking? Please have mercy on us, Bella. We love you, and we're deeply concerned about your safety. Your father said it precisely and correctly. We've been on pins and needles. Please don't punish us, Bella. We love you, and we're deeply concerned about you."

"Enough already, you two," Bella objected. "I know you love me, and I love you both. I'm fine. I'm taking care of myself. People don't talk much in here. The food is not so good, compared to yours, Momma, but it's edible and sustaining. I've only talked to Kelly and one other woman. Everyone seems to be very nice, although pretty standoffish." Silence filled the space between them, although inaudible words rattled around in the background. "That's about it . . . not much to tell."

"We'll ignore the elephant in the room for the moment." Rod shook his head several times out of frustration. He fought with emotions that he usually kept far from the surface. "I'm not sure why you want to avoid talking about what is in your heart, in your mind. We can't and won't pressure you." Again, Rod paused. He took in a deep breath and let it out slowly with a kind of hiss. "Let me say here, one day, perhaps, you'll have children. I hope you never have to feel the doubts, the concerns, the worry that we feel, Bella Joy. We reluctantly agreed with your little experiment, and your avoidance about your feelings is making us regret letting you do this."

"I'm hungry, Papa. Can we eat? Let me get something in my stomach, and then I'll do my best to tell you what I'm thinking."

"OK. Deal."

Bella did not wait to be served. She grabbed the Subway bag. The first wrapped sandwich was marked 'Turkey.' "This must be Papa's." She placed it in front of Rod. He did not move. With the second wrapped sandwich marked 'Veg,' Bella announced, "Veggie Delight must be Momma's." Bella deposited the stack of napkins in the middle of the table. "Club. That's me. Perfect." Bella opened her sandwich first and quickly took a healthy bite. "Mmmm. That's so good," she mumbled with her mouth full. They each ate a few more bites of their sandwiches without words. Marci and Rod decided to let Bella take the time she needed or wanted.

Bella finished chewing and swallowing her bite. She placed her half-eaten sandwich down on the wrapper and took a sip of her drink. Marci and

Rod followed suit, not wanting any distraction from listening to their daughter. "First off, I'm not trying to hide anything. I'm not trying to avoid any discussion. Now is no different to me than our previous discussions since the incident in Minville. I'm just uneasy and apprehensive. I want you to be proud of me, and I certainly recognize that entering this indulgence camp is seriously stretching your tolerance and acceptance. I know I owe you the best I can give you . . . all of it. But I'm still figuring things out. So, I don't have answers to some things and can't give you answers that I don't have." Bella paused. Rod nodded his head in agreement. Marci did not respond. "The feelings I shared or at least tried to express the last time we talked remain valid. I'm grateful to have this unsupervised time. This is my step, not yours. My experimentation in your house makes you liable in a form. My experimenting here does not leave you open. It's all me."

"Thank you for that," Rod added.

"Ditto," Marci said.

"So, to your elephant, Papa."

"Not my elephant, Bella Joy," Rod objected. "The elephant. We're in this together."

"Thank you for that as well. I've quietly and without any fanfare or support of anyone else tried to answer the questions that have been in my thoughts for some time now." Bella paused, as if she wanted one of her parents to ask a question. Marci and Rod again agreed without words to allow Bella her own space and time, to tell her story at her own pace. Rod and then Marci took another bite of their sandwich, as they waited. Bella did the same. Several minutes trickled away until Bella finished her lunch and her drink. She went to the machines and retrieved another drink for each of them.

Bella popped the top and took another sip. "Thank you for lunch," she said to both her parents. "That was far better than what we get here." Bella audibly sucked in a deep breath and let it hiss out slowly, quite like her father did on occasion. "OK . . . to the elephant. Let me start with the end. This is not what I see for my life, not even in the remotest sense." She took another deep breath and released it. "I've no interest in staying here, but I don't know how much longer I'll remain in this place. I'm not quite done."

"Done with what, Bella?" Marci asked.

"With my experiment."

"What experiment?" asked Rod a little more harshly than he intended. The shock on Bella's face made Rod step back. "I'm sorry. That came out a little too sharply. What were you seeking? What are you trying to accomplish?"

"I'm learning my boundaries. The IC's . . . well, the state's list of regulated substances. I've eliminated quite a few. I don't like the feelings, the sensations . . . the effects. A few of them I've found useful. I'm just trying to figure out my limit, my thresholds of tolerance . . . my boundaries."

"Why do you need any of them?" Rod asked.

"Have you tried any of them?" Bella queried.

Damn, I hadn't expected that question. She's challenging me. "Alcohol," Rod answered. "I've never tried smoking, nicotine—tobacco. No interest. I'll confess to smoking a joint before I entered the Marine Corps. But that's it. I've found no interest in trying any of them. A few years back, I used to arrest people for even possessing a gram of those substances—not very much. I don't see the attraction."

"Daddy, look at me." Rod hesitated and then looked into and held his daughter's eyes. "Perhaps, your fear of these drugs was learned . . . taught to you. If you've not tried them, how would you know? They're not some devil's brew, Papa. Knowledge is far more powerful than ignorance. What they used to say about these substances is flat-assed wrong, and by 'they,' I mean the government. They lied to us, Papa. They outright lied to us. They tried their best to keep us ignorant. They did not want us to know the truth. Thank goodness, our state has made it safe . . . safe to consume, safe to learn."

"What else are you learning?" Marci asked.

"I wish I could talk to other women . . . and men . . . in here. I know there are people here who favor every single one of these substances. There are reasons they like them. I'd like to understand them all. I've read the side effects on each substance, and some of them scare me. I've learned a lot from Kelly. I know the benzos are of no interest to me, based on her experience with those. Heck, she's even gotten them out of her system. I've tried meth. I didn't like it, but I recognize that it could be useful in certain circumstances. I've not yet found any purpose to PCP, psilocybin, or LSD."

"Silly what?" Marci asked.

"Psilocybin is the psychoactive component," answered Rod, before Bella could respond, "of certain varieties of mushrooms—a hallucinogenic."

"Right," Bella added. "Some artists find those substances very stimulating to their creative side. I don't feel any of that attraction."

They sat in silence, each of them lost in their thoughts.

"Do you think this has been worth it?" Rod questioned.

"So far, I would say yes. But the question really belongs at the conclusion," Bella responded.

"And when is that going to be?" asked Rod.

"Not today, but soon. I must say, I'm extraordinarily grateful that you've allowed me to have this space, and to the state for this facility. Thanks to the state's generosity, I've resources to find answers that neither of you had. I'm finding the answers I need."

"Then what happens next?" asked Rod.

"You mean, after I finish here?"

"Yes."

"I can't imagine being here more than a few more days or weeks. This is definitely not where I belong."

Where do you belong, Bella Joy?

"Before you ask," Bella continued, "I belong at home. I need to finish high school and get ready for college. Drugs aren't going to be part of my everyday life. But to be honest with you, some of this stuff is beneficial for certain things . . . certain activities. You really should try it sometime. You might find you like it and can use it."

"Ain't gonna happen," protested Rod.

"Papa, don't be so closed-minded." Bella just smiled at her father. "You know you might actually learn like I did that you've been lied to by the government all of your life."

"Perhaps," Rod said with uncharacteristic meekness. "I've certainly seen enough in the last few years to recognize that there is some degree of veracity to your words and observations. I can't deny that . . . or those facts. But Bella Joy, we're not the issue here. You're the one who voluntarily entered this drug camp." Rod swung his left arm, and then he swung both arms around the room. "We can talk about that dimension once you're past this phase. I'm reluctant to speak for your Momma, but we've done nothing but worry about you since you decided to do this. We're trying our best here, Bella." Rod took a sip of his drink, held it close to his lips, and then took another swig before placing the can back on the table.

"I echo your father's words, Bella," Marci added. "We're here to calm our fears, to hear about your experience, and to help you get past this phase."

"I think I've proven consumption of these substances is not dangerous, if consumed properly, in either the immediate or chronic perspective. As I said earlier, most of this stuff is beyond any interest of mine. I had to prove all this to myself . . . and to you. There are quite a few professionals who support this camp who know far more about the single and long-term use of these substances. I've learned a lot." Bella searched the eyes of her parents. "I can't imagine staying for more than a week or two more. I've started talking to a few of the counselors about some of my thoughts. I've been truly amazed at how supportive they are . . . not supportive of consumption, but of finding my own way. What works for me, and what doesn't. They've really helped me see things that I'd not thought about before. Kelly has been extraordinarily helpful. She's dealing with a lot of stuff I'm not, and she's been very open and candid with me. I've learned from her what I don't want in any relationship."

Wow! I wonder if Raoul realizes any of this. Several thoughts rumbled through his consciousness. *I also wonder if anyone says stuff like that about Marci and me. I've got to put these thoughts out of my mind, for now. I've got to change the subject.* "Have you seen real addicts in this place?" asked Rod. "I mean, these camps were originally designed and intended for hard addicts—people who are truly dependent on these substances."

"Yes, quite a few . . . mostly men, some women. The ones who are like walking zombies are the scariest, but they appear to be stable, meaning the same every day, every time I see them wherever. I just can't imagine how they feel anything . . . but I suppose that is the point. At least they've found a steady, reliable source and don't have to search or dig for what they need. I've not seen one of those heavy users in anyone, not one, of the meetings I've been to since arriving here. It's good to see and hear others across the full range from the zombies, as I call them, to the poor or unemployed who don't have access or can't afford the substances they seek. Kelly has been the most helpful to me in understanding what I see and hear."

"Why is she here?" Rod asked, unable to resist his curiosity.

"She is hiding."

"From what?"

"From her husband. She's found peace, freedom for her, and she thinks she's found a path to a better life. She's a very kind and gentle woman . . . wise in many ways. But it's evident she hates . . ."

"Wait, wait," protested Rod. "I shouldn't have asked that question. We can talk about her, and us, well, and anyone else, but right now our collective focus must be on you. So, let me ask, what do you think you're going to take away from this journey you're on now?"

"I'm going to be much smarter, more informed, more knowledgeable about life, about my body, and about other people. I expect to be more compassionate and more understanding of other people."

"You really think all of that is coming from your unsupervised consumption of illegal . . . no, wait, not illegal . . . your consumption of psychotropic substances?" Rod questioned with a stern tone.

"No, Papa. The consumption is not the issue or the process. It's only a tool . . . like a microscope to see small objects. I've heard you say things, and I've heard many others tell me what it was like before the law changed. Your generation and Grandpa's generation were repeatedly told that marijuana was a gateway drug. Take one puff or eat one brownie, and you're headed to heroin and oblivion. I'd be willing to bet good money that my children will be better informed than me."

"Wait . . . ," Rod protested.

"No, Papa, you wanted to know how I feel. I need to finish my thoughts. These are very important to me. I recognize and acknowledge that I quite probably wouldn't be here without the direct support of both of you. If I had shown up here by myself, they probably, and I'll add rightfully, would've called child services rather than admit me. I'm here because you believed in me enough to stand with me when I entered. I've heard real addicts talk about why they're dependent . . . and wish to be dependent. I've heard those people express their gratitude that they no longer have to steal, sell tainted drugs, and sell their bodies to obtain what they sought and what they felt they needed. I've seen hardcore meth addicts whose teeth are so rotten they can barely chew what food they consume. I've seen heroin addicts who are literally wasting away because they care more about the euphoria and oblivion of consumption over the food they need to sustain their lives. I'm learning so much from other people, things I couldn't learn from you. Yes, I know you've seen the worst of humanity. You've seen the consequences of addiction before the law changed and after. I've heard you say more than once that the new normal is far better than the old normal. I wasn't old enough to even be aware of the old normal as you call it. I've listened to what both of you have taught me, but I've also listened to real people who've lived that old normal. I have a very blessed life I'll be forever grateful for, but I want my children to learn about life better than I did. I want my children to be better informed. Those feelings lead me to a sense of activism . . . to help other people not as well informed as the two of you to learn . . . ," Bella paused, holding her right index finger to her quivering lips, as tears descended her flush cheeks, ". . . to learn that the government lied to you, lied to Grandma and Grandpa, and lied to me. The government sought isolation and ignorance. They, whoever they are, didn't want us to know the truth. Worse, by our forced ignorance, they wanted us to be afraid . . . to fear what we did not know. To be honest, this experience makes me want to be president, to lead this great country to a more enlightened and informed future, a better future for my children."

Marci and Rod could only stare at Bella; their mouths agape as if in speech, but no words came from them. They looked at each other several times and then back at their daughter, whose expression changed from satisfaction to curiosity, as she was asking with her eyes—well. Rod could only think, *oh my God, what have you done with my daughter? Where has she gone? Where did this young woman come from without us seeing? Why have we never seen her before?*

"Are you going to say anything?" Bella asked, glancing quickly at each of her parents, searching their eyes.

Again, Rod and Marci looked at each other and then back at Bella. Neither one of them could speak.

Bella's expression shifted again from curiosity to concern and then apprehension. "Did I say something wrong?"

"No!" Marci and Rod said simultaneously. "We . . . ," again, they said together. Marci nodded to Rod for him to respond.

"Bella Joy, I'm struggling to find the words. The only word that comes to me after listening to your words is a British slang word—gobsmacked. I'm literally gobsmacked. It means utterly astonished—astounded. You've shown us far more awareness and wisdom than people four times your age. We didn't teach you any of that. You've far outgrown us. You've perceived things that neither of us has felt. Yes, gobsmacked is the relevant word. Your Momma and I have a lot to talk about, to process, from what you've said. I can't predict the future, or how Momma and I will feel tomorrow, but I think we . . . no, here, I'll not presume to speak for your mother. Your words inspire me, Bella Joy."

"As am I," Marci added. "I share your father's sense of wonderment and amazement that you've grown up so fast. My apprehension has vanished. I know you have a handle on all this," she said, circling her head around the room. "We can leave here, trusting your judgment. You're a grown woman now, Bella Joy. I'll presume to speak for your father; we're very proud of you, enormously proud of you. And we eagerly look to the future and your accomplishments."

"Well said, Momma," Rod pronounced. "I'll only add, when you do run for president, you'll have my vote--proudly."

"And mine," added Marci.

Bella smiled broadly. "Wow! Really?"

"Yes, really," Rod said with strong emphasis that made others in the room look around at him. "I still can't believe those words came from our little baby daughter. I agree with Momma. You're a grown, mature woman. You've jumped from the nest, and you're flying like the powerful eagle you've become. That fact alone is impressive to watch." Tears descended his cheeks—not tears of pain or sorrow, but tears of immense pride. He did not attempt to wipe his tears away or hide them. "Momma was precisely correct. Our apprehension has vanished. You're far more in control of yourself than either of us could've ever imagined."

Now, Bella apparently needed a break. She stood. "I'll do the dishes." Bella grabbed the wadded-up wrapper balls and the empty cans. She walked to the trash bin and deposited the residue of their lunch in the proper bin.

"You're such a sweet, young woman," Marci observed. "We're so proud of you."

"You said that before," Bella chuckled.

"And we can't say it enough," Rod contributed. "I think we've accomplished what we hoped to do. We've got a long drive back to town.

We would like to assure you, we're ready to come get you when you're ready. Call us day or night. We only have a few years left with you before you leave the nest for good, for your own life. We want to enjoy every day we have remaining."

"That sounds so final."

"It's not, Bella Joy. It's just recognition that you're almost fully grown up, and our task is nearly done. As Momma said, we're very proud of you. We can't say it enough. I'm compelled to add my sincerest, deepest, most genuine apology to you for doubting your handling of all this. I was wrong, and for that, I apologize to you."

"Thank you, Papa. Thank you very much. That means an awful lot to me."

"We're always with you, Bella Joy. Just let us know how we can help you."

"Thank you, Papa . . . Momma."

"You're welcome," Marci and Rod said together.

"I don't want to see you go. I'm tempted to leave with you. You need to get back home before dark."

"That's OK. We don't turn into pumpkins when the sun sets."

"I know, but you know what I mean." Bella giggled.

Rod stood. Marci and Bella followed. They hugged and kissed each other, and then they hugged together. Marci and Rod walked Bella to the lobby. They hugged and kissed again, and then watched Bella pass through the door to the interior. She waved and smiled as the door closed.

Rod embraced Marci and kissed her forehead. He nodded to the receptionist and left the air-conditioned lobby for the heat of the exterior. Rod quickly scanned the horizon all around them. The thunderstorm cell he had noted early had dissipated and not been replaced by others. Rod started the car and gave it a minute or so to cool down before they closed the doors. Neither of them exchanged words until they were several miles down the road.

Marci was the first to speak. "That was not what I expected."

"Me either."

"How did she learn all those things?"

"I've no idea," Rod replied. "It's certainly something we should ask her when we get her home. I'm quite frankly staggered by how much she has seemingly grown in the last few months, incredible, simply incredible."

"There's so much I want to ask her, but that wasn't the time. She's so far beyond me."

"And me, truth be told. Heck, Marci, I've learned from her. I suspect I've got much more to learn from her."

"You and me, both. I think she clearly has been doing a lot more research and thinking about this stuff than we were aware of until now."

"You've got that right," Rod added. He drove several more miles before he continued. "She's made me think. I've got more homework to do to catch up with her. She used the word 'lied.' In a legal sense, lying requires intent. I've had the feeling for some time now that what we were being told was wrong, but I hadn't and still haven't gone as far as lying—willfully using falsehood to mislead the conversation. She knows far better than me how to use the Internet for research purposes. I suspect she may well be correct, but I've got to convince myself with evidence. Today, much of the congressional record is available to us on-line. We didn't have the benefit of the Internet when we were her age. I also have access to experts that I didn't have a few years ago. If she is correct, her observation changes the dialogue and the agenda. Ignorance is never good."

"What are you going to do?" Marci asked.

"Learn more about how we got to where we are."

"What do you mean?"

"There is one phrase I remember my parents telling me as a teenager, and I've seen it in various print documents about drug abuse when I was a young man. Marijuana is clearly not a gateway drug. It doesn't belong on the Schedule One list with other narcotics. But that is where it stays even to this day. If the government lied to us about marijuana, what else did they lie to us about in all this? We see more and more empirical evidence the rationale for the Controlled Substances Act is wrong in its entirety and probably based on emotion rather than hard evidence. I suspect Congress of that day reacted to the destruction of contraband substances that had no quality control, no regulation, no controls whatsoever. The Congressional Record is available to us today. It really wasn't available just a few decades ago. Thank you, Internet. Anyway, I've got so much reading to do."

"I guess I should read with you, then."

"That would be good."

"I think we both feel the same, Rod. Bella has leaped out in front of us a long way. We both need to catch up with her. We're both very proud of her."

"Yes, we are."

They drove a couple of dozen miles lost in their thoughts. Driving back into the setting sun was not the best choice, but it was what it was. Rod was noticeably less critical of other drivers on the road. Marci chuckled every time someone did not signal for a lane change, or drove too slow in the left lane, or cut them off, and Rod just shrugged his shoulders and let it pass.

"You know, sweetheart, I must confess I never really considered that we'd be learning from our daughter."

"Yeah, me either. She amazes me . . . so much more mature than I was at her age."

Rod laughed hard. "Me either." He laughed more. "We seem to be saying that a lot lately."

"Thanks to Bella," Marci said, smiling broadly.

"Indeed! I certainly feel a lot better than I did this morning."

"Ditto, my dear."

They rode along for several more miles with their thoughts.

"When do you think we're going to get her out of there and home with us?" Rod asked.

"When she's ready."

"Yeah . . . but when?"

"My guess is as good as yours," Marci answered. "She said days to a few more weeks. So far, she's done everything she said she was going to do. We have to be patient."

"Easier said than done when our daughter is involved."

The rest of the drive home was uneventful, and the day passed into night and contented sleep.

—

22

If it had not been for Kelly's short telephone call, Laura would have refused Raoul's request for her to accompany him to IC12 to visit his wife. Kelly had only asked for Laura to come with Raoul. She had not said it explicitly, but Laura believed Kelly wanted her to be a witness. Kelly clearly did not want to talk about her thoughts or feelings over the telephone, so Laura had not pressed her friend for more information. Laura had no idea how Raoul discovered or determined Kelly's location, but obviously, something had changed. Kelly might have told him for all she knew. He might have used his law enforcement contacts to track her down. Regardless, the telephone call from Raoul precisely stated that Kelly had invited him to visit her at the camp and that he was to bring Laura. There was nothing more of substance in their short conversation.

Last night had been a very productive and profitable night, although it ended later than expected—early this morning. Sleep had been deep, peaceful, and sound, but it had been far too short. She agreed to accompany Raoul, but she did not want to regret the comparatively early morning hour. After her shower, a bowl of cereal, brushing her teeth, but before she donned her plainest farm boy conservative attire, Laura removed the single foil-wrapped packet from her purse. She stared at it for a minute. The plain, sans serif, block lettering plainly and distinctly on the wrapper:

METH

Methamphetamine
single dose
30 mg / 70 kg body wt

Laura tore the wrapper, removed the single white pill, and swallowed it with water. Time: 7:45 AM. She knew it would take 30-45 minutes to feel the jolt of energy. The extra dose in her small shoulder purse might be required later in the day to keep her awake and alert. Laura instinctively knew it was going to be a long day, and she had appointments that began in the early evening. Her loose-fitting Levi's, sneaks, light blue tank top, and medium blue, light flannel over-shirt gave her a nice feel. Laura rolled up the shirt sleeves to just below her elbows. She checked her appearance in the floor to ceiling mirror. *That works.*

Just as she reached the living room window to check on Raoul's arrival to pick her up, a royal blue, slick, expensive-looking, Mercedes-Benz sedan pulled up to a stop. *That's the same kind of car Ted Graves had, just a different color.* That has to be Raoul. Laura grabbed her small, leather purse, put the long thin strap over her head and across her chest, and closed up her apartment.

Raoul had just stepped out of the car when Laura exited the building. They waved in recognition. As Laura neared the vehicle, Raoul opened the passenger door. He leaned forward and extended his left hand, clearly intent upon a more personal greeting. Laura felt his hand on the small of her back and offered her right cheek that Raoul kissed briefly.

"Nice car," observed Laura.

"Yep . . . an S-560," Raoul responded, as he closed the door. He walked around, settled himself in the driver's seat, and buckled his seatbelt. As they drove away to begin the day's journey, Raoul added, "Very powerful car . . . 460 horsepower . . . handles like a dream. . . sweet ride."

"I'll bet . . . a lot more car than my Mini." They both laughed.

Distant road noise in the well-insulated vehicle offered the background to their silence until they were on the freeway headed out of the city. Laura had questions, but she really did not want a conversation with Raoul. He broke the silence 30 minutes into their drive to IC12.

"Thank you for going with me," he said softly at almost an inaudible level.

"I'm doing this for Kelly."

"I know. She told me she wanted you to be there."

"She asked me to attend, but I didn't say much else," Laura said. She waited for several more miles and a comfortable gap in the moderate traffic. "If I may, how did you find her?"

A grin passed quickly across his face. He kept his eyes on the road and did not look or even glance at Laura. "I didn't. She called me, told me where she was and had been since she left, and asked to meet."

"Did she say what this is about?"

"I was going to ask you the same question. You're the one who talked to her after she left."

"We talked about a lot of things, Raoul. But my conversation a couple of days ago was quite short, and she offered no explanation . . . just her request."

"I'll bet you can guess what she wants to say."

"No, I don't, and I'm certainly not going to speculate. Kelly will tell you soon enough, and I'll hear whatever it is at the same time as you. So she told you where she was?"

Again, a grin quickly flashed and disappeared. "Yes. She said she left to enter the camp. I asked a bunch of questions, but she refused to answer any of my questions over the telephone. I'm not sure why. I can't imagine any surveillance warrants that would allow wiretapping, but I didn't check, and the issue is moot. You've visited her?"

"Yes, once, several months ago. I've also talked to Kelly several times before and after my visit."

"Was she happy?"

"Raoul, I understand your desire to know, but it's not my place to express her feelings."

"No. I'm just asking your impression . . . your opinion."

"My opinions are based on her words. I'm not going to discuss her words or even my impression of her words with you. Further, I'm absolutely not going to get into your relationship. I'm only a listener, a witness, at Kelly's request; nothing more."

"So," Raoul said and looked directly at Laura, "a hummer to relieve my tension is not in the offing?"

"No, it's not." *Ya gotta hand it to the guy; he's got balls.*

"A handie, perhaps?"

"Ain't gonna happen. You're welcome to jack it if you want an off so much."

Raoul did not respond. He did not challenge or press his request farther. They drove the rest of the way in silence. He did not attempt to relieve whatever tension he was feeling. Neither of them suggested stopping for food, drink, or relief.

They arrived ahead of their mid-morning requested meeting time. They checked in and had no problem finding an open table in the nearly empty visitor's lounge. Kelly must have been waiting for them, as she arrived shortly after they sat down. Laura stood to embrace her. She whispered to Kelly's right ear, "I hope you're OK with all this."

"I'm fine," Kelly responded more for Raoul than Laura.

Raoul stood and started to come around the table to embrace his wife but stopped when Kelly raised her right hand, palm out. Kelly sat across from Raoul, placing Laura in the middle.

"How have you been, sweetie?" Raoul asked.

"I'm fine . . . never been better, but now, I'm going to speak, and I want you to listen 'til I'm done. OK?" Laura glanced at Raoul to see his wordless acknowledgment. "I chose to leave you for a host of reasons, Raoul, not least of which was to clear my head, figure things out for myself, and find my path forward. I'll say at the outset that I appreciate all you've provided, but material wants have never been my objective. I was practically a zombie zoned out on Xanax. It took me several months to ween myself off of the benzos. I have truly appreciated the isolation of this place and genuinely appreciate the tolerance of the state in allowing my entrance and access without judgment or restriction. I'm not here for the drugs, and the managers of this facility have figured that out. They finally got around to asking the question, so I surmise my days here are numbered. They've not asked me to leave, but I can feel the question hovering out there."

"Are you coming home?"

"Raoul, stop. I asked you to listen, to let me talk. I'm not finished. I asked you to come here to listen. I've rehearsed my little speech for weeks now. I freely admit and confess that I've not been a model wife or marital partner. I know that. I admit it freely. At best, I was perhaps adequate arm candy for a rising district attorney. I was in a perpetual depression for years until I found solace in benzos, specifically Xanax. Eventually, the benzos began eating my soul. So, there I was . . . damned if I did, damned if I didn't. I know they let me in here because of the drugs, and I can't possibly express my gratitude to the state and the people of the state, for allowing me this retreat. But I didn't come here for the drugs. I came here to get away."

"Kelly!" Raoul protested.

"Stop, damn it!" shouted Kelly. "You're never going to intimidate me again, Raoul. I came here to get away from you." It was as if she had instantly slapped him in the face very hard. The genuinely shocked expression on Raoul's face surprised both women.

He had no idea she was that unhappy, Laura thought. *That expression speaks volumes; it seems to me.*

"It's not my intent to criticize you," Kelly continued, staring intently and directly into Raoul's eyes. "You're who you are. You're who your parents raised and taught. I've no interest, desire, or energy to change you. You're who you are," she repeated. "What I am here to state emphatically, without equivocation or qualification, is I'm not going to take it anymore. The compromises I had to make to live with you were the source of my depression. This place and these legal drugs helped me realize what I must do. First, I'm not finished with my search for discovery, so I'm going to stay here as long as they'll allow me, or until I've a clearer view of my path forward. What I do know is, I'm not going back to the way it was."

"Kelly, I can change."

"Shut the fuck up!" she shouted quite loudly and angrily. So much so, the matronly receptionist came to the door and said with a commanding voice. "Is there a problem here?"

Kelly bowed her head and waved her right hand that everything was OK. Apparently satisfied, the woman left them alone. Kelly took a couple of deep, cleansing breaths to calm herself.

"I'm sorry," Raoul said softly and rather meekly, causing Laura to glance at him.

Again, Kelly waved her hand dismissively. She placed both hands flat on the table and raised her head to once again stare into his eyes with defiance in her eyes. "I'm not going to debate any of your personality flaws or mine with you . . . not now, not ever. As I said, you're who you are. I just know now that I can't live with that man. So, here is what you're going to do. I abandoned you, not the other way around. You're going to file for divorce. You can dictate whatever terms you feel are appropriate for our years . . . our dysfunctional years . . . together, and for my abandonment. I don't care what those terms are. I truly don't. Once that is done, I'll leave here and move on to the rest of my life, whatever that may be." Silence filled the space between them.

Damn, I wonder what the hell she's thinking. Is she seriously considering the profession of pleasure and flesh? What does she want to do after walking away from everything she had? I have so many questions I want to ask her, but I don't dare interrupt her thinking . . . and certainly not in front of Raoul.

After several minutes, Raoul gestured as if asking Kelly if she was done. Kelly stared at Raoul with her forehead lowered and a stern determined expression for several seconds, and then nodded her head in consent.

"First, we're not going to divorce," he declared. Kelly's expression did not change. "Second, you take whatever time you need to get yourself straight, and then you'll come home to me."

Damn, he just doesn't get it, Laura thought without expression or reaction.

"Third, I forgive your transgressions without qualification. Fourth, we'll get you whatever professional assistance you need to see things more clearly and help you realize that I love you very much. I don't want to lose you."

You lost her a long time ago, you idiot!

Kelly just stared at him with the unflickering stony expression. She's not budging. "Raoul, let me try once more to make this as clear as I possibly can. Your *machismo* bullshit and your days of lord and master crap are over, period, full stop, do not pass GO, do not collect $200."

Good for you, honey. You go, girlfriend.

"I'll die," she continued, "before I return to your abusive male bullshit."

"Abusive!" shouted Raoul.

Oh, dear, please don't say that. He's not worth it.

The receptionist appeared in the doorway again. This time Raoul waved his hand dismissively at her. She did not move until Kelly gave her a thumb's up sign. The woman returned to her desk without speaking.

I suppose she is accustomed to expressive emotions in this place.

"*Ve a buscar a una linda chica*," Kelly nearly spit out in Spanish.

Wow! I've never heard her speak Spanish before. Will wonders ever cease? Laura thought. *This is beginning to worry me, maybe even scare me.*

"No! I have you. I have a wife."

"No, you don't. You've not had a wife for more years than I choose to count. It's time for you to move on as well, Raoul. Let me go! You know I'm right. It's just better for your career if you divorce me for my abandonment than if I divorce you for your abuse and seek a temporary restraining order."

That got his attention. Laura noted his discernible change of expression. "You wouldn't."

"Oh yes, I would, and I suggest you don't want to test my newfound resolve. If I ever held any sway over you, that power has vanished. I've no control over what you do or don't do. As they tell us in here, 'Grant me the serenity to accept the things I cannot change, the courage to change the things I can, and the wisdom to know the difference.' I possess that serenity today with crystal clear sobriety and resolve."

Raoul could only stare at her with a strange admixture of expressions—wonderment, fear, and apprehension.

After several minutes, Kelly added, "You take all the time you need, Raoul. I've nothing but time in here. If there's one thing you take away from this visit and our conversation, it should be clear that my mind is made up. Do not try any of your legal shenanigans. One crucial thing I've learned in this place, in this indulgence camp, is they finally respect my freedom of choice. You no longer have any control over my actions, my opinions, my beliefs, or my thoughts. We're done, Raoul. I suggest we part ways peacefully, amicably if possible, and without rancor or dispute. As I said earlier, I abdicate full control to you in this final action of our relationship. I loved you once. I do not love you anymore. Best you recognize reality, give me what I want and what you wish to give me, and move on."

"Sweetheart . . ." He stopped when she raised her right arm shoulder height with her palm out.

"I've said what I needed to say. We're done." She looked directly at Laura. "Thank you for coming." Kelly stood. Laura followed. The two women embraced in a warm and intimate hug. Kelly backed away just enough to raise both hands to grasp Laura's head gently, stared into her eyes for a moment, and then kissed her passionately for longer than expected. *Wow! That was some kiss.* Kelly did not release her grasp on Laura's head, but she withdrew her head just enough to look deeply into Laura's emerald green eyes. She kissed her quickly one more time, and then silently said with her lips, thank you very much. Kelly gave Laura one last peck, and then she turned sharply and marched boldly, confidently, and without hesitation out of the visitor's lounge, and back into the camp. She did not even acknowledge Raoul's presence.

Once Kelly disappeared behind the entrance door, Laura looked over her shoulder at Raoul. His expression had mutated from shock and disappointment to anger.

"Sit!" he commanded.

"I'm thirsty. Do you want a drink?"

He thought for a moment. "Sure. Coke, please."

Laura went to the free vending machine. She retrieved a Coke for him and a Diet Coke for her.

When Laura sat, and they both opened their cans with the characteristic pop-cush, he said, "What the hell was all that?"

"I think she was quite clear, Raoul. You're a man of words. I do believe you understand the English. I've not heard her speak so cogently and precisely in many years."

"Are you two lovers?"

Laura laughed hard, deep down from her belly. When her laughter finally began to subside, she answered, "No, but we certainly could be with a kiss like that." Laura shook her head and chuckled some more. "Just like a man, all men, you're more concerned about the sex than the substance."

"An easy accusation to make, but that little display surprised and perhaps shocked me. I don't think she has kissed me like that ever."

"Your loss."

"So, what do I do now?"

"It's not for me to say, Raoul, but my opinion is, you should do exactly as she says."

"My faith doesn't allow divorce."

Laura smiled broadly and held Raoul's eyes. "I've never known you to be a man of faith."

"Maybe not, but my parents are, and they'd never forgive me."

Laura chuckled inaudibly but visibly. "Time you grow up."

"That's not a very nice thing to say, Laura."

"Perhaps not, but it's the truth. I'll not be so generous or respectful as Kelly was. You've got an abusive, domineering streak in you that is no longer relevant or tolerable. The days of coverture have long been over legally, for decades now, and as an accomplished lawyer, you must know that. The last of the head and master laws were struck down by the Supreme Court in 1981. I don't care, and neither does Kelly, what you were taught as a child, but you're no longer the king of your realm. To be blunt, you've spent Kelly's generosity and tolerance. She obviously has nothing left to give you."

"I'm not that way."

"Then perhaps you're incapable of self-assessment or self-awareness. I've seen it myself, Raoul, personally and firsthand. Even your sexual conduct is domineering and definitely not respectful. I'm not alone in that observation, just from the women I know you've been active with recently." Laura paused to think about how much farther she wanted to press this argument. *If I'm going to help her, I need to make him understand her.* "I don't know what she said in Spanish, but I believe I caught the drift."

"She said, go find a pretty young woman."

"Sounds like good advice. I'm sure there are plenty of women out there who are willing to submit to your *macho* bullshit. Kelly is not one of those any longer. And I'm not either, no matter how much money you've got. I think she was excessively generous to you and your profession."

"Do you think she is really that hardened?"

"Yes."

Raoul lapsed into contemplation. He did not even sip his drink, although Laura took several good swallows of her soda.

Laura looked out the window at the desert landscape of the terrain surrounding the indulgence camp facility, as she waited patiently. She checked the wall clock—1:17 PM. *We need to be heading back pretty soon, or I'll have to make other arrangements for my customers.*

Raoul eventually looked up from the table and at Laura. "So, you think I should give in to her?"

"Don't think of it that way. Think of it as respecting her wishes."

"Has it really come to this?"

"Yes."

Raoul again lapsed into cogitation. Laura was willing to give him space, but her sense of irritation and reaction were rising to the level of awareness, and it was heading toward the threshold of tolerance. *I've got to give him space. This is not my time. If we don't head back by two, I'll either have to call my customers for this evening, or perhaps I can get Blondie or Juli to service my customers tonight.*

Laura finished her drink, placed her aluminum can in the recycle bin, and then she sat back down and folded her hands in front of her. She waited patiently, without expression, staring out the window.

"Oh my, look at the time. I suppose we must be going. I need to get you back for your . . . your . . ."

"Appointments."

"Exactly . . . your appointments."

"It's up to you. I came on this little adventure for Kelly and for you. Whatever you want."

"I need a good poke."

Laura smiled.

"Well, that's better than an 'ain't gonna happen' rejection."

"Don't get your hopes up, Hoss. Ain't gonna happen. Better?" They both laughed. "My position has not changed, Raoul. So, if you need more time here, we'll take the time. I'll just need to make some calls."

"No, no, no need. It's not fair of me to keep you from your work." Raoul stood and gestured to the door.

They both made a pit stop before hitting the road and then checked out as another family arrived. The drive back to the city began with silence. Laura did not really want to talk to Raoul, but she recognized that an utterly silent journey was not likely. Neither of them showed any sign of needing to stop for food, drink, or relief. The respite just could not last.

"Am I going to get you back in time?" asked Raoul eventually.

Laura glanced at her smartphone time and compared it to the vehicle clock. "Yes. Barring any bad traffic between here and home, I should have plenty of time to prepare."

"What do you do to prepare, if I may ask?"

"The gory details serve no purpose. Let it suffice to say that I make sure my body is smooth, thoroughly clean, inside and out, and ready to give a customer whatever pleasure he or she desires."

"You have female customers?"

"Yes . . . more than a few."

That answer apparently satisfied his curiosity and perhaps gave him some different subject matter to think about as he drove. Laura was grateful for the silence they had for the remainder of their drive.

Raoul pulled up in front of her apartment, left the engine running presumably for the air conditioning, released his seat belt, and shifted in his seat to face Laura. She unbuckled her seat belt but did not exit the car.

"Thank you for going with me," he said.

"You're welcome." *No need to add anything more.*

"Can I call you sometime?"

"You can call me anytime you wish . . . for a chat . . . not for sex or intimate contact."

"I'll take what I can get. I imagine I'll need your counsel as I work through this mess."

"Life is messy, Raoul. Don't fret over it. Just move on. Kelly gave you extraordinary latitude, probably because she prefers no resistance rather than assets. That said, I hope you can find it in your heart to give her a generous settlement, but that is your choice entirely. As she said, she doesn't care and places herself at your mercy."

"I've got a lot to think about."

"Yes, you do. I'd really like to know what you decide, if you don't mind sharing it with me."

"I see no reason not to do so. You've certainly been the closest to this very personal affair."

"Thank you." Laura reached for the door handle.

Before she opened the door, Raoul said, "Can I at least have a kiss?"

"Nope," she responded, as she opened the car door and stepped out. From the curb, she bent over to connect with Raoul's eyes. "Eventually, you'll give up."

"Perhaps, but not yet. Enjoy your work tonight."

"I will," she answered and firmly closed the door. As she walked toward the entrance door, Laura did not hear his engine start. *He's probably watching my butt as I walk. Good move, my dear, wearing loose-fitting Levi's.* Laura did not look back at him. *I'm not going to give him the satisfaction.* She walked up the stairs and entered her apartment. Out of curiosity, Laura surreptitiously looked out the front window. His car was still there. Laura went back to her front door and engaged the deadbolt for an extra measure of safety . . . just in case.

As was her routine, Laura went to her work telephone. She had three messages. The first two were for future appointments next weekend that she would confirm on Monday. The third one was from Kelly.

"Laura, this is Kelly. I know you're traveling back to the city with Raoul, so I couldn't call your cellphone. Please call me as soon as you are able at 945-233-1756. That's the IC12 message service. Leave a message telling me your available time window. They get me a message note within minutes. Thanks, sweetie. It was so great seeing you again. Sorry it had to be in such difficult circumstances. Until we talk, bye-bye." Laura wrote down the number on a notepad.

I need to get ready for work first, and then I'll call Kelly.

Laura showered, and she tended to all of her usual hygiene and preparation processes. Her routine was well-rehearsed and practiced, and surprisingly did not take much time to complete. She chose a lightweight, airy, short, floral print dress with no undergarments. They always got lost or were retained as souvenirs, so it was no longer worth the pretense. Laura checked herself in the mirror—front, sides, and back. *Ready.* The clock told her she had 45 to 60 minutes at the outside before she had to leave to begin the evening's pleasure.

The call to IC12 was easy enough. The operator indicated the number was manned 24/7. The young man took down Laura's message and told her he would deliver it promptly. *It seemed odd given contemporary telephonic technology that they're using a manual messaging service. I suppose it's to control and regulate communications rather than the retention of old methods.* Laura made herself a single piece of peanut butter toast with a bottle of chilled water. It was not a proper meal, but it was best to keep the contents of her stomach low for this evening's activities. She planned to take her second Meth tab before she left her apartment.

The *Game of Thrones* theme song ring tone announced a cellphone call. Laura looked at the number. It was probably Kelly. She touched the green accept spot on her screen. "Hello."

"Laura, it's me."

"Hiya, kiddo. How are you feeling?"

"Good, actually. Thanks for calling back so quickly. How was your drive back?"

"For the most part, quiet. He is struggling with what he should do."

"That's his problem," Kelly said, with a definite sneer to her voice. "It's really quite simple. I made it as easy and straight forward as I possibly could."

"Yes, you did, overly so in my humble opinion. He did ask me if he could call to talk about things."

"He didn't call you for a poke?"

"Oh, he's asked several times, Kell. I did him once for business after you left, and it's never going to happen again."

"He's got a shitload of money, Laura. You might as well get some of it."

"He doesn't know how to enjoy the pleasures of the flesh with a woman."

"Maybe he's really into men." They both laughed hard through a couple of waves.

"Perhaps. We'll never know. So, what are you going to do?"

"Well, the first order of business is satisfying the powers that be here so that I can stay. I'm not untouchable by him in here, but this is about as close as I can probably get. Then, I'll wait for his decision—his next move. Thank you so much for being my witness, Laura. It means so much to me."

"That's what friends are for, Kell. Have you thought about what you are going to do when you get through this rough patch and leave IC12?"

"Like I told you before, I thought about your profession. All I've got to do is spread my legs."

Laura chuckled softly. "It takes a lot more than that for most men and for all women."

"Yeah, probably so. You, of course, know quite well. I've got a nice and worthy body, but I just don't enjoy sex like you do."

"That is pretty much a requirement. You need to really enjoy it or be an exceptional actor, but the latter option just seems like a dead-end road to me. Our customers today can very quickly detect a service provider who is not into it or enjoying herself . . . or himself for that matter."

"Anyway, to answer your question, no, I don't know what I'm going to do. That very question is at the top of my 'to do' list while the asshole is figuring out what he's going to do."

"Is there anything I can do to help?"

"Just be a good friend."

"That's easy. By the way, that was one helluva kiss when you left."

"Heartfelt . . . truly."

"I could tell. You know, Kell, in that kiss, I felt the fires of passion smoldering within you. You might search your soul. Maybe your distaste for sex is a direct product of Raoul's peculiarities and limitations. Perhaps there is a beautiful bloom within you just waiting for the right moment to spread her glory."

"Maybe, but I just can't imagine that potential at the moment."

"Understandable. I only mention it because I felt it in our kiss this afternoon."

"I'm so glad you felt it, because that's exactly what I felt at the moment, and I still do feel it."

"I must say, Kell, that Raoul didn't miss the moment either. He was somewhat shocked by what he saw, and especially with your departure."

"Good. I wanted him to see and know that I'm a lot more than what he allowed me to be—an awful lot more."

"I think he got the message."

"Laura, the kiss was for you, not for him."

"I felt that."

"I just wanted you to know how I felt. One last thought, 'cuz I know you've got to go." Laura glanced quickly at the wall clock. *She's right. I need to be getting along here.* "If you really think the potential is within me, perhaps I could apprentice with you . . . learn to really enjoy sex."

"Sure. I'm game. I've got a few worthy clients who would truly enjoy a 'two-fer,' and I think I could coax the bud to blossom in all her glory. There is more within you, Kell. I just know it, and you may not be aware of your potential."

"I'll keep that in mind as this sordid affair plays out. One more one last thing," she giggled, "if you do talk to Raoul, you're free to disclose our conversations to him. I'll tell you directly if there is something I don't want him to know. Other than that, everything is fair game. If you do talk to him, I'd appreciate knowing what he's thinking and planning, just to get my head straight and prepared."

"Sure, no problem whatsoever. I think he kind of expects it. Anyway, after that kiss, he asked me if we were lovers."

Kelly laughed hard. "I'll bet he did . . . that sordid pervert of a man. If you only knew, Laura."

"I don't know, and I really don't want to know unless there is something you want to share with me. He's caught up in that old-world, male-dominant thinking."

"Exactly. He's from a previous century . . . thanks to his parents. They never liked me . . . and I guess they were right."

"Don't say that Kell. You're a whole lot of woman, much more than he deserves. All that *macho* nonsense he seems to believe in is from an era long past. The more you're able to see that, the quicker your recovery will be, my friend. You're not what he has allowed you to be, and you're so much more than that. Although we've not really talked much about your experience in the camp, I sense that you've touched upon your own awakening. Only you can know if it is true, but I sense that you have come to realize that he is the source of your depression. Once you felt the freedom that the camp has given you, the more you have felt that reality. From my perspective, keep doing what you're doing. You're on the path of your own discovery. You've got a very bright future, Kell. Look to tomorrow and putting this time behind you. You've learned. You know what matters to you, and more importantly, what doesn't matter to you. The tide has changed."

"It's always so rejuvenating when I get to talk to you. You're an extraordinary woman, Laura Lynn Simmons."

"Thanks, sweetie. Now, I've got customers waiting for my exceptional services." Laura giggled softly. "I really must be going."

"Sure. I understand. Thank you so much for calling me back and for coming today. I can never repay you for your friendship and caring."

"No need, Kell. You're in my heart. Call me whenever you need me. I'll be there for you."

"Thanks. Laura."

The two women offered well-wishes and said goodbye. Laura took several deep breaths. I sure hope she makes it. She grabbed a little filtered water and swallowed the other Meth pill to keep her going this evening, and she added an MDMA pill—Ecstasy—for good measure. She could not allow the reality of only three hours of sleep in the last 42 hours to interfere with her performance this evening. It would probably be another eight hours before she had any hope of sleep. *Tomorrow is definitely going to be a crash recovery day for me.* She was out the door and on her way to her first appointment.

—

23

The chief had called Rod off another embezzlement case he was working for an unscheduled, unplanned meeting with him and the mayor in the latter's office. He knew the irritation he felt would subside as he neared city hall. Rod had no idea whatsoever exactly what topic was on the table. *Have I done something wrong? Is there some sensitive political issue associated with one of my open, active cases?* The chief had not given him any head's up, which was not characteristic for Chief Harris. He was an accomplished and respected chief of police. He was also a tough taskmaster when it came to the job and responsibilities of policing. Rod used his keyed ID card to access the City Hall underground parking garage and took one of the reserved police parking spaces next to the elevator. He was alone inside the elevator and pushed the number '10' for the top floor.

"Detective-Sergeant Ramirez," he said to the mayor's secretary. "I was called to the mayor's office by Chief Harris."

"Yes, Detective. They're expecting you." She stood, went to the large double doors, knocked, and stepped partially inside to announce Rod's arrival.

"Please send him in." Rod heard from inside the office.

His secretary stood back, opened the door wider, and looked at Rod to nod him inside. Both men were standing. Harris shook hands with Rod first, and then Mayor Geraldo 'Gerry' Garcia. "Great to see you again, Detective," Garcia said.

"Likewise, Mister Mayor," Rod responded.

Garcia gestured to the leather overstuffed chairs around a small, round coffee table. "Would you like any coffee, water, bourbon?"

Rod smiled. "No, thank you, sir."

"Ah yes, on duty."

"Yes sir."

"The chief and I were discussing an upcoming conference I'll host on the local assessment of the state's drug policy. This is part of an initiative generated by the Domestic Policy Subcommittee of the House Oversight and Government Reform Committee in DC to collect information from the local governments in our state. The unofficial word is enough House members are interested in updating and reforming federal drug policy based on our experience. The chief reminded me that you were selected to be and are a member of the governor's commission."

"The chief is correct."

"Excellent. I asked the chief if you could join our drug policy assessment conference, thus his request for you to join us this morning. Will your caseload allow you to participate?"

"Yes sir. I think I can manage."

"Excellent. If I'm informed correctly, you've some personal experience with the major elements of reform as well as your law enforcement exposure."

Is he indirectly asking me about my daughter? How would he know about Bella? I've not even told the chief. "Yes sir. I requested authority to escort my first convict to Black Hole Confinement Number Seven and arranged for a tour—quite an eye-opener. Well, actually, my tour was limited to the control room and video screens. We've referred quite a few, but I've not counted how many citizens have gone to Indulgence Camp Number 12. They don't have tours or even the sophisticated surveillance capability that BHC7 has available to them. I've not followed-up on all of those individuals to see the success rate. I know some emerge, having broken the cycle of abuse. I think a fraction of those going in have chosen to remain. I've had enough on my plate to keep me busy, and I'm not aware of any professional study of recidivism at IC12, and the term is moot with BHC7."

"You're far ahead of me or the chief either," Garcia said, pausing to glance at Harris for a confirmatory head nod, "for that matter. Neither of us has seen those facilities. Let me ask you, should we visit them?"

"Neither of them does tours, but I think a visit could be arranged."

"Yes, but should we . . . ?"

"That's your choice entirely," Rod responded, looking at both men. "If you're asking me if such a visit was vital to your jobs, I'd say no. It's not really essential to my job either, but my curiosity and my work with the governor's commission compelled me to learn more."

"Tell us just a little about both types of facilities, if you would," the mayor said.

"With the SCIP Act, the indulgence camps were set up to be a middle ground between normal life and prison. The commercial sales of formerly controlled substances that were restricted by the federal Controlled Substances Act have seriously reduced, but not eliminated, the criminal aspects of drugs. The indulgence camps have further reduced drug-associated crime by collecting up junkies, so they don't have to resort to crime to feed their habits. The black hole units were added at the far end of the penal system. The convict I mentioned earlier was possessed by his efforts to avoid the camp, so much so that it made me wonder how he learned about what was meant by confinement in a black hole facility—he really did not want to go into the block. Several stints in prison didn't cure him or convince him to amend his ways, but BHC7 will end his threat to our community."

"From what I've heard, those black hole units are rather brutal," observed Garcia.

"They're supposed to be," Harris added.

"That is certainly what drove the convict and his antics to avoid entrance. He believed the black hole was cruel and unusual punishment, and he and his lawyer contended the black hole system violated his Eighth Amendment protections. But I must say, other than the convict in question, the place was quite peaceful, ordered, and rather non-descript. I was surprised if I must say. I've not seen hard data yet, but I'll bet when the data are collected, it may well show our recidivism rate is demonstrably lower after the SCIP Act and the advent of the black hole facilities. To my knowledge, the changes created by the SCIP Act have done precisely what they were intended to do. This is not to say that improvements can't be made, or additional tweaks may be necessary, but I feel safe to say that the changes made in this state have greatly reduced the consequences of drug smuggling, drug addiction and abuse, and the associated crime. At the bottom line, our community is safer and more peaceful because of the SCIP Act."

"Do you think you can collect the data to prove that statement?" Garcia asked.

"I don't know, Mister Mayor. I'm just a cop."

"One helluva cop I must add," Harris contributed.

Rod nodded in recognition to the chief. He looked back at Mayor Garcia. "The governor's commission has a data collection office with a half dozen specialists. I can call them to see . . ." Rod's smartphone rang and vibrated in his inside jacket pocket. It was the ringtone that gave him a start. His initial reaction was embarrassment that his phone interrupted the mayor and chief's meeting, but the ringtone was unique to one person on the face of the planet. "Excuse me, Mister Mayor, Chief, that is Marci, and it must be something rather important. Would you please excuse me?"

"By all means," the mayor responded. "Family first."

Rod extracted his phone as he stood and walked to the door. He hit the 'Accept' button and put the phone to his ear. "Standby, Marci." He kept the phone at his ear, although there were no words. Rod waited until he was in the hallway at the far end near the large, picture window that covered the entire end of the hallway overlooking the city. "I'm sorry, Marci. I was in a meeting with the mayor and the chief. What's up?"

"Rodrigo," she said with stuttering emotion, "I just got a call from Bella. Something has happened. She would not tell me what it was or why, but she was crying and very upset."

"Is she in any danger?"

"I don't think so, but I've never heard her so upset and emotional. I'm scared, Rod."

A million thoughts flashed through his consciousness as he considered the possibilities. "Did she want us to do anything?"

"She wants us to go get her."

"When?"

"Now!" Marci shouted.

Rod kept very quiet and calm. Fortunately, there were very few people in the top floor hallway, so there was no noise of movement or discussion. *I need to give her a few moments to calm herself.* "Let me go tell the mayor and chief I've got a family emergency. They'll understand."

This time, Marci was quiet, as her mind was probably grinding through the options. "No, no," she finally said. "It must be important." *It's not that important*, Rod thought. "I'm sorry to have interrupted your meeting. Please convey my apologies to the mayor and the chief. I think I can drive. I'll go get her. I don't want to wait for you to be available. Let me get her home, and then we can talk to her tonight."

"Are you sure?"

"Yes, I'm sure. I've calmed down a little, but it was very upsetting to hear her like that, Rod."

"OK. I'll pass along your apology, and I'll keep my phone on. You must not hesitate to call me if there is anything wrong, or you even have a flat tire. I can turn my lights on in the department car and be there far faster than you. Also, I want you to call me when you arrive, when you've got her, and when you get home. Can you remember all that?"

"Yes," she answered dismissively. "I just can't imagine what would've upset her so much."

"Who knows? There are many things that it could be, but I've never heard of anything dangerous or threatening in an indulgence camp. If it's nothing dangerous, then it was probably emotionally unsettling for her. Let's get her home and safe, and then we can talk to her."

"OK. I'm leaving now."

"Take some extra water and something to eat, a few snack bars, or something quick and easy."

"Sure. Good idea. OK. Again, I'm sorry to have interrupted your meeting with the mayor. I'm leaving now. I'll call you when I get there."

"Thanks, Marci. Be safe. Don't speed. Keep your mind on the road and traffic. Don't allow yourself to be distracted. I should be done with this meeting by the time you arrive, so please do not hesitate to call me."

"I won't."

"I love you. Give Bella a hug and kiss for both of us when you get her."

"I love you, Rod. Oh, I'll probably overdo the hugs and kisses." They both laughed. *A good sign.* They said goodbye, and Marci disconnected.

Rod took a very deep breath and let it out audibly in a long hiss. He held his phone's sound volume button down to silence his phone. *I'll just have to take the risk. I can't accept another interruption of the mayor, especially with the chief in attendance. I'll check for calls and turn my phone back on after we're done.*

When he reentered the mayor's corner office, he noticed the fantastic view out the panoramic windows. *There are perks.* "Excuse me for the interruption, but I needed to take that one."

"Is everything OK?" the chief asked.

"Yes sir, well, more or less. Our daughter is having a bit of a crisis, apparently. Marci is going to pick her up."

"If you need to leave, Rod," the mayor said, "don't hesitate."

"Not necessary, sir. I think Marci has it, and she asked me to pass along her apologies for pulling me out of your meeting."

"Nonsense, Rod. These things happen. I'm just glad it's not serious."

It was sure serious to her, but I'm not going to say that to you.

Garcia paused to think for a moment. "Very well, then, you were talking about the governor's commission data collection specialists," Garcia reminded him.

"Yes. Thanks. They're a pretty good bunch. I'll pose the questions to them and see what they can come up with for answers."

"Excellent. You might also talk to Betty in the Registrar's Office. I don't know what they've got her working on, but she's a pretty good ferret. She might find something valuable, as well."

"Sure. I've talked to Betty more than a few times. She's usually overloaded, but I might catch her with an opening."

"Excellent." *He likes that word*, Rod thought. "So, you'll be able to join us?" Garcia asked Rod.

Detective Ramirez took a quick look at Chief Harris, who nodded his consent. "I believe so."

"Perfect. We'll convene a week from Thursday in the Council Chamber." Mayor Garcia stood. *The meeting is apparently over*, Rod thought. Chief Harris and Rod stood as well. The mayor extended his right hand to both Harris and Ramirez, shaking hands with each man. "Thank you for joining us, Detective. Great suggestion, Chief," the mayor acknowledged and nodded his head toward Rod. "I look forward with eager anticipation to our meeting."

The two police officers said their goodbyes to the mayor and his secretary. Once in the hallway, Chief Harris gestured toward the large window at the end of the hallway and asked, "Do you have a few minutes to spare for me?"

"Of course, Chief."

Harris gestured for them to sit on the long, oak bench in front of the window. "My apologies for no head's up on that meeting. The mayor sprung the topic on me as well."

"No problem, Chief. I'm at your service." They sat.

"You've become our leading voice on the SCIP Act implementation."

"Not my choice, sir."

"Understood, but nonetheless, here you are. I've not had the occasion to convey my gratitude for your efforts to help us all understand the consequences of these changes in our community. I also wanted you to know that I personally and professionally support your representation of these changes. I confess to my skepticism early on in this process."

"I was as well," Rod added. "The data convinced me."

"Quite so. The mayor didn't explain to you how all this came about, and I thought that would be important for you to know. The governor held a telecon with the mayors of the state to inform them of the House initiative. None of us are overly optimistic that the feds might change course, but it's progress for them to at least ask some questions. According to the mayor, the governor believes the House effort may stimulate other states to join us."

"That would be a huge step forward, but in my view, it seems remote at the moment."

"Why is that do you think?"

"I've thought a lot about that. In thinking through the changes and the field data we've collected, I had to reconsider the source of my opinions. I believe the resistance is the extraordinary bias taken by Congress in the late 60s and early 70s. We see physical evidence that the foundational rationale was false, based on emotion rather than hard science. I think we've seen enough hard evidence that the drugs were never the problem. They've a useful purpose if used properly and respectfully. Our state has taken on a monumental effort and risk to illuminate reality, and to correct the grievous errors of 50 years ago. We're slowly but surely bringing the truth to the public stage, but I also think we'd be grotesquely naïve if we think our experience will overcome the social conservative bent that still holds sway through most of the country."

"Yes, but wouldn't you say, we're making progress. I mean the fact that the House of Representatives would even allow an investigation or public hearings on drug policy seems like progress."

"Yes, I agree, Chief. But hearings aren't legislation and change."

"Long journeys begin with small steps, Rod."

"So true, and we've got a very long journey with a rough ride ahead of us. It took just 14 hard years for us to learn that prohibition of alcohol was not achievable in a free society, and by that prohibition, we produced an entire criminal subculture that caused its own destruction. We've been at this war on drugs for better than 50 years with nothing to show for our efforts but a broad path of destruction from individuals to nations. Our war on drugs has degenerated marginal states in Central America into the chaos that produced a flood of refugees overwhelming our dysfunctional immigration system. How much more destruction will it take for us to learn—we're a free society. We cherish our freedom. We've implemented laws to address the abuse of alcohol while respecting the freedom of choice of every citizen. The SCIP Act is a noble effort to do the same with psychotropic substances. We've given up far too much freedom to validate the moral outrage of a willful minority. I've had to think about and read far too much about this question. From my perspective, the bottom line is that the SCIP Act is the first *bona fide* effort to recognize reality."

"Very well said, Rod. It sounds like you should be running for president."

"No sir. Absolutely not. My chosen profession is hard enough on the lives of my wife and daughter. I couldn't in good conscience add to their burden."

Chief Harris glanced at his wristwatch. "I'm afraid I'm late for another meeting. Thank you for the chat, Rod. Let me close here by saying, you've got my support. If you run into any obstacles that I might be of assistance in overcoming, please don't hesitate to call me directly. I'll take the obligation to inform your chain of command of this directive. Thank you, again, and keep up the good work."

"Thank you, sir."

Chief Harris stood and stepped out smartly. Rod stood and saluted the retreating posterior of Chief Harris. Detective Ramirez walked at a more casual pace toward the elevator. He extracted his smartphone to check for any messages from Marci—none. The time told him Marci had another 20 minutes or so before she should be arriving at IC12. *I'll feel a whole lot better once I know Bella is safe.* Rod rechecked the phone's sound was full-on. He took the elevator down to the top floor of the basement parking garage.

Rod figured he would reset his day and return to the office to catch up with the team. He stopped at his favorite street vendor's mobile canteen to buy a small *carne asada burrito*—the regular size was just too big. When he was roughly halfway through the remainder of his drive to his precinct office, his telephone ringtone announced Marci's call. Rod quickly pulled over to the curb and placed his vehicle in Park.

"You just arrived?"

"Yes. The drive wasn't too bad," Marci said. "As requested, I wanted to call you. I just got here, and I'm getting ready to go inside to pick her up."

"Are you OK?"

"Yes. I'll either call you from inside or in the car. I'd suggest we don't question her, Rod. Let's let her tell us what she wants to tell us."

"Agreed. I'm on the road. I should be back in the office in 10 minutes or so."

"OK. I'll call you shortly."

"I'll be standing by." They disconnected. Rod reached for the shift handle but hesitated. *It's only going to be a few minutes, and I'd rather take the next call with more privacy than I have in the office.* Rod pulled his right hand from the shift lever. He quickly looked around to make sure he was in a safe area. Satisfied, Rod turned on the car's commercial radio for some rock-n-roll music behind the routine police radio chatter. As was his nature born during his service as a Marine, Rod continuously scanned the space around his vehicle, making good use of the car's mirrors and windows. He no longer thought about the personal surveillance task; it was just something he did when he was in public. His phone rang—12 minutes, not long. He immediately turned the volume to zero on both radios.

"Do you have her?"

"Hi, Papa. Yes, she does," Bella chuckled. "Mom's got me. Thank you for picking me up."

"Your Mom did that. I'm so glad that you're safe, Bella Joy. It'll be great to have you home."

"Thanks, Papa. Mom wants a word." Marci's phone was presumably transferred.

"As agreed, I have her, and we're in the car. We'll be heading out as soon as I hang up. We'll probably stop for lunch," she paused, "yes, we'll stop for lunch. Bella is rattling her eyeballs with the vigor of her agreement. We should get home about mid to late afternoon."

"OK. Be careful, sweetie. Take it nice and slow. I'll try to knock off early and be home when you two arrive. I sure will be glad to have this episode behind us."

"Me too, Rod. I love you. See you soon."

"I love you."

Rod put away his phone, turned up the police radio to absorb the activity, and shifted the car into Drive. He had at least a couple of hours to get caught up and process his incessant paperwork. The field team, although the field was a computer screen for this team, had collected sufficient evidence to arrest a half dozen people on a rather clever embezzlement scheme. As agreed earlier this morning, the team had already presented the evidence to the district attorney's office. They expected to have the necessary warrants later this afternoon, ready for execution in the morning. Rod felt good about the case and fully expected they would have all of the perpetrators behind bars in a month or so. Somehow, Rod always felt better about prosecuting white-collar crime, since it seemed to have a far more lasting and profound effect on society than the spot damage of violent or property crime.

Rod briefed Captain Johnston on their case and the plan to execute the warrants in the morning. Everything was in order. He also informed his boss on the surprise call from the chief and the meeting in the mayor's office. Johnston had not yet received the call from the chief or his commander, so Rod chose not to open that box—that was the chief's business. The captain seemed satisfied. Rod asked to knock off early for personal reasons. Captain Johnston had no objections but asked for Rod to keep his cellphone on and handy, just in case. Cleared to go, Rod gathered some reports he could review at home. He wanted to be there ahead of the earliest possible arrival time and expected to wait for an hour or so. Rod logged off and shut down his computer, and then he secured his desk.

It was unusual but not unprecedented for him to arrive home to an empty house. He grabbed a snack bar and a glass of iced tea. He opened the living room curtains, including the inner veil curtain, before settling into the single overstuffed chair at the far end of the couch. He wanted a clear view of the driveway in his peripheral vision. Rod ate the granola bar and drank half his tea, and then he opened the folder containing the reports he needed to read. It did not take him long to figure out that he did not bring enough reading material home. He retrieved the house mail from the curbside mailbox—nothing special. Next, Rod cleaned, dried, and put away a few pans, plates, and utensils Marci had left when she left in a hurry with the morning's higher priority task.

Rod returned to his perch, observing the driveway and allowed his mind to wander among the myriad, scattered thoughts about what might have disturbed Bella so much to want out of IC12 so suddenly. *There were no police reports of any noteworthy events. Could one of the residents have attacked her? Had she taken something that scared her? Had she seen something that fundamentally changed her mind about the place? What the hell was it? It's highly unlikely anything from outside could've produced that reaction. What the hell was it?* He kept asking himself. Rod repeatedly reminded himself that he had to resist questioning or interrogating her. *Marci is precisely correct. We have to let her open up to us at her own pace when she was ready. It's going to be too late to make dinner. Are they going to be hungry? Where do we go? What the hell was it? Did someone hurt her or threaten her? What the hell was it?*

Rod heard the garage door open before he saw the car in the driveway. Rather than go outside, Rod went through the kitchen to the interior garage door. Marci was slowly pulling the car into the garage. Bella practically jumped out of the vehicle before it was completely stopped and ran to leap into her father's outstretched arms. They held each other until Marci shut off the car and joined them in the family hug.

"Are you OK?" Rod asked softly.

"Yes, Papa. I'm fine."

Rod kissed Marci on her forehead and kissed Bella on her left cheek. "Welcome home, Bella. You're safe now."

"Thanks, Papa. It's great to be home."

"Shall we go inside?" asked Rod.

They disassembled. Marci led the way. Rod retrieved the small sports bag Bella had dropped and used for the few things she had taken with her.

With the garage doors closed, Rod deposited Bella's bag on the dining room table and returned to the kitchen. "It's a little late to make dinner. Are you ladies hungry?"

"I'm not," Bella offered first.

"Me either," added Marci. "How about I make you a couple of fried egg sandwiches? I think Bella wants to talk." Rod looked at Bella.

"I know you're curious and probably dying to ask me about what happened. I really need to put your worries to rest. You two were so generous with me. It's time for me to pay you back."

"Yes, you know me well."

"Why don't you two sit down at the breakfast bar or the kitchen table, so I can listen while I cook you up a couple of sandwiches. I've heard some of this, but probably not all."

"How about the kitchen table? I'd like to see your eyes and face."

Bella responded without words, taking her usual seat facing the kitchen. Rod did not take his usual seat and took the chair facing Bella, with this back to the kitchen. Marci instinctively knew they would both need drinks—Fanta Grape for Bella, iced tea for Rod. "OK, where to begin?" Bella took a few seconds to consider the question. "First, let me say, thank you, thank you, thank you so much, to both of you. I know it was not easy for you to let me go to the camp. It'll take me a few days or weeks to process everything, but as I sit here now, I think my experience answered a lot of questions in my mind. So, thank you for allowing me the space to find answers for myself." Rod only nodded his head in recognition, not wanting to interrupt Bella's thoughts.

"I know you're most concerned about what happened today, as Mom told me in the car. I was doing well until this morning. I've been feeling the completion of my search was nearing, but this morning three things happened in rapid sequence. First, a woman in my block was found dead in her bed first thing this morning. I heard the medics say she had been dead for hours. It was horrible seeing her distorted face before they covered her and took her away. Then, at the end of the morning meal, some guy went berserk. Something set him off. I've no idea what it was. One of the ladies in my building said she thought it was a PCP OD." Marci placed a plate with two fried egg sandwiches and another large glass of iced tea in front of Rod, but he did not eat. Marci pulled a chair over and sat next to Rod. Bella continued, "He was hitting everyone within reach. It was horrifying. Some of the male residents tried to subdue him, but he wound up knocking out all of the subduers. He was a one-man rampage. I've never seen anything like it, and it scared the hell out of me. I wanted to run, but I was spellbound by the violence and spectacle of it. He was tossing grown men around like they were ragdolls. There were moments I couldn't see the man, but I could see the bodies flying around, and he was moving toward me. Kelly tried to get me to leave, or at least to move, but I couldn't."

If that asshole touched her, touched . . . Rod took the first bite of his sandwich.

"The security guys came. It took six of them and some stun devices to subdue the man finally. They sedated the man. The police came, put him in a straitjacket, and dragged him away. I think all of the medical people and most of the staff were out there tending to the injured. I was told that two residents died and a dozen more were taken to the hospital. It was terrible, Papa. There was blood everywhere. When they took care of the injured, they shooed us away. Kelly and I walked back to our block. Just as we reached the area of our cubes, a woman whose name neither of us knew, started shaking, went rigid, foaming from her mouth and nose, and keeled over hard as a board, hitting the floor with a terrible thud. She continued to shake in continuous convulsions. Someone called the medics. They arrived in seconds that seemed like hours. It was shocking to see. They tried to save her, but she died right there in front of us." Bella lapsed into contemplation as a steady stream of tears descended her cheeks. Marci finished cleaning up and sat down next to Rod. Neither of Bella's parents moved or spoke. Bella eventually nodded her head, wiped her tears with back of her hand, and then looked at her mother and father. "Just this morning, I've seen more people die and dead people than I've seen in my whole life. For the last few days, I'd been thinking about leaving, but what I saw this morning decided for me."

A dozen or so seconds passed in silence with no words or even twitches. Bella remained in her thoughts. Marci was the first to break the silence. "Can we ask questions?"

"Sure. Shoot."

"Let's start with what you've learned from this morning's events?"

"I don't know what caused those fatalities, or why they did what they did?"

"No, Bella. I mean, what did you take away from those events?"

"Because of where we were, I've no choice but to assume that at least the two women I saw were drug overdoses, and quite likely, they were intentional. Kelly felt the same, too. The drugs on the list can be dangerous if misused. But I also know that if they are used properly, they have benefits."

"Like what?" asked Rod.

"I can go through how I've reacted to some of these drugs, but I'd rather have that discussion after I've gotten a good night's sleep. The beds they have at IC12 are not the best and certainly not as good as my bed."

"OK. Fair enough. So, does this mean you're finished with the indulgence camp?"

"As you've told me more times than I can count, I can't predict the future."

"*Touché*, as the French like to say in such circumstances," Rod observed.

"Let me answer your question this way. I've absolutely no desire to re-enter IC12 . . . or any other camp. I think I've seen what I needed to see, so the best answer I can give you is yes, I think I'm done. I can't imagine the circumstances where my desire to reenter the camp would rise to action."

"Now, a bit of a side note to today's events . . . ," Rod said and paused. "I didn't go with Mom to pick you up because I was in a meeting with Mayor Garcia and Chief Harris. The mayor will be holding a meeting regarding our experience with the SCIP Act changes that includes the indulgence camp system, among other aspects. To that end, your experience, your observations, are relevant to the purpose of that pending meeting. With that as background, do you think the ICs are a good service? Do they do what they're supposed to do? Should the IC system be extended? Can it be improved? Let's start with those."

"Does this mean I'll be a part of your meeting?"

"Yes."

"Well, then, I think I can answer from my perspective. Yes, I absolutely believe the camps are a good, worthy, and necessary system. I don't have any direct memories of what it was like before the indulgence camps came into existence. I was too young. But from everything I've heard from others who are old enough to know, I'd say the ICs are far better than the way it was. Kelly

Henry is the one to answer that question. She lived both. From my view, I think the ICs, wait, I guess I should say IC12 since I don't know about the other camps, is doing far more than they're supposed to do. The people who run the camp and take care of the residents are extraordinarily generous with their time, assistance, and compassion. Some residents are perpetually zoned out. They appear to have only one interest, staying zoned out. But many others like Kelly are seeking something far different. Yes, absolutely, the ICs should be extended, supported, and encouraged. You know far better than me what the drug law changes have done to lower crime. To your last question, yes, I'd say there's always room for improvement."

"Like what?" Rod asked again.

"Better beds." They all laughed robustly. When their laughter subsided, Bella continued, "I'll have to think about what could be improved. I certainly was impressed with the efficiency of the operation, the care of the people as I mentioned earlier, and the respect I felt while inside the facility. I was impressed, to be frank. No one, not one, made any distinction for me or my age. It was nice to be treated as an adult."

"You're not one yet," Marci interjected.

"I know, Mom. The law says 18. All I'm saying is they didn't care, and they never asked. They treated me like an adult, and I appreciated that respect."

"What's next?"

"Unless you have any objection, I'd like to take a few days to a week perhaps to rest and digest my experience. By the way, I should mention that I kept a daily journal of what happened, and my thoughts about things along with my feelings. I need to read through what I wrote to make sure there is nothing too private, but assuming not, reading my journal might be useful."

"I'd like that, if you're willing to share," Rod said.

"Me too," added Marci.

"I'll see. If necessary, maybe I can black out the sensitive stuff."

"No need, Bella," Rod said, jumping in quickly. "I think it's better that you preserve your spot feelings than for us to read them. Let's just say, share what you wish to share, but don't worry about Mom and me."

"Great. I know it's early, but if y'all will forgive me, I'm exhausted, and I'd like to take a shower and go to bed. We can talk more in the morning."

"Sure, honey," Marci said.

"Have a good night's sleep, Bella. We're so glad and grateful to have you home safely."

Bella stood, followed by her parents. They hugged and kissed each other, and then Bella headed off to her room, which was just as she had left it.

Marci and Rod compared impressions of the conversation with Bella. Marci also added a few items that Bella mentioned during the drive home that she had not mentioned in the family chat. Rod washed his plate and glass, dried them, and put them away. They both headed to bed early as well.

—

24

Captain Tim Sullivan arrived early for his shift. He entered the control room and received a head nod recognition from his colleague Captain Jason 'Jay' Billings, the supervisor of BHC7 Team Two. "Mornin' Jay. What's up this bright and shiny morning?"

"We've a deposit . . . about 30 minutes ago."

"What happened?"

"Seems the new guy exceeded the threshold of their tolerance. He got his thrashing beginning at 23:17 last night. It took about 18 minutes. They really wanted to make him suffer. They left him where he fell until about 30 minutes ago. Four of the residents carried him into the transfer chamber and literally dropped him with an audible thud. We didn't have enough time to retrieve the body, so I decided to leave it for you."

"No problem, Jay. We'll take care of it pronto, as soon as my tac team guys assemble and get suited up. New guy . . . I presume that's Jurgensen?"

"Yep, the one and only."

"We kinda saw that one coming."

"You got that right. He either had a death wish, or he was really slow on the uptake. They gave him plenty of warnings—three thumpin's that I recall."

"Yeah, at least that. The same attitude that got him in here. I'll go check his file. I'll wait until we get the body out here for our medic to examine and verify." A couple of the Team Three members entered the control room to begin the daily transfer of responsibility. Tim sat at the parallel supervisor's workstation. He pushed the intercom button for the duty room. "Team Three, prepare for deposit extraction. Confirm when the Tac Team Three is assembled, suited up, and ready to go."

"Wilco," he heard in response.

Tim logged into his supervisor's account. He called up Jurgensen's file and went directly to the next-of-kin page. "I'll be damned."

"What've you got?" asked Billings.

"Jurgensen listed his last arresting officer as his next-of-kin."

"Strange . . . but not without precedent. I guess they wanted the collar cop to know they're gone."

"The first time I've seen it. Odd thing is, I met the guy. He volunteered for the escort detail, and I gave him the cook's tour of our little camp. This is probably going to be a bit of a shock to him as well. He told me Jurgensen was his first Black Hole perp." Sullivan opened a new window on his computer screen and called up the team's status page. All green, ten minutes before the scheduled shift change. "Looks like we're all good. We'll assume the 'conn' to clear the deposit, so we don't interfere with their food delivery." Tim selected and printed a full, color picture of Jurgensen's face file photograph.

"The packet is ready when you are."

"Thanks, bud."

"You've got the 'conn.'"

Sullivan activated the duty button for Team Three. Billings logged off and shut down his workstation.

"Tactical Team Three ready to rock-n-roll," came the confirmation without Tim asking.

"Roger." Sullivan hit the control room button on his intercom. "Are we ready for extraction?"

"Ready." The captain heard two voices not quite simultaneously.

"Tac Team, deploy for extraction."

"Wilco," came the response.

Several minutes passed before the Tac Team, along with the medic identified by a large red cross covering his back and front as well as his helmet, appeared in the transfer tunnel. They were heavily armed with 9mm automatic weapons and pistols. The medic carried his kit bag as a matter of routine. They pushed a cart they would use to transport the body and a second cart with the four packages for meals for each quadrant. Once they arrived at the access lobby, the Tac Team and controller stepped through their rehearsed procedures to ensure the lockout chamber was secure. They quickly lifted the body, placed it in a heavy plastic zipped body bag, and then set the black bag onto the cart. The team quickly and efficiently cleaned and sanitized the area, and then they withdrew to the access lobby so the doors could be locked. The medic promptly checked for life signs.

The medic spoke, and his voice was heard, "No pulse. No respiratory activity. No reflex response. No pupil response. The subject is deceased."

"Time noted: 07:13," Sullivan responded for the record.

While the medic secured the body, the Tac Team stepped back through the entry procedures to deliver the packets of freeze-dried meals for the day to all four quadrants of BHC7.

"Tac Team complete."

"Recover," commanded Sullivan. Once the team was clear of the access lobby and in the tunnel headed back out, Tim left his workstation to meet the team at the medic station. He waited for a couple of minutes for the team to arrive. "Good job, guys."

"He took a hard beating, Skip," announced the medic.

"Let's take a look-see," Tim said.

They pushed the cart into the room and closed the door as they left. The Tac Team headed back to the duty room, where they would remove their weapons and protective gear. The medic unzipped the bag and opened it beyond his shoulders.

It was Jurgensen based on his arm and shoulder tattoos, but his facial features were barely recognizable. He held the paper sheet image of Jurgensen's face next to the head of the corpse. "Hard to pick out distinguishing facial features, but I think the hair, ears, along with arm and shoulder tattoos are sufficient identification."

The medic checked the available evidence. "I concur."

"The deceased is positively identified as Resident Maxim Georgi Jurgensen," Captain Sullivan declared. "I'll take care of next of kin notification. Notify the county coroner."

"Will do, Skip."

By negotiated procedures in such circumstances, the coroner would make the trip out to BHC7 to validate the death and perform a minimal autopsy for the official death notice. The facility had four refrigerated lockers for corpses. The camp would retain the body for 14 days or retrieval by the next of kin, whichever was sooner. The medic went about his task to prepare the corpse for cold storage preservation, including removing the body bag and his clothing, taking detailed high-resolution photographs of his overall body plus close-ups of his visible injuries before and after cleaning.

Sullivan returned to his workstation. He completed his portion of the report. Calling up Jurgensen's next of kin page, Sullivan took a few minutes to consider exactly what he wanted to say to the deceased resident's designated next of kin.

Rod Ramirez barely had time to sit and log into his department account when his desk landline telephone rang. Lifting the handset, he answered, "Ramirez."

"Detective-Sergeant Ramirez, this is Captain Sullivan, the shift supervisor at BHC7. It is my duty to inform you as the designated next-of-kin that Resident Maxim Georgi Jurgensen has deceased this morning."

Rod laughed. *This has to be some kind of joke.* "What is this, some kind of punk?"

"I understand your reaction, Rod, but I can assure you this is no joke. Jurgensen listed you as his sole next of kin. It's unusual but not without precedent. He left no instructions or will. He clearly specified you were to be notified on his passing—no one else."

"I'll be damned. I've never heard of such a thing. What happened?"

"We've completed our preliminary review of the available evidence. By the way, the state will conduct a separate thorough review in accordance with the law that will be the official final assessment. So, this is preliminary information. At 23:17 last night, a group of six residents gained entry to Jurgensen's room and beat him to death with their fists and feet. The assailants had no discernible weapons. They left him where he died until 06:21 this morning when a group of four different residents carried his body from his room to the Quad Three lockout chamber and literally dropped him on the floor at the center of the chamber. Using our standard operating procedures for such events, our duty tactical team was dispatched to retrieve the body. Once they had the corpse secure, our medic checked for vital signs, found none, and Jurgensen was pronounced dead at 07:13 this morning. The medic and I examined the corpse and positively identified him, although I must say they were not gentle or reserved in their assault on the man. His face was barely recognizable—not a pretty sight, I must say. Lastly, the county coroner will perform a minimal examination and autopsy here this afternoon. You're welcome to observe if you so desire."

"I can't say I'm surprised. No, I've no desire to see the body. I've seen enough dead people. I'm not needed for identification, am I . . . as the designated next of kin?"

"No, not necessary. I think we all saw this coming. It was just his nature, and he refused to adapt."

"So, what happens now?"

"We await your instructions for transfer of Jurgensen's body."

"Hang on a sec, Captain." Rod quickly typed in Jurgensen's name to call up their available file information for Maxim. He quickly scanned every relevant page. "OK. I've checked our files. We've got no additional information with respect to relatives, friends, or acquaintances who might have an interest. What are my obligations here?"

"To be blunt, you were his designated next of kin regardless of any existing family or relations. Your only obligation under the law is to decide what you want to do with his body. That's it."

"What are my options?"

"You have two options. One, you can send a funeral home service to retrieve the body to inter him as you wish. Or two, you can declare no action, in which case, we'll cremate his remains and scatter his ashes in the desert on our property. Well, I guess there is a third option, you can do nothing. After 14 days from today, option two will be exercised."

"Option two is sufficient."

"Very well. Just to verify and confirm, you're directing us, as Jurgensen's designated next of kin, to cremate his body and scatter his remains."

"Yes sir. That is my direction."

"Thanks, Rod. It shall be done per your authorized instructions later today after the coroner completes his findings, or perhaps tomorrow morning, depending upon when the coroner finishes his work."

"And thank you, Captain Sullivan."

They said their goodbyes. Rod entered some notes into the Jurgensen file to reflect the relevant content of his conversation with Sullivan. With that task done, Rod turned his attention to an Internet search for any familial relations for Jurgensen. He found the press reports of Jurgensen's many arrests, trials, and convictions. There was no biographical information available for the man, and after spending 20 minutes on his searches, Rod found nothing helpful—not even a clue or lead. *Oh well, he died alone. He chose his path.*

Rod looked up the number for Jurgensen's public defender lawyer. He entered the phone number he had.

Surprisingly, he answered his own phone. "Public Defenders' office. Houseman."

"Counselor, this is Detective Ramirez."

"What can I do for you, Detective?"

"I wanted to let you know that I received a call this morning from Captain Sullivan at BHC7 to inform me that Maxim Jurgensen died this morning."

"He's not my client anymore. How did it go down?"

Rod recounted the information Sullivan had provided him along with the odd detail of Rod's designation as Jurgensen's next of kin.

Houseman asked several related questions. "Thank you for the courtesy of your call, Detective, but I'm no longer Jurgensen's attorney of record." Hank Houseman indicated his appeal case had been transferred to another *pro bono* law firm. Houseman stated he would pass along information to his current lawyer for any potential action.

"If you have a moment . . ."

"Sure. Shoot."

"If I may ask, what is the status of Jurgensen's Eighth Amendment appeal?"

"Good question. His new lawyer agreed to explore the potential of Jurgensen joining an expanded class action appeal challenging the Eighth Amendment implications involving the Black Hole Confinement Camps."

"Do you think they will be successful?"

Houseman chuckled audibly. "I gave up a long time ago trying to predict the outcomes of judicial proceedings. While I believe those camps are indeed cruel and unusual punishment, and thus unconstitutional, I don't think the courts are going to allow the constitutionality of the camps to be taken in isolation, in other words, without the context of the penal reform instigated by the SCIP Act. Do you have an opinion?"

"Yes, I do. Jurgensen's death and especially his mode of death tends to complement your constitutionality perspective. However, strangely, I think inmates have more freedom in the Black Hole camps than they do in traditional prisons. The difference is the interactions between the inmates and the staff. Conventional prisons are based on, or at least should be based on, rehabilitation of the individual that requires education and training. The Black Hole camps recognize some people are not recoverable. They refuse to be rehabilitated. That was Jurgensen."

"Perhaps so, but those inmates executed Jurgensen without due process."

"Therein lies the rub, huh?" Rod responded. "Jurgensen, by his decisions and actions, chose to disobey and defy the rules of civil conduct, as least as defined in that facility. The state simply accepted the reality of Jurgensen's choices and allowed him to live the rest of his natural life by the rules he imposed on the rest of civil society. I think those camps basically recognize that reality."

"Interesting argument."

"I don't know everything that happened to him in BHC7, but from what I do know, he was given multiple warnings by other residents that his conduct inside Quad Three was disruptive to their quadrant's stability. He apparently refused to conform to the internal rules, so the group finally took action to end the problem."

"That is hardly due process."

"No, it isn't by our legal standards. But he chose to live by different rules, and he suffered the consequences."

"Do you think those camps should be retained?"

"The law enforcement officer in me understands the law and the enforcement of our laws. However, these habitual criminals present a unique challenge to our society."

"Assault is assault. Murder is murder. They are crimes," Houseman insisted. "Those crimes shouldn't and mustn't be tolerated in any segment of our community, or in any civilized society for that matter, including these so-called Black Hole camps."

"Noble objectives, I must say, Counsellor. However, in the small subset of our population, as represented by your former client, these individuals have received ample due process consideration repeatedly and consistently until they crossed the threshold of being declared a habitual criminal . . . also by due process. As I said earlier, those comparatively few individuals who cross that threshold are simply being allowed to live by the rules they've inflicted upon the rest of the peaceful, law-abiding citizenry. They got what they want."

"Hardly."

"Well, in that sense, they seek the beneficent treatment they receive in a free and open society to carry out their criminal activities. They want to be free to do what they wish to do without constraint, restriction, or obstruction."

"Why isn't life without parole sufficient?"

Rod smiled. "Good question. If we accept the fact that conventional prisons are modeled to rehabilitate criminals, and habitual criminals have repeatedly demonstrated their unwillingness to be rehabilitated, why should society allow a habitual criminal to take up a valuable slot in a conventional prison when there is no hope of redemption?"

"A valid point," Houseman acknowledged. "I hadn't thought of it that way. I need to think that through. But I'll confess to my bias to contemporary jurisprudence rather than the progressive approach of penal reform."

"I'll add here as well, Mister Houseman, like most citizens I think, initially, I thought just the same that the Black Hole facilities were likely going to be brutal places with so many bad men in a closed environment and no supervisory controls applied. Certainly, Jurgensen's blunt force trauma death in BHC7 qualifies as brutal, and taken in isolation, it would be considered cruel and unusual punishment as the Constitution prohibits, and the Supreme Court has interpreted. However, taken on the whole, I no longer see it that way. Today, I admire the elegance of that terminal facility. Not only are the bad guys removed from peaceful society, but they're also removed from the potential contamination of other individuals who are still in the rehabilitation process."

"If I read between the lines, you don't think an 8th Amendment claim will be successful."

Rod chuckled softly. "As you said, Counsellor, I'm unable to predict the judgment of juries and judges. From my lay perspective, I don't see the Black Hole camps as cruel and unusual punishment."

"Being beaten to death is not reasonable punishment," Houseman observed with solemnity.

"No, it isn't. However, Jurgensen made his choices, and given the rules he lived by, that was the outcome. The states did not impose the punishment."

"There's a reason we use the word custody to describe conditions of restraint and incarceration. It means the state assumes responsibility for the safety and well-being of individuals committed to its custody. The state had an obligation to intervene once they witnessed a crime being committed upon an individual in its custody."

"Respectfully, Mister Houseman, we need to shift our thinking. Men who enter BHC7 are lost souls. The state is protecting them, and importantly, protecting peaceful, law-abiding citizens from the ravages of predatory habitual criminals. The state provides sustenance without qualification. The state demands nothing from them. They have no obligations, no work responsibilities, or no duties. We expect nothing from them. They're free to live as they wish, and we leave them alone with their thoughts. Jurgensen made his choices. No one made his decisions for him. Jurgensen chose not to live by the rules of Quad Three. He was warned several times that I'm aware of, and Quad Three tended to its rules without the need for state intervention."

"All nice thoughts, Rod, but those men are in state custody. They don't enjoy freedom of choice, freedom of movement, or anything close to the other freedoms we enjoy and are constitutionally protected."

Rod laughed more out of frustration than humor. "Well, Counsellor, I think they do . . . just within a secure space where their free choices don't threaten any other member of civilized society beyond their little community of like-minded habitual criminals."

"Another interesting argument," Houseman responded. "Unfortunately, Detective, I've taken more time than I should have, and I must get back to my overloaded stack of indigent cases. A public defender's job is never done."

"Thank you for the chat, Mister Houseman. Just for the record, the Jurgensen file is closed and will be sent to the archive."

"Understood. Agreed. Quite appropriate."

"Have a good day, Mister Houseman. Take care."

"Thanks, Rod. Same to you."

They disconnected. Rod hung up his handset.

"Interesting discussion," Rod muttered to himself.

Detective Ramirez returned to his work, collecting clues, facts, and even hints on a number of his open cases for the remainder of his day. At the end of the notional workday for detectives, Rod called Marci. She informed him that Bella found a good job and would not be home until later this evening. So, they were going out to dinner. He agreed, logged off his computer, and closed up his desk.

Marci was waiting for him with her purse over her shoulder when he walked into the kitchen.

"So, tell me about Bella's new job," Rod said.

"In the car," she answered, pointing to the garage. "I'm hungry, and the 'hangries' are nipping at my civility. I'll tell you during the ride."

Rod gestured toward the garage. "We don't want that. Let's be on our way." Rod opened the passenger door for Marci. He backed out of the garage, closed the garage door remotely, and headed out. "Where are we going?"

"Wherever you want."

"Don't do that to me. You know you're far more sensitive, and shall we say picky. Just tell me where you want to go."

"OK. I'm feelin' shrimp salad at the Blossom Petal. How does that work for you?"

"You don't want to go to Bella's new job?"

"No, definitely not. This is her first day. We need to give her time to settle in and gain confidence in her new job before doing that to her. The Blossom Petal will do."

"Works just fine, sweetheart." Rod adjusted his path accordingly. Several miles passed without a word from Marci. "Are you going to tell me about Bella?"

"Oh yeah, sorry, yes. She went down this afternoon to interview at a couple of restaurants and even with Burger King. The owner of the Griddle Plate hired her straight away and asked her to start immediately. She called me to say she wouldn't be home until about 10 or 11 tonight. She seemed really excited."

"Good for her. She seems to be getting her life back on track."

"Definitely, Rod. She decided she needed a job without any encouragement from me. She's talking about college."

"Has she started looking and setting her sights?"

"Yes. Her focus at this point in time has been on Ivy League universities."

"Oh my."

"Yeah. Could be a bit pricey, but I'm quite reluctant to constrain her ambitions."

"Agreed. We'll figure out a way to make it happen if she gets admitted to any university she wants."

"That's a pretty bold statement, Rod."

"Perhaps, but that's how I feel about it."

"I feel the same sentimentally, but sooner or later, practicality will show its ugly face."

"We'll see. First things first, and one step at a time. She has to apply and get admitted first."

"OK, but I'd suggest we leave it a little looser when the topic comes up with Bella."

"Agreed. We've done a lot to prepare . . . well, maybe not quite to Ivy League levels, but we've been at it since Bella was in your belly . . . a most beautiful and gorgeous time of our lives."

"So, I'm not beautiful and gorgeous now?" she teased.

"You know what I mean."

Marci laughed hard. "Yes, my darling, I do know what you meant, and I thank you for the compliment and your love."

"That part's easy."

They drove the rest of the way without words. Upon arrival, Rod parked. They held hands as they walked to the restaurant. The exceptional meal was made better by their light-hearted conversation about their garden, the vegetable section fenced off from varmints, and news of the neighbors that Marci thought appropriate. The wine added to their sense of satisfaction. By the time they returned home, they figured they had an hour or so before Bella was due home, and they mutually decided to renew the intimacy of their relationship.

—

25

Laura sat in her small living room, enjoying the last of her afternoon tea. She was prepped and dressed for the evening's work. A cable news network program offered up the latest information from around the world. Laura was not really paying attention. Her thoughts drifted in and out to the customers she would service this evening. Her first one was a weekly regular who had been consistently gentle and conventional for several years now. He was always very respectful of her moods and feelings that made it so much easier to please him. Her second and last appointment for the evening was one of her favorites—a party with two married couples she knew well. The events of any particular party were always different, great fun, and with ample pleasure.

The bell ring of her private telephone startled Laura from her euphoric thoughts. "Hello."

"Laura, this is Raoul. I'm glad I caught you." There was an unusual hesitation in his voice.

"Just barely. I've got work tonight. I'm leaving in a few minutes."

"Kelly is dead," Raoul shakily and softly announced.

The words struck Laura like a hard slap across her face. She sucked in a deep and quite audible gasp. "What!" she exclaimed, as if she had not heard him correctly.

"The director of IC12 telephoned me 45 minutes ago to inform me. According to him, she took her life by a purposeful overdose of heroin after consuming benzodiazepine around mid-day. She had a valid DNR on file, so they let her go. I'm going out to identify her body and collect up her belongings. The director also said the only note she left was explicitly addressed to you alone and private. I'll not ask you to go for this visit. If you don't want to go, I'll have them mail the note to you."

Millions of disparate thoughts flashed and streamed through Laura's consciousness. She had so little time to adjust. *Do I try to find a substitute? Do I just call them and ask if they want me to find a substitute? Do I just beg forgiveness and give them a freebee at their convenience?* "I want to go. I owe it to Kelly. But I'll need to call my clients for tonight and make other arrangements? I'll just drive out myself," Laura thought aloud.

"No, no, not necessary. It'll take me 20 minutes or so to make arrangements on my end and drive over to your place. Is that sufficient time for you?"

"I think so."

"OK. I'll pick you up in 20 to 30 minutes. See'ya then." He hung up and did not wait for a response.

Laura took a dozen minutes to calm her thoughts. So many questions clouded her thinking. She chastised herself. *Get a grip, girl.* She called her clients consecutively and informed them of what had happened in general without the details. The widower understood and said he would reschedule. He appreciated the offer of a substitute or a freebee, but neither was necessary, nor wanted. The wife of the sponsoring couple, who had originally scheduled Laura, was disappointed, but she also understood. She asked about the potential substitutes, but after some discussion with her husband and Laura, they decided they would reschedule, also. Both of them repeatedly offered their condolences for Laura's loss of her friend.

Once her business obligations were settled and set aside, Laura had a little less than ten minutes before Raoul planned to arrive. She quickly changed out of the sex outfit into her casual Levi's and a T-shirt. Laura opened a bottle of excellent cabernet sauvignon, poured herself a healthy glass, and sat down to sip her wine and consider her thoughts. She had barely consumed a quarter of her wine when she saw Raoul's Mercedes pull to a stop at the curb in front of her apartment. Laura placed the partially consumed glass of wine on the kitchen counter, grabbed her small shoulder purse, and placed it across her chest. By the time she exited her building, Raoul was at the door reaching for the call button.

Raoul started to lean in to kiss her cheek but stopped when Laura held up her left hand to stop. He swung his arm, gesturing to the car. They got situated, buckled in, and on their way without words. Neither one of them felt the urge to speak, so they drove along in silence with no music and only the muffled road noise for background.

It was 50 minutes into the drive to IC12 when Raoul broke the silence between them. "How have you been?"

"I'm not up for small talk, Raoul."

"OK. Let me say, I've no idea what to expect when we get there. Did she contact you in the last few days? Do you have any idea why she would've done this?"

"None, Raoul, none. I've not heard from her since the last time we visited her. I've no clue why." Laura's thoughts drifted toward a far darker place. She turned her head and stared at him. Raoul eventually sensed her gaze and quickly glanced at her, gesturing with his eyes for her to continue. "She was in good spirits when we left. Have you done something stupid since then?"

"No, of course not."

"Something changed to cause her to take such a dive, and you're the only source of her discontent I can think of for such a drastic change in her."

"I don't want to lose her."

"Well, you have, haven't you? She's gone to both of us, now."

Raoul changed the subject. "We're supposed to meet with the director even though it is after hours. Maybe she left a note to explain what happened, although the director didn't mention a note, other than the sealed envelope to you, and I didn't have the presence of mine to ask."

"Who's the director?" Laura asked.

"Duncan, Michael Duncan. He goes by 'Mike.' He's apparently been the director since the camp opened six years ago. Nice guy, if a telephone voice is any indicator."

Laura nodded her head in recognition and lapsed into the thoughts about what lay ahead. She was troubled by what could have driven Kelly to such drastic, final action. There was nothing Laura could do for her friend now other than remembering. Raoul asked her if she wanted something to eat. As was her usual practice, Laura had a very light dinner in preparation for the evening's work, so she was tempted but ultimately declined. She would be fine until they got back home. Darkness had enveloped the scenery until they crested the last rise and saw the lights of IC12 in the middle of the moonless, dark, unseeable landscape.

Raoul parked his car near the entrance. Numerous people were coming out of the administration building.

Must be shift change time, Laura thought.

Raoul introduced themselves to the receptionist, whose expression changed from cheerful to somber as soon as she heard the names, although he did not mention the event that brought them to IC12. The middle-aged woman immediately called presumably the director and said, "They've arrived." When she hung up the telephone handset, she gestured to the couches and added, "Please take a seat. The director will be with you shortly." Neither of them responded other than to sit on the opposite ends of a couch.

Not quite five minutes later, a late-middle-aged man in a tan suit but no tie emerged from the interior followed by an older woman, dressed conservatively, with short curly grey hair. Another man, younger, perhaps early 40s; his charcoal, well-cut suit and solid medium blue tie suggested he was probably the house lawyer. They walked directly toward Raoul and Laura, whom both stood.

"I'm Director Mike Duncan. This is Doctor Lisa Blackman, and Jack Dunbar, our chief counsel." The five of them shook hands. "If you'll follow me, we'll go to a more private conference room, so we can talk freely." Duncan did not wait for an acknowledgment. Raoul followed, then Laura, and Blackman brought up the tail. They went down an interior hallway and into a rather barren small conference room with a rectangular table and six chairs. Once they were all seated, with Mike, Lisa, and Jack on one side, and Laura and Raoul on the other side, Duncan said, "Please allow me to offer my condolences." Raoul nodded.

Laura said, "Thank you."

"At times like these, we've found it best to answer your questions. We don't want to give you more than you want to hear."

"Where is she?" asked Raoul.

"She's in our medical clinic. We've positively identified her, so it's not necessary for you to identify her, but you're welcome to view the body, as is your right."

"Yes, I would like to see her one last time."

He doesn't deserve to see her ever again, Laura thought.

"We can do that whenever you're ready." Raoul nodded his head slowly. "We need . . ." Duncan stopped when Raoul held up his left hand. "Yes?" Duncan asked.

"Let's get the hard part out of the way. Shall we?"

"You want to view the body now?"

"Yes."

"Very well," Duncan said and stood. The others did the same. The group followed Mike Duncan to the adjacent building. The sign by the door identified the medical building. They made their way to a medium-sized room that was outfitted with three metallic tables that appeared to be surgery or examination tables. Along the wall opposite the door, three rows of five large, stainless steel lockers. A male nurse/medic knew why the director and the others came to visit his duty station. He went to the middle locker of the middle row. As he stood with his hand on the door handle, he turned to look back. A man and a woman stood behind him on each side. The leaders of IC12 remained back by the door, presumably not wanting to intrude upon this difficult moment for the visitors.

The nurse said, "Are you ready?" He looked at Laura and Raoul. Both nodded their consent. The man opened the door and pulled out the bare stainless steel tray. Kelly's naked body lay peacefully, with no visible signs of trauma. Laura could feel the cold and shivered. There was no doubt the corpse had been Kelly. The IC12 medical staff had clearly carefully arranged the hair on her head, and they made sure she was clean and in the best appearance she could be.

Raoul stepped toward the tray. Laura noted the tears descending his cheeks. He placed his left hand on her left breast and withdrew it sharply as if he had touched a hot pan. "She's so cold," he said softly to no one. Raoul leaned over, kissed her forehead, and then kissed her lips. He hovered over her and stroked her colorless left cheek. Standing up straight, Raoul looked first at the nurse and then at Director Duncan. "This is my wife, Kelly."

"Agreed," Laura added her identification confirmation.

The nurse pushed the tray back into the cold storage locker and latched the door.

The group returned to the conference room.

Raoul opened their continued discussion. "Surely, you've completed your preliminary investigation. What happened?"

Duncan answered. "Miz Henry planned this action very carefully. She convinced three residents to witness and take notes on each step. Kelly took a standard dose of benzodiazepine at 12:36 after eating a noon meal, presumably to calm herself. She said her goodbyes to the witnesses. At 13:21, she administered 10 successive doses of heroin from a new inhaler. She lapsed into unconsciousness at 13:26. The witnesses repeatedly checked her pulse and breathing until they noted that her vital signs had ceased at 13:43. One of the witnesses called the medical department at 13:51 to report Kelly's overdose. The medical staff responded within a few minutes and confirmed that no vital signs were present. She had a valid DNR, and they took no further action."

"Then those witnesses are accomplices to suicide and must be prosecuted," Raoul growled.

Duncan looked at Jack Dunbar to respond. "This facility is based upon respect for the freedom of choice of each resident. There's no doubt whatsoever based upon Kelly's preparations that she was unreservedly exercising her freedom of choice. The witnesses were present again by her choice. They bear no culpability and won't be prosecuted."

"We'll see about that!" Raoul declared.

"Counselor, you're free to take whatever action you feel appropriate. I'll only say that the provisions of the SCIP Act, including the operating guidelines for indulgence camps, have been tested multiple times before the bar. The state sanctions our rules, and we've operated within those rules."

Raoul huffed and puffed in his frustration. He was used to intimidating people and was unaccustomed to being confronted. "What now?"

"The next step is deciding what to do . . . what . . . this is a bit tricky here." Duncan looked directly at Joubert. "To our knowledge, you're still legally Kelly's next of kin."

"Yes."

"But she made it quite clear that she was separated from you."

"Not legally."

"Jack," Duncan said, looking down the table, "I think it appropriate for you to take over here."

Dunbar cleared his throat. "Mister Joubert, this situation is rather unusual but not without precedent. Kelly—here I'll not refer to her as your wife or spouse—was quite explicit. She was separated from you in body, mind, and spirit. She was waiting for you to divorce her. She designated Laura," Dunbar said, glancing at Laura, "as her next of kin, and Miz Simmons was to make all decisions regarding the disposition of her remains and as the executor of her estate, the disposition of her worldly assets."

"You can't be serious," Raoul shouted. "She was my wife."

"Mister Joubert, you understand the law as well as I do. Your former wife's . . ."

"We aren't divorced," protested Raoul, loudly. "She's still my wife."

"Your wife's instructions were quite clear."

"Was there a note or something?" Raoul asked.

Dunbar looked at Duncan. Mike took the baton. "The only note we could find in your wife's few belongings here was actually and explicitly addressed to Miz Simmons only." Duncan opened the folder in front of him and extracted an envelope, placed it on the table, and pushed it across the table to Laura. Raoul reached for it.

"Ah, ah," Dunbar said, wagging his raised right index finger and looking directly at Joubert. "That envelope is addressed explicitly to Miz Simmons only." Raoul hesitated and then withdrew his outstretched hand.

Laura raised the envelope that read:

This note is for Laura Lynn Simmons <u>ONLY</u>.
<u>PRIVATE!</u>
Strictly no one else.

Laura extracted the single page note, handwritten.

June 7th

My dearest Laura,

I'm terribly sorry I've done this to you. You're my best friend in the whole world. You don't deserve this. I owe you the best explanation I can give you.

I gave everything to Raoul. I asked for nothing other than for him to let me go. You were my witness. The bottom line is that it was not good enough for him. He decided to take my future from me, just to punish me and intimidate me to abandon the divorce. I knew it was a mistake to let him know where I was, but that is water under the bridge now. I can't hide out here for the rest of my life, and I believe he will eventually use his legal connections to get me kicked out of ICI2, if his intimidation didn't work on me, which it won't. What I'm about to do is all I have left. I'm doing this with a free and unburdened mind. I'm finally free, Laura.

Thank you for being my friend. Please forgive me. I hope you'll understand.

With great love,
Kelly

P.S.: Three last thoughts:
1. Whether you show this to Raoul, or anyone else, is your choice entirely. The deed is done.
2. As a last favor to me, please contact Bella Joy Ramirez for me. Tell her I'm terribly sorry. Perhaps you can explain to her why I did this. I don't want her hurt by what I had to do.
3. My one true regret in all this, I didn't have the pleasure of making love to you. I think I truly love you, Laura.

Tears ran like small streams down her cheeks and wet her T-shirt above her breasts. Laura stared at the table, unable to look at anyone else as she struggled with her emotions. She did not attempt to wipe away her tears. *Raoul has done this. Raoul made her take her life. I'll never forgive him for whatever he did precisely to make her so despondent.* Laura placed her hands on top of each other over Kelly's note.

"That's the only known note Kelly left," Duncan added.

Raoul reached for the note. This proved to be the proverbial straw that broke the camel's back.

Laura snatched the note and sprang to her feet, knocking her chair over and backpedaling until she hit the wall behind her. "How dare you!" she shouted. Everyone else in the room held expressions of shock. Raoul's shock was mixed with traces of fear. "You killed her, you bastard."

"Laura!" he protested.

"She gave you everything. She asked for nothing."

"Laura, please," Raoul spoke softly, attempting to calm Laura.

"No! I won't be silenced. You can't intimidate me, you asshole. You killed her as surely as if you put a bullet threw her brain."

Doctor Blackman stood and stepped toward Laura.

"No!" Laura shouted. "I'm not hysterical or emotional. I speak the truth. He," she said, pointing her shaking right index finger at Raoul, "killed her. She gave him everything. She asked for nothing," she repeated, "except for the divorce she sought."

"Laura, you can't . . ."

"Shut the fuck up, you little prick. I'm going to haunt you for the rest of your fucking life. I owe that much to Kelly, to her memory." Again, Laura pointed her accusatory finger at Raoul, again, and shook it. "That was not good enough for him. He threatened to ruin the rest of her life. This asshole tried to intimidate her into remaining married to him. He's an abusive man who killed Kelly Henry."

"Joubert," Raoul interjected.

"No! Dammit! She sacrificed her life to your arrogance and misogyny. Her family name is Henry, as she was born. She chose Henry when she entered this camp." Laura looked directly at Duncan. "I want her death certificate, her name, recorded as Henry, not Joubert. She hated that man," she growled, as she pointed and shook right index finger at Raoul, "and what he had done to her."

"Laura, stop!" Raoul commanded.

"No! You don't deserve to be here. You've no right." Laura paused to glare at him, sending angry, icy daggers with her eyes. "You've got one chance. Leave now, or I'll tell these witnesses the rest of the story."

"You can't do that," struggled Raoul.

"I most certainly can and will, if you don't leave now. Get the fuck outta here," she shouted and pointed at the door."

"I drove you here. I'm your ride back home."

"So the fuck what! I'll find my own way home. I never want to see you again, ever, for any reason."

Raoul Joubert stood, held up his hands in a don't shoot gesture, and backed toward the door. He opened the door and was gone, slamming the door behind him.

Laura held her clenched fists in front of her as her body shook as if she was on the verge of an epileptic fit. Doctor Blackman went to her without resistance this time. The doctor embraced Laura and tried to soothe her. Eventually, Blackman's efforts succeeded. Laura stopped shaking, lowered her hands, and nodded to Blackman. The doctor released her embrace. Laura pointed to her chair and sat back down.

Director Duncan cleared his throat. "In light of these developments, I think it is probably important for us to see Miz Henry's last missive and ask you a few more relevant questions." Laura nodded her head but did not move to comply. "It seems obvious to me that there is relevant information in the letter," Duncan continued.

"Yes, but there is also sensitive personal information as well, and Kelly said in the letter that disclosure was my choice entirely."

"Miz Simmons, you've accused an assistant district attorney of murder."

"I saw no wounds on Kelly's body. I believe she was secure in this place. But I think he psychologically convinced Kelly that she no longer had a reason to live. He abused her during their entire marriage. She knew exactly what he was capable of doing. If we include psychological tools or weapons, then yes, I'm accusing him of murder."

"Does Miz Henry's letter indicate exactly what he said to her?"

"No."

Duncan looked at Dunbar. Jack shook his head and said, "That's not enough for charges or prosecution. At best, it is knowledgeable conjecture. We could subpoena the letter, but given what we know, I wouldn't recommend it."

Mike Duncan nodded his head. "Very well, then. To satisfy my curiosity, Miz Simmons, perhaps you could read the applicable portions and avoid the sensitive parts."

Laura thought about the request for a few seconds, and then removed the letter from the envelope and unfolded it. She read aloud, "I gave everything to Raoul. I asked for nothing other than for him to let me go. You were my witness. The bottom line is that it was not good enough for him. He decided to take my future from me, just to punish me and intimidate me to abandon the divorce. I knew it was a mistake to let him know where I was, but that is water under the bridge now. I can't hide out here for the rest of my life, and I believe he will eventually use his legal connections to get me kicked out of IC12 if his intimidation didn't work on me, which it won't. What I'm about to do is all I have left. I'm doing this with a free and unburdened mind. I'm finally free, Laura." She folded the letter and put it back in the envelope.

"What were you a witness to in all this, if I may ask?" Duncan pressed gently.

Laura stared at Mike Duncan with no expression but a sense of disbelief. *Why do I feel the tentacles of legal action touching me? I really don't want this letter to become a dispute.* "Five days ago, Kelly asked me to come out for a meeting between her and Raoul. She wanted me to witness what she was going to tell him. I was surprised that Kelly had told him where she was. Kelly had been cautious not to disclose her location when she left him, and she swore me to secrecy. During that meeting, Kelly told Raoul she wanted him to divorce her. She wanted nothing from him—no alimony, no spousal support, no assets, nothing. She just wanted a peaceful, no-nonsense divorce."

"So, what do you think happened?" Dunbar asked.

"The legal answer is, I don't know," Laura responded curtly.

"I'm not asking on a legal basis."

"Mister Dunbar, you're the chief counsel for IC12. I already sense the law closing around me and this letter," she said, holding up the envelope. "I'm not going to speculate in front of the three of you, and especially the chief counsel of IC12."

Duncan quickly jumped into the exchange. "Miz Simmons, please accept my apologies. None of us has any intention of intruding upon your privacy or your relationship with Miz Jo . . . Miz Henry. I imagine you can see the loose ends that exist in this case."

"Have you interviewed the three witnesses that watched her die?"

Duncan smiled nervously. "Yes, we have."

"And what did you learn?"

Duncan fidgeted in his seat. "I'm afraid we can't discuss an on-going investigation."

This time, Laura smiled broadly and confidently. "There'ya go." She pointed her right index finger at Director Duncan. "That's exactly what I'm talkin' about. My senses have exposed the troll under the bridge. You have me here by myself, without legal counsel, at a time of enormous grief. Whether you choose to subpoena this letter," she said, tapping her finger on the envelope, "is your choice entirely. I voluntarily read you the relevant paragraph. The rest of the note is personal and private. I think we're done here." Laura stood. "Now, I've got to figure out how to get home," she said and turned to leave.

"Wait," Duncan said firmly. "Please sit." He waited through her hesitation until she sat down. "I'm terribly sorry that we misstepped. We meant no harm or risk to you. With a death such as this and your accusation that her husband may have been involved in her demise, we've no choice but to pursue an investigation."

"I can see that. I don't feel comfortable in this conversation without legal counsel."

"We don't want you to feel uncomfortable, Miz Simmons. I'm terribly sorry, on behalf of myself and the staff of IC12, that we made you feel uneasy, especially at this time of your grief." Laura nodded her head in recognition. "One last item of official business, as Kelly Henry's designated next of kin, may we ask what your intentions are with respect to her remains?"

"How much time do I have?"

"Take whatever time you need. I'd like to have this settled and closed within two weeks if that isn't too difficult for you."

"I intend to take a day or two to process all of this. I don't think it's fair to Kelly's parents and family to just decide this on my own, even though I may be allowed to do so by law. I expect I'll call her parents, perhaps meet with them and the family, and do what they want me to do for them. I'd like to think I can have an answer to you by the end of next week."

"That should be sufficient," Duncan said. "The hour is advancing, and you've got a two-hour drive ahead of you. Two things. First, please accept our sincerest apologies for making you feel uncomfortable. That was never our intention, and I'm terribly sorry that our curiosity got the better of us. To that end, after you've had time to reflect and perhaps seek legal counsel, your accusation is a loose end that can't be ignored. We'd like to tie that off as soon as possible." Laura again nodded her head in acknowledgment. "Second, we can generally get Uber transportation out here just about all hours of the night. We'd be happy to arrange that for you. However, in recognition of the hour and your patience with us, I'd like to offer a driver and one of our cars to take you home."

"Thank you, Mister Duncan. I accept your offer."

"The camp car?" Mike asked for confirmation.

"Yes."

Duncan left the room, presumably to make the arrangements. Laura noted Lisa Blackman's eye gesture to Jack Dunbar for him to leave.

"I'll excuse myself, Miz Simmons." He extended his right hand to Laura, who took it. "I'll add to Director Duncan's apology. I'm terribly sorry we made you feel uncomfortable." Laura only nodded. Dunbar left the room.

Blackman said, "I'm also sorry this meeting turned out the way it did. Strange times. I wanted to tell you personally and privately that I met with Kelly several times myself during her time with us. We were all impressed with her sense of reform, shall I say. She was an intelligent and vivacious woman. In here, she had access to all the drugs and intoxication she might have wished for, but she was what we refer to as a minimal consumer. Her death came as an extraordinary shock to all of us as well. In that light, I must tell you privately that I felt your reaction to reading what amounts to Kelly's suicide note. I fully believe you're correct—Raoul Joubert did some unspecified something to evaporate any sense of future she might have felt a week ago. I'll add on a personal note, woman to woman, I'd love to see a man who would do that to a woman he presumably loved, prosecuted to the fullest extent of the law. If you should decide to pursue his culpability, I want to assure you that I'll do my best to help with the information I have of some of our discussions with Kelly. She was a very good woman who didn't deserve to be treated as she was."

"May I ask, did you or any of your medical staff talk to her after the drastic turn? I mean, did she seek professional counseling for what was her suicidal thoughts."

Blackman lowered her head and shook slightly. "No. I truly wish she had. I know we could've helped her."

"She didn't reach out to me either," Laura added. "I really feel like I failed her at her moment of greatest need."

"No, no, Laura. Please don't take that burden. Neither of us has fault here. If she had felt any need, she would've reached out, of that I'm certain." Blackman removed a business card from her jacket pocket and wrote down a series of numbers on the back. She handed the card to Laura. "Here are my numbers, eMail and such, as well as my personal cell number on the back. Please don't hesitate to call me, day or night, should you need a worthy ear to listen."

"Thank you, Doctor Blackman."

"Lisa, please. I felt a connection with Kelly, and I grieve with you. I feel a connection with you as well, Laura."

"Thank you. I'll remember . . ." A knock on the door preceded Duncan's return.

"Your transportation awaits," he announced. The two women stood and hugged. Blackman and Duncan escorted Laura to the car, offered their apologies and condolences, again, and then they said their goodbyes.

The ride back into town was peaceful, easy and nearly wordless. The driver tried several times to initiate conversation, but Laura was just not up for a chat. He also offered to buy her dinner, but she declined. The driver had calmed her. By the time she entered her apartment, she was ready for bed. The tension of the evening had been exhausting.

Laura took the next day entirely to herself and her thoughts. The only concessions to the world outside were calls to her clients for the next few days. Most of them offered their condolences and simply agreed to reschedule. A couple of her more active male clients accepted the offer of Blondie Baker's services. One actually told her he would make arrangements with Sweet Thomas, which kind of surprised her.

The following day, Laura called Mrs. Henry to make arrangements for a visit with her and her husband that evening. Mrs. Henry invited Laura to have dinner with them and to make their evening fully available to Laura. She met with the Henrys. They had not been informed of their daughter's passing. Laura took the time to recount what she knew, although she chose not to disclose Kelly's personal note. The conversation made for a very somber dinner, but the Henrys handled their grief with dignity. After dinner, Laura asked them the hard question, what did they want her to do? They decided they wanted to cremate her remains and save her ashes in a decorative urn. Laura thought the same thing, but she acquiesced to the Henrys' wishes. Laura told them she would contact Director Duncan with their decision tomorrow morning. Before she left, Mrs. Henry asked Laura to return for dinner in a week. They knew Laura and Kelly had been best of friends since school, and they thought it would be useful for all of them to reminisce about the good times with Kelly. Laura agreed, and so they left it.

After her short conversation with Director Duncan, Laura made arrangements with a local funeral home to fulfill the Henrys' wishes. All of the administrative tasks were done, at least for now. Her thoughts returned to Kelly's note. She reread it several more times. Although Kelly had not given her a choice, Laura felt the full obligation her friend had asked her to perform. She thought about contacting Mrs. Ramirez, but she ultimately decided the best course to initiate the next task was to call Detective Ramirez since they had met several times previously, even though under less-than-ideal circumstances.

"Detective Ramirez," he answered her telephone call.

"Detective, this is Laura Simmons. You may not remember me."

"Oh, I do remember you, Miz Simmons. You're not an easy woman to forget."

"Thank you, I think."

"What can I do for you?"

"Please bear with me, please. My best friend, Kelly Henry, committed suicide three days ago."

"I'm terribly sorry," he interjected.

"Yes, thank you. She left me a personal and private note. In that note, she asked me to talk to your daughter, whom she had befriended while they were together in Indulgence Camp 12. I'm calling to make arrangements with you and your wife, as Bella's parents, to speak with Bella . . . to fulfill my obligation to Kelly."

Silence deadened the telephone line, although she could hear muffled, indistinguishable conversations in the background of what had to be his office.

"Detective?"

"I'm here. I'm just trying to process all of this."

"I understand. Take your time." Laura waited several more seconds.

"Tell you what, let me call my wife Marci. I'll let her know what's up. I'm not sure of Bella's schedule. She works now. Anyway, let me call Marci. I'll call you right back."

"That's fine. I'll be waiting for your call."

After they hung up, Laura went to her refrigerator. She extracted a bottle of raspberry-flavored sparkling water and a sweet Honey Crisp apple. Laura had eaten the apple and nearly finished her water when Rod Ramirez called back.

"If you are agreeable, we'd like you to come to dinner tonight. We asked Bella to take the evening off, but we didn't tell her what it was about. We thought it best to allow you to say what you need to say. Both of us wanted to ask you explicitly if it is OK for us to listen and perhaps participate?"

"Yes sir. I expected that you would want to do so. I've no problem with any of that."

They set the time, and Rod gave her the address. Laura instinctively knew it was not going to be an easy evening, but she owed it to Kelly.

Laura decided to wear her well-tailored, tan silk slacks with matching jacket and a nice, modest, white silk blouse. She wanted to appear professional, perhaps a little elegant but subdued.

Laura arrived ten minutes early. She decided to wait in her pink Mini car, not wanting to impose upon the family by being early. She had barely shut off the engine to wait, when an attractive woman dressed in an airy summer dress appeared at the door to the Ramirez house. She waved for Laura to come. Laura secured her car and walked to the small porch.

As she approached, Marci said, "You must be Laura Simmons."

"Yes ma'am."

"Please, Marci, Marci Ramirez. I'm Bella's Mom," she said, extending her right hand to Laura. "Please do come in, no need waiting in your car for the appointed time."

"Thank you."

After serving iced tea to both of them, they sat in the living room. "Rod is running a little late. I hope that isn't too difficult."

"No ma'am . . . sorry, Marci. Quite all right."

"Bella is in her room, working on something. We've not told her about you or the purpose of your visit, only that we're going to have a guest for dinner." Laura nodded her head. "My curiosity is rampaging, but I'll wait for your discussion with Bella. By the way, Rod didn't properly inform me. You are a very attractive young woman."

Laura felt her cheeks flush. "Thank you."

"He also tells me you are a professional woman if that is the proper way to say it."

"Rod informed you correctly. I'm a prostitute and proud of my profession. I have been all of my adult life, which isn't yet quite so long."

"That's a whole other topic of discussion. I'd love to talk to you about it, but I'll not distract you from the purpose of your visit."

"Any time you wish. I've no qualms talking about what I enjoy doing."

"Excellent. If you'll permit me one preparatory question." Laura nodded her consent. "Do you know why your friend did what she did?"

"Not in any certain terms, but I've very strong suspicions. She was despondent."

"Over what, may I ask?"

"Her husband pushed her off the proverbial cliff."

"Oh my. Her husband was Raoul Joubert?"

"Yes."

"Oh my," Marci kept saying. "I should say before we get started with Bella that Rod and I have discussed your profession, but we've not mentioned it to Bella. Neither of us has any problem discussing that aspect of your life with Bella if it comes up. That is your choice entirely. We've tried to be very open with our daughter."

I guess so, letting her go to an indulgence camp, Laura thought. She only nodded her head in recognition.

Marci must have heard the sound she was waiting for to arrive. "Rod's home." Marci went to the kitchen to greet her husband.

Laura stood in anticipation. After what seemed like a long, quiet minute, Rod and Marci returned to the living room. Greetings were exchanged. Rod retrieved a beer for himself and freshened the two iced teas.

"Shall we get started?" Rod offered.

"Dinner is ready when we are," interjected Marci. Laura noticed for the first time that the dining room table was set for four.

Marci went to Bella's room and returned with their daughter. Laura was introduced to Bella only by her name, nothing more. Marci nodded to Laura to begin.

"Bella, I asked your parents to visit with you to fulfill an obligation to my best friend, Kelly Henry."

"Henry?" asked Bella.

"Her family name. Bella, it is my sad duty to inform you that Kelly has passed away."

Bella sucked in a heavy, quite audible gasp that almost verged upon a cry. "No! That can't possibly be. What on earth happened?"

"She took a serious overdose of heroin at IC12."

"No!" Bella screamed and jumped to her feet. "That's impossible. She was so happy when I left."

"Kelly asked me specifically to inform you and explain why she did what she did."

Tears were streaming down Bella's cheeks, and Laura felt her own tears. She did not attempt to hide them or wipe them away. "Are you telling me she took her own life with drugs?" asked Bella

"Yes. Kelly had arranged for three witnesses who corroborated the information."

"Why?" Bella cried as her sobs and tears continued.

"Something happened between her and her estranged husband that left her feeling she had no other path ahead."

"She was so happy. She taught me so much. We were talking about getting together once Kelly decided to finally leave IC12. What the hell did her husband do to turn her so dark like that so quickly?"

"We don't know. She didn't tell me, and apparently, she didn't say anything to anyone else either. I talked with the director and medical director a few days ago when they informed me. They were equally as shocked. I so wish I could've talked to her to save her possibly, but she chose not to give me that opportunity."

"Did she talk to any of the counselors at the camp?"

"No. No one . . . that was part of the problem."

"What did that asshole do to her?"

"Bella Joy!" protested Marci. "That language is uncalled for and not appropriate."

"But it's true, Momma. Kelly told me a little about the problems she was having with her husband. He was why she went to the camp, to get away from him . . . well, and she wanted to be rid of her addiction to Xanax. He was not a nice man."

"I can attest to that. He was raised in the old way, the very old ways. The last of the state's head and master laws was declared unconstitutional in 1981, but it takes generations to unravel the grip those antiquated laws have on people. He hasn't been able to grow out of them. I don't give him a pass, and I only offer my observations to understand. He is a product of how he was raised."

"Is someone going to punish him for what he has done?" asked Bella.

"Not so fast, Bella," Rod interjected. "He's the assistant district attorney. He is the law."

"So, let me get this straight . . . because he is a powerful man in the law, he gets to abuse women and force the woman he supposedly loves into a corner so tight that she felt she had no choice but to take her own life . . . without talking to her best friend, or me, her newest friend, or anyone who could have helped her."

"It's not that simple."

"Isn't it? Does his position put him above the law like the president?"

"We seem to have diverged from the purpose of Laura's visit," Marci declared. "Perhaps we should have dinner."

Rod helped Marci serve the prepared and chilled *salade niçoise*. Their conversation as they enjoyed the flavors of their salads remained light and unrelated. Laughter punctuated their words. *This family is so amazing. They've welcomed me like a longtime friend or a related family member.* When they had all finished, Laura offered her genuine compliments to Marci for the care and attention she had devoted to the uniquely French salad. Rod cleared the dishes and rinsed them for the dishwasher, as the ladies conferred about the latest fashion trends. Rod sat back down at the dining room table and tolerated the chit-chat, having nothing to contribute.

Laura eventually reached the point where she felt she had spent a respectable amount of time with the Ramirez family. She thanked Marci for the perfect meal. Marci and Laura set a date and location for lunch the next day. Bella hugged Laura. They agreed to keep in touch and called it a night.

—

26

Detective-Sergeant Ramirez entered the large City Council Hall amphitheater. The mayor and ten council members were not at their seats behind the expansive dais. He was early and chose to stand at the very back of the large room with his back against the wall between the two sets of double doors. As he watched, a quarter of the seats were filled, and people trickled into the hall, spreading out to open seats and finding friends. Several uniformed police officers entered the room, one at each set of doors. They both nodded to Rod, who nodded back. He did not know either officer, but they knew him. The stream of attendees increased as the start time neared. The auditorium was close to half full when Rod saw Marci and Bella enter. They did not see him standing in the back. He would join them when the doors closed. Rod still wanted to measure the people in the room. Most were casually dressed. A few wore business suits, both male and female. Hank Houseman walked in, noticed Rod standing at the back, and he waved to say hello.

Laura Simmons entered and stopped. She took a couple of steps to the side to avoid blocking the aisle. The light, elegant suit she wore made her appear entirely professional, like the owner of a small business that she was very proud of creating and owning. Laura scanned the room and did a double take when she saw Rod. She waved and then walked gracefully toward Rod. "Great to see you, again, Detective."

"Always a pleasure to see you, Laura, and please, I do believe we're familiar enough for you to call me Rod. Rather dashing today, aren't you?"

"Rod, it is then, and thank you very much."

"This should be an interesting hearing."

"I hope so. The purpose is right."

"I haven't seen you since you came to dinner. I wanted to thank you again for your patient reflection with Bella."

"Not the best of circumstances, but I think it went well. By the way, didn't I see Marci and Bella toward the front on the right?"

"Yes, you did. I'll join them once the doors close."

"Always the warrior . . . on guard," Laura giggled softly.

"Nature of the beast, I'm afraid . . . too many years of looking over my shoulder to keep track of what was around me."

"Thank you for your service to this great country."

"The honor is mine." Rod continued to scan the arrivals and filling room. He noticed that Marci had saved a seat next to her. Raoul Joubert walked in, saw Rod standing with Laura, and started to walk toward them. Rod shook his head as subtly as he could while holding Raoul's eyes. The widower got the signal and pulled up.

Laura picked up the gesture, looked over her shoulder, noticed who it was, and then looked back at Rod. "Thank you for that, Rod. He is not my favorite character."

"So I've gathered," he answered. Rod watched Raoul walk quickly down the aisle to the front row of seats. "Not mine either, but I have to work with the man."

"Maybe not much longer. There's an election coming up."

"There is that isn't there?"

Mayor Geraldo 'Gerry' Garcia led the full council into the hall. The police officers closed the doors. Rod estimated that only ten percent of the seats were empty, and a half dozen people stood around the periphery. Chief Harris followed the city council members, but he turned, descended the short stairs, and took a reserved seat in the front row.

"We'd better take our seats. Looks like there's an extra seat where Marci and Bella are. Would you join us?"

"Sure. Thanks."

The shuffling sounds of people taking their seats and muffled conversations dampening signaled the beginning of the meeting. Bella politely asked the couple next to her to move over one place. Laura sidestepped past Marci and Bella after saying hello. Rod sat in the open seat next to Marci on the aisle. He leaned and kissed Marci, and then he leaned a little farther to pat Bella's knee.

"This special meeting of the Council will come to order," Garcia announced. The last of the sounds in the hall evaporated. "We expected a large group. We're relieved that the Council Hall can accommodate everyone. Thank you for coming.

"The singular purpose of this special meeting is to collect observations, opinions, and beliefs from our citizens with respect to the controlled substance consumption within our jurisdiction. For the record, the catalyst for this meeting was a unique request originating from the House of Representatives' Domestic Policy Subcommittee of the Oversight and Government Reform Committee. The House committee is seeking evidentiary data, which we're collecting, as well as the effects on citizens along with the citizen's view of the state reforms. The House request was officially made to the governor. With the sanction of the legislature, the citizen's view portion of the information request was opened up to the counties and cities that wished to respond. So here we are.

"The central reform at issue here is the changes implemented by the state under the Psychotropic Substance Reform Act, also known as the Substance Consumption Improvement Program (SCIP) Act, passed by the legislature and signed into law by the governor seven years ago. The SCIP Act provision took effect six years ago. The law is somewhat complicated and is beyond the scope of this meeting. However, in a very broad summary, the SCIP Act provides for the retail sale of various regulated substances with strict controls on labeling, packaging, content, quality, and dosage. The retail systems use processes identical to those in place for decades for alcohol and tobacco to ensure sales to only adult citizens. The law also created what is known as indulgence camps to provide support for those citizens who are unable to consume responsibly in exchange for their removal from the public domain. The concept is intended to reduce the collateral crime associated with drug addiction, as we knew it before the SCIP Act implementation. Related to these changes are several legal and judicial reforms to recognize the fundamental shift in the state's treatment of drug consumption.

"With those introductory remarks, the council has voted unanimously to make this a listening session. We've agreed to refrain from making political statements regarding our views or positions. Council members may ask questions for clarification, but we're here to listen. These proceedings are being recorded and will be transcribed for our final report to the state and the U.S. House of Representatives. Our report, as well as the state's report, will be available in print and online in roughly one month's time.

"One last administrative item, I'd like to acknowledge several important guests. Landry Harris . . ." The chief raised his hand. ". . . our chief of police is with us to provide law enforcement information should it be needed to support our discussions today. I notice we have Assistant District Attorney Raoul Joubert in the audience." Raoul raised his hand. "Lastly, I am pleased to introduce Rodrigo 'Rod' Ramirez. Please stand, Rod."

"Damn it all. I don't need this," Rod muttered to himself. He did as he was asked.

"Rod is the only member in attendance serving on the Governor's Drug Policy Commission that has been active for the last several years."

The audience applauded, which surprised Rod. He waved his hand, bowed his head slightly to acknowledge the recognition, and then he sat back down. "What was that all about," he mumbled to Marci.

Marci leaned toward her husband and whispered, "Just be grateful for the recognition."

"Are there any preparatory remarks from the Council?" Garcia asked and scanned the dais panel on either side of him. Most members shook their heads, and a few offered no response whatsoever. "Very well, then, the floor is open to the public. To those who wish to contribute, I ask you to state your name and confine your remarks to two minutes. We potentially have quite a few contributors today. The large red digital time displays on all the walls will signal your time remaining. Very well, let's begin."

Several people stood and went to the standing microphones—three women and one man initially.

"My name is Betsy Wokowski," the first woman, who appeared to be in her mid to late-20s. "I wanted to take this opportunity to publicly thank the governor, the state legislature, and all those workers at Indulgence Camp 12 for their compassion and expertise. The state enabled the camp, and the people at the camp saved me from certain destruction. I've been sober and clean for almost five years now. Thank you." Betsy returned to her seat.

The first man to stand was next. "My name is George Harrison—no relation." Everyone laughed at his little quip. "My son never made it to one of those camps. His name was Billy, well William, we just called him Billy." More nervous laughter punctuated George's remarks. "He died six years ago just as the indulgence camps were opening up. The autopsy showed he had a kind of a heart attack from the crystal meth he ingested, but it was some toxic contaminant in the drugs he took that day that killed him. We tried numerous times to intervene, to stop him, but we couldn't help him. We tried, oh, I don't know, maybe a half dozen detox programs at three different rehab centers over the years and nothing could break the grip that damned stuff had on him. When I heard that Mayor Garcia and the Council were going to hold this public hearing, I knew I owed it to Billy's memory to say something. I don't know if one of those indulgence camps would've saved Billy like it saved Miz Wokowski, but it surely would've been a better place to die than the rathole where he was taken from us." A conservatively dressed, middle-aged woman stepped toward George and tugged on his left shirt sleeve. "My wife," he said, nodding to the woman who sat back down, "always says I talk too much." More laughter filled the hall. "We lost our son to the scourge of drugs, but I want to say, on behalf of my wife and me, I'm convinced the changes in our approach to drugs would've helped our Billy. I'm . . . no, we're . . . certain these changes are good. We're all the better for them. There's always room for improvement, I'm sure, but neither of us would like to see a regression to those times that took our Billy's life." George hesitated for a couple of seconds, nodded his head, and then he sat down with his wife.

The other two women offered their short statements of gratitude for the changes in drug policy they saw as positive and helpful to them and to their families. You could feel the passion in their voices.

An older man in a red, checkered, flannel shirt and well-worn bib overalls spoke next. "With all these rosy, feel-good, testimonials, it's time for a little reality. My family has lost too many members to these damn drugs. Oh, I forgot, my name is Homer Johnson. I own a farm in the Sugarwood district. We lost a son before the change, and we lost our daughter and a niece after the change. These drugs are bad. There's nothing good about them, no matter what color of lipstick you try to paint on that pig. I'll acknowledge the improvement in the various aspects of the crime rates, but the cost in human life to achieve those reductions can't, by any measure, be worth it. I say let's scrap this nonsense and get back to banning these drugs for human consumption. No one should be taking any of these damn drugs. That's it. Stop all this bullshit!" He finished what he had to say, stepped away from the microphone, and left the hall.

Bella leaned across Marci, to speak softly to both her parents. "I want to speak."

Oh crap! We'd not discussed her offering any testimony. Rod searched Bella's determined gaze. He glanced at Marci, who raised her left eyebrow and canted her head slightly. *What the hell is she going to say? I don't need her to make wild statements and expose the family.* He looked back at Marci and received exactly the same gesture. *Damn, no help there.* Rod swallowed hard. "OK, Bella," Rod answered in a tone just above a whisper. "You've a right to speak, but nothing too personal." Bella nodded her agreement and stood. Surprisingly, Laura stood with Bella and shuffled past Marci and Rod. Laura stood behind and to the left of their daughter, more as if in line rather than in companionship with Bella.

Bella looked around the room to see if anyone else was going to speak. She stepped to the standing microphone. "My name is Bella Joy Ramirez. I'm 15 years old. I think I understand Mister Johnson's feelings and opinions, but I think he misses the essential element of this whole question. I started trying drugs and alcohol without my parents' permission; at first, out of peer pressure. My friends were trying them, and they encouraged me to try them. I eventually did. I learned well from my parents that freedom of choice has its responsibilities and obligations. They also taught me to respect and cherish our freedom of choice, not just for ourselves selfishly, but also for everyone else. We learned about Prohibition in school. I don't think anyone would disagree that it was a terrible time for the country. Citizens made their choices, not hurting anyone, and then the government made them criminals. I'm certainly no expert. I'm only a young woman who has tried to learn, to educate myself regarding these substances. Prohibition is not the answer; it never was and never will be the answer in a free society. Education is. From my observations, a few people will succumb to the attraction of these drugs; most folks will not. We need to offer treatment for those who wish to break the grip of addictive substances. Oh, I should amend that part of my statement, these substances are not addictive if they are used properly. Addiction is a function of abuse or excess. Let's respect every person's freedom of choice and deal with individual excesses rather than denying the choice to everyone." Several people in the audience applauded Bella's words as she sat down. Rod squeezed her hand as she shuffled past him. She looked around, and Rod mouthed a well done to her. She nodded and smiled. Marci patted her thigh.

Laura waited for the applause and commotion to die down before she stepped to the microphone. "I'm Laura Simmons. I'll publicly confess that I'm living proof that the use of these controlled substances, well, at least some of them, is not dangerous or even injurious as long as they're used correctly. I've occasionally and purposefully used them for a handful of years now, and I'm not dependent and don't regularly use any of them . . . well, except maybe alcohol. I do enjoy a glass of wine with dinner." Muffled laughter seemed more nervous than humorous. "I came down here to listen and perhaps to learn. I've not been disappointed. I've learned that a 15-year-old young woman has wisdom well beyond her years. After listening to Mister Johnson, I felt compelled to say a couple of things. First, I offer my sincerest condolences to Mister Johnson and his family for their losses of loved ones. Second, my best friend admitted herself to IC12, not because she needed to but because she wanted to, just to rid herself of her addiction to benzos and escape her abusive husband." *Damn, she's publicly indicting Raoul Joubert.* Rod looked over to Raoul's seat. He was shaking his head and twisting in his chair. *Is he going to rebut this?* "She took her life with an intentional overdose of heroin while she was still in IC12. I say this to recognize her passing and to offer tribute to the extraordinary work of the medical personnel at IC12, but none of us were able to intervene, not because we didn't want to, but because she felt she had no choices left. One of the improvements I would recommend is better, much better, mental health treatment for the general public."

"Excuse me, Miz Simmons," interrupted Mayor Garcia. "Your time has expired."

"My apologies, Mister Mayor. I concede." Laura made her way back to her seat.

Rod looked at Raoul again. It seemed like he started to rise. *Don't do it, Raoul.* Joubert appeared to settle back into his seat. He did not look around at anyone. A lull stopped the rhythm of the meeting. The mayor and council members scanned the hall but remained silent. Several minutes passed. No one moved or made a sound.

Eventually, an older, rather slight, woman dressed in a modest, striped dress rose and shuffled awkwardly to the nearest microphone. "My name is

Roberta Higgins. I live over on Generous Avenue. I wasn't sure I really wanted to speak, but here goes. For many years, far more than I choose to count, I witnessed young drug dealers selling their stuff at a vacant lot near an intersection not far from my house. I called the police I don't know how many times. About half the time, they did nothing, and when I called back, they said their patrolmen had higher priority tasks. Then, about five years ago, those drug dealers just up and disappeared. I can't say exactly why, but as I read various reports in the newspaper and on the TV news, I believe it was moving the sale of that stuff from the street to the store that made the difference. I don't know if I'm safer, but I surely feel safer without that nonsense going on so close to my home. So, however that happened, I wanted to publicly say thank you for cleaning up the streets. I'm glad those hoodlum drug pushers are gone. Thank you very much." The old lady returned to her seat.

Houseman moved to the standing microphone halfway down the left aisle. "I'm Hank Houseman. I'm here and seek to testify as a private citizen. My remarks do not represent those of my employment or my employer. I wanted to offer my opinions regarding the Black Hole Confinement facilities." Houseman's words caused a stir among several members of the council. "I believe the whole of these units violate the Constitution's 8th Amendment against cruel and unusual punishment. I want to illuminate this publicly . . ."

"Excuse me, Mister Houseman," interjected Garcia. "The Black Hole Confinement facilities are beyond the scope of this meeting. The changes that brought them into existence were part of the judicial reform process. This hearing is about the state's drug policy as it applies to our community."

"I know what the law is, Mister Mayor, but the public needs to know what is being done in their name."

"I will now say you're out of order, Mister Houseman."

Raoul Joubert stood and without a microphone loudly proclaimed, "Let him speak. He's correct, and the people need to know. This is all tied together."

"Very well, we'll yield to the assistant district attorney. Proceed, Mister Houseman. You've one minute, 37 seconds remaining." Raoul sat back down.

"Thank you, Mister Joubert, and thank you, Mister Mayor. The legal reform brought on by the SCIP Act created several legal process changes with the state's criminal justice system. Most of the changes were positive in that we eliminated simple possession or consumption as felonious crimes. When we made those substances legal and subject to regulated retail sales, we dramatically reduced the burden on the justice system, and I do believe placed consumption in a more flexible environment. Many of the drug-related offenses we used to deal with were victimless crimes, but those violations of existing law at the time demanded an inordinate amount of time and effort away from the prosecution of more serious crimes. Even our prison reforms have had positive effects in substantially reducing our recidivism rate by finding alternatives to incarceration for victimless crimes, most notably simple possession. Where I depart from endorsing these positive changes is the addition of the so-called Black Hole confinement camps. I understand the sentiment that led to the BHCs, but that doesn't justify the "Animal Farm" approach to incarceration. For those who may not know," Houseman paused to quickly look around the hall, "Black Hole camps are facilities that leave inmates without protection, support, or treatment. A recent client of mine was literally beaten to death inside BHC7, and the minimal guards maintaining the perimeter did nothing to intervene or stop the murder. The public needs to be aware of what's happening in those places. I apologize for exceeding my time." Houseman sat down, and Joubert jumped up.

Raoul went to the microphone near his seat and said softly to the woman standing before the microphone, "Excuse me, madam. I need to respond to that." The woman nodded her head and stepped back two paces. Raoul stood to the microphone. "I'm compelled to add to Mister Houseman's soliloquy. Criminals committed to the BHCs are formally and legally classified as habitual criminals who have repeatedly refused the state's generous opportunities to reform and rehabilitate themselves. The BHCs simply recognize and acknowledge the consistent choices of those bad men. Yes, Mister Houseman's former client was indeed beaten to death by other inmates inside BHC7. However, it is important to note that the inmates generally remain calm and orderly, but there are exceptions. Habitual criminals should be allowed to live as they wish without endangering peaceful, law-abiding citizens. Thank you for your forbearance, Mister Mayor." Joubert sat down.

"Well said, Raoul," Rod muttered.

Marci leaned toward her husband. "You need to tell me more about these BHC places they were talking about." Rod nodded his head in consent.

The woman whom Raoul stepped in front of stood to the microphone. "My name is Julie Baker. I learned something from that," she said, nodding to Houseman and Joubert. "I need to do more research to learn more. Anyway, I've a couple of things I wanted to say. My son is 15 years old and a sophomore in high school. Somehow, he was able to acquire several cocaine inhalers. We tried to find out where and how he got them, but we were unsuccessful. We've sought expert professional assistance to help him deal with his attraction to that stuff, but that's not the point of my testimony. As I understand the law, retail shops are prohibited from selling those drugs to children—less than 21 years old. I'm not sure what the right answer is but my suggestion is some kind of serial number or tracking number that would allow law enforcement, or even us," she said, waving her arm about the room, "to track down where the illegal sales are coming from and take corrective action. Thank you." Ms. Baker returned to her seat.

The public testimony continued for another two hours, and then the mayor extended the session to allow everyone who wanted to speak to do so. Most folks remained for the whole session, with perhaps a dozen leaving after they testified and lost interest.

Rod had not taken notes, but his impression of the afternoon's hearing left him feeling the pros outweighed the cons by three or four to one. Even some of the negatives offered encouraging words. A few of the pros believed the changes enacted by the SCIP Act had not gone far enough. He was surprised at the degree of positive and supportive comments. The positivity was not what Rod perceived, perhaps from his day job, and definitely not what he expected.

Mayor Garcia spoke, "Are there any other citizens who would like to contribute to this hearing?" The mayor and council surveyed the audience for a dozen seconds. No one offered any sign of further contribution. "Would members of the council like to offer any closing comments?" Garcia looked both ways across the dais. None of the council members chose to speak. "Very well, then. I would like to thank everyone for their attendance, for the contributions of those who chose to speak, and for the orderliness of the assembly. We'll compile a summary of the public testimony and collected data. The full transcript of this afternoon's testimony will be included as an appendix. Our objective is to complete and release our final report by the end of the month. With that said, we are adjourned."

With the cacophony of departure blooming in the hall, Rod turned his head to the ladies and said, "Let's stay put for a few minutes to let the crowd dissipate." All three of the women nodded. Rod looked into Marci's eyes. She instinctively knew what he was going to ask and simply nodded her consent. Leaning forward enough to catch Laura's eyes, Rod asked, "Would you like to join us for an early supper?"

"If I would not be intruding," Laura paused to get a negative gesture from Rod, "thank you for your generous offer. I would be honored to join your family."

Interesting that she phrased her answer like that. "Excellent."

Most of the council members departed, but a few met with people on the floor. Mayor Garcia stood at the edge of the dais until he caught Rod's eyes and awareness. He held up his right index finger. *He wants me to wait.* Rod nodded his head. Garcia descended the stairs to the floor, paid his respect to Chief Harris and Assistant District Attorney Joubert. Presumably, after the pleasantries, Raoul took the farthest aisle to leave and did not even glance toward

Rod and his nemesis Laura. Rod saw the mayor gesture toward him. Chief Harris walked with Mayor Garcia toward Rod and the ladies. The audience ahead of them had cleared, so Rod felt comfortable stepping into the aisle and allowing the ladies to stand and join him. Rod introduced the mayor and chief to Marci, Bella, and Laura.

"Thank you both," Garcia said to Bella and Laura, "for testifying today. I'm fairly certain there is much more we could all learn from both of you."

"Very cogent observations, Bella," added Harris.

"Thank you, sir."

"We didn't need to call on you this afternoon," the mayor said to Rod, "but, thank you for being available. How are you doing with the crime statistics task?"

"Progressing well, Mister Mayor. We should have all the data in hand by early next week. I'll try to organize the numbers and summarize what they tell us by the end of next week."

"That should work just fine," Garcia responded. "I look forward to reading your report."

"We're going to an early supper. Would you like to join us?" Rod asked Garcia and Harris.

"Thank you so much for your gracious offer, but I'm afraid I've got a prior engagement," Gerry answered.

"Likewise," added the chief. "Thank you for inviting us."

Rod nodded his head.

"By the way," Garcia said, looking directly at Bella, "you should consider running for political office when you're a little older."

"Thank you, sir. I've never considered civil service in my future."

"You should. I was quite impressed with your testimony, Miz Bella. You're a natural . . . a very rare trait these days. Thank you all," the mayor added, and then he shook everyone's hand.

Chief Harris did the same and saluted Rod. "Well done, Detective."

"Thank you, sir."

Garcia and Harris walked out together. The hall was pretty much empty except for a half dozen folks talking with a couple of council members.

"Well," Rod exclaimed. "That was quite an afternoon. Since you seem to be the woman of the hour, Bella Joy, how about you pick our dining establishment."

Bella did not hesitate. "How about The Green Room?"

The local family restaurant specialized in Mediterranean cuisine of various flavors from Spanish to Greek with a smattering of common Arab dishes. The proprietors had also taken extra care to polish the ambiance.

"I know Marci's good with that, as am I. How does that work for you, Laura?"

"One of my favorites," Laura responded, and then she looked at Bella. "Good choice, Bella."

"Thanks. I've always liked it."

Laura followed the Ramirez family in her car to the restaurant. They had to wait for 15 minutes for a booth to open up, so they ordered drinks. Bella asked for a glass of wine, and her parents consented. Eventually, they were seated at a nice, somewhat secluded booth. They reviewed the daily menu and ordered their food. They also refreshed their drinks.

"While we've a moment, I'd like to propose a toast to our two stars of the afternoon. Well done, ladies." Glasses clinked, and gratitude conveyed.

"I was surprised you didn't testify, Rod. You've plenty of insight into the topic," Laura observed.

"I've had plenty of opportunities to express my opinions. I didn't need to take up everyone else's time."

"I've not really heard you speak on the topic before."

"My opinions are part of the public record now, but thank you for that."

"I've heard him talk plenty on the topic," Marci said and winked at Bella sitting next to Laura. "But I want to hear about these Black Hole places."

"Me too," Bella and Laura said simultaneously.

Rod smiled and nodded. "Not exactly the best dinner conversation, but since you asked, let me preface my answer with Hank Houseman seems to be on a bit of a crusade, and I do believe he is ill-informed. He's correct in that the cruel and unusual punishment question is making its way through the courts, undoubtedly to the Supreme Court eventually, so I suppose the Court will decide. That said, I visited Black Hole Confinement Camp Number Seven some months back. I was fortunate enough to get the cook's tour of the place and watch a little of its operation. The essential issue is the government's responsibility for the safety and welfare of inmates in its custody. What separates the Black Hole facilities from all other prisons is the lack of inside supervision. They've a small guard staff, but their task is predominantly to maintain the walls and confinement. The residents, as they call them, are left to their own processes. As Houseman testified, one man was beaten to death by other residents. He contends that the state, in the *persona* of the guards, should have intervened to stop the crime."

"Why didn't they?" asked Marci.

"Well, I suppose the best way to answer that question is, none of those men lived by the law on the outside, so they can live as they choose on the inside."

"That seems rather violent," Bella commented.

"In the case of Maxim Jurgensen, it was very violent, but there's little doubt in my mind that he brought it upon himself. He was a bad man who committed multiple injurious and property crimes, was in and out of regular prison several times, and given numerous opportunities to amend his criminal behavior. He chose not to live like the rest of us, and a judge and jury convicted him and categorized him as a habitual criminal in accordance with the law."

The waiter delivered their meals. Rod was pleased to see Bella switch to iced tea. Their first several bites were enjoyed and praised. *Good choice, indeed, Bella.*

"Anyway," Rod continued between bites, "while I was there and according to the captain of the guard, the quads where they're isolated remain peaceful and well-ordered." He took another couple of his couscous ambrosia, a uniquely Tunisian dish according to the menu. The combination of the grainy couscous and a variety of dates, pomegranate kernels, olives, and diced apples made a delightful and flavorful amalgamation. "I guess my point is to close out my answer that the more I learned about them, the more I saw the elegance of simplicity in the facilities."

"Why do they call them Black Holes?" asked Bella.

"It's a direct reference to the astronomical phenomenon. What goes in never comes out."

"What do they do with the dead?" Laura asked.

"They remove them, using a well-rehearsed, almost military-grade process. They specifically try not to interact with the residents. If families don't claim the remains, they're cremated, and their ashes scattered on the grounds outside the walls."

"Wow!" Bella exclaimed.

"Did that answer your question?" Rod asked, looking at Marci.

"Yes but produced many more. I need to think about all of that. We'll talk later."

"May I ask . . . ," Laura said, looking directly at Rod, who nodded for her to proceed as he ate more of his meal. "Where do you think this is going? What lies ahead?"

Rod finished chewing and swallowing his bite, and then he washed it down with a sip of his beer. "First, Mayor Garcia was precisely correct. The Black Hole legal question has nothing to do with the drug law reforms, other than I imagine a fraction of those confined in the Black Holes are there because of illegal drug-related violence. Now, the best I can offer is my opinion, since it's impossible to predict what Congress is going to do." Laura nodded her head that Rod's opinion was good enough. "I'm very encouraged that at least the

House of Representatives is asking us for comments and evidence regarding our experience with drug reform. Based on what I heard today, and my work on the Governor's Drug Policy Commission, I'd say the prognosis is good. I've a hard time imagining how the feds might change their policies, but anything would likely be better than the nonsense of the so-called war on drugs. I like where we've come to in these changes. I believe we're a safer, more peaceful, more secure community because of these changes."

"Freedom of choice seems rather important to me," Laura contributed.

"Yes, it is! For decades, we've forgotten that reality. For far too long, we were asked and expected to give up our freedom and rights to impose the socially conservative agenda on everyone. That's not how it's supposed to work in a free society."

"I sure hope they get the message," Bella added.

Rod chuckled softly. "That's yet to be determined. It'll sure make all of our lives easier if they do. But, like I said, I've given up trying to predict congressional action. I think the best we can hope for, at least in my generation, is a more enlightened position by the feds. There are too many very conservative states to expect broad reform. We need to be more than the only state. Like Sir Winston Churchill at the darkest hour for the British people so eloquently said, 'The life of the world may move forward into broad, sunlit uplands.' We can only hope."

—

Author's Postscript

My intellectual unease with the so-called war on drugs grew with time, and the mounting collateral damage many of us, if not all of us, have witnessed for decades. In recent years, my unease has transformed into active opposition. This book is the consequent product.

On Tuesday, 27.October.1970, President Richard Nixon signed into law the *Comprehensive Drug Abuse Prevention and Control Act of 1970* [PL 91-513; 84 Stat. 1236]. The operative element of the Act for this story was Title II known as the Controlled Substances Act (also known as CSA) [84 Stat. 1242]. The CSA became the enabling legislation.

Eight months later, the president announced the specific reorganization of the federal government to enforce the CSA. In that statement, Nixon declared:

> "America's public enemy number one in the United States is drug abuse. In order to fight and defeat this enemy, it is necessary to wage a new, all-out offensive. I have asked the Congress for legislative authority and funds to fuel this kind of offensive. This will be a worldwide offensive, dealing with the problems of sources of supply as well as Americans who may be stationed abroad wherever they are in the world. It will be government wide, pulling together the nine different fragmented areas within the government in which this problem is now being dealt with." 17.June.1971

So began the war on drugs. I could and probably should chronicle the extraordinary collateral damage done in the United States, and in Central and South America as well as other source areas throughout the world, but that task is simply too large and beyond the scope of this humble novel. My focus in this work is a notional solution to drug consumption and the disastrous attempt at prohibition.

It is important to note at this juncture that the societal context of the federal government's actions is and should be debatable. At the root, a large portion of American society condemned drug use. The socially conservative element represented by President Nixon and the majority of Congress at that time believed it was necessary to pass and enforce the CSA because the consumption of psychotropic substances was corroding the fabric of society. Whether we choose to recognize it, the argument became a "chicken-or-egg" conundrum, i.e., was the consumption of drugs the root problem or the prohibition of consumption? It can also be argued that there were more suspect motives for the so-called war on drugs that were political. Nixon saw marijuana usage as popular among the "hippies" and the anti-war movement, and heroin as the drug of choice among Americans with dark skin pigmentation. Arguably, the combination of these motivations amid the societal turmoil of the civil rights and anti-war movements of the Vietnam War era drove the genesis of the war on drugs.

The United States began its legislative penchant for the projection of moral prohibitions into the private lives and conduct of its citizens during the Victorian era that had a profound impact on American culture. The first significant law was *An Act for the Suppression of Trade in, and Circulation of obscene Literature and articles of immoral Use* (also known as the Federal Anti-Obscenity Act of 1873, or the *Comstock Act*) [PL 42-258; 17 Stat. 598], signed into law by President Grant on 3.March.1873. The law was used by law enforcement of the day to prosecute what they deemed immoral conduct well beyond erotic photographs or writing, as originally intended. The first federal effort to regulate all ingestible substances other than for medical purposes was the *Pure Food and Drug Act* [PL 59-384; 34 Stat. 768], signed into law by President Theodore Roosevelt on 30.June.1906. The law required proper labeling for all ingestible substances and was used to prosecute worthless products like Clark Stanley's Snake Oil Liniment. The first federal law to prohibit non-medical use of a psychotropic substance was An Act To prohibit the importation and use of opium for other than medicinal purposes (also known as the *Smoking Opium Exclusion Act*) [PL 60-221; 35 Stat. 614], signed into law also by President Theodore Roosevelt on 9.February.1909. The 18th Amendment to the U.S. Constitution prohibited the production, distribution, sale and consumption of alcohol in all its forms, as the Temperance Movement reached its peak in the post-Victorian era of moral projection. The joint resolution of Congress [S.J. Res. 17; 40 Stat. 1050] was passed, certified, and sent to the states for ratification on 18.December.1917. The constitutional amendment was ratified when the 36th state—Nebraska—approved the law on 16.January.1919. The 18th Amendment took effect one year later—at 00:01 EST [R], 17.January.1920. One last law of note in the background of this novel is the Marijuana Tax Act of 1937 [PL 75-238; 50 Stat. 551], signed into law by President Franklin Roosevelt on 2.August.1937, and became the first federal tax on the sale of marijuana. There are myriad other laws passed by Congress after the CSA, but this background should suffice to reflect the expansiveness of federal laws regarding the production, distribution, sale and use of an array of psychotropic substances.

In the CSA, the federal government declared Schedule I compounds had:

A.) a high potential for abuse,

B.) no accepted medical use, and

C.) no accepted safety for use.

Consequently, all research into these substances was banned; in essence, the federal government chose to keep us blind and ignorant of anything other than its *dicta*. The legislators of the day who concocted this law refused to believe, recognize, understand, or even acknowledge that there might be or could be other uses of these substances. They (Congress of the day) chose to construct an elaborate façade of legitimacy to protect their imposed morality, not the rights and freedoms of We, the People. Cracks in this imposing structure began to appear, e.g., Colorado's approval of medical marijuana use in 2000 and recreational use in 2012. As the consumption of other Schedule I substances began to bubble up into public awareness, we began to see the fallacy of the whole disguised prohibition, i.e., medical use is not the only reasonable purpose for using such materials. Before Congress chose to take the action it did in 1970, it should have funded comprehensive studies to establish and document other reasons for taking these materials, and whether a safe dosage threshold could be established, more along the lines of tobacco and alcohol. So here we are, five decades later, with the federal government very deeply into our private lives, our private choices, and the very essence of our freedom and liberty. We have generations of American citizens who have grown and procreated, and they have known nothing but the falsity of this contemporary prohibition.

When President Nixon initiated the "war on drugs," I was serving on active duty as a lieutenant of Marines toward the end of the Vietnam era. I witnessed firsthand the consequences of the unregulated consumption of psychotropic substances along with the erosion of good order and discipline in our national security apparatus. In the beginning, I was all-in "to wage a new, all-out offensive" against illegal drugs. In those days, I only saw the objective as articulated by the moral projectionists—not the means or consequences of that offensive. I confess to my inability or unwillingness to consider or contemplate the collateral effects or consequences in those early days.

As the ancillary damage mounted, I began to question the foundation as well as the basis of the "war on drugs." At its very root, I saw many similarities to Prohibition (of alcohol). As I learned more, the similarities became more evident. The prohibition of private conduct in a free society is an oxymoron of sorts. However, can anyone be free to choose what matters to them in their private lives? Just as history recorded during the prohibition of alcohol era, consumption demand fueled the criminal subculture that was all too willing to feed the demand. Rather than the government confining its actions to the public domain or public safety, the lawmakers and prosecutors stretched the meaning and definition of public safety far beyond the public domain. Thus, in the name of the "war on drugs," the government imprisoned people who had done nothing to injure or endanger anyone in public or in private. The government confiscated property without due process of law. The "war on drugs" began to take on unconstitutional dimensions under the guise of the stretched interpretation of public safety. Further, it can be argued that the persistent migration of Central and South American citizens toward the United States has been amplified by the criminal subculture generated in those countries to feed demand in the United States. The growth of violent activities in neighboring countries can be directly attributed to the "war on drugs."

At the root level, I can see little difference between alcohol & tobacco and other psychotropic substances; they all temporarily alter the brain's cognitive function in one way or another. History has recorded the tough lessons we learned the hard way during the Prohibition era (1919-1933). In a free society, demand would be met by one means or another. The criminal subculture took on very graphic and public dimensions, facets and aspects—speakeasies, gangsters, moonshine stills, rumrunners, bank robbers, outlaws, *et al.* American society eventually came to its senses and repealed the 18th Amendment to the Constitution (21st Amendment). Unfortunately, we have yet to correlate the lessons of the Prohibition era with the contemporary prohibitions of the "war on drugs."

This story sprang from one simple contemplative question: there has to be a better way? While the fictional changes reflected in this story may not be the answer we need, they are a humble attempt to articulate a more enlightened path to eliminate, or at least seriously reduce, the enormous penalty our society continues to pay for what amounts to moral projection in an attempt to prohibit freedom of choice. *Indulgence* takes place in an unspecified state at some time in the near future. In this notional community, Congress has repealed the prohibition provisions of the CSA and associated laws, allowing the states to adopt different approaches. As a result, our notional state implemented a serious, comprehensive, reform law we shall call the Psychotropic Substance Reform Act, also known as the *Substance Consumption Improvement Program* (SCIP) Act. A few other states implemented other changes, but our notional state stood as the most progressive. The new law had been tested in the courts and implemented by the state to various degrees. The principal characters in this story are immersed in various aspects of the SCIP Act implementation. We join them in that experience.

If this story does nothing else beyond stimulating the public debate, then it will be successful beyond imagination.

This book has been percolating in my little pea brain for several decades. It took me more than a decade to construct a story around the central notion and gather up the will to write this book. I was also under no illusion that it would be easy to write or would be readily accepted in our socially conservative society. I was driven by one foundational belief: the so-called war on drugs has no hope of being successful in a free society—either freedom or oppression. Underlying the central premise was the driving motivation that there has to be a better way to deal with the negative consequences of psychotropic substance consumption.

This story was written predominantly during the COVID-19 pandemic of 2020 [AKA novel coronavirus 2019, 2019-nCoV, SARS-CoV-2]. With the pandemic crisis as a background surrounding the writing of this story, the negative consequences of freedom of choice were on graphic display. The shelter-in-place orders imposed hodgepodge across the country after the president's emergency declaration [13.March.2020] demonstrated, in part, the benefit of breaking the chain of infection. However, the rapidly rising rates of infections, hospitalizations, and fatalities showed that far too many people failed to comply with the restrictions to break the chain of infection. Our freedom of choice, in this instance, inflicted injury on others. Freedom of choice is not the freedom to be stupid or to disregard the potential threat to other, more vulnerable citizens. There are responsibilities and consequences for individual freedom of choice, and that reality applies equally to the psychotropic substance consumption issue. The government struggles to deal with that reality. Yet, the government has attempted to suppress psychotropic substance consumption with prohibition, and the data proves our failure.

Indulgence is a novel—a work of fiction. The book, this story, is not and never was intended to be a definitive treatise on constitutional or common law, psychotropic substance consumption, the morality of prostitution or suicide, or any other related societal issue beyond every citizen's fundamental right to privacy and freedom of choice. Hopefully, the story offers enough of a glimpse into what might be or could be, if we shift our focus from prohibition to dealing with reality in an intelligent, informed manner. Freedom of choice is far too important and precious to be sacrificed at the altar of moral projection.

As is with novels of this sort, a comprehensive treatment of a complex societal question is not within the scope of a page-count bound novel. Thus, it was with this project. The constraints of this novel were no different. And yet, I feel a profound obligation to the topic for a broad host of reasons. I simply could not end the book without acknowledging just some of the other aspects of the subject that could not be sufficiently addressed in this story.

First and foremost, among those unspoken aspects of this story has to be mental health detection, intervention, and treatment. Mental health factors should not, and perhaps must not, be contributors to the diminished capacity intoxication or abusive use of psychotropic substances. The mental health dimension adds a unique and complex matrix of considerations that must be balanced with every citizen's fundamental freedom of choice and right to privacy. There are genuine physical and/or mental reasons some folks are drawn to one or more of these substances; the spectrum of reasons is far too broad for any reasonable treatment here. Let it suffice to say that each individual is driven by their own internal forces, demons, pleasures, fears, pain, or whatnot, to seek the benefits (to them) of one or more of these substances. Many of those motivations seem to be tied up in mental health aspects of one form or another. The essential question: how far do we let things go before state intervention becomes necessary or required? The mental health domain affects so many segments of society, far beyond the consumption or abuse of psychotropic substances, and the United States has backed away from more aggressive mental health treatment. Continued reticence toward mental health intervention will only exacerbate any psychotropic substance reform effort. Concomitantly, any drug reform effort that does not include societal mental health treatment improvements will be relegated to the half-measure arena with the deck stacked against success.

Second among the omitted aspects of this novel is the societal economic elements of the drug policy reforms depicted. The retail sale of these substances would be priced by simple supply and demand forces as any other commodity; they would pay for themselves. The economic impact of the notional SCIP Act centers upon the indulgence camps portrayed in this story. Society pays for the maintenance and operation of the ICs, and the supply of products to residents for consumption. A detailed, comprehensive analysis of the costs and treasury funds transfer is well beyond the scope of this novel. Further, because drug consumption and addiction have been hidden from both the government and the public, the costs of the current prohibition enforcement are difficult to identify and therefore offer as counterweight. For example, what are the costs of an addict who steals from family, friends and common citizens to gain sufficient funds to feed his drug habit? What are the costs of deploying DEA agents around the world in a futile attempt to suppress substance production? What are the costs of drug cartels and gangs that our drug demand created and motivated with obscene profits? What are the costs of 'no knock' warrants executed to find drug dealers, and wind up entering the wrong address and killing an innocent woman? None of these costs are tangible enough to offset the hard costs associated with building and operating indulgence camps. Associated with the hard physical costs of operating indulgence camps are the personal, familial, and societal costs of sustaining non-productive citizens, i.e., residents of the IC are not contributing to society and only draining. The ICs are not holiday resorts; they are austere minimalist facilities, designed for one purpose only—the removal of addicts from society. Some people so inclined will find attraction. For those individuals in that cohort, I respectfully submit that it is better for society to have them in a controlled, supervised place rather than free to wreak havoc in our communities. I do believe most folks will be like Bella Joy Ramirez; they will find their bottom and seek their way out of an IC. Taking alcohol or tobacco as examples, adult citizens have free, unfettered access to as much of those materials as they wish to pay for, and a comparative very small portion of the population become dysfunctional in their consumption. For the sake of argument, let us assume my assumption is incorrect, i.e., the number of citizens seeking the attraction of zoning out, without the costs, overwhelm the capacity. The austerity of the IC will not be attractive to the majority of people. In such circumstances, if they were to occur, a triage process would be required to ensure access for those individuals who present the greatest threat to society. At the end of the day, the economic question comes down to how best to spend our precious tax dollars. I respectfully submit that providing a safe place for addicts to consume as they wish out of the public domain is far better than having them mixed in among us.

As history recorded during the Prohibition era (1917-1933), a powerful criminal subculture will always evolve and flourish where there is societal demand despite banning any particular conduct. Consumption of alcohol continued throughout the 1920s even though it was a federal crime to produce, trade, possess, or consume alcohol. Moonshiners, smugglers, rumrunners, speakeasies, and the hoodlums that drive those deliveries to meet demand generated lawlessness, which in turn contributed to the burgeoning of other collateral crimes including murder, robbery, extortion, bribery, corruption, *et cetera ad infinitum ad nauseum*. The death and destruction of that era remain sad testimony to the consequences of imposing prohibitive moral constraints without education to alter behavior. We have seen five decades (so far) of precisely the same results as banning psychotropic substances. Demand has not waned despite a concerted governmental effort to portray drug consumption as villainous. Demand finds a way to be fulfilled. I think it safe to say that we have proven without question that the prohibition of psychotropic substances and the associated law enforcement of contemporary prohibition has not reduced demand. In fact, the effort has stimulated escalating measures that impose upon the freedoms and rights of all of us regardless of whether we are consumers. Our ancestors recognized reality and went through the extraordinary process of amending the Constitution to rescind the prior amendment that enabled the Prohibition era. We have failed to learn the exact same lessons. Our modern-day prohibition has been unable to suppress demand or supplant the criminal subculture that flourishes to feed demand.

Tragically, our criminal subculture is not confined to the United States. We have exported comparable stimulation to neighboring countries and, arguably, across the globe, e.g., the opium trade in Afghanistan. Drug gangs or cartels have grown into powerful, militia-enforcement entities, violent organizations with one primary purpose, carve out their share of the obscene profits available from the drug trade to feed demand in the United States. The gangs have become so strong and violent that citizens flee their homeland to escape the violence and seek asylum in the United States. They perceive a better, safer life awaits them in the U.S. And we blindly wonder why all these people from Central America are flooding to our borders, pleading for asylum. We tell ourselves they want to come here because we are so prosperous. We are fed a steady diet of American exceptionalism, and we believe. Our demand for psychotropic substances has corrupted the social infrastructure of far too many countries around the world and especially in the Western Hemisphere. We bear direct responsibility to fix what we have broken, and perhaps the best way to do that is to help these illegal sources become legitimate, proper, regulated suppliers.

Wrapped up as a subset in our understanding of psychotropic substances, but an entire arena for study is our consumption of prescription medicines and specifically opiates and opiate derivatives, including synthetics. It is difficult to ignore the issue with the plethora of news programs illuminating the scourge of prescription opiate consumption and abuse. We cannot ignore the specter of malpractice by medical professionals, yet in no small measure, like so many other aspects of the 'supply system,' the doctors are responding to the pressure of demand around them. I am living testament to the fact that powerful opiates have very important medical uses (with the caveat of proper usage). I used them when I broke my back. There is zero doubt in my mind that they enabled my full and healthy recovery; I did not become addicted. However, as it is well known in the medical community, opiates can lead to addictive dependence if not used properly. Respectfully, Congress was wrong in 1970; many substances on the Schedule I list have medical and non-medical uses, and they can be safely used if consumed with the proper purity, dosage, and frequency.

A very touchy, sensitive, and emotional related issue that probably should be a subset of the mental health matter, but I have chosen to address separately is suicide. The subject is inseparable from the broader topic of psychotropic substance consumption. As with the character of Kelly Margaret Joubert, née Henry, in this story, individuals with suicidal thoughts occasionally choose the sedative effects of opiates as the method to end their depression/ desperation. The societal aversion to suicide may have its genesis in religion; however, I choose to believe the basis is the greater compassion for our fellow man (in the generic form). In reforming the consumption of psychotropic substance laws, we cannot and must not ignore the societal matter of suicide. I freely confess my unqualified support for death with dignity laws. We must separate end of life events from suicide in general. However, death with dignity is not and should not be within the scope of general suicide. Intervention processes exist today, but they are largely passive, i.e., they seek to talk the individual off the ledge. Respectfully, we need more effective means to identify and intercede well before the action phase begins. We must also conclude an essential shift in our thinking; simple consumption is not a suicidal action. Like so many societal problems, We, the People, must actively care for our fellow citizens. As most citizens know to call 911 for emergencies, we should also know a quick and ready means to deploy professional help when signs of depression, mental health problems, or suicidal tendencies appear. The difficulty with this subject beyond the very personal human dimension is the very fine balance point between our disapproval of suicide in opposition to every citizen's fundamental right to privacy and freedom of choice.

Tied up in all of this are the collateral and associated police reforms to remove law enforcement from the mental health aspects of life and out of our private lives. As an instrument of the state, the instructions, guidance, and direction from elected politicians of one form or another channel the efforts of law enforcement agencies within our communities. We need the police out of the private domain, out of morality enforcement, and focused on the public domain. The realignment of law enforcement is much broader than the private-public separation, but it is a worthy start.

A keystone element of psychotropic substance reform is the strict quality control of raw production materials to retail sales to eliminate injurious contaminants and uncertain dosage. The consistency of controlled substances will not eradicate overdose events, but it will undoubtedly reduce mistakes and inadvertent injuries and overdoses. Regulation of the content will not alter intentional events, which is directly related to the mental health and suicide treatment noted above. Mixed in the material quality issue, informed consent becomes a critical element of consumption. Every consumer must be informed of the proper dosage and effects, as well as the consequences of overdoses. Whether the individuals were adequately informed of the consequences of misuse is debatable. Yet, at the end of the day, those individuals chose to overdose on those high quality, controlled substances. We must recognize and acknowledge that such consumption is a personal freedom of choice action.

The U.S. Constitution defines the system of governance for the United States of America. It defines the authority of the federal government. Four years after the Constitution's ratification, the first ten amendments, also known as the Bill of Rights, defined specific rights retained by We, the People. Some of the inalienable rights illuminated in the Declaration of Independence are not mentioned in the Constitution—Life, Liberty, and the pursuit of Happiness. Those terms have not been defined, but they can easily be interpreted as including the fundamental freedom of choice and the right to privacy. Underlying the topic of more responsible consumption of psychotropic substances rests those inalienable rights not delineated in the Bill of Rights. Further, morality is often defined as what we do when no one is watching. The question of right or wrong rests with each individual and not with state legislatures or Congress, except as those matters affect the public domain. Whether any individual chooses to consume psychotropic substances is a private choice, as long as that choice has no effect on another citizen's choice(s) or property. We should respect choices of others, not as our choice but as theirs, and a representation of the freedom of choices that each of us possesses. We must learn to respect the choices of others, not as our own, but as a reflection of our freedom of choice that we wish others to respect. Yet, we cannot forget that one individual's freedom of choice must never risk or threaten another person's safety, rights, or freedoms. Intoxication by any substance for any reason can never be tolerated in any individual who is entrusted with the lives of others, e.g., pilots, doctors, bus drivers, police officers, *et al.* Zero tolerance must be staunchly enforced. But what individuals do in private is their business—not ours.

Social conservatives love to validate their beliefs by imposing their choices, their morality, their principles of life on every living soul regardless of borders. The moral projectionists are the enforcement arm of the social conservatives. They use the law to carry out their work. And We, the People, pay the price.

I hold absolutely no intention of avoiding critical aspects of the psychotropic substance consumption issue or the myriad ancillary matters. The notional system depicted in this work of fiction is not intended to be a comprehensive plan to remedy the disastrous war on drugs. In this story, the only purpose was to stimulate thinking and debate, consider the possibilities for the recovery of our essential freedoms, and find a better, far more enlightened way to deal with consumer demand. It is long past time to respect the choices of individual citizens. The 91st Congress believed they knew better than individual citizens, and they chose to enact what evolved to be draconian impositions on the freedom of choice for all American citizens then and for perpetuity (until We, the People, decide there must be a better way). They made a dreadful mistake; it is time for We, the People, to right the ship.

To paraphrase Henry Ford's observation more than a century ago, if we continue to do what we've always done, we will continue to get what we've always got. Prohibition does not and will never work in a free society. Let us mature and deal with individual freedom of choice with respect rather than contempt. We are better than the wasteful and destructive war on drugs that has been imposed upon us in our name, whether we realize it. We shall overcome.

Respectfully yours,

Cap Parlier

Author
—

About the Author

Cap Parlier

Cap and his wife, Jeanne, live in the warmth and diversity of Arizona. Their four grown children have established their families and are raising their grandchildren, who in turn are graduating from college and beginning their adult lives.

Cap is a graduate of the U.S. Naval Academy, a retired Marine aviator, Vietnam veteran and experimental test pilot, and has finally retired from the corporate world to devote his time to his passion for writing a good story. He has numerous other projects completed and, in the works, including screenplays, historical novels as well as atypical novels at various stages of the creation process.

—

Interested readers may wish to visit his website at http://www.Parlier. com for his essays and other items, or subscribe to his weekly Blog: "*Update from the Sunland.*" Cap can be reached at: Cap@SaintGaudens.Org

—